Captive of My Desires

JOHANNA LINDSEY

Captive of My Desires

DOUBLEDAY LARGE PRINT HOME LIBRARY EDITION

POCKET BOOKS
NEW YORK LONDON TORONTO SYDNEY

POCKET BOOKS, a division of Simon & Schuster, Inc. 1230 Avenue of the Americas, New York, NY 10020

ISBN-13: 978-0-7394-6906-4
ISBN-10:   0-7394-6906-1

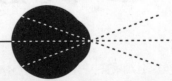

This Large Print Book carries the
Seal of Approval of N.A.V.H.

In memory of Birdena Doyon.

Captive
of My
Desires

Chapter 1

She'd been told to hide, and stay hidden. That had been Gabrielle Brooks's first thought as well after the noise had drawn her up to the deck and she'd seen what was causing the commotion. It wasn't the captain who'd given her the order, though. He'd been nothing but confident that he could lose the ship bearing down on them. He'd even laughed about it and shaken his fist at the Jolly Roger flying from the attacking ship's mainmast, which was visible now to the naked eye. His enthusiasm—and dare she say delight?—had certainly relieved her mind. Until the first mate pulled her aside and told her to hide.

Unlike the captain, Avery Dobs didn't appear eager for the upcoming confrontation. His complexion as white as the extra sails being swiftly hoisted by the crew, he hadn't been gentle about shoving her toward the stairs.

"Use one of the empty food barrels in the hold. There are many of them now. With any luck, the pirates won't open more than one or two, and finding them empty, they'll move on. I'll warn your servant to hide as well. Now go! And no matter what you hear, don't leave the hold until someone whose voice you recognize comes for you."

He hadn't said until *he* came for her. His panic was infectious, his roughness surprising. Her arm was probably bruised where he'd gripped it. It was such a change from the courteous way he had treated her when the journey began. He'd nearly been courting her, or so it had seemed, though that was unlikely. He was in his early thirties and she was barely out of the schoolroom. It was just his deferential manner, his gentle tone of voice, and the inordinate amount of attention he'd paid her during the three weeks since they'd left London, that gave her the impression he liked her more than he should.

He'd managed to instill his own fear in her, though, and she'd raced toward the bowels of the ship. It was easy to find the food barrels Avery had spoken of, nearly all of them empty, now that they were nearing their destination in the Caribbean. Another few days and they would have sailed into St. George's harbor in Grenada, her father's last known whereabouts, and she could have begun her search for him.

Nathan Brooks was not a man she knew well, though all her memories of him were fond ones, but he was all she had now that her mother had died. While she'd never once doubted that he loved her, he had never lived at home with her for any length of time. A month, maybe a few months at a time, and, one year, an entire summer—but then several years would pass without a visit from him. Nathan was captain of his own merchantman with very profitable trade routes in the West Indies. He sent home money and extravagant presents, but rarely did he bring himself home.

He'd tried to move his family closer to where he worked, but Carla, Gabrielle's mother, wouldn't even consider it. England had been her home all of her life. She had no family left there, but all her friends were there, as well as everything she valued, and she had never approved of Nathan's seafaring occupation anyway. *Trade.* She'd always spoken the word in disgust. She had enough aristocracy in her ancestry, even if she bore no title herself, to look down on anyone in *trade,* even her own husband.

It was a wonder they'd ever married. They certainly didn't seem to like each other much when they were together. And Gabrielle would never, ever mention to him that his long absences had led Carla to take a . . . Well, she couldn't even bring herself to think the word, much less say it. She was so embarrassed by her own conclusions. But Albert Swift had been a regular visitor to their two-story cottage on the outskirts of Brighton during the last several years, and Carla had behaved like a young schoolgirl whenever he was in town.

When he'd stopped coming around and they heard the rumors that he was courting an heiress in London, Gabrielle's mother had undergone a remarkable change. Overnight, she turned into a bitter woman, hating the world and everything in it, crying over a man who wasn't even hers.

Whether he had made Carla promises, whether Carla had intended to divorce her husband, no one knew, but her heart seemed to have broken when Albert turned his attentions to another woman. She had all the signs of a woman betrayed, and when she took sick in early spring and her condition had worsened, she'd made no effort to recover from it, ignoring her doctor's advice and barely eating.

Gabrielle was heartsick herself, having to watch her mother's decline. She might not have approved of her mother's obsession with Albert, or her unwillingness to try harder to save her marriage, but she still loved her mother deeply and had done everything she could think of to cheer her up. She'd filled her mother's room with flowers that she scoured the neighborhood for, read to her mother aloud, even insisted their housekeeper, Margery, spend a good portion of her day visiting with her, since she was such a chatty woman and usually quite funny in her remarks. Margery had been with them several years at that point. Middle-aged with bright red hair, vivid blue eyes, and a host of freckles, she was opinionated, outspoken, and not at all awed by aristocrats. She was also a very caring woman, and had taken to the Brookses as if they were her own family.

Gabrielle had thought her efforts were working, that her mother's will to live was returning. Her mother had even started to eat again and stopped mentioning Albert. So Gabrielle was devastated when her mother passed away in the middle of the night. "Pined away" was Gabrielle's personal conclusion, because she'd been on the mend from her illness, though she would never mention that to her father. But her mother's death left Gabrielle feeling utterly alone.

Although she'd been left a lot of money, since Carla had been quite well-to-do herself from a family inheritance, Gabrielle wouldn't see any of that money until she reached her majority at the age of twenty-one, and that was a long way off. Her father did send funds regularly, and there was the household money that would last quite a while, but she'd just turned eighteen.

She was also going to be turned over to a guardian. Carla's solicitor, William Bates, had mentioned it at the reading of the will. In her grief, she hadn't really paid attention, but when she'd been given the name, she was appalled. The man was a philanderer and everyone knew it. The rumors were that he chased his maids all over his house, and he'd even pinched Gabrielle's bottom once at a garden party, when she'd been only fifteen!

A guardian, and he in particular, wouldn't do a'tall. She still had one parent living. She merely needed to find him, and so she set out to do just that. She'd had to conquer a few fears first, of sailing halfway around the world, of leaving behind everything *she* was familiar with. She'd nearly changed her mind twice. But in the end, she'd felt she had no choice. And at least Margery had agreed to go with her.

The trip had gone very well, much better than she'd anticipated. No one had questioned her traveling with just her servant. She was under the captain's protection, after all, at least for the duration, and she had implied her father would be meeting her when they docked, just a small lie to keep any concerns at bay.

Now, thinking about her father and finding him kept her current fears in check for only a short while. Her legs had fallen asleep, curled into the barrel as she was. She'd had no trouble getting all of herself into the container. She wasn't a big woman at only five-four, and was slender of frame. A splinter had pierced her back, though, when she'd scrunched down into the crate just before she'd pulled the lid back over it, and there was no way to reach it even if she had enough room to try.

And she was partly in shock that it was even possible for a ship to fly a Jolly Roger in this day and age. Pirates were supposed to be extinct. She had thought they had all been routed in the last century, either pardoned or hung. Sailing the warm Caribbean waters was supposed to be as safe as walking down an English country lane. If she hadn't been certain of that, she never would have booked passage to this side of the world. And yet, she'd seen the pirate flag with her own eyes.

There was a tight knot of fear in her belly, which was also empty and adding to her discomfort. She'd missed breakfast and had intended to remedy that at lunch, but the pirate ship had arrived before lunch was served, and now it was hours later. At least, it seemed like she'd been cramped in the barrel that long, and there was no indication of what was going on topside.

She had to assume they were staying far ahead of the pirate ship, but if they had lost the other vessel, wouldn't Avery have come to tell her so? Suddenly a blast shook the entire ship, and another, and more, all exceedingly loud. There were more indications that a battle had begun, the smell of gun smoke from the fired cannons that seeped into the hold, the raucous yells, even a few screams, and then, a long while later, the horrible silence.

It was impossible to determine who had won the battle. It was nerve-wracking. As time passed, her fear grew. She'd be screaming soon, she was sure. In fact, she didn't know how she'd managed not to succumb to that urge already. If they had won the day, wouldn't Avery have shown up by now? Unless he was wounded and hadn't told anyone where she was. Unless he was dead. Did she dare leave her hiding place to find out?

But what if the pirates had won? What did pirates do with captured ships? Sink them? Keep them to sell or man them with their own crews? And their current crew and passengers? Kill them all? The scream was bubbling up in her throat when the lid was torn off of her barrel.

Chapter 2

Pirates! Gabrielle got undeniable proof that pirates weren't extinct when one of them yanked her by her hair out of the barrel where she was hiding, dragged her topside amongst a lot of laughter and cheers, and dumped her on deck at the feet of the ugliest pirate of them all, their captain.

She was so terrified by that point that she couldn't imagine what was going to happen to her next. But she was sure it was going to be horrible. The only thought that entered her mind was to jump overboard in all haste.

The man looking down at her had thin, scraggly brown hair that fell to his shoulders, and on top of his head was an old tricornered hat with a dyed pink feather that hung down limply, as it was broken in at least two places. If that wasn't odd enough, he was also wearing a bright orange satin coat and flowing lace cravat right out of another century. The garments were in such appalling condition, they probably were that old.

Before she could get to her feet to dive over the side of the ship, he said, "M'name's Captain Brillaird, at your service, miss." He paused to laugh. "At least that's the name I'm using this month."

If he was picking names out of a hat, she thought he ought to try Moles. She'd never seen so many on someone's face.

Still trembling, she made no reply, but her eyes flew back to the ship's railing.

"You can put your fears to rest," he added. "You're too valuable to be harmed."

"Valuable how?" Gabrielle managed to ask, coming slowly to her feet now.

"As a hostage, of course. Passengers are much more lucrative to dispose of than cargoes that might rot before we can find markets for them."

She was starting to feel a smidgen of real relief, just enough for her to stop eyeing the railing. "What about the men?"

He shrugged. "The captain and the officers of a captured ship generally bring decent ransoms, too."

She couldn't tell if he was deliberately trying to put her mind at ease, or if he just liked to talk, because he proceeded to hold forth on the subject of ransoming prisoners.

Gabrielle learned that she and Margery were to be ransomed by her family. The captain never asked her if she had a family, he simply assumed that she did. It just remained for her to tell him whom to contact for the ransom money, and he seemed in no hurry to obtain that information. He and his cronies had other business to dispose of first, like the rest of the captured crew.

Gabrielle looked around the deck. If any of the crewmen had died in the battle, the evidence had been removed before she'd been dragged topside. Avery was lying on the deck, apparently unconscious from a gash on his head, tied up like the other officers and passengers, waiting to be transferred to the other ship. Theirs had sustained severe damage and was already starting to take on water.

Margery was there, too, also tied up, but she was the only prisoner who was gagged as well. She'd probably been too vocal with the pirates, chastising them for their temerity. She didn't care whom she offended when she got the notion to complain.

As for the common sailors, they were given a choice, to join the pirates and take their oath then and there, or to pay a visit to Davy Jones's locker, which meant they'd be tossed into the sea to drown.

Not surprisingly, most of them elected rather quickly to become pirates. One of them, a stout American, refused, and was quite nasty about it.

Gabrielle was forced to watch in horror as two of the pirates approached him, each taking one of his arms and dragging him to the rail. She didn't doubt he was going to be tossed over it. But he didn't change his mind and continued to curse them all right up until they smashed his head against the rail, knocking him out. The pirates laughed uproariously. She didn't see what was the least bit funny about making the man think he was going to die, then not killing him, but those pirates certainly did.

The American was still tossed into the water, but not until the next day when there was land within sight of the ship. It was an uninhabited island, but land nonetheless. He'd probably still die eventually, but at least he was given a chance. He might even be able to hail a passing ship and get rescued. It was a better fate than what Gabrielle had thought would befall him when he'd defied the pirates.

Later that same day they came to another island, which also appeared to be deserted. They'd sailed into the crystal clear waters of a wide bay. Nearly in the center of it was another small island. But as they approached it, Gabrielle could see it wasn't an island at all but a floating jungle of trees, many of them dead, and thick plants, most of them thriving in the dirt and other debris that was piled high on top of boards, not land. It was almost like a cluttered wharf, and yet it was a thickly built jungle, designed to conceal the ships anchored on the other side of it from any passing ships out in the ocean.

The flag of death was hoisted on the two ships that were there now, indicating that there had been disease on them, which might account for their abandoned look.

It didn't take long for the pirates to make their own ship look the same before the small boats were lowered into the water and the prisoners were rowed to shore—and they hoisted a flag of death on their ship as well. Gabrielle realized then the ships were nothing but a ruse to keep any other vessels that might sail into the bay from investigating the abandoned ships.

"Where are we going?" Gabrielle asked the pirate who helped her and Margery out of the rowboat. But apparently he didn't feel it was necessary to answer her. He just nudged her forward.

They began a trek inland. They weren't waiting for everyone to get off the ship, but thankfully, Avery was in the first group to go ashore. It was the first chance she'd had to talk to him since they'd been captured.

"Are you all right?" he asked as he walked alongside her.

"Yes, I'm fine," she assured him.

"No one . . . touched you?"

"Really, Avery, I haven't been hurt in any way."

"Thank God. I was so worried. You can't imagine."

She gave him a reassuring smile. "I'm to be ransomed. Captain Brillaird made it clear to me that I'm too valuable to be harmed. She pointed to the large open cut on his forehead. "How does your head feel? I saw you got knocked out yesterday."

He gingerly touched his wound. "Oh, that's just a scratch."

But Gabrielle could tell from his wince that it must be painful. "From what I gathered from the captain, he plans to ransom you, too."

"I don't know about that," Avery replied with a sigh. "I don't come from a wealthy family."

"Well, I'll speak to my father when he collects me," she said. "I'm sure he'll be able to arrange something to gain your release as well."

But she wasn't the least bit sure that Nathan could even be located. What would happen to her and Avery if the pirates couldn't track down her father?

"That's very kind of you," he said, then added urgently, "but listen to me, Gabrielle. You may have been given assurances, but from listening to this pirate crew, I understand there will be others of the same ilk where we're going. Your best way to come through this safely is to simply not draw attention to yourself. I know that will be difficult, as beautiful as you are, but—"

"Please, you needn't say anything more," she cut in with a blush. "I understand that we won't really be safe until we've seen the last of these cutthroats. I will remain as inconspicuous as possible."

They were separated then when one of the pirates pushed Avery to hurry him along.

The first sign that the island was inhabited was a watchtower they passed along the beaten path. It was built of logs, and was tall enough to have a clear view of the sea in at least three directions. They were climbing into the hills behind it. The tower was occupied, but the fellow in the tiny hut on top of it was asleep as they walked by. Not a very diligent guard, Gabrielle thought as one of the pirates kicked the tower to wake him, while another swore at him in fluid French.

Margery added her own opinion as she came up beside Gabrielle. "Lazy no-goods, the lot of them. Let's hope when help arrives, the guard sleeps through that as well."

Gabrielle would have liked to share that optimism, but the chance of their being rescued before they were ransomed was slim. "Once they find my father—"

"*If* they find him," Margery cut in. "Since we weren't even sure that *we* could, what are the chances of that, eh? We never should have undertaken this journey. Didn't I warn you it would be dangerous?"

"You could have stayed home," Gabrielle reminded her. "But it wasn't supposed to be dangerous. Would you have believed that pirates still exist in this day and age if someone had told you? No, you would have scoffed or laughed at them."

"That's beside the point," Margery replied. "But listen to me, before we get separated again. Look for a weapon, any sort, even a fork if you can get your hands on one, and keep it on your person at all times. If one of these bastards starts anything with you, you stick it right in his belly, hear? Don't hesitate."

"I'll remember that."

"You better, girl. If anything happens to you, I don't know what I'd do."

It looked like Margery was about to cry. She was more upset than she was letting on. And her distress was contagious. Gabrielle would have liked nothing better than to cry on her friend's shoulder just then, but she managed to restrain herself and dredged up some courage for both of them.

"You worry too much. We're going to be fine. Captain Brillaird has assured me of that."

That wasn't exactly true, but it was what Margery needed to hear and it got a weak smile out of her.

About a half hour later, they reached a large settlement of sorts high in the hills, surrounded by trees. There was one big building at its center, built of actual lumber that she was to learn had been obtained from one of the ships the pirates had plundered at sea. The rest of the buildings spread out around it were mostly just small thatch-roofed huts. Gabrielle could see through the open doorways that many of the huts were filled with chests and crates, serving as storage sheds for the pirates' ill-gotten gains.

Avery and the other male captives were shoved into one hut and Margery was led away to another, but not before she shouted back at Gabrielle, "Remember! In the belly!"

"Where are you taking her?" Gabrielle protested.

The pirate who was pushing her toward

the big building sneered. "Servants don't bring ransoms, but she'll be released with you once the captain's demands are met. You're valuable, so you'll go in here, where it'll be easier to guard you. Don't want any of the mates touching you and interfering with the high ransom you're sure to fetch." He winked at her lewdly, and Gabrielle couldn't help but cringe.

Once inside, the pirate led Gabrielle to a long table in the large room, pushed her down into a chair, then walked away. A bowl of food was set in front of her by a female cook, who remarked in a friendly tone, "Hope you got someone to pay for you, dearie. I delayed as long as I could before I finally had to admit that I didn't have any family left, and that's why I'm still here."

The middle-aged woman who introduced herself as Dora sat down and chatted with Gabrielle for a few minutes. She'd been allowed to stay on the island to work off her ransom. She cooked for the pirates, and apparently serviced them in other ways if she felt like it, all of which she mentioned in an offhanded manner.

She'd been there for two years now and even considered herself one of them, volunteering, "They're not out to make a name for themselves, not like the pirates you might have heard of from the last century. In fact, they change their names frequently, change their ships or the names of them, use disguises. They're in the business of making money, not getting hung. They operate in secrecy now and even change their base every few years."

"Is that what this is, their base?" Gabrielle asked curiously.

Dora nodded. "This one is on an island so remote it's never been named. It's a nice island, too nice actually. A time or two they've had to scare away settlers who also thought so."

"Who leads them?"

"No one. The captains have equal say, and jurisdiction only over their own crews. If something needs to be decided that affects them all, they vote on it."

"How many captains share this base?" Gabrielle asked.

"Five now. There was a sixth, but he died of natural causes last year and his crew joined up among the others."

Gabrielle expressed surprise that the

number was so few for what seemed such a large settlement.

"They don't want too many crews here. Figure the more people there are, the greater the chance someone will go rotten and give away the location of the base."

The woman moved away as soon as Captain Brillaird entered the building. Gabrielle had never been given his real name, nor was she to ever learn it. He changed his name so frequently that his men just called him Captain, so she had, too, when she found it necessary to address him. But he merely took note of where she sat, then ignored her for the rest of the day—and the days that followed.

Five days later the captain still hadn't asked her whom to contact for her ransom. She was left to worry over how to explain that while she knew her father would meet their price, she simply didn't know where he could be found. She really didn't think the captain would believe her, and she couldn't imagine what would happen if he didn't. Dora explained that she hadn't been questioned yet because the captain didn't need the information until he was ready to set sail again, and when that would be was anyone's guess. The captain's wife lived on the island and he hadn't seen her in two months.

The pirates ate, slept, drank, gambled, fought, joked, and told stories. Gabrielle slept in a tiny room at the back of the main building, and she was allowed access to the main room each day, so she couldn't complain that her time there was boring. Nerve-wracking, but not boring. Margery was brought in to visit her for a couple of hours each day, and Gabrielle was relieved to see that her former housekeeper was weathering her captivity well, although she complained incessantly about the thin straw mattress she was forced to sleep on and the poor quality of the meals.

On the sixth day of Gabrielle's captivity two more ships arrived and the main room actually got crowded with the new crews. And much more disturbing. There was nothing friendly about the newcomers. Several actually chilled her with a glance. And one of the two new captains stared at her so long, and so intently, she didn't doubt he meant her harm.

Tall and muscular, he was likely in his late thirties or early forties, though it was hard to tell with his full black beard that was so matted, she doubted a comb had ever passed through it. She heard people call him Pierre Lacross, though he probably wasn't really French. So many of the pirates pretended to be something they weren't, and none of them used their real names. But then she found out he was the exception to that rule. He really was French. He had a strong accent that he couldn't turn on and off like the others could. He wasn't ugly, but the cruel glint in his blue eyes marred what might have been a handsome visage.

There was something evil about this man, and she wasn't the only one to recognize it. The other men moved out of his way and avoided catching his eye. But his icy blue eyes kept coming back to Gabrielle, until she was nearly trembling with the fear he managed to inspire.

Gabrielle had left England quite innocent of men's desires. Her mother had never explained what she could expect when she married one. She probably would have done so before Gabrielle had had her Season in London, but Carla had been caught up in her romance with Albert, and then consumed with her own misery at the end when he'd betrayed her. But Gabrielle had learned a tremendous amount about men from the pirates.

They didn't curb their language when she was within hearing distance, and they loved to boast about their sexual conquests. So she had no trouble understanding the motives of the evil captain Pierre Lacross when he leaned over her the day after he'd arrived and said, "I'm going to buy you from my friend. Then it will be my choice what to do with you."

She wished she hadn't understood what he was implying, but she did. Would Captain Brillaird care where the money for her came from as long as he was paid? Did she dare to promise him more than Pierre could possibly pay? That was the only way she could see to avoid being "owned."

There was nowhere to run even if she could manage to sneak out of the building, no way off the island except with the pirates. Captain Brillaird was still her only help and yet she knew he wouldn't help her out of the goodness of his heart. What goodness? He was a pirate! Money was his only concern.

But she knew instinctively that she would come to serious harm if Pierre had his way with her, which was why he terrified her so much. And she was unfortunate enough to witness his cruelty when he disciplined one of his own men. He whipped the man right there in the hall, and not with just any whip. A cat-o'-nine-tails it was called, and it shredded skin as easily as a knife. The look in Pierre's eyes as he wielded it left no doubt in her mind that he was enjoying it.

Pierre grew impatient, waiting for her captain to show up so he could make the transaction. He sat next to her at her table and taunted her with what he planned to do to her.

"Why do you not look at me, *chérie*? You ladies, you are filled with too much pride. You will have none left when I am done with you. Look at me!"

She didn't. She'd avoided his gaze since that first day. "Go away, please."

He laughed. "So refined you are. So polite. I wonder how long that will last after I make you my pet. Will you be an obedient pet, *chérie,* or will I have to punish you often?" He heard the gasp she couldn't hold back and added, "You saw what I am capable of, but do not worry for your sweet, aristocratic skin. I would never mar your beauty. There are other ways to train a pet . . ."

He taunted, but he never touched her. He was careful not to do that with so many witnesses in the room. But it was obvious he wanted to. Dora told her the forced restraint was causing him such considerable frustration that he got so drunk each night he would stumble outside to pass out somewhere, and not return until the following afternoon.

It was an incredible piece of luck for Gabrielle that Captain Brillaird's wife kept him occupied until the last of the five captains sailed into the harbor. The fifth captain arrived on the island. He entered the building with Captain Brillaird one morning, both of them laughing heartily over something one of them had said. He noticed Gabrielle immediately. He paused and stared at her, then he put his arm around Brillaird's shoulder and offered to buy her. Pierre wasn't there to cry foul, that he'd thought of it first. She was sure he would have, and that there might even have been a fight. But he was still sleeping off his overindulgence of the night before. And Captain Brillaird didn't seem to care one way or the other, just as she'd guessed he wouldn't. She saw him shrug before the two men shook hands and the fifth captain tossed a purse of coins to him.

Gabrielle was in shock. It all happened so quickly. She found out later that the new captain was a middleman. It wasn't the first time he'd bought up hostages on the isle and returned them to their families for a tidy profit. It worked agreeably for all concerned, allowing the other captains to get right back to the business of capturing more ships, instead of dealing with the business side of their trade. He was good at the business side, and disguises. She almost didn't recognize him . . .

"What in the blazes are you doing here, Gabby, and where is your mother?"

He'd taken her out of the settlement immediately and was pulling her down the well-worn path to the bay. Most of his crew were still anchoring his ship, but a couple of his men whom they passed on the trail were ordered back to the ship without an explanation. When Gabrielle dug in her heels and explained that her housekeeper needed to be rescued, too, one was sent to collect Margery.

She had a thousand questions for him, but they were all forgotten with the reminder of her loss. "She died, Papa. That's why I left England. I was coming to find you, to live with you," she cried. "But not on this island, if it's all the same to you," she added primly.

Chapter 3

Gabrielle's father was extremely embarrassed the day he rescued her. All these years and she and her mother had never known, never suspected, that he'd been living such an adventurous life. Nathan Brooks the pirate. That took quite a bit of getting used to.

He looked so different now. It really had been difficult to recognize him. Whenever he had come to England to visit her, he'd cleaned himself up, shaved his beard, cut the long hair he was sporting now. That was the only man she'd ever known, and she'd thought she'd taken after him, at least in terms of her coloring. His hair was just as black as hers, his eyes the same pale blue.

She hadn't inherited his height, though, which was fortunate, because he was a tall man, a bit over six feet, while her size was the same as her mother's at five feet, four inches. But this man looked nothing like the father she knew and loved. He was actually as flamboyant in his dress and looks as all the other pirates she'd met. He even wore a small golden earring in one ear!

He quickly removed the earring. That's how embarrassed he seemed to be that she'd found out about his secret life.

A couple of hours after they sailed out of the harbor, Gabrielle realized her father's ship had slowed down. She went up on deck to see what was happening and walked right into Pierre Lacross! His ship had pulled abreast of her father's ship. Pierre had followed them from the pirate base!

She hadn't yet mentioned him to Nathan. There hadn't been much time for them to talk yet, and besides, she was still trying to deal with her shock over finding out her own father was a member of that pirate confederacy. But she'd at least felt safe after her father had rescued her and had been so certain she'd never see the likes of Pierre again.

But now here he was on the deck of *The Crusty Jewel,* standing next to Nathan and talking to him as if they were old friends. It dawned on her that they must be old acquaintances at least, since each of them was one of the five captains who shared that base.

Pierre's cold, avid gaze latched onto her immediately, pinning her to the warm deck boards. Her fear rushed back to her. She must have turned pale, because her father moved to her side and put his arm around her protectively.

"You sailed off with her too quickly, *mon ami*," Pierre said, making no pretense about his reason for being there. "I was going to buy her for myself."

"She's not for sale," Nathan said.

"Of course she is. You paid for her, I will pay you more. You will make your profit, we will both be happy."

"You misunderstand. She's my daughter," Nathan said coldly.

Pierre looked surprised. There was a very tense, silent moment while he seemed to assess the situation, his eyes shifting back and forth between her and her father. He must have realized he couldn't have her without a fight and decided against it; he laughed and complained about rotten luck in what for him was probably as good-natured a tone as he could muster. Pierre's tone seemed to assure her father that he knew Gabrielle was off-limits to him, but Gabrielle wasn't fooled. She had a feeling that Pierre viewed the conversation with her father as only a temporary delay. He sailed off, but she was very much afraid this wasn't going to be the last time she ever saw him.

Margery wasn't shy about expressing her wholehearted disapproval of her father's occupation. With all the nasty looks she was giving him those first few days, Gabrielle quickly found herself defending him. He was her father, after all. That he was a pirate didn't mean she could stop loving him.

She and her father didn't get a chance to talk until they reached his home port in St. Kitts, an island central to his sailing routes. He kept a small house there on the beach, far enough from town that he could anchor his ship offshore and row in if he had to. But he never had to. St. Kitts was an English port and he was an Englishman who'd never once fired on English ships. The French, the Dutch, the Spanish, those ships were all fair game.

His house was rather unique, like a fine English cottage that had been adapted to the warm climate, with large airy rooms and windows open to catch the breeze no matter which direction it came from. Gleaming hardwood floors, palm trees in large urns, thin, wispy drapery, these things added a touch of local color, but the furnishings were elegant and quite English in design, and everything was kept spotless by his small staff of servants who looked after the house when he wasn't in port. The paintings on the walls were tasteful and so reminiscent of those her mother had collected that she felt right at home.

The bedroom she was given was much larger than the one she'd had in England. The old wardrobe in it was an antique with cherry wood and ivory inlays in its doors; the canopy bed had carved posts and was draped in sheer white mosquito netting. And the view of the ocean and the harbor in the distance that could be seen from her balcony was magnificent.

The dining room also overlooked the ocean, and dinner that night was a tasty local dish of stuffed crab with plantains and spicy tomatoes, served with a fine French wine. A balmy, scented breeze entered from the open windows, as well as the soothing sound of ocean waves. She had a feeling she was going to love living there. But it didn't appear that Margery would. She spent the entire dinner glaring at the servants and insisting she was going to catch the first ship back home.

As soon as Margery took her sour looks to bed, Nathan led Gabrielle out to the beach for a walk so she could ask all the questions that had been running through her mind. He made no excuses for the career he'd taken up, but he did explain how he'd come to choose it.

"I was just a young sailor on a merchantman when we went down in a storm," he told her. "There were only a few of us who survived. We'd been floating for days when the pirates found us."

She thought she understood. "So you felt beholden to them because they rescued you?"

"I wouldn't exactly call it a rescue, Gabby. They were merely short on hands."

"Otherwise they would have sailed on without stopping?" she guessed.

"Exactly. And we were given the standard offer, join or get back in the water. So I joined."

"But you didn't have to stay with them, did you? When you reached a port, you could have gone your own way?"

"We didn't make port, at least not one that didn't belong to the pirates, for a long time. By the time we did, well, truth be told, I was enjoying the life. I found it exciting. So I had few misgivings about staying, and I worked my way up through the ranks until I had a ship of my own."

"Was this before or after you met Mama?"

"Before."

"And she never suspected?"

"Not in the least."

"What were you doing back in England, to have met her?"

He grinned at that point. "Treasure hunting. The captain of that first ship got me addicted to it."

"Treasure hunting in England?" she said in surprise.

"No, it was a missing piece of one of my maps that led me there. It took me years to find out that her family was known to be in possession of that last piece of it. I married her in order to facilitate my search."

"Did you not love her at all?"

He blushed slightly. "She was a fine-looking woman, but no, my only love is the sea, lass. And she was just happy to have a husband. She'd begun to fret about it, having gone through a few seasons without catching one. I wasn't up to her standards, of course, and couldn't claim the same fine bloodlines that she could, but I was rather dashing back then, if I do say so myself. But I think she surprised us both when she accepted my proposal. The bloom wore off rather quickly. She was glad to see me sail off."

That certainly explained a lot. Gabrielle had always wondered what had drawn her parents together, since they'd seemed to be nearly strangers to each other whenever he visited. That hadn't been far from the truth. She had a feeling that while Nathan had used the marriage for his own purposes, so had Carla. She'd wanted a child and she'd needed a husband to get one. Never once, though, through the years, had she doubted her mother's love. Even at the end, when Carla became so bitter because of her lost lover, she never took that bitterness out on her daughter.

"Did you ever find the missing piece of your map?" she asked curiously.

"No," he mumbled. "But I stayed too long searching for it. You were conceived before I left, and you were the only reason I ever returned over the years. I never regretted that, though. You've been a very bright light in my life, Gabby, my one true source of pride. I'm so sorry about your mother, and that you had to go through that alone. And then for you to risk coming here to find me—that was very brave of you."

"I didn't feel I had any other choice."

They'd stopped to stare out over the moonlit ocean, waves lapping near their feet. A warm breeze ruffled the hem of her skirt. His arm slipped about her shoulders, gathering her close.

"I'm sorry, too, that you were captured, but I'm not sorry at all that you're here with me now, daughter. It's where I've always wanted you to be."

Tears formed in her eyes as she put her

arms around him to hug him back. She was home, finally, really home.

Gabrielle found life on St. Kitts exhilarating. Every morning she woke up to a day full of sunshine and adventure. At her father's insistence she learned how to swim and did so nearly every day in the warm, blue Caribbean. She also rode the horse he bought her along the beach, sometimes not coming home until dusk so she could enjoy the magnificent sunsets.

She loved it there, even though the heat could become oppressive at times. But it was all new to her, and at her young age, she found it all fascinating. The food was different, the climate was certainly different, the locals were colorful and friendly, the entertainments, even dancing in the streets, were nothing she could ever have imagined back home in England.

She even discovered that she liked sailing, and was an old hand at it now, sailing with her father often when he was chasing down clues to one of his many treasure maps. She came to understand why he'd taken up the life he did. He could easily experience more fun and adventure in a single week than some men experienced in a lifetime! She might not approve of his pirating activities, but she began to view them in a different light, especially after she learned that some of the hostages that Nathan handled might never be returned to their families if he didn't intervene, playing the middleman, as it were. And he no longer captured ships himself. He spent most of his time chasing down treasure.

She was even with him when he actually located the landmarks on one of his maps and was finally able to zero in on the bright red mark that indicated where the treasure was hidden. It was incredibly exciting to watch her father and his men dig at that spot on that little island and then find the large chest that was buried there. But it was quite disappointing to see them open it and find it empty.

It was to be expected, though. The maps he had collected over the years had passed through many hands before they came into his possession. Most of Nathan's maps were very hard to decipher because each owner of the treasure who drew the maps used very few landmarks, just enough to lead himself back to his loot, but not enough for anyone else who might get hold of the maps to figure them out. And some of his maps had been torn apart to make them next to impossible to figure out, the pieces hidden in different places, or given to different members of a family, the meanings of them lost over the years, so some people didn't even know what they possessed. Her father had two maps that were missing pieces.

Margery never did catch that ship back to England, as she'd sworn she would do when they'd first arrived in St. Kitts. Although she hadn't taken well to the heat in the islands, she'd stayed because she wouldn't leave Gabrielle alone among "pirates." She got to know some of those pirates quite well herself, though, at least the members of Nathan's crew. They both did. Gabrielle even considered a few of them dear friends. Actually, most of the members of Nathan's crew were surprisingly quite decent and honorable, though perhaps too free-spirited and adventure-loving to fit into proper society.

Nathan did a good job of shielding her from unsavory men, like Pierre Lacross, though she never did lose her fear of that man, not even after she'd heard he'd taken up with the female pirate called Red. And she did see him again once, at sea, when she and her father had been treasure hunting. Pierre had just captured a ship. That was when she found out that if Nathan didn't take Pierre's hostages off his hands, he would have killed them. And before Pierre departed, he managed to get close to her for a moment and whisper, out of her father's hearing, "Do not think I have forgotten you, my pet. Our time will come."

That was probably the only black mark on a spotless tapestry of wonderful experiences she enjoyed while living with her father in the islands. She knew it wouldn't last forever. She'd get married eventually, was even looking forward to it. She dearly wanted what she'd missed as a child—to have a stable, loving family who stuck together. She even had a few flirtations with handsome sailors, but they always sailed away, which was fine with her because during those first couple of years on St. Kitts all she really wanted to do was spend time with her father and make up for all the years they'd been apart.

For nearly three years she'd felt that way, until Charles Millford returned from his schooling abroad. The very handsome son of a fine English family who owned a sugar plantation on the island, Charles had seemed quite interested in her as well—until he found out who her father was and was rude enough to explain why he couldn't further their acquaintance. And it wasn't that Nathan was a pirate! No one on St. Kitts knew that. It was because they considered him a commoner. The Millfords were snobbish enough to presume that she wasn't good enough for their only son because of that.

Gabrielle was crushed when Charles gave her the cold shoulder after that, though she hid it well. She wasn't about to let her father know that the one man who'd made her seriously think about matrimony wouldn't have her because of him.

But it was a small island. Somehow Nathan found out about it. She should have guessed by his suddenly pensive mood, which was so unlike him, but since he said nothing, she was loath to bring it up herself. It was when she mentioned that she'd soon reach her majority and Ohr, one of Nathan's loyal crew members, overheard her and re-marked, "And she isn't married yet?" that Nathan actually paled and she was sum-moned to his study that very night.

After his reaction to Ohr's remark, she guessed he was going to talk about her matrimonial prospects on the island. She never could have guessed the decision he'd already made.

No sooner did she sit down across from him at the other side of his desk than he said, "I'm sending you back to England."

Her reaction was immediate. She didn't even have to think about it. "No."

He smiled at her. It was a sad smile. And he didn't try to argue with her. Since he liked making her happy, she usually won any dis-agreements they had.

He simply explained, "You know your mother and I were a mismatched pair. She was gentry, while I came from the other side of the coin. I've nothing to be ashamed of, mind you, not where my rearing was con-cerned. I grew up in Dover. My parents were good, hardworking people. But your mother never saw it that way and made up grand stories for her friends about my background and why I was rarely at home. She didn't even want her friends to know I was in trade, which wasn't the case, but was what she thought."

"I know all that, Papa."

"Yes, I know you do, but you see, you have aristocratic blood due to your mother's lineage. However, no one is going to believe that in this part of the world. And besides, I realized today what I've denied you by keeping you with me, a Season in London, all the grand balls and parties a young girl of the upper crust can expect—everything your mother wanted for you, including a fine gentleman for a husband."

She lowered her head. "You know about Charles Millford, don't you?"

"Yes," he said quietly. "I even toyed with the idea of calling old man Millford out."

Her head shot up. "You didn't!"

He grinned. "Actually I did, but I thought I ought to ask you first if you really loved the boy."

She gave that a moment's consideration, then admitted, "Not really. I'm sure I could have, but to be honest, I think I was just ready to fall in love, and Charles was the first man I've met here that I felt would make a fine husband."

"Whether he would have or not, Gabby, think about what you just said. In all your time here, he's the only one you've even considered for matrimony. That's an appalling number of choices, my dear, when you should have dozens of young men to choose from, and in England you will have. No, you're going back to claim your inheritance and have the Season your mother always planned for you to have, and in the process find a proper husband."

She knew he was right, that she probably had no other options. But an English husband meant living in England again and she hated the thought of giving up her idyllic life here. On the other hand, if she got really lucky, she might find an Englishman adventurous enough to move to the Caribbean for the sake of love. Now *that* would be perfect and even made her feel excited about the journey.

"You're right," she said. "I would like to meet someone I can fall in love with and marry, but how can I do that in England without an entrée into society?"

"Not to worry, my dear. I may not have the

connections that your mother did, but there's a man I know who owes me a favor and he's upper crust with all the right connections. His name is Malory—James Malory."

Chapter 4

"D' you think Drew will mind?" Georgina Malory asked her husband as she prepared for dinner.

"You intend to ask him?" James replied.

"Well, certainly."

"You didn't ask me," he reminded her.

She snorted. "As if you'd let me go alone."

" 'Course I wouldn't, but there was the possibility that I would have told you to stay home."

She blinked in surprise. "Was there really?"

He groaned inwardly. She'd miscarried their last child. They didn't talk about it, but it had been recent enough that James would have agreed to anything she wanted, even though he could barely tolerate her brothers, and the thought of sailing with one of them when he wouldn't be in control of the ship himself was the last thing he would have normally agreed to do.

In fact, he was considering buying another ship himself so he wouldn't have to, though he wasn't sure he could manage that in the short time frame Georgina was planning on. Then again, taking her to America himself wouldn't give her the extra time with her brother, which she was also looking forward to. Bloody hell.

"I've already agreed, George, so it's moot. But he's your brother. What do you think?"

Georgina bit her lip, though she didn't appear to be worried. "It is perfect timing, isn't it?" she asked, wanting a little reassurance. "Drew was already scheduled to sail in a couple weeks, and not off on one of his Caribbean routes, but home to Bridgeport, so he'll have room for passengers this trip, and won't have to go out of his way to oblige me. And I'm sure he wouldn't mind sailing a week earlier. He was only going to stay here longer to visit with me."

James raised a single golden brow at her.

It was an affectation that used to annoy his wife before they married, but now she found it quite endearing.

"And you wouldn't have asked him otherwise?" he queried.

"Well, certainly I would have. There's no better time to go, after all. It's late summer, so we'll be home before winter. And the date for Jeremy's wedding in a few days is even accommodating. We'll be back in London from the wedding with plenty of time to pack if we sail next week. I just wouldn't have felt as comfortable asking him to make a detour to take me to Bridgeport, but since he's already going there . . ."

"You forget, he adores Jack. He'd do anything for her, if not for you. And like you, he'll be delighted with the notion of taking her to Connecticut to see firsthand where the barbaric side of her family comes from. For years now your brothers have been mentioning that she ought to make the trip. If they had their way, she'd be raised there, not here."

She ignored the "barbaric" remark to point out, "I don't think they meant for her to go while she's this young, though. If you must know, they're hoping she'll marry an

American, so they wanted her to make that particular visit when she'd reached an age to attract a husband."

"Bite your tongue, George. She's going to marry an Englishman—if I allow any of them to get close enough to her to make her acquaintance."

The last was said in a mumble that had Georgina grinning. "Well, the thought was that if she fell in love with an American, you wouldn't prevent the marriage. You'd object, of course, but since the little darling fits in one of your few soft spots, you'd give in, in the end."

"Appreciate the warning."

Since he didn't elaborate, she frowned. "In other words, you won't allow her anywhere near Connecticut when she reaches a marriageable age?"

"Exactly."

The frown eased. She even chuckled. "I hate to inform you of this, but more and more Americans visit England these days. And you can be sure that when the time comes, my brothers will be trotting every eligible one of them by here to meet their beloved niece."

"I wouldn't place any wagers on that, m'dear."

She sighed, imagining how unpleasant it would be if her husband and brothers put aside their truce. It was only a grudging truce, after all. It wasn't as if they liked each other or hadn't tried to kill each other in the past. In fact, her brothers had trounced James soundly, all five of them at the same time. Of course, they wouldn't have succeeded if they'd been fair about it, but they had been furious when he'd announced to them that he'd compromised their only sister, *and* they'd been quite willing to have him hanged for piracy if he didn't agree to marry her. Not a very good start to the wonderful marriage they had now, but she certainly couldn't say getting to know James Malory, ex-rake, ex-gentleman pirate, hadn't been incredibly exciting.

She finally tsked and complained, "I don't know how we got onto the subject of Jacqueline's future marriage, which is years away. We should be discussing Jeremy's instead, which is only days away. You do know he's coming to dinner, right? And that he needs cheering up? I've also invited Percy and Tony and his family."

James came up behind her and wrapped his arms around her. "You mentioned all that at breakfast. What I didn't know was that you were nervous, and don't deny it. You wouldn't be repeating yourself if you weren't. Fess up, George."

"I'm not nervous a'tall. I expect Drew to be quite pleased to take us on as passengers once I mention it to him, and I'll do that tonight."

"Then what is it?"

She sighed again. "It's occurred to me that we're getting old, James."

"The devil we are."

She turned around, put her arms around him as well, which was no easy task considering how wide and solidly muscled James Malory was. "We are," she insisted. "With Jeremy getting married, I don't doubt he'll make us grandparents soon, and I'm going to feel positively ancient when he does!"

He burst out laughing. "What a silly chit you are, and I thought you only get that way when . . . you're . . . pregnant. Good God, George, you aren't pregnant *again,* are you?"

She huffed. "Not that I know of. Really, I don't think so."

"Then stop being silly, or must I remind you that Jeremy is only your stepson, *and* that he's only a few years younger than you are. You're only going to be a step-grand-mother. And don't even think of calling me ancient again, or were you planning on serving shoes for dinner?"

She pushed out of his arms, laughing at the memory of his chasing her around his desk on his ship, *The Maiden Anne,* after she'd told him "if the shoe fits" in relation to his being ancient. He'd told her he was go-ing to make her eat that shoe, and he prob-ably would have, too. She'd wounded his vanity, after all, quite deliberately, of course. But shoes and the eating of them were a standard joke with them now.

"And of course the youngun needs cheer-ing up," James agreed. "His future mother-in-law all but kicked him out of her house and refuses to let him see the bride before the wedding. I'm deuced if I would have al-lowed your family to keep me away from you after the wedding date was set."

"Very funny, James. We didn't get to set a wedding date and you know it. We both got shoved up to the altar the very same day my family met you."

"And a good thing, too, but then barbarians are *so* predictable."

She burst out laughing. "Let's not inform them that you did the forcing that day, when they really thought it was their idea."

"They wouldn't believe it anyway, and thankfully, you only have one brother here at the moment—one too many, but one I can tolerate."

"You'll never admit that my brothers aren't as bad as you thought, will you? Drew even recently helped extricate Jeremy from the leg-shackle that he didn't want, and without being asked, too."

"His help was noted. Hate to say it, but I do owe him one for that. Just don't remind him that I do. I bloody well hope he forgets."

"Oh, posh. He doesn't expect payback. Andersons aren't like that and you know it."

"Beg to differ, George. *Everyone* is like that if the need is great enough. Fortunately, he's got four other brothers to depend on before he'd think of turning to a brother-in-law for help. And it sounds like Tony has arrived," he added with a wince as they both heard the noise from downstairs. "You really should point out to our daughter that squealing is a habit of pigs, not young girls."

Amused by her husband's reaction to the din their daughter and Tony's daughter were making, she grinned at him. "Won't do any good. You know very well Jack and Judy are inseparable. If they haven't seen each other for a few days, they simply can't help being excited when they do."

"And make that unearthly racket."

"Which reminds me. Jacqueline is really looking forward to this trip, but I don't think it's occurred to her yet that she won't see Judith for the couple of months that we'll be gone."

James groaned inwardly, quite aware of where her thoughts were going. "You're leaving the twins with Regan, but now you want to add to the passenger list? My brother will never agree. You may depend upon it."

" 'Course he will. It's going to be an educational trip, after all, for the girls to visit America. They've never been out of England, either of them."

"What's that got to do with Tony missing his only daughter?"

"Just remind him that it will give him some time alone with Rosalyn."

He pulled her back into his arms. "And when do I get some time alone with you?"

"Do you want some?" she almost purred, wrapping her arms around his neck as she leaned into him.

"Always."

"Then I'll think of something, and *you* may depend upon that."

Chapter 5

"Two weeks ain't the least bit depressing, and you only have three days to go before the wedding. Gives you time to have second thoughts, don't it? Her mother is a genius if you ask me. You may end up thanking her."

All four men stared at Percival Alden as if he were daft. This was not an unusual occurrence. It happened all the time, actually. Percy, as his friends called him, could be counted on to say the most ridiculous things, or worse, to say things he shouldn't to the wrong people, which usually resulted in one of his friends getting in deep water. And oddly enough, it was never intentional, it was simply Percy being Percy.

Right now, only Jeremy Malory was glaring at Percy for the remarks he had just
made. The other men in the room were
greatly amused, though most of them tried
admirably not to show it. But Jeremy was
the one in the dumps over being denied access to Danny, the woman who'd won his
heart, while her mother arranged their wedding.

Some private time alone with her daughter was Evelyn Hillary's real motive when
she'd told Jeremy almost two weeks ago to
go home to await the day of his nuptials. He
shouldn't begrudge her that, she'd said,
and he didn't really. Mother and daughter
had been separated for many years, after
all, Danny having grown up in the London
slums, unaware of who she was or that she
still had one parent alive when she'd
thought them both dead. And they'd only
just been reunited.

Knowing that made the separation no
easier to bear for Jeremy. He'd only just realized that what he felt for Danny was real,
and Malorys didn't succumb to love easily.
They were a family that had produced some
of London's most notorious rakes, Jeremy
included, and not one of them had ever

treated that emotion lightly once they'd experienced it.

Drew Anderson was the only one in the drawing room, where the men had gathered after dinner, who didn't try to conceal his amusement over Percy's remarks. Out of all the Malorys he probably liked Jeremy the best, since they had so much in common, or at least they did before Jeremy decided to give up his bachelorhood. Jeremy was also his nephew by marriage, or stepnephew, but family nonetheless.

What was even more amusing was that Jeremy, known to have such a high tolerance for alcohol that he'd never experienced a state of real inebriation, even when drinking everyone else under the table, looked to be on his way to changing that amazing record tonight. He'd arrived with a bottle of brandy in hand, had gone through another during dinner, and was fast making his way through a third. It was incredible that he wasn't passed out on the floor and that his words weren't slurred, but there was a telltale glaze in his eyes that warned he was foxed, as the saying went here, for the first time in his life.

His father, James, hadn't noticed yet. His

uncle Anthony was too busy trying not to laugh to notice. Percy only noticed things he shouldn't, so he wouldn't be remarking on it. But Drew, being an Anderson in the enemy's camp, as it were, had no trouble spotting Jeremy's misery and what he was attempting to do about it.

Sorrows drowned in drink. It was too funny. But Drew could almost sympathize. The bride was incredibly beautiful, and he'd considered pursuing her himself when he'd thought she was just Jeremy's upstairs maid. But Jeremy had already staked a claim and had made that clear. And no woman was worth fighting over in Drew's opinion. If he couldn't have one, another would do. He wasn't particular, and wasn't about to get caught in an emotion that was foreign to him.

In every harbor he sailed into, there was a woman waiting to greet him with open arms. It wasn't that he'd made a deliberate effort to have a "sweetheart" in every port, as his sister was fond of putting it. He was just a man who loved women, all women, and those he favored tended to hope he'd make their port his permanent one. Not that he ever gave them any reason to think he'd ever settle down. He told them no lies, made them no promises, and when he was at sea didn't require they be any more faithful than he'd ever be.

Georgina and Anthony's wife entered the drawing room before Jeremy got around to blasting his friend. Now, there was another fine-looking woman, Rosalyn Malory, Drew thought. He had heard how Anthony had won the lady. She'd been in need of a husband to protect her from an unscrupulous cousin who was trying to steal her fortune. Anthony had volunteered, to the amazement of his family. He was another rake they'd thought would never marry.

Drew could say one thing for the Malory men: they certainly had good taste in women. And James Malory had made the best catch of all, in his opinion, because James had managed to get the Andersons' only sister to fall in love with him. He didn't deserve her, of course. None of her brothers thought he did. But it couldn't be denied that he made her happy.

Drew wasn't looking forward to being confined on a ship with his formidable brother-in-law, but he was certainly delighted that he'd be spending more time with his sister and niece, since he didn't get to London that often. Too bad James couldn't be left behind. He ought to suggest it. He could take care of James's family well enough, since they were his family, too. And he was sure James didn't really want to go, when he had such bad memories of the last time he'd been in Bridgeport.

Wouldn't hurt to suggest it, Drew thought. It would be another week before they sailed, enough time for James to at least consider staying home. There was time enough for Drew to watch Jeremy tie the knot, too, and lament that another confirmed bachelor was leaving the ranks. If he ever got that stupid, he hoped someone would shoot him first.

Chapter 6

Drew was in a hurry. He had just been told that his brother Boyd's ship, *The Oceanus,* was anchored in the harbor waiting for dockage. It would be days before it was given a berth because the line of incoming ships was long. But that didn't mean Boyd hadn't rowed ashore already, and if not, Drew would find a dinghy himself to pay Boyd a visit.

He hadn't known Boyd was scheduled to stop in England, but his timing couldn't have been better. The family had just returned to London yesterday from Jeremy's wedding and would be sailing to Connecticut in less than a week. Drew had come down to the docks today to let his first mate know they would be sailing sooner than planned.

He'd actually expected to find *The Oceanus* in Bridgeport, since it usually transported sugar and tobacco from the West Indies to the northeastern states. He'd been looking forward to a reunion with his youngest brother. That was his main reason for sailing to their home port himself.

If Boyd had come to England merely to visit with Georgina, then he might like to sail home with Drew this trip. Now, that was a pleasant thought, especially since their brother-in-law, James, hadn't taken the hint and was still determined to sail with his wife and daughter. Drew could use some rein-forcements with that particular Malory aboard.

Georgina and Boyd were the only two Andersons who didn't captain their own ships. She'd never been expected to and would probably have had quite a fight on her hands with all five of her brothers if she'd ever suggested it. Boyd simply didn't want to. He loved to sail, he just had no desire to take command.

They'd always thought it was nervous-ness and he just needed time to outgrow it, and that eventually he'd become captain of his ship *The Oceanus* when he was ready. But he'd finally admitted he saw no need to ever take that step, that he preferred to simply enjoy the voyages without the responsibility of being in charge, and since he paid his captains from his own pocket, his brothers had no reason to complain. Since Boyd was not needed for *The Oceanus* to set sail again, he might be agreeable to traveling with him and Georgina and her family on *The Triton.*

Hurrying along the crowded wharf to the Skylark Office, where he expected to find Boyd if he'd already come ashore, Drew didn't pay much attention to the traffic, other than to avoid it. But it was hard to miss the woman about to fall right in his path.

It was a mere reflex to grip her arm to keep her from falling. He wasn't really paying attention to her because his eyes were on the two fellows walking behind her who charged forward just as Drew set her back on her feet.

"Let go," she growled at him, and he did.

Drew wasn't sure if the two men were really with her, because now that she was standing steadily on her own two feet, they hung back behind her, trying to appear as if they weren't keeping an eye on her. Odd. Drew glanced back at the woman to see why she'd been unappreciative of his help, and forgot about her escort entirely.

The palest blue eyes he'd ever seen surrounded by black lashes were glaring at him. They were eyes so startlingly beautiful that it took him a moment to take in the rest of the package.

Drew wasn't often given pause. Piqued, certainly. But being rendered speechless just didn't happen all that often to a man who'd pursued the loveliest of the lovelies across the world. This one was pretty, yes, but many could outshine her. A pert nose, black brows barely arched, probably because of her frown. But full, lush lips boldly red, though not from any paint. Because she'd been biting them would be his guess.

Her black hair was tightly contained in an artful coiffure. Her blue dress and hat were nearly as pale as her eyes. She was dressed like a lady in the height of fashion, and yet she had a rich, golden tan that the ladies of England simply wouldn't acquire. He'd wager she'd been in a warmer climate recently.

Was that what surprised him, the deeply tanned skin that was darker than her eyes? Or those sinfully lush lips? Or perhaps it was simply because she was glaring at him when he'd helped her, for crying out loud.

"Should I have let you tumble at my feet, sweetheart?" he asked.

"Excuse me?"

"You were about to fall," he reminded her. "Or has that slipped your mind? I know I do have that effect on women, scattering their thoughts every which way," he added with a boyish grin.

Instead of charming her out of her ire as he expected, his remark had her drawing in her breath indignantly and claiming, "You've bruised my arm, you lout."

"Did I? Let me see."

She jerked her arm out of his reach. "I think not. If you were indeed trying to be helpful, I thank you. But next time don't be such a brute about it."

His smile gone, Drew replied, "There won't be a next time, because if you stumble again, I'd definitely think twice about trying to catch you. In fact, I'm sure I'd let you fall. Good day, miss."

He heard her gasp of outrage as he

walked away. It was a sweet sound, but it didn't bring back his smile. Ungrateful wench, he thought. He was so annoyed he felt no urge to look back at her, which was unusual for him when he encountered a beautiful woman. He just barreled past her escort, if indeed the two men really were her escort. Too bad neither of them took exception to it.

Chapter 7

The London dock was teeming with activity, but it was no different from the last time Gabrielle had been there, when she'd set off three years ago for the Caribbean, so confident that she could find her father. The arriving vessels accounted for most of the extra wagons that late in the day, transporting cargoes from ship to warehouse or straight to market. The sounds, the smells were almost familiar, and had so distracted her that she hadn't seen the cart that had nearly knocked her over, or the man who'd prevented her from falling. Perhaps if she had seen him first, she wouldn't have been so surprised by the immediate attraction she'd felt, and wouldn't have made such a blun-

dering fool of herself because of it. Good
grief, she'd never in her life behaved so out-
rageously before, and all he'd tried to do
was help her!

Her ship had sailed up the Thames early
that morning, but it had taken most of the
day before the passengers were rowed to
the dock. She was glad of the late hour. It
allowed her to get a room for the night and
to delay delivering the letter in her pocket.

Two of her father's crew were trailing at a
discreet distance behind her, the two he
trusted most, Richard and Ohr. They'd been
sent to England with her to protect her, and
to make sure the lord to whom she was delivering the letter complied with the favor
her father was requesting of him. The men
made two of the most incongruous chaperones imaginable, and yet, if they weren't accompanying her, she doubted that she
would go through with this.

She was to go husband hunting in the
grand style favored by the English ton.
She'd been sent ahead with her chaperones
to get started on a magnificent new wardrobe for that very reason, and to catch the
tail end of the summer Season. Her father
was in the middle of ransoming two hos-

tages, so he couldn't leave just yet, but he'd promised to join her in a month or two. She'd argued that she could wait for him. He'd argued that this couldn't wait. He'd won.

Margery had come as well. It wasn't surprising that the middle-aged woman had staunchly refused to let her travel to England without a *real* chaperone, as she put it, but then, unlike Gabrielle, she'd missed their homeland terribly. She'd been excited during the whole trip about finally going home. As soon as they'd reached the dock, she'd rushed off to find them a carriage to hire, no easy task with so many arrivals that day, but she maintained she knew exactly how to *not* take no for an answer and it took her only an hour to prove it, which Richard had teased her about all the way to the inn.

Gabrielle tried not to think about what was causing her such apprehension right now. Instead she thought about her time in the Caribbean with her father. Not until recently had either of them considered the disadvantages of her staying in that part of the world with him, that she would be missing all the things a young marriageable Englishwoman should be doing after reaching eighteen. She couldn't say she regretted it, though. Not for anything would she have missed those wonderful years with her father.

The two men joined her and Margery for dinner and stayed to keep Gabrielle company. Ohr was playing cards with Margery, who had worn herself out with her excitement over being home, so she wasn't paying much attention to the game or the conversation.

Out of Nathan's crew, Ohr had been with him the longest. He used a host of fake names, too, as they all did, but Ohr happened to be his real one. If a last name went with it, he never bothered to mention it.

Most people assumed he was calling himself a nautical term when he introduced himself. Gabrielle had certainly thought that herself. Which was why he always volunteered, without being asked, that his name was spelled with an *h*. That he had the look of a half-breed Oriental, even wore his excessively long black hair in a single braid down his back, kept anyone from questioning it. They merely assumed, without knowing any better, that it was an Oriental name.

Over six feet tall, he had a face that

seemed ageless. He mentioned once that his father had been an American who often sailed to the Far East. Ohr had joined the crew of an American ship sailing back to the Western side of the world, with the thought of finding his father, but he'd never gotten around to trying, had become a pirate instead.

The second crewman who her father had sent to watch over her went by the name of Jean Paul and a host of other names. But he'd revealed to her in secret when they'd become friends that Richard Allen was his real name. He'd told her that much, but no more about his past, or where he really came from, and she'd never pressed. He wasn't much older than Gabrielle, and he stood out among the pirates not because he was so tall and handsome, but because he was always meticulously clean, both his person and his clothes.

He wore his black hair long and queued back, kept his face shaven except for a trim mustache. His clothes were as flamboyant as everyone else's but spotless, and his high boots always shined. He wore no gaudy jewelry, though, just a single silver ring with some sort of crest on it. He had wide shoulders but was slim of build, and his green eyes sparkled. He seemed to always be flashing his white teeth with a smile or a laugh. Gabrielle found him to be appealing, a very lighthearted young man.

Richard practiced his French accent constantly, though it was still as atrocious as it had been when she'd first met him. At least he'd stopped slipping with the "bloody hells" when he got emotional, which were a dead giveaway to his real nationality.

She'd asked him once why he bothered to pretend to be a Frenchman when the fake names were enough for most of the pirates. He'd merely shrugged and said he didn't want to be like the rest of the pirates and he was determined to master the disguise before he gave it up.

Richard had told her once that while he had wanted to make romantic overtures to her, he was afraid her father would kill him if he did, so he'd managed to resist the urge.

She'd laughed. He was a charming young man, humorous and daring, but she'd never once considered anything more than friendship with him.

But that she'd only formed a platonic relationship with such a handsome young man as Richard Allen didn't mean she hadn't succumbed to a few romantic attractions over the years in the Caribbean. It was just as well that most of them had been sailors, though, aside from Charles, because a seafaring man was the last kind of man she wanted for a husband, having grown up with firsthand knowledge of how infrequently they were ever at home.

When she did marry, the man would have to actually share a life with her. That's how she envisioned marriage. If he was gone for months at a time the way sailors were, if she ended up being left mostly alone, then what would be the point of marrying?

Her mother had had a similar opinion. So often over the years, she had told Gabrielle that it was pointless to love a man who loves the sea. The competition was too great.

"Why did you let him upset you, *chérie*?" Richard asked as she paced the room.

She knew exactly whom he was talking about—the handsome man she'd encountered on the dock—since she'd been trying to keep "him" out of her mind. But she didn't have an answer that she cared to share, so instead she said, "I wasn't upset."

"You nearly took his head off."

"Nonsense. I was just shaken," she replied. "That cart would have knocked me over, if he didn't grab me. But he pinched my arm so hard I think I would have been less hurt if I'd fallen to the ground, so he wasn't really the least bit helpful."

It was a blatant lie. Richard raised a brow to indicate he suspected that, causing her to blush and try a different reason, one that was true.

She continued, "I've been quite nervous ever since we set sail."

"Hoist the sails!" Miss Carla squawked.

All four pairs of eyes turned toward the bright green parrot in the little wooden barred cage she was occasionally kept in. The bird had belonged to Nathan. She was a sweetheart when she was on his shoulder, but everyone else she regarded as the enemy.

During the first year, whenever Gabrielle tried to pet the bird or feed her, she usually yanked back fingers dripping blood. She'd been persistent, though, enough so that Miss Carla had eventually defected to the enemy camp, as it were, and Nathan had gifted her with the bird her second year in the islands.

The parrot's vocabulary until then had merely been nautical—and disparaging about her mother. Even the name Nathan had given the bird had been a deliberate insult to his wife. He'd found it amusing to teach her phrases like "Carla's a dumb bird" and "I'm an old biddy," and the worst one, "A copper to drop me drawers."

He'd been so embarrassed when she'd first squawked "Carla's a dumb bird" in front of Gabrielle that he'd immediately marched the bird down to the beach to drown her in the ocean. Gabrielle had had to run after him to stop him, though she was sure he wouldn't really have killed Miss Carla, and they'd both been able to laugh about it later.

Ohr tossed his dinner napkin at the bird's cage, getting three hard flaps of her wings and a "Bad girl, bad girl" out of her.

Richard chuckled at the parrot, but then got back to the subject at hand, asking Gabrielle, "You're nervous about getting married?"

That question threw her off. "Married? No, I'm actually looking forward to meeting all the dashing young men who will be in London for the Season. I hope to fall in love with one of them," she added with a smile.

That was true, but she just wasn't sure she wanted to live in England again, when she'd loved the islands so much. And she certainly didn't like the idea of living so far away from her father. But she was still hopeful that she could convince the man she married to move to the Caribbean or, at the very least, spend part of each year there. "But calling in this favor from a man I don't know and my father barely knows, well, I really hate the idea of doing that," she added. "He could just close the door in our faces, you know." She could hope.

"We're here to make sure he doesn't do that," Ohr said quietly.

"You see!" she exclaimed. "Then we'd be forcing his hand, and you just don't do that with English lords. Do either of you even know him, or know how my father helped him to incur this favor?"

"Never met him," Richard replied.

"I have, though I didn't know he was an aristocrat," Ohr said. "My experience of lordly types, minimal as it is, is that they are mostly popinjays who crumble at the least sign of aggression."

She couldn't tell if Ohr was joking or not, but Richard made a sour look to that remark, which was very telling. Good grief, was her friend an English lord without ever having let on that he was? She stared at him hard, but he merely lifted a brow at her. He probably had no idea he'd stirred her curiosity with his reaction to Ohr's comment.

She shook the thought from her mind. It was absurd, anyway. Englishmen might become pirates, but English lords certainly wouldn't. And the lord they would be visiting tomorrow could be the veriest dandy, but that didn't erase her reservations. She was simply mortified to have to collect on a favor that wasn't owed to her personally. She was the one who was going to end up being beholden, and she hated the idea of that.

She'd grown and changed a lot over the last three years. She'd found out that she could be resourceful, that if something needed to be done she could get it done. She'd survived a hurricane that had struck while her father was away, and she and Margery had pitched in to help the town recover from it. She'd been left alone with just Margery for weeks at a time when her father sailed without her, and she had liked making her own decisions.

She'd enjoyed treasure hunting with him, and she'd miss those adventures once she married. But mainly, she disliked reverting back to depending on others to get things done for her. So it simply went against the grain now to have to ask this English lord to help her.

"We could always hold him ransom until he finds you a husband," Richard said with a grin.

She realized he was only teasing her now and she returned his grin. She'd say one thing for Richard, he had no trouble a'tall getting someone's mind off of what they didn't want to be thinking about. And she needed to stop thinking about that tall, handsome fellow she'd encountered on the docks today.

Good heavens, that man had been startling. She'd been broadsided, as her father might have put it, blasted right out of the water. It was no wonder she'd made such a fool of herself. But she would have been much more embarrassed if he'd noticed her ogling him, as she'd caught herself doing before he glanced her way.

He'd been a giant of a man with unruly golden brown curls. And she could have sworn his eyes were black, they were so dark. Such a fine figure of a man, but he was handsome, too.

She hadn't meant to be so sharp with the man, but her heart had still been pounding from that cart that had bumped her, causing her to lose her balance. His grip on her arm had been rather tight, too. And she'd been afraid that Ohr and Richard, being so protective of her, might cause a scene because he had his hand on her.

Which wasn't a silly fear. They'd already done so just ten minutes earlier when a sailor had merely jostled her. They'd nearly tossed the man over the wharf into the water. She'd told them then to be more discreet and walk behind her the way English servants were supposed to do.

Then, when the tall, handsome man had looked down at her with those dark eyes, his gaze turning sensual, she'd become more unsettled. And if that wasn't bad enough, when he'd given her that engaging grin, she'd felt something stir deep inside her. So flustered by then that it took her a moment to even grasp what he was saying, her tone had come out sharper than she'd intended, enough to turn him rude.

She sighed to herself. She'd probably never see him again. She'd met enough Americans in the Caribbean to recognize his accent. Americans visited England, but they didn't stay here, and most of them didn't even like the English. Why, it hadn't even been that long since the two countries had been at war with each other! So if she ever saw that particular American again, she would be amazed. Every bit of embarrassment she'd felt today over her own behavior would come rushing right back to her—and probably have her acting the fool again.

Chapter 8

Gabrielle's nerves were nearly shredded by the time they knocked on the door in Berkeley Square. The townhouse was in the upper-crust end of town. It had taken half the morning to find out where the lord lived. Her father certainly hadn't known, as he hadn't seen the chap in more than fifteen years. All he knew was that the man had moved back to England quite a few years ago with his son.

She'd tried to look her best for this meeting, and Margery had helped, getting the wrinkles out of her clothes, but her nervousness was making her feel like she wasn't up to scratch. And she was cold. Good grief. It was still summer in England! But she was too used to the warmer climate of the Caribbean now, and, unfortunately, her current wardrobe reflected that.

She had only a few stylish dresses and even those were made of lightweight materials. Long ago she'd tossed away just about her entire wardrobe that she'd left England with, because it was much too warm for the Caribbean. Now her trunks were filled with brightly colored casual skirts and blouses, and not even one petticoat.

She had a purse full of money for her new wardrobe, but that wasn't going to help her make a good first impression today. She was hoping no one was home, that the man wasn't even in England. If Richard and Ohr weren't with her, she wouldn't be standing here biting her lip. She would be on the first ship back to St. Kitts.

The door opened. A servant stood there. Then again, maybe he wasn't a servant. With a scraggly gray beard, cutoff pants, and bare feet, he looked like he belonged in the islands more than they did.

"Wot's it to be then and be quick about it," he said quite rudely.

Ohr, without expression, said, "A letter for

your master, to be hand delivered. We'll wait inside."

He wasn't giving the man a chance to disagree. He took Gabrielle's arm and pushed past the fellow.

"Now just a bleedin' minute," the man protested. "Where's yer calling card, eh?"

"The letter is our—"

"Is there a problem, Artie?"

All eyes turned to the woman who appeared in one of the open doorways off the long entry hall where they now stood. She was no bigger than Gabrielle, maybe an inch or so shorter, with dark brown hair and eyes. She looked to be somewhere around thirty years of age, with a face that would be exceptionally lovely at any age.

The three visitors were so taken by her beauty that they were speechless, giving the servant called Artie a chance to say, "They barged in, George, but I'll be giving them the boot now."

The woman—George—tsked and said, "There's no need for that." And then she smiled at Gabrielle and added graciously, "I'm Georgina Malory. May I help you?"

Gabrielle's embarrassment prevented her from answering. She felt like a bloody beggar. She didn't care what her father had done to help Lord Malory, it couldn't be enough of a favor to expect these people to take her in and sponsor her for the Season. And it might even take her two Seasons to find a husband!

The launching of a debutante was a major undertaking. It required attending party after party, planning, acquiring a new wardrobe, arranging suitable escorts and chaperones. She and her mother had talked about it often—before Carla had met Albert. And Carla had known the right people. She'd been looking forward to her daughter's Season in London. Gabrielle had, too, back then, and even on the trip here. But now that it was time to call in favors, she just wanted to go back to the Caribbean.

Richard spoke up with a charming smile, even doffed his jaunty hat for the lady. "We have a letter for Lord Malory, madam. Dare I hope he isn't your husband?"

"Yes, I am," came a deep voice in a distinctly unfriendly tone from the top of the stairs. "So get your eyes off of my wife or I will have to tear you apart limb by limb."

Gabrielle glanced up the stairs and actually took a step back toward the door. Good grief, she'd never seen a man quite so solidly built, or so menacing. It wasn't his unfriendly tone. Not at all. It wasn't even the lack of expression on his face. There was simply an aura about the man that warned he was dangerous, even deadly . . . that they should be looking for the nearest exit.

With no telling expression, the man didn't appear to be jealous, yet his tone smacked of jealousy. It was regrettable that Richard had posed his question in such a way that implied an interest in the lady, and even more regrettable that her husband had heard him.

Gabrielle shook her head. No, this couldn't be the man she was to ask this favor of. There had to be some kind of mistake on her father's part. Of course! There must be more than one Lord Malory in London. They'd come to the wrong house.

That thought gave her such relief; she was about to say so when Ohr said, "We meet again, Captain Hawke. It has been so many years, you may not remember—"

"I never forget a face."

Gabrielle turned to give Ohr a surprised look. Blast it, so they did have the right house. But Ohr could have told her what the man was like instead of mentioning fops to mislead her. And she didn't doubt Malory had been just like this when Ohr had met him all those years ago. Dangerous just didn't go away.

"We don't use that name anymore," Malory continued coldly. "So strike it from your memory, or I will."

That was clearly a threat, the second one in as many minutes. If the first hadn't produced a reaction in her two escorts, this second one certainly did. The tension was now palpable in all three men.

Of all the ways Gabrielle had envisioned this meeting going, this wasn't one of them. But then she'd had a completely different view of English aristocrats. She'd met many over the years growing up, and not one of them had been the least bit intimidating. This man was more than intimidating. Big, blond, and so muscular it wouldn't take much for him to tear someone limb by limb.

Malory continued down the stairs. Gabrielle was ready to leave before any more threats were uttered. Ohr wasn't. He didn't mention the letter, but he shoved it at the man when he was within reach.

She groaned inwardly. She knew she

should have kept that letter herself, instead of letting Ohr carry it. It was sealed. None of them had opened it. She didn't even know how her father had phrased his request—as a favor, or a demand? Good grief, he wouldn't have dared make a demand of a man like this, would he?

She held her breath while Lord Malory opened the letter and scanned it quickly. "Bloody hell," he muttered when he was done. Gabrielle was mortified.

"What is it, James?" his wife asked, frowning curiously.

He said nothing, merely handed the letter to her so she could see for herself. She didn't utter any oaths. In fact, she amazed Gabrielle by smiling.

"Why, this sounds like fun," Georgina declared, and it looked like she actually meant it. She then glanced at her husband. "Didn't you read it all?"

"Yes, but I see you haven't grasped the implications yet," he replied.

"That there will be many parties to attend?" she queried.

"No."

"That we're going to be a bit crowded

here, with two of my brothers visiting as
well?"

"No."

"Then what's got you annoyed, aside
from the remark that provoked your charming display of jealousy?"

Gabrielle could guess. Although she
hadn't said a word yet, Malory must have
assumed that as the daughter of a pirate
she was utterly unsuitable to be foisted on
the ton.

And yet all he said was, "Bite your
tongue, George. I am not, nor will I ever be,
charming."

He didn't deny the jealousy, though,
which brought a flush to Richard's cheeks.
Nor did he answer the question, which
prompted his wife to make another guess.

"You must be feeling guilty, then, for making so many unnecessary threats."

It was such a provocative statement. How
did the woman dare to talk to him like that?
For that matter, what was a petite, perky
woman like her doing married to such a big,
menacing bruiser? Granted, he was handsome, with his long blond hair that reached
his shoulders and those sharp green eyes.

But he was deadly. There was absolutely no doubt in Gabrielle's mind.

And yet, all he did was snort at his wife and say, "The devil I am."

"Glad to hear it," Georgina said in a chipper tone, then added by way of explanation to the others present, "He's impossible to live with when he's feeling guilty."

"I'm bloody well not guilty, George."

It wasn't just the words but the tone that lent truth to that statement, and yet the woman said, "Yes, yes, and I can depend upon it, too, I'm sure you'd like to add, though we both know better."

"George."

Such warning in a single word, but the women still ignored it and said briskly to Gabrielle's escorts, "You gentlemen can be at ease now. My husband isn't going to tear off any limbs today."

"You might, m'dear, when you realize that you'll have to cancel your trip to accommodate this request."

Georgina frowned. "Oh, dear, I hadn't thought of that."

"Didn't think so," Malory replied.

"Ah, so *that's* why you're annoyed? You think I'm going to be disappointed?"

He didn't deny it, and actually confirmed it by saying, "Aren't you?"

"Not a'tall. Jack probably will be, though. You know how impatient children can be. But next year will do just as well for that trip."

Gabrielle had blanched with the realization that this favor was going to interfere with their plans. She finally spoke up.

"Please don't change your agenda on my account. My father probably didn't consider that you might not be available to assist me. His decision to send me here was made on the spur of the moment. We can make other arrangements and wait until he arrives to figure out something else."

"When will that be?" Georgina asked.

But Ohr said at the same time, "No we can't. He's still in the Caribbean and won't be coming here anytime soon."

"Well, that won't do a'tall," Georgina said with some finality.

But Malory clinched it when he said, "You'll stay." And that settled that. However, he wasn't finished. With a look and tone that left no room for argument, he told her escorts, "You won't. You've done your duty. She's in my care now. There's the door."

Ohr and Richard hadn't intended to stay in this part of town. Gabrielle quickly hugged them good-bye. She felt bad that James Malory had all but kicked them out the door, but she was sure it was Richard's stirring up Malory's jealousy that resulted in their having to leave sooner that she would have liked.

Alone now with the lord and lady, she felt her nervousness increase tenfold. But Georgina put her more at ease when she asked, "Shall we adjourn to the dining room? If you haven't eaten yet, the buffet is still hot. We eat at odd hours here, so breakfast is served for most of the morning. In any case, let's have a cup of tea while we get acquainted."

Gabrielle followed the lady, and unfortunately, James Malory followed her. She was sure she wasn't going to be able to relax with that man in the room. He was far too intimidating, and besides, she was still so embarrassed about intruding on their lives that she could barely get out the apology she felt she owed them.

"I'm very sorry that my arrival has disrupted your plans like this."

"Not another word, m'dear," Malory replied, his tone much more congenial now. "At the risk of earning a scowl from George, I don't mind admitting your timing couldn't have been more perfect."

"You weren't happy with your plans?"

When he didn't answer, Georgina laughed and explained, "He's still worried about that scowl he mentioned. You see, while he'll go above and beyond in his efforts to please me, the trip I wanted to take was rather quickly arranged, to take advantage of my brother Drew's ship being in London. But my husband doesn't actually get along famously with my brothers—"

"No need to wrap it up nicely, George," Malory interrupted. "I despise her brothers and they despise me. It's pleasantly mutual."

Gabrielle blinked, but Georgina rolled her eyes. "He's simplified it, but they really do *try* to get along."

"What she means is we stopped trying to kill each other years ago," James added.

He sounded serious, but Gabrielle simply couldn't believe that he was. And assuming that he was joking managed to put her somewhat at ease.

"At any rate," Georgina continued. "James

wasn't happy about sailing on my brother's ship, so yes, he's no doubt delighted to have our trip postponed to a later date."

Amazingly, they'd managed to remove most of Gabrielle's guilt for foisting herself on them. Not all of it, but she was certainly feeling much better about it.

"I have a maid who will need to stay here with me," she told them.

"Certainly," Georgina said. "I would have hired one for you if you hadn't brought yours."

"Thank you. I'll only need to avail myself of your hospitality for a few weeks, until my father arrives and finds us other accomodations. That you're willing to sponsor me for the rest of this Season is most appreciated. By the by, if you don't mind my asking, how do you and my father know each other?" she asked James.

"He didn't tell you?" James queried.

"No, it was all so sudden, his decision to send me here. And then I was quite disappointed that he couldn't sail with me because he had some business to finish up. I wanted to wait for him, but with the Season already under way, he wanted me here soonest. Anyway, I never got around to asking him."

"I'm rather curious myself," Georgina admitted, glancing at her husband. Just what is this debt you owe? That letter didn't say."

"How do you put a price on a life? Brooks saved mine. I didn't ask him to."

"When was this?" Georgina asked.

"Long before I met you. I'd picked a fight in the wrong place at the wrong time, had about twenty drunken sailors trying to tear me apart."

"Only twenty?" She snorted. "And you consider that life-threatening? To you?"

James chuckled. "Appreciate the vote of confidence, m'dear. But they'd already stabbed me, shot me, and pronounced me dead."

A frown of concern immediately appeared on her face. "Were you really almost dead?"

"No, but one of the sailors had also cracked my head open, so I was no longer paying attention, and they were too drunk to notice I was still breathing."

"You were unconscious?"

"Quite. But since they were convinced I was dead, they were determined to get rid of the evidence. They tossed me off the wharf there in St. Kitts. It was a deep dock. And the water didn't revive me. Apparently I had no trouble sinking to the bottom."

"So Nathan Brooks fished you out?"

"To hear him tell it, he nearly drowned himself trying," he said.

"But he obviously succeeded."

"It was luck all the way around, m'dear. His ship was docked there. I'd happened to be tossed in the water right next to it. But it was late at night. No one was around, and he wouldn't have been there either to hear the commotion if he hadn't come back to his ship to fetch some map he'd forgotten. Nor would he have bothered to fish out a dead body, but he happened to hear one of the crowd ask if they were sure I was dead. So he dove in to check. I woke up soaking wet, lying under the dock where he'd left me."

"Then how do you know—"

"Let me finish. He'd been unable to carry me farther. He's a tall man, but I'm rather heavy at a deadweight. He'd left to get one of his men to help, the Oriental you met today. Then he took me to his house to mend. And there you have it."

"A very simple favor he's asked in return,"

Georgina said with a smile. "I would have paid him a fortune if he'd asked for it, for saving your life."

James gave his wife a very tender look, which appeared rather odd to Gabrielle, on the countenance of such an intimidating man. "That's because you love me, George, so I'm bloody well glad he didn't ask for it."

Chapter 9

Having turned their unexpected guest over to the housekeeper to get her settled, Georgina promptly dragged her husband into the parlor to find out what he really thought about this turn of events. But she'd forgotten Boyd was still sleeping on the sofa in there. And Judith, Anthony's daughter, had spent the night. Both she and Jacqueline had sneaked into the parlor and were amusing themselves in a corner of the room.

The girls had been quiet enough not to wake Boyd, and he'd also slept through the noise in the hall. He had stumbled in that morning right after she and James had come down for breakfast, had given her a sloppy kiss and hug, then promptly passed out on the sofa in the parlor. She hadn't bothered to wake him to tell him to go find a bed. He'd still been quite foxed from a full night of revelry.

Two years older than she was, Boyd was the youngest of her five brothers. He was also the prankster in the family. He'd pulled some good ones over the years, some that were really funny, some quite embarrassing, even a few that she, at least, had considered dangerous, though her brothers hadn't thought so. But she'd only for the briefest moment wondered if Gabrielle Brooks might be one of his pranks gone awry, because he wasn't awake to put a stop to it before it got out of hand. Unless he'd been so drunk when he'd set it up that he hadn't thought to add contingencies to assure that the joke was revealed before it went too far. No, she couldn't believe the young woman's arrival was his doing. He liked pranks, but he wasn't stupid enough to irritate her husband with one.

Boyd was, however, the most hotheaded in the family now. Their brother Warren used to have that distinction, until he'd married Amy Malory. Hardly anything disturbed

Warren these days, he was so happy in his marriage.

Georgina turned to find a different room where she and James might talk, but James wouldn't budge. He stood solidly in her path as he said, "You can fess up now, George. You put a good face on it, but we both know how much you were looking forward to that trip to Connecticut."

"Yes, I was, and I still will be. We can just as easily go next year."

"This year was convenient, even if it was a spur-of-the-moment decision on your part, because one of your brothers was here to take you. Next year they might not be."

"True, so I'll just have to make sure that my own ship, *The Amphitrite,* will be in port to take us next year. I'll have plenty of time to arrange it. I'm sure you'd like that better anyway, since you could captain her."

"Absolutely," he agreed.

"I should wake Boyd, don't you think?" She wrapped her husband's arms around her waist, belying her intention to tend to her brother.

"Leave him. He hasn't had enough time to sleep off whatever he drowned himself in last night. And other than standing in as a punching bag for me, there's not much else he'd be good for."

She hadn't thought of that, but having Boyd and James in the same house when James was seriously annoyed was going to make for a powder keg. And only James could control that, since Boyd was too impulsive, throwing punches before thinking.

She glanced at her husband sharply. "That wasn't the least bit funny. You will try to contain your annoyance."

It was an order, not that he'd obey it, but she felt he should know her druthers.

"You worry too much, George," he said laconically.

"That statement might work at any other time, but you know very well—"

"Lower your tone before the girls hear you."

She refrained from snorting and merely rolled her eyes instead. "When those two are whispering to each other, the rest of the world ceases to exist."

He glanced at the two girls sitting cross-legged across the room, their shoulders touching, their heads, one blond, one copper with golden streaks, leaning toward each other. Jack was grinning as she whispered to her cousin. Judy was nodding, then laughed softly and quickly put a hand to her mouth to stifle it. Both immediately glanced at him and slightly blushed, as if they were worried they'd been overheard. Which was an impossibility. No one ever overheard those two. They had whispering down to a fine art.

"Beside the point," James conceded, which almost brought a grin to her lips. But then he squeezed her slightly before he let her go and added, "And you might want to convince one of your brothers to extend his visit for a while. Or I will."

She blinked. "You? Why? You're usually pushing them out the door!"

"Because I know you're going to want an escort for all those parties that will soon be on your agenda, and it bloody well won't be me."

She laughed. "I see. The debt is yours but I get to pay it back single-handedly?"

"You'll have to admit, this is your cup of tea, not mine. Think I didn't notice that gleam in your eye when you said this sounds like fun?"

"Don't look for an argument." She grinned at him. "I quite agree. And since you'd never mentioned any of this before, I take it you incurred this favor during your wild and reckless days at sea?"

"I was never reckless, George."

"Considering the occupation you took up, you most certainly were," she disagreed. "Which is the part I don't understand. How the deuce did this man know to find you here, if he met you in the Caribbean? You weren't in the habit of going by your real name back then, were you?"

" 'Course not. Hawke was the only name I used back then. But apparently I did some talking in my sleep due to the medications I was given to help with my wounds, and some of it was about my family. He gained knowledge of who I was and ended up telling me his life story as well. We actually became friends after that."

"So who is he? An Englishman? Is that why he sent his daughter here for her coming out?"

"Do you really need to know?"

She frowned at that answer. "To launch her and find her a husband *here,* yes, I do need to know her background. You know how damned particular you aristocrats are about bloodlines," she added with some disgust.

"Don't include me in that package, just because you Americans don't like aristocrats. You *did* marry one, and I *didn't* marry one. I rest my case."

She laughed and punched him lightly in the chest at the same time. "Just answer my question."

"You won't like it. In fact, you just might be slamming doors shut on me again."

"Oh come now, it can't be that bad."

"Beg to differ, m'dear. She's the daughter of a pirate, not one who just dabbled at it like I did, but one who's made it his life's career."

"Who's the daughter of a pirate?" Drew asked as he entered the room behind them.

Chapter 10

A party already? Gabrielle hadn't yet had a chance to relax since she'd arrived at the Malory townhouse. Her nervousness might have decreased a bit during her talk with James and Georgina Malory, but it hadn't dissipated completely. And she was expected to attend a party tonight?

After she'd been shown to a room upstairs, she'd done nothing but pace until Margery had arrived a few hours later. The housekeeper had elected to stay behind at the inn when they couldn't find a carriage big enough to accommodate all of them that morning, and to come over later with the baggage and Miss Carla.

She missed Ohr and Richard already.

They hadn't intended to stay in the same house with her, merely to make sure she was welcome. But Malory had made it clear *they* weren't welcome. Her friends wouldn't be deserting her entirely, though, just the neighborhood. The original plan included their waiting in England until Nathan arrived, since it was quite possible he'd be on his way to join them before they got back to the Caribbean, so they were going to rent a flat near the docks where they could watch for *The Crusty Jewel*'s arrival. She'd guessed her father had simply ordered them to remain here to keep an eye on her.

Her father took care of incidentals like that without telling her, though she usually found out. His overprotective nature had been a surprise to her, had even included having reports sent to him regularly over the years about her progress and activities as she was growing up. Her mother's gardener had been in Nathan's pay. No wonder that old man had always questioned her extensively about what she was up to!

When Nathan had fessed up about the gardener, she'd realized he must have also been informed about her mother's affair with Albert. He didn't say so, and she cer-

tainly didn't mention it, but she'd felt bad for
months, thinking about it, and had a feeling
that his parrot hadn't been taught derogatory remarks about Carla until after her father had knowledge of her mother's unfaith-
fulness.

Georgina Malory came up with Margery
when she arrived, to tell Gabrielle they
would be attending a soiree that night being
given by her niece by marriage. "I wasn't in-
tending to go," the lady admitted. "Regina
has so many parties when she's in London
that I don't feel the need to attend more'n a
few of them. But as it happens my brothers
Drew and Boyd are both in town for a visit
and would make fine escorts. So it occurred
to me that this will be the perfect opportunity for you to get your feet wet, as it were.
So we'll go."

Gabrielle would have preferred to keep
her feet dry, but she wasn't rude enough to
say so. She had several perfect excuses to
decline, such as no suitable wardrobe yet
and exhaustion from her trip, but she didn't
use them. She'd already inconvenienced
this nice lady with her presence, which had
forced Georgina to cancel her own plans.

She was determined not to disrupt her plans in any other way.

"Your brothers don't live in London?" she asked.

"London? Goodness, no, not even in England. In fact, while our family home might be in Connecticut, you could say all five of my brothers actually live at sea. My family owns Skylark Shipping, you see, and each of my brothers commands his own vessel."

Sailors, Gabrielle thought with some amusement. She couldn't get away from them even in England. But at least these two from Georgina's family were only visiting. And she might even like them. She'd never marry one, but she did have a lot in common with sailors, after all.

"About the party tonight," Gabrielle said. "I have one dress that would be appropriate, but I'm going to need to visit a seamstress tomorrow. I've brought the funds with me for a wardrobe for the Season, so I really should get started on that right away."

"I agree, and you needn't wait until tomorrow. I'll send for mine today. She's very good at producing miracles on short notice."

"That would be wonderful," Gabrielle allowed. "I'll just need to know how many ball gowns I should order. Can you hazard a guess?"

"A half dozen at least."

Gabrielle blinked and gasped out, "That many this late in the Season?"

"Oh, yes," Georgina said with a roll of her eyes. "It's due to the competition among the ladies who typically host these gatherings. If one of them outdoes another who's already given her ball, then she simply *must* give yet another ball to get back in the lead of who's ball was the best of the Season. It's all quite silly in my opinion, but it's why we get deluged with so many invitations near the end of summer. By the by, why *did* you wait so long to come to London? There are only a few weeks left of the bigger gatherings. You do realize that many of the best eligible bachelors will already have made their choices and be committed?"

Gabrielle nodded and added, "I'd be surprised if the pickings weren't thin. The timing wasn't by choice, it was merely my father suddenly realizing that I'm long overdue in getting this done and sending me off posthaste."

Georgina chuckled. "Getting this done? That's a rather unique way of looking at it."

Gabrielle grinned. "Well, to be honest, coming here wasn't my idea. I would have preferred to find a husband at home in the islands. But I'm rather excited about this now that I'm here. I just hope that I can persuade whomever I do marry to at least take me back to the Caribbean occasionally. I know I'm going to miss my father dreadfully if I only see him rarely like before."

"Before?"

"I missed out on his presence while growing up. I lived here with my mother; he works out of the West Indies. It was very rare that he came to visit us."

"Ah, that explains it, why your diction is so cultured. So you actually grew up here in England?"

"Yes, near Brighton. My mother would have seen to my being launched into society. She knew all the right people. But she died when I was seventeen, so I went to live with my father. He didn't explain this in the letter?"

"No, he didn't mention your background at all."

"Good grief, you've taken me in without

even knowing that my credentials are up to snuff? You're too kind, Lady Malory."

Georgina laughed. "No, I'm an American. We don't put much stock in titles where I come from, so please don't use the one my husband saddled me with. If I could get rid of it without getting rid of him, you can be sure I would."

Gabrielle wasn't surprised. She'd met enough Americans in the Caribbean to know that they preferred to stand on their own merits, not those of their ancestors. But in England people took bloodlines much more seriously, at least the nobility did, especially when it came to marriage.

Before she could reassure the lady, Margery glanced up from her unpacking to volunteer, "She's got a couple earls she can dig out of the pantry."

Gabrielle blushed to hear it put that way, but felt it prudent to add, "Several generations removed, so I have no title. But then I'm not looking for a title either."

"But you wouldn't turn one down if it comes to that?"

"No, of course not."

Georgina grinned. "I only asked because *I* would have."

"But you didn't."

"Only because I was already married before I found out James has a title!"

Gabrielle didn't know whether to commiserate with Georgina or congratulate her, but Miss Carla saved her from remarking on it when Margery moved her cage off of the next trunk she was about to open, and the bird squawked, "Lemme out, lemme out!"

Georgina gasped and said, "Is that what I think it is?"

Gabrielle decided to uncover the cage so the lady could see for herself. It was better to be forewarned anyway, because the parrot could be quite loud, and she didn't want anyone breaking down her door to find out what the racket was. But the oddest thing about parrots was that women found it hard to resist talking to them, and Georgina Malory was no different. She came over to the cage to examine Miss Carla and immediately started saying hello to her.

"Dumb bird," the parrot replied.

Gabrielle's cheeks went up in flames, but Georgina burst out laughing and said, "That was amazing. Does it say anything else?"

"Too much," Gabrielle mumbled. "She belonged to my father. He gave her to me after I got attached to her, but he'd already taught her some outlandish phrases, all of which are too embarrassing to mention."

Georgina raised a brow. "Too vulgar for young ears?"

"I would say very much so."

The lady sighed. "Well, that's too bad. I would have suggested you bring her downstairs occasionally to amuse my family, but my oldest daughter is only seven and too impressionable. She already hears more than she should from the men in this family."

"I'll try to keep her quiet."

Georgina chuckled. "And I'll try to keep Jack from investigating."

"Jack?"

"My daughter Jacqueline."

"Ah, I see."

"No, you don't, but then nobody understands my husband's propensity to give the females he's fondest of unusual nicknames."

"Not unusual, George," James said from the open doorway. "Just names that no one else would consider. Now come along and let the girl get settled. She'll want to rest before you drag her off to Regan's tonight."

"Regan?"

"Another one of those names, this one for his favorite niece, Regina," Georgina explained, then added with a frown, "Do you need to rest?"

"No, I'm fine."

"Good, then expect the seamstress within the hour. I'll send for her now."

Chapter 11

Gabrielle went downstairs at the appropriate hour. Her powder-blue tulle dress, which
nearly matched her eyes, was too thin for an
English evening. Unfortunately, the only
coat she had was her sturdy wool traveling
one, which wasn't at all appropriate to wear
to a party.

Her new clothes would start arriving tomorrow, though, the seamstress had assured her, and would continue to be delivered over the next week, so she wasn't
going to worry about being a little chilly this
one evening. And her hair was done up
nicely. She was rather good at arranging
artful coiffures for herself, which was fortunate, since Margery wasn't really a maid.

She was merely acting in that capacity for the time being.

It appeared she was the first to arrive downstairs, so she moved into the parlor to wait for the Malorys to join her. She thought she was alone until she saw two small heads poke up over the back of the sofa. One was golden haired; the other was golden, too, but streaked with bright copper. She could say quite honestly that she'd never seen more beautiful children.

"I'm Jack," the golden-haired girl said to her. "This is my cousin Judy. You must be the pirate's daughter."

Gabrielle didn't know whether to be embarrassed or amused at the child's candor. Good grief, did everyone in the household know about her father's occupation?

"I suppose that would be me, yes," she said.

"Are you a pirate, too?" the other girl asked.

She managed not to laugh. "No, but I've dabbled in treasure hunting."

"Oh, that sounds like fun!" both girls said nearly at once.

Gabrielle grinned. "It is indeed."

"And I'm sure she'll tell you all about it,

but not tonight," James Malory said from the doorway. "Run along, younguns, your dinner awaits."

The girls filed out of the room with only a few mumbles of protest. Gabrielle had been relaxed before Malory arrived, but now she tensed up, which made her wonder if she would ever be at ease in his presence.

"George will be down shortly," James informed her nonchalantly. "She's browbeating her brothers into joining you this evening."

"You" instead of "us" meant *he* wasn't going. Her relief was instant. "Then you aren't going?"

"Good God, no. I adore my niece and wouldn't miss one of her family dinners, but that's not what this party is. Doesn't bother me a bit to fess up that I abhor social gatherings of this sort, so I will be doing my utmost to avoid all the events my wife has on the agenda for you."

"Which means I'll get stuck as . . . your . . ." A deep, masculine voice trailed off. The man who lost his tongue stood next to Malory, staring at her incredulously. Her own expression probably mirrored his. Good grief, him? The blond giant from the wharf whom she'd been so rude to? Recalling her behavior that day brought a rush of color to her cheeks. Blast it, she'd known she would be mortified if she ever ran into him again, and here he was, in the house she was going to be living in for the next several weeks. She was most definitely mortified.

"I take it you two have met?" James said dryly, glancing from one to the other. "Or dare I guess I'm witnessing love at first sight?"

Drew recalled himself first and snorted. "Love? Not a chance. I merely rescued her from a nasty fall on the docks yesterday when she was clumsy enough to nearly tumble at my feet."

Fortunately, he managed to remove all signs of embarrassment from Gabrielle's cheeks with that remark. Or perhaps her swiftly rising ire did that.

"Clumsy?" she shot back. "It wasn't my fault that a cart nearly bowled me over. But you were a brute about your so-called rescue."

"Brute?" James said with interest. "Now that doesn't surprise me. He *is* an American, after all."

"Don't start in on me, Malory," Drew almost growled. "Now isn't a good time."

"Beg to differ, dear boy," James replied. "Anytime is a good time to mention how barbaric you—"

"James Malory, don't you dare." His wife arrived to interrupt him as she pushed her way between the two men. "I swear, can't I leave you two alone in the same room for five minutes?"

" 'Course you can, m'dear," James replied. "He's still standing, isn't he?"

The large blond man and Georgina both made a rude sound in reply. Gabrielle didn't know what to make of their bickering and James Malory's implied threat. It sounded serious, and yet none of them looked serious.

In fact, Georgina leaned up to kiss James and tell him, "We'll probably be late, so don't wait up."

"I'll wait."

His expression turned sensual and his arm went around her waist, pulling her closer to him. The handsome giant rolled his eyes at them. Georgina just chuckled and pushed away from her husband.

"Come along, Gabby," she said, taking

her arm. "I can't wait to introduce you to Regina. She's an incorrigible matchmaker, you know. I don't doubt she'll find you a husband in no time." But then she glanced back at her husband to warn him, "I almost forgot. Boyd begged off from joining us, so do try to avoid him. He said something about his voyage having been longer than expected and that he wouldn't be fit for proper socializing without at least three nights of carousing."

"What rubbish," James and the giant said almost in the same breath.

"Yes, that's what I said, but his head was still pounding from his first night of overindulgence, so I didn't press the matter."

"Only because you'd already roped me in for the chore," the giant complained, though he kept his tone light.

Gabrielle realized he must be Georgina's brother Drew, whom she had mentioned earlier. And from the sound of it, he wasn't very pleased about being their escort tonight either. He just hadn't been able to come up with an excuse to bow out as his brother Boyd had. She would have felt bad about that if she wasn't still smarting over his remark about her being clumsy.

Georgina quickly got them under way. The ride to Park Lane was very short, which allowed for little conversation in the coach. That was fortunate. Gabrielle was having a hard enough time dealing with the knowledge that the man she'd been so attracted to on the docks who had made an utter fool of her was not only sitting next to her now, but was staying in the same house she was, and that she was probably going to see far too much of him in the coming weeks.

She wondered if she should adjust her attitude and try to make amends for her rudeness that day. But explaining her uncharacteristic behavior was out of the question, since it required revealing how attractive she found him. May be she could come up with a plausible excuse for it.

She recalled his charming smile and how it had affected her. He'd turned rude only after she did. Was that the only reason he was still surly? Or did he *really* object to escorting her and his sister?

As soon as they entered the large townhouse that belonged to Nicholas and Regina Eden, Georgina moved off to find Regina, leaving her temporarily alone with the giant. He steered them into the parlor, which was quite crowded, and hailed some-one he knew, but he didn't leave her side.

He didn't seem to be paying her the least bit of attention, though, so she almost man-aged to relax. Then out of nowhere he asked, "Are you really here to catch a hus-band, pirate lady?"

She drew in her breath. So he'd been told about her father, too? Was he simply insult-ing her by calling her a pirate—or did he really believe she was one?

Actually, as a seafaring man, he wouldn't doubt that there were women pirates and had likely heard of such females during the heyday of piracy in the Caribbean. Pierre even had such a woman with him now. Red, they called her, and she could fight as well as any man, even more viciously, it was ru-mored. He probably liked that about her, as evil as he was himself.

Gabrielle shivered at the memory of that particular captain. And she never did lose her fear of him while she remained in the Caribbean, even when she'd heard that he'd taken up with Red. But having returned to England now, she was sure she never would see him again. England was a whole ocean away from his normal haunts, after all.

"Cold?" Drew speculated. "Or maybe you don't want a husband after all?"

He'd noticed her shiver. Why would he relate it to his first question about her looking for a husband? And why did he sound a tad hopeful? His question was far too personal for her to answer, especially after he'd addressed her with the derogatory term "pirate lady."

"Look, Captain—"

"It's Drew," he cut in. "Drew Anderson."

"Yes, I know," she said. "I had a long chat with your sister today."

"Did you? I'm amazed she's agreed to help you. In fact, I'm surprised she'd even deign to consort with a pirate long enough to *chat.* Then again, damn, I must take that back, she's done it before."

He'd started out by insulting her, which had got her hackles up, but he'd ended with an intriguing comment that piqued her curiosity. She doubted he would elaborate if she asked for further detail.

Her curiosity prompted her to try anyway. "What brought that about?"

"It was quite unintentional. She didn't

know she was dealing with a pirate. Actually, to be fair, I should say ex-pirate."

"Her husband, I suppose? How did she come to marry such a brute?"

Even before he frowned at her in such a way that warned she'd stepped out of bounds, she regretted the question. It was natural enough for her to be curious about the people she was staying with, but since those people happened to include him, she'd just as soon he not be made aware of it. And she really shouldn't be making disparaging remarks about his brother-in-law, the very man she'd foisted herself upon. That had been rude of her.

Before she could apologize, he surprised her by asking, "Do you really think he's a brute? My brothers and I have always thought so, but personally, I've wondered how a woman perceives James Malory."

"A definite brute. But I suppose your sister doesn't think so."

"No, she adores him," he replied. "Hard to imagine, isn't it?"

She detected the humor in his tone and wondered briefly if it was at her expense, or because they were sharing the same opinion. She decided not to find out and kept her eyes off him. The man was far too attractive for her to be able to look at him indifferently.

"Actually," she said after a moment, "if you can get past the feeling that all he wants to do is clobber you, then I'd have to allow he's a handsome man."

"I wouldn't go so far as to say *that.*"

"To say what?" Georgina asked as she returned to them with her niece in tow.

Gabrielle's cheeks reddened. Considering how disagreeable the man had been to her, she didn't doubt that he was going to confess all. It was the perfect opportunity to embarrass her, and he seemed determined to do that. He might have let up enough to have a conversation with her, but she hadn't forgotten how it had started.

Again he surprised her, by making light of it and only mentioning, "She thinks that brute you married is a handsome fellow."

"Of course she does," Georgina replied. "I've never met a woman who didn't. But I wish you'd remove the word 'brute' from your vocabulary."

"Not until he removes 'barbarian' from his," Drew said with a smile.

The woman with Georgina chuckled. "I'm glad my Nick isn't present to hear this."

Regina Eden was quite stunning. She had black hair and the most amazing cobalt-blue eyes that were slanted just enough to appear exotic. And her chuckle left behind a smile that was warmly welcoming.

Georgina explained to Gabrielle, "You'll find that Reggie's husband doesn't like mine very much. They used to try to kill each other."

Georgina spoke in such a teasing tone that Gabrielle didn't take her comment seriously. But then Regina added, "And nearly succeeded a few times, but they get along famously now—at least in comparison."

"I wouldn't call it famously," Georgina grinned. "But I'll allow it's probably just old habits dying hard. They still go toe-to-toe verbally. My brothers are the same way," she added with a disapproving look at Drew.

He didn't appear at all abashed, even grinned cheekily. "I know when I'm outnumbered, which is a good time to go find some libation while you ladies get acquainted."

He sauntered off, but only one of them watched him go. Gabrielle caught herself staring after him and groaned inwardly. It was going to be a problem, keeping her eyes off that man when he was around. He'd insulted her enough that she should want to ignore him at all costs, but she simply couldn't. She was so powerfully attracted to him that even when he raised her ire, he affected her in other ways she couldn't control.

But she was going to have to figure out how to deal with his proximity. The man wasn't just a sailor who might, with enough incentive, be convinced to give up the sea. He was captain of his own vessel and his family even owned their own shipping company! He couldn't be a more inappropriate man for her to get better acquainted with.

Chapter 12

"Did we miss her?"

"Has she not come down yet?"

Drew put his fork aside and smiled at the two young girls who'd just run into the breakfast room. Their excitement was obvious. And he didn't need to ask whom they were talking about. He'd just been thinking about the same female and asking himself the same questions!

He told his niece, "If you mean the pirate, she's probably still abed. We returned rather late last night from your cousin Regina's party."

"Did she have fun there?" Judith asked.

"Probably," he replied, and managed to keep his tone neutral, though he found the thought irritating. "She was swarmed by every bachelor in attendance."

"She said she's not a pirate," Jacqueline corrected him as she came over and swiped a sausage from his plate.

"But she's a treasure hunter!" Judith volunteered.

"And Papa said she'd tell us all about it," Jacqueline added.

He stared pointedly at his niece, but she merely gave him a cheeky grin, then promptly finished off the sausage anyway. He shook his head with a chuckle. Jack was an adorable minx, graceful, not the least bit gangly, and too lovely by half for her age. She was going to be an incorrigible handful when she got older, he was sure.

"This late in the morning and you two haven't eaten yet?" he asked.

"Oh, we did, long ago," Jacqueline said.

"We've just been checking back," Judith explained. "Didn't want to miss the lady. And I go home today. I'll be ever so disappointed if I don't get to hear about the treasure hunting firsthand."

"If I see her, moppets, I'll send her straightaway to find you both."

They took him at his word and ran back

out of the room as exuberantly as they'd entered it. But with the room quiet again, his thoughts went right back to where they'd been, centered on his sister's guest.

Her arrival had changed Georgina's plans, and thus his as well. Since his sister and her family wouldn't be accompanying him on the voyage back to Connecticut, he could revert to his original schedule, which allowed him to spend another week or two with his sister here, but he wasn't sure if he should stay now. He could visit Georgie at another time. He didn't feel comfortable staying at her house while she had a houseguest that he was attracted to, especially since his sister's unexpected guest was off-limits to him.

Pirates. He'd never run into any himself, but his brother Boyd had. Pirates had stolen his cargo at sea. The same thing had happened to his brother Thomas, who'd had to limp back to port, his ship had been so damaged in that fight. It hadn't upset Thomas, though, but then nothing ever did. He was the most patient of all six Andersons.

Ironically it had been James Malory who'd tangled with both his brothers at sea and won. They all laughed over it now, though not at the time. A gentleman pirate, he'd called himself back then.

For a decade James had amused himself on the high seas, indiscriminately bedeviling any ship that appeared to offer a challenge, even English ships. It had been a game to him, a test of his skills, and according to Georgina, for a man who'd gotten so jaded being one of London's most notorious rakes that even duels couldn't stir his emotions anymore, the life of a gentleman pirate had been his salvation.

Drew found it amazing that Gabrielle Brooks had actually guessed that James was the pirate that Georgina had consorted with in the past. Pirates recognizing pirates? He didn't think so.

When James and Georgie had explained their houseguest to him, James had admitted that the girl's father didn't know that *he'd* been a pirate as well, merely that he'd gone by the name Captain Hawke back then. It was his real identity he'd revealed in his delirium. So it was more likely that Gabrielle had merely been sarcastic when she'd made her guess and called James a brute.

Rude, ungrateful wench. The strikes against her were adding up, but the worst one was that she was here to find a husband. If not for that, he might have made an effort to patch things up with her. But he didn't want them patched. Hell no. He needed the buffer of her disagreeable disposition to remind him that she was off-limits.

Not that he needed much reminding when the mere sight of her yesterday had instantly recalled how annoyed he'd been with her on the dock. Which was odd. It just wasn't in his nature to let things affect him to such a degree that he couldn't shrug them off. He was too carefree. He could even withstand arguments and knockdown fights with his brother Warren, who used to be so glum he could annoy a saint, and not be bothered by them at all. But this wench bothered him too much.

Boyd appeared in the doorway and tried to lean on it, but nearly fell into the room instead. Drew had been so deep in thought that he hadn't heard the front door open, but it was obvious his brother was just getting in. He looked as if he hadn't slept all night.

Boyd had the same color hair as he did—light brown with golden highlights—but his brother hadn't cut his since he'd docked, probably hadn't combed it either by the shaggy look of it. While Boyd's brown eyes were lighter than his own, they were also quite bloodshot at the moment. Of the five brothers, only Boyd and Thomas hadn't inherited their father's extraordinary height.

"You haven't been to bed yet?" Drew guessed.

"I slept, just no idea where," Boyd replied.

"Is that what happened the other night? You deserted me for a soft bed?"

"Very soft, I vaguely recall, but I'm sure you found your way home without me."

Drew chuckled. "Yes, at a decent hour, too." But then he shook his head. "You really go overboard when you reach port. Was your last trip really that long?"

"No; I just had a passenger that drove me mad with lust for two damn weeks."

Drew raised a brow. "Couldn't do anything about it on board?"

"She was married, had two children with her, and was so damned pleased to be on her way to meet her husband that I wasn't going to let her know how I felt."

"Well, got it out of your system now?"

"Ask me that after I sober up," Boyd said, but then added with a snicker, "But how was your evening?"

"Why don't you ask *me* that after you meet the pirate," Drew shot back.

"No thanks. I've already got a long list of excuses lined up for our dear sister. She won't be dragging me to any of these virginal affairs. I've been taking notes from Malory on how to avoid them. Besides, you're much better than I am at being bored."

Drew burst out laughing. "You're all heart, brother. But what do you want to bet you'll change your mind—after you meet the pirate?"

Boyd just grinned at him. "I'm not falling for that. If she was such a great looker, you'd be making sure my ship sails tomorrow."

"Suit yourself," Drew said with a shrug.

Boyd narrowed his eyes on him. "*Is* she pretty?"

"What's it matter?" Drew countered offhandedly. "The wench is here to catch a husband, remember? Or are you ready to settle down?"

Boyd gave that a moment's thought. "Unlike you, I don't have a sweetheart in every port, so I wouldn't mind having a pretty wife to sail home to. Remember, I'm not the one who said he was never getting hitched, that was you. But when I do settle down, it sure as hell won't be with a wench whose father is a pirate."

"Good point," Drew agreed. "Considering we're in shipping of the legitimate sort, I'd say Clinton might object if you try to bring a pirate into the family. No reason to get permanently on his bad side, after all."

"Oh, so now you're making it a dare?" Boyd said in a belligerent tone.

Drew rolled his eyes. "Go on to bed. If you're looking for a fight to round off your overindulgences, at least wait until you're sober."

"Bad idea," Boyd grumbled. "Then I'll feel it too much. Maybe Malory will oblige me instead."

"Oh, well, why didn't you say you just want to die," Drew replied dryly.

Chapter 13

Gabrielle looked around the glittering ball-room. A soiree one night, a grand ball the next. When Georgina had told her that they probably wouldn't spend a single evening at home for the rest of the Season, she hadn't been joking. Which was fine with Gabrielle. She wanted many choices for the matrimonial list she was going to create, and the more events they attended, the more bachelors she would have a chance to meet.

She'd already met two new gentlemen this evening, and three more had signed her card. She would be able to talk to them later when they danced. But just now she was staring at the man across the ballroom whom she couldn't get out of her thoughts.

For an American sea captain, Drew Anderson certainly made a dashing figure in his black evening clothes. She was surprised at how well he fit in, as if he were a member of the ton. It was actually impossible to tell he was American until you heard his accent. Not that it mattered to the women present. The man was far too handsome. He had women, young and old, trying to catch his eye.

Right now he was talking to a lovely lady he'd just finished dancing with. He hadn't asked *her* to dance. He'd barely said two words to her, actually, since they'd arrived at this ball.

Of course, her dance card had filled up immediately, but he could have asked her to save him a dance before they arrived. They'd ridden there in the same coach with Georgina, after all. He'd had plenty of opportunity. And it was the polite thing to do, even if he didn't really want to dance with her. But all he'd done was give her a nasty look when she'd come downstairs earlier, and she knew she looked exceptionally pretty in the new ball gown that had arrived just in time this evening.

Icy-blue satin in color with embroidered

roses in a glittering pink thread that trailed along the seams, the gown had arrived with matching slippers and matching ribbons for her hair. She'd already heard several people say that she was definitely *the* sensation of the evening. But did Drew Anderson think so? Evidently not, she'd say, after the nasty look he'd given her, and after what she'd overheard today.

She'd heard too much. And to think, she wouldn't have heard any of that conversation between the two brothers if she'd just slept a little longer, as Margery had suggested. But no, she'd woken up hungry after only picking at the plate of food Drew had brought her at Regina's soiree last night. Not that she hadn't been hungry then, too, but he'd somehow managed to fill her plate with every food she didn't like.

She'd come downstairs this morning in time to hear Boyd Anderson tell his brother, "You're much better than I am at being bored." Drew didn't look bored now; he looked quite interested in the lady he was still talking to, but the remark had been in relation to her and his having to escort her. "Considering we're in shipping of the legitimate sort, I'd say Clinton might object if you try to bring a pirate into the family."

They both found her contemptible, obviously. That didn't hurt her—not too much, anyway. But it did infuriate her. They didn't know her, they didn't know her father. How dare they judge either of them out of hand like that!

"A sweetheart in every port." "Never getting hitched." She understood perfectly now. Drew Anderson was a cad. And he found *her* contemptible?

"You're scaring all the eligible men away with a scowl like that," she heard Drew say. "A penny for your thoughts."

She looked up and saw him standing beside her. She'd stopped staring at him for only a moment. How had he managed to cross the room so fast? If she'd seen him coming, she would have moved off in another direction. She didn't *really* want to talk to him.

"My thoughts would cost you more'n that," she said in a dismissive tone, and glanced away.

"How much more?" he persisted.

"More than you can possibly afford."

"A pity. I was hoping for some sort of amusement to break the tedium."

She drew in her breath sharply and glanced back at him. "So you think my thoughts would amuse you? You think they're filled with silly—"

"I never said that," he cut in.

"You didn't have to. It was implied in your tone," she said, then added under her breath, "No more than one can expect from a brute."

Apparently he heard her, because he actually sighed. "Is every man a brute to you?"

"No, but you're the one who manhandled me so roughly you bruised my arm."

His eyes narrowed at that accusation and he demanded, "Show me your bruises."

She hadn't bothered to look at her arm to see if she had any, and was about to say so when he grabbed her arm and turned it. His expression changed immediately. She glanced down to see the bruise as well. It was just a tiny one. Good grief, she'd never in her life been happy to see a blasted bruise, but she certainly was now.

"I told you," she said with the utmost pleasure.

"Yes, you did," he replied quietly, and he

actually looked contrite, no, *actually,* he looked stricken. "I apologize, Gabby. It certainly wasn't my intention to bruise you, merely to help you that day. I'm sorry you bruise so easily."

The last remark gave her pause. She didn't bruise easily, and in fact, his grip that day hadn't been *that* strong and shouldn't have left a mark . . .

She drew in her breath, recalling that she'd been jostled sharply in the carriage on the way to the Malory townhouse when the vehicle rolled over a rather large pothole, enough that she'd cried out and Ohr had remarked on it. There was no doubt in her mind now that that's how she'd gotten the bruise.

She wasn't going to tell him. She rather liked his current conciliatory expression . . . *Oh, bother!*

"I was mistaken," she said sharply. "So you can retract your apology."

"Excuse me?"

The blush came despite her irritation with herself. "I've just remembered that I got that bruise in a carriage the day after I saw you on the docks. But that doesn't mean you aren't a brute," she added firmly.

He burst out laughing. It drew too many eyes. A big man like him, his laugh was deep, robust, and damned if it wasn't distinctly sensual, too. She was barely able to ignore the shiver it sent down her back.

"I see I managed to break your tedium after all," she grumbled.

"Yes, but I was only hoping for some witty remark that I'm sure you're capable of. I certainly wasn't expecting a feast of . . . silliness."

His engaging grin said clearly that he was teasing her now. It flustered her, but what surprised her even more was that she wanted to grin back at him.

The man's moods shifted quickly, and she found this winsome one more disconcerting than his earlier antagonism. It reminded her of that very real smile he'd given her on the docks, which had caused her stomach to flutter strangely.

She needed to get away from him. Her stomach was starting to flutter again. She looked for her current dance partner, who had gone off to procure some refreshment for her. Peter Wills—Willis, or something like that. But he was nowhere in sight. She wasn't surprised. She'd wanted a break from the dancing before her feet got sore in her new slippers, and had noticed how long the line was for refills of champagne before she sent him off for some.

"Why are you standing here alone?" Drew asked. "I was only joking about that scowl, you know. It certainly wouldn't have kept me from approaching you—if I were interested in making your acquaintance. So why aren't you dancing?"

"I was parched. I sent—"

"Excellent," he cut in, and twirled her onto the dance floor before she could object. "I was wondering how I could manage a dance with you. And the music will be over before your partner returns. A shame to waste it."

He was touching her. Her hand was grasped warmly in his, while his other hand rested firmly on her waist. She felt his touch so keenly that for a moment she could think of nothing else and barely heard what he was saying.

His eyes—they really were black. The light in the ballroom was fairly bright from an excessive number of chandeliers, and standing this close to him, she could detect no other color in them. Quite disturbing, those eyes. They started that fluttering again in her belly—no, it was probably just him. The attraction she felt was more powerful than anything she'd ever experienced before.

His shoulders—good grief, they were so wide. He was such a tall, strapping man, and far too pleasing on the eyes. That fluttering inside her wouldn't stop. She really should get away from him, but it would be too rude of her to end their dance abruptly, and oh, God, she didn't *really* want to.

He smelled so good, like exotic spice. They were dancing too closely. And yet she lacked the will to break the contact with him or mention that it was highly improper. Why, their chests were so close they were nearly touching; in fact, her breasts did graze against him at one point and instantly tingled in response.

"You never did answer my question," he said softly near her ear. "Did you really come back to England just to get a husband?"

Her salvation! Such a perfect subject to get her mind off of what he was making her feel. "Yes, but don't worry, I won't be setting my sights on you. I'm aware that you're just a Lothario."

"Am I? And where did you hear that?"

She wasn't about to admit that she'd eavesdropped on him and his brother this morning and had hurried away before they'd noticed. "Your sister must have mentioned it."

"No, she wouldn't have. She could be furious with me but would never use a word like that to describe me."

"A sweetheart in every port?"

He chuckled. "I concede. That's indeed something Georgie might have said." But then he gave her a knowing look and guessed, "Ah, I understand. *You* related that to being a Lothario."

She shrugged and managed to sound nonchalant. "If it's merely the word you object to, 'philanderer' works just as well, don't you think?"

He winced. She was immediately contrite. Did she really need to ruin these few minutes with him? The dance was almost over. She'd go back to getting her feet trampled by the long list of partners on her dance card. He'd go back to arranging an assignation with another woman for later in the evening. She didn't doubt that's what he'd been doing earlier with that lady she'd seen him talking to.

She debated confessing the truth to him, that it hadn't been her idea to come back to England, and certainly wasn't her idea to appeal to his family for help. But that really wasn't something he needed to know and it wouldn't make the least difference in what relationship they were allowed—which was none at all. Because she *did* want to get married, preferably to a man she could persuade to live part of each year in St. Kitts so she could still see her father regularly, but *Drew* didn't want to marry ever.

"I see another Malory has shown up," Drew remarked just as the dance ended.

"How many are there?"

"Too many," he replied with a chuckle. "But this one, like James, doesn't care to be dragged to affairs like this, so I wonder what he's doing here, unless . . . Did you meet them when they picked up Judith today?"

"Her parents? No, I was getting last-minute fittings for this gown."

"They may just be here to meet you, then. And that's a very pretty gown, by the way."

His dark eyes ran up and down the length of her, pausing at her bosom.

She wished he hadn't said that. She wished he hadn't looked at her like that. It accounted for the blush she was wearing when he deposited her in front of the Malorys he'd just mentioned. Georgina had already found her relations by marriage and made the introductions.

Anthony Malory was incredibly handsome, but oddly, he looked nothing like his brother James. Taller, and certainly darker, he sported the same black hair and blue eyes that his niece Regina had. His wife, Rosalyn, was simply breathtaking, with red-gold hair, lovely hazel-green eyes, and a trim though voluptuous figure. It was obvious now where Judith got her coloring from.

"You must be the pirate," Anthony said baldly.

His wife gasped. "Anthony!"

And Georgina scolded, "Not so loud, Tony. And don't say that *word* in public when referring to Gabby. We don't want to ruin her chances of making a good match."

But Gabrielle saw that no one other than the Malorys was nearby to have overheard him, and the poor man was beginning to look contrite, even though she was sure he had just been teasing. So she grinned and said, "Yes, bloodthirsty and all that. It's a shame there are no planks around here so I can prove it."

He chuckled. "Well said, m'dear."

But Drew whispered behind her, "He thinks you're teasing, but I actually wish you weren't. Pirates aren't virgins and don't give a damn about convention, so you could prove you really are one by spending the night with me."

Gabrielle's blush was immediate. But when she turned to rebuke Drew, she almost gasped, seeing his expression. There was such heat in his eyes, as if he were already imagining her in his bed. And, good heavens, she started to do the same thing. Her stomach wasn't just fluttering now. Her whole body felt warm and as if it were trembling! She put her hand on her chest to try to contain the pounding there.

Behind her, Georgina was telling Rosalyn and Anthony about some of the parties she intended to take Gabrielle to over the next couple of weeks. But Anthony must have noticed the interaction between Gabrielle and Drew, because he remarked, "It shouldn't take long to find her a husband. She seems to find the men in London agreeable, even the American ones."

Hearing that, Georgina looked curiously at her brother, then her eyes flared slightly and she asked him, "You've been behaving, haven't you?"

He gave her a boyish smile. "Don't I always?"

Georgina snorted. "No, you don't. But see that you do, henceforth."

He rolled his eyes at her, as if she were making something out of nothing, but Gabrielle was very aware of the hand he put on her waist to turn her back toward his relatives. It was a very casual touch to anyone who might have noticed it, but not to her. She felt the slight squeeze of his fingers just before he let go.

Wilbur Carlisle had to say her name twice to gain her attention. She'd been too busy wondering why Drew had just touched her in what was a distinctly possessive manner to notice that her next dance partner had arrived to claim her. Had Drew seen the young gentleman approaching and touched her like that just to make a subtle point? Wilbur *did* glance at Drew a bit curiously. No, she was being silly and making something out of nothing herself.

She gave Wilbur a bright smile and her full attention. Now, here was a nice chap. If she had to make a choice immediately, she would choose Wilbur as a husband. He was handsome, amiable, and witty. She could find no fault with him, other than he didn't make her stomach flutter the way Drew did. She'd met him last night at Regina's and had enjoyed their brief conversation. He'd even made her laugh several times, something none of the other men she'd met so far had tried to do. She was pleased that he was there tonight so she could get to know him a little better. Without a doubt, he was the most handsome of the gentlemen who had flocked to sign her dance card as soon as she arrived. Not as handsome as Drew, of course, but . . . Good grief, she had to stop thinking of philandering rakes like Drew Anderson and keep her mind focused on the men who were as interested in marriage as she was.

Chapter 14

Gabrielle got very little sleep that night. Rolling through her mind repeatedly and keeping her awake was Drew's remark. Prove she was really a pirate by spending the night with him. She should have been scandalized. But she wasn't. When she took the time to think about it after she got home, she was too pleased by what she'd read between the lines—he wanted her. And what a remarkable effect that knowledge had on her. One moment she felt so excited she became almost giddy, and the next moment she experienced the deepest despair. Because she couldn't do anything about Drew's desire for her. Nor would he.

Margery woke her the next morning earlier than she would have liked. She almost shooed the older woman out so she could get a few more hours' sleep, but she remembered that Margery hadn't been home much the last couple of days. She had many old friends in London she wanted to visit. So now would be a good time to talk to her and get her opinion on her prospective suitors, in case Margery was going out again today.

"Help me figure out which qualities I should be looking for in a husband," she said as Margery riffled through her wardrobe to pick out her day dress.

"Just use your common sense, girl," Margery said, and held out two dresses. "The pink or the blue?"

"The pink," Gabrielle replied without glancing at the dresses. "But common sense doesn't really tell me what to look for, it merely helps me determine what I find agreeable about a man after I meet him."

Margery tsked. "Kindness, tolerance, patience, honor, compassion—"

"Wait!" Gabrielle threw up a hand. "Some of those qualities aren't going to be obvious or come to light easily. I could know a man for years and not find out if he's honorable or not. Or is there a way to tell that I'm not thinking of?"

Margery tossed the pink dress on the bed, then moved to the bureau to fetch some underclothes. "You're asking me if there's a way to find out if a man has honor? Lord love you, lass, if I knew how to do that, I'd bottle it and sell it."

Gabrielle sighed. "What else should I be looking for?"

"Your personal preferences, of course."

"You mean like a good sense of humor? I'd really like that in a husband."

"And?"

"A fine physique. I'm partial to that."

Margery rolled her eyes. "No, you're not. That Millford heir had a rotund gut to go with his handsome face."

"Only a slight one and let's not mention that snob," Gabrielle said indignantly, then gasped, "Snobbery, of course! I won't tolerate that!"

"What else?"

"A sallow complexion won't do. I swear, half the men I've met here look like ghosts, they're so pale."

Margery chuckled. "And how would you know what a ghost looks like, eh?"

"You know what I mean."

"Well, I wouldn't be discounting complexions, girl. Stick a man out in the sun for a few days and that takes care of that, don't it?"

"True."

"Have you started that list, then, that you were thinking of making?"

"That's what I'm doing now."

"Well, don't be making this husband hunt more difficult than it is by listing a whole slew of names. You want a few choices, not a headache sorting them out. How many are you starting with?"

"Just a few," Gabrielle replied, then frowned. "I think you're right, though. These other two men I was going to put on the list, I'm not really interested in. And that leaves just Wilbur Carlisle for now."

"You like him?"

"He's almost too perfect," Gabrielle replied with a frown. "There's nothing about him not to like."

Margery chuckled. "Don't you dare find fault with that, Gabby, so get that frown off of your brow and remember you've only been to two parties so far."

Gabrielle grinned. "I know. Georgina has

assured me there are many more men for me to meet. But I hope Wilbur will come by so you can have a look at him. I'd like your opinion—"

"All right, but my opinion won't matter one bit and it shouldn't," Margery said. "Because you've already answered your own question, haven't you? You know exactly what you want in a man. So go ahead and make your list, but trust your heart in the end."

Margery said no more on the subject and helped her to dress as she did each morning, then went off for a cup of tea while Gabrielle sat down at the vanity to fix her hair in the simple coiffure she preferred for daytime. But Margery's last remarks stuck in her mind, in particular, that she already knew what she wanted in a man. It struck her as odd that she'd said *man,* rather than husband, but she didn't find it odd at all that the only name that came to mind for a *man* was Drew. And back came the giddiness, and the despair, that had kept her awake so long last night.

But remembering how good it had felt when he'd held her in his arms while they'd danced, she soon began thinking about ways she might get around her own objections to him—and overcome his. Her main, no, really her only objection to getting involved with Drew was that he was a sailor, and that was an objection because she didn't want to spend her life pining away at home, month after month, wailing for her sailor to come home, just as her mother had done. *It was pointless to love a man who loves the sea.* That advice had been drummed into her since she was a child, and she'd taken it to heart. But that was before she'd gone to sea and discovered that she loved to sail. So where was it written that she had to stay at home and let her man go off to sea alone? Why couldn't she live at sea with her husband?

As soon as that thought occurred to her, the despair was gone, leaving only the giddiness. His objections to getting involved with her were minor. So he didn't want to get married. Maybe he only *thought* he didn't. And maybe that was because he'd never had a reason to give marriage serious consideration.

She could give him that reason, if she'd stop pushing him away with every other word out of her mouth. But she'd have to circumvent his own agenda first. *A sweet-heart in every port.* That phrase was so very—annoying. She didn't doubt he would have tried to make her his sweetheart in his English port if she weren't actively seeking a husband. His outrageous remark about spending the night with her implied that he would.

The same thoughts followed her around the rest of the morning and into the after-noon. They were going to the theater to-night, but that didn't distract her either. It was a new play, so even James would be attending. Which meant Drew wouldn't have to escort her and Georgina. She wasn't sure if she'd see him at all today, but she was anxious to find out if it was even possible to get rid of the antagonism that had grown between them.

It was actually a relief when Richard showed up to check on her that afternoon, not because she was glad to see him, which she was, but because she knew he would take her mind off of Drew, and he did that quickly enough with just his attire. She barely recognized him!

"Look at you!" she exclaimed when she

came downstairs to find him in the entry hall, and gave him a big hug.

Richard was dressed as finely as any young lord. He'd even cut his black hair, or it appeared that he had, until he doffed his hat and his braid tumbled down his back.

"You've been shopping," she continued.

"One of us had to, if we are going to keep coming to this end of town to check on you, and Ohr refused to go anywhere near a suit. So, have you found us a husband yet?"

She laughed. "Us?"

"Well, we have a vested interest, don't we? If you've got your husband picked out by the time Nathan gets here, then we can head home right after the wedding, and I don't mind telling you, the less time I spend here the better."

She raised a questioning brow at him, but he went right on to the next subject as if he hadn't just admitted he was nervous about being back in England. She wondered if she'd ever find out what he was running away from.

"Have you seen your solicitor yet?" Richard asked.

"No, but I have an appointment tomorrow."

A servant came down the hall. Gabrielle took Richard's arm and led him out back to the large garden behind the house, thinking they wouldn't be disturbed there, but he noticed immediately that it was already occupied.

"Wonderful," he said. "I was so hoping I'd see her while I was here."

"Her?"

"Lady Malory," he answered.

She followed his gaze to where Georgina was sitting on the edge of a fountain, trying to read a book and keep her eye on the two younger children, Gilbert and Adam, she had with her. Energetic tykes; Georgina wasn't getting much reading done.

Gabrielle had been introduced to the twins and their nurse just yesterday. She didn't know why the nurse was absent today; perhaps the lady just wanted to spend some time alone with her children.

But it took her only a moment to recall the jealousy Richard had inspired in James Malory upon their arrival. She glanced at him, wondering whether she should laugh or clobber him.

She finally said, "Richard, she's a married woman."

"Yes, but look who she's married to," he replied. "She can't really be happy with a brute like that. Wouldn't you agree?"

Absolutely, was her first thought, and yet she'd witnessed the way the couple behaved together, just as Richard had, and while he might not have read between the lines, she certainly had. In addition to their obvious physical attraction to each other, she'd also sensed the emotional closeness between them, and the utter lack of fear on Georgina's part. Any woman who could talk to her husband the way Georgina Malory spoke to James knew that she was loved and obviously reciprocated the sentiment.

But Gabrielle saw that her friend appeared to be serious, so she replied cautiously, "You'd think she'd be intimidated by a man who so easily inspires fear in others, wouldn't you? But I never got that impression from her, just the opposite, actually. And I've spoken with her several times in private. She might not be happy with the current situation I've placed her in. They did have other plans, after all. But she hasn't let on that I've inconvenienced her and seems happy enough otherwise. But then you *were* just basing your opinion on who she's married to, right?"

He didn't answer that and said instead, "I should talk to her."

She realized suddenly that he hadn't taken his eyes off of Georgina since he'd come into the garden. It made her try to see the woman as a man would see her. Georgina Malory *was* beautiful. Childbearing hadn't disturbed her figure at all; it was nicely trim and curved where it should be.

Gabrielle became alarmed. "Be sensible, Richard. You said it yourself. Look who she's married to. Do you really want that particular man after your blood?"

"He'd never know."

"Richard!"

"And I'm not thinking of stealing her away from him. A single dalliance will do."

That statement managed to infuriate her. Trust a man to think of taking his pleasure and then never giving the woman another thought. Richard intended to give in to his temptations.

She watched him move briskly through the garden to approach Malory's wife. She should have stopped him, but she was sure he was going to be rebuffed, so it was better he find that out and put the lady from his mind. He had no time to be subtle about it, after all, since Gabrielle was going to be there only a few weeks herself, and he couldn't come by every day without James's noticing. So he'd have to forgo subtlety and get right to the point.

He sat next to Georgina. They talked for quite a while. She even noticed the lady laughing. Well, Richard was quite handsome and could be very amusing. But she'd been right. After a little warm-up, her friend must have got right to the point.

Even if she hadn't seen it, the slap Georgina gave Richard was hard enough to be heard across the garden. She winced for her friend. She just wasn't surprised. She hoped he wasn't too disappointed, though. Actually, knowing him, he'd probably try again. But she was sure that he'd continue to fail. Georgina Malory wasn't just a married woman. She happened to be a happily married woman who loved her husband, too.

"I suppose I should apologize to you."

Gabrielle jumped, she was so startled. She groaned inwardly before she turned to face James Malory, who'd come up silently beside her. "Apologize?"

"I'm going to have to hurt your friend," James said.

She was afraid he was going to say that. But he didn't really sound or look angry. She just didn't know him well enough to realize that his expression was never an indication of his true feelings.

"Must you?" she asked. "He's really harmless. And Georgina has already dashed his hopes."

"He's trespassed. I'm afraid I can't allow that."

Richard, looking disappointed, started to walk back to her. But then he saw James standing with her and bolted in the opposite direction. It was almost funny, how quickly he went over the high wall that separated the garden from the neighbors' property.

"Very wise of him," James said. "I don't climb walls."

She would have been relieved, but she had a feeling Malory wouldn't leave it at that. "Would it help if I gave you my word that he will never approach your wife again?"

He raised a brow. "While I don't doubt

your word, m'dear, I must point out that one person can never fully control another's actions."

"True, but what I will do is get *his* word. Once he's given his word, he's quite trustworthy."

"Very well. That will suffice to keep me from tracking him down. But you might want to warn your friend, it won't suffice if I ever see him again."

She nodded, grateful for the clarification. And if Richard didn't pay attention when she visited him this afternoon to warn him how close he'd come to dying, it would be on his own head.

Chapter 15

Later that afternoon Gabrielle met the other Anderson brother who was visiting the Malorys. Actually she ran into him, since he barged out of his room upstairs just as she was passing it. The collision didn't knock them over, but it drew an immediate apology from him, then a very telling pause as he looked her over.

Boyd Anderson was a surprise to her because he didn't look anything like his brother Drew. He was shorter and a little stockier than Drew, and even his facial features were different from Drew's. In fact, only the brothers' hair color was the same—golden brown.

"Well, hell," he said, leaning a hand

against the wall, which pretty much blocked her from proceeding. "I can see I had a good reason to avoid you after all."

She stiffened instantly. Was he going to be as insulting as his brother tended to be?

"Did you?"

"Yes," he said. "You're far too pretty. I could have gotten along just fine without finding that out."

She relaxed, even chuckled. "And now?"

"I just may have to get in line." He grinned. "How long is it?"

"Not long a' tall."

He seemed incredulous, then slapped his forehead. "That's right, you've only been here a few days."

"It's not that," she admitted. "There's been ample interest, but only a few men who have piqued my own interest so far."

"I'll consider that a boon. What's on your agenda for tonight?"

"The theater."

"Really? I just happen to love the theater."

The Malorys certainly did, they even had their own box on the upper level with a splendid view of the stage. She was to find that Drew loved the theater as well, at least that was the reason he gave for joining them that night, when he didn't have to. Gabrielle didn't doubt it was just an excuse. Obviously, he'd found out his brother was going. What wasn't so obvious was why that would make any difference to him, but she was sure it did. The competition between them was subtle, but it definitely existed. And as the night progressed, it was as if Drew was determined to make sure Boyd couldn't find a single moment alone with her, and vice versa.

When James and Georgina went to speak with some friends during intermission, leaving her alone with an Anderson brother on each side of her, she mentioned some refreshments. She actually was parched after laughing so much during the first acts of the comedy the theater was presenting tonight.

"A splendid idea," Drew said, and stared pointedly at Boyd, making it obvious he wanted his brother to do the fetching.

But Boyd just stared back and even nodded a few times toward the door, making the same silent suggestion.

Gabrielle caught on to what they were doing and sighed. "Don't get up," she said dryly as she got up herself. "I'll fetch something myself."

Drew came instantly to his feet. "An even better idea. I'll join you."

"So will I." Boyd jumped to his feet as well.

Gabrielle hid her smile and didn't wait for them to follow. Downstairs, she was delighted to find the Honorable Wilbur Carlisle waving at her and she moved across the lobby to speak with him.

"How nice to see you again, Wilbur."

"The pleasure is entirely mine, Miss Gabby. I tried to gain your attention earlier, but you were quite enthralled by the play—and the gentlemen with you."

There was curiosity in his tone, or was it censure? But she realized he didn't know who Drew and Boyd were. She glanced back to see that they'd temporarily lost sight of her in the crowded lobby, *and* were looking around for her. She wasn't going to have long alone with Wilbur.

"I'm with the Malorys, Wilbur. The two gentlemen are Lady Malory's brothers."

"Ah, yes, I believe I've heard of them. In shipping, aren't they?"

"Yes, her whole family is. But tell me," she said, glancing up at him flirtatiously, "why haven't you come by to call on me?"

He actually looked quite uncomfortable suddenly. "I wanted to, but, well, dash it all, I suppose I must confess that James Malory is the reason I've stayed away."

"You know him?"

"Not a'tall," Wilbur replied. "But I've heard so many things, well, that is to say, I've been trying, desperately, to get up the nerve to enter his domain, and I will. I assure you I will. I just need a few more days to remind myself that rumors are rarely true and that he's likely harmless—"

"Not harmless at all," James said behind them.

Gabrielle almost laughed, James was looking so aggrieved to have come upon two people discussing him, and not in a very positive light. She just didn't know that under any other circumstances, he probably would have picked Wilbur up by the scruff of his neck and tossed him out the nearest window. But because of her, and because Wilbur was obviously one of her suitors, James Malory was determined to be on his best behavior. So the blades on his witty tongue were mostly sheathed for the evening.

Gabrielle noticed that Wilbur was blushing profusely. James noticed as well and said, "I was joking, Carlisle. Please feel free to come by to call on Gabrielle this week. As long as she has only good things to say about you, you'll be welcome in my home."

A warning and an invitation in the same breath. Amazing how Malory could do that. But Gabrielle was sure he'd extended the invitation just for her sake. And Wilbur didn't seem to catch the warning. His fears somewhat put to rest, he thanked James and mentioned that he would be pleased to accept the offer before he hurried off.

"Not very brave, is he?" James remarked as soon as Wilbur rushed off.

"Is any man in your presence?" Gabrielle said in Wilbur's defense.

James burst out laughing. "Touché, m'dear." But his laugh had drawn Drew and Boyd's attention, and with them both heading in their direction now, James added, "Except for those two, though I could wish it was otherwise."

"You found her," Boyd said, reaching them first.

"You lost her?" James replied.

"Not as disastrously as you lost Georgie

that time in the Caribbean," Drew replied as he came up on Gabrielle's other side.

"I didn't lose your sister, you ass, you sailed off with her."

"Right under your nose, too." Drew smirked.

"Careful, Yank. I never did get even for that."

Gabrielle felt her body tense up. She was certain that upon seeing the expression on James's face, any other man would have backed off and run the other way. But the two Americans just laughed at their reminiscing. They really weren't afraid of James Malory. Because he was their brother-in-law? Actually, as they continued ribbing him, she realized it was because they'd tangled with him before and lived to tell the tale.

"Malory, you are, without a doubt, superlative with those lethal fists of yours," Boyd said with some very real admiration.

"Don't ever mention that in front of my brother Tony," James replied. "He thinks he's as good as I am in the ring."

"Now, that's a fight I'd love to see," Boyd said. "And wasn't Warren taking lessons from him there for a while?"

James nodded. "Your brother Warren was determined to take me on."

"Did he ever get around to it, before he owned up that he was in love with your niece?" Drew asked curiously.

"Indeed. One of my fonder memories, too, that fight."

"Warren was always pretty good with his fists. We rarely beat him, Drew and I. And you took him by surprise, that time you fought us all in our home in Bridgeport."

"You have a point to make in all that rambling?" James asked dryly.

Boyd chuckled. "Just wanted to know how badly you wiped the floor with him in that last fight."

"You don't give your brother enough credit. He acquitted himself rather well."

"But still lost?"

"Of course."

"Who are you raking over the coals?" Georgina wanted to know as she joined them.

James refused to answer, merely raised a brow at her brothers. Boyd explained, and as James had probably guessed, she began scolding both brothers for discussing violent subjects in front of Gabrielle.

Drew, whether teasing or not, pointed out, "A pirate's daughter would be used to hearing even worse subjects discussed. Isn't that right, sweetheart?" he asked Gabrielle.

Somehow she dredged up a smile for him. "Oh, certainly. We don't thrash our victims with fists, we gut them with swords."

She walked away before he realized he'd insulted her, and she was gratified to hear Georgina begin to chew his ear off for using that *word* again. But he'd already used it an awful lot tonight, without Georgina overhearing. To get a rise out of her? Or to remind Boyd of her background? It was hard to tell. But she wasn't going to forget the conversation she'd overheard the other day in which Boyd had said, "When I do settle down, it sure as hell won't be with a wench whose father is a pirate."

While Boyd seemed not to share Drew's aversion to marriage, he did seem to harbor more resentment against pirates. Not that it mattered. She might find him quite handsome, and he seemed to be taken with her despite his feelings for pirates, but he didn't cause any fluttering in her stomach like his aggravating brother did.

She was still having fun, despite the little annoyances. And she didn't care why Drew was there, she was just glad that he was. Actually, she was glad Boyd was, too. In their bickering and in trying to outdo each other for her benefit, the brothers inadvertently were revealing things about the Andersons and the Malorys that she might never have heard of otherwise.

She learned that one of the Malory ancestors had actually been a gypsy. This was apparently a rumor that had circulated for many years, but the brothers confirmed it was true. They called James an ex-pirate, but it was said in jest, so she didn't believe it. They implied the head of the Malory clan, Jason Malory, Third Marquis of Haverston, had married his housekeeper! She didn't believe that either. Drew and Boyd talked about their three other brothers and mentioned that they were straitlaced New Englanders, though Boyd teased that Drew certainly didn't fit that mold. She had no trouble believing that.

She was also able to begin her campaign to end the animosity between her and Drew. Not a single sour look crossed her countenance, and she managed to control her sensitivity to Drew's teasing. Even when he told his brother earlier in her hearing, "Stop apologizing for every 'blast and damn' out of your mouth. Pirates win hands down when it comes to vulgarity," Gabrielle had managed not to pay him back in kind, though she had to grit her teeth to keep her mouth shut.

The rest of the play was just as amusing as the first two acts. It was a story about an English family trying to marry off their daughter. She didn't relate it to her own situation at all and wouldn't have if Drew didn't lean close during the last act to whisper, "Who do you think the heroine is going to choose? The safe, proper young lord, though damn, he's clumsy, isn't he? Or the blackguard she keeps swooning over?"

She shouldn't have answered him. Really, it wasn't a serious question. He was merely rubbing it in, her own situation, since *he* obviously related it to the comedy they were watching.

Without really thinking, she said, "The suave blackguard will win hands down."

She heard his softly indrawn breath before he asked, "Why?"

"For the obvious reason. She loves him." And then she grinned. "Care to bet?"

He sounded annoyed now when he answered, "No, you're probably right. It's a comedy, after all. The silly chit is being portrayed as not having any sense, and certainly not enough to realize she'd never be happy with a rogue."

"Nonsense," she disagreed. "She could go through the rest of her life without realizing what a blackguard he is, or she could find out and not care. Happiness is a matter of the heart, after all."

"Is it? You think you'll be happy when you fall in love?"

There was no longer any pretense that they weren't discussing her. And while they'd been whispering, and leaning a little closer to each other to do so, she hadn't looked at him once, had kept her eyes on the stage. But she turned to look at him now and gasped when she saw he was closer than she'd thought. Their lips nearly touched and his gaze was so intense, it nearly mesmerized her.

But she answered him, rather breathlessly now, and just as softly, "I know I will be."

"How do you know, Gabby?"

"Because if the man I love loves me in return, then nothing will stand in the way of our happiness. It's inevitable. And besides, I can always make him walk my father's plank if he doesn't make me happy."

Drew burst out laughing. Fortunately, so did the audience just then, so no one knew his humor had nothing to do with the play.

Later that night, while Margery helped her prepare for bed, Gabrielle evaluated her own performance that evening. That's what it had been. She'd had to resist countless urges to upbraid Drew severely for his careless remarks, teasing or not. But she'd persevered and merely smiled at him. She *was* going to change his opinion of her—if she didn't clobber him first.

Chapter 16

Gabrielle went to bed that night with a smile on her lips, quite a change from the night before. She felt the evening at the theater had gone splendidly, all in all. There'd been a few rough moments, at least where her patience was concerned, but in the end, she'd accomplished what she'd set out to do, which was let Drew know that their little war was over as far as she was concerned. Now, if he'd just draw in his own cannons . . .

Gabrielle and Margery went downstairs at midmorning the next day to meet Georgina, who was going to accompany them to the solicitor's office. She wasn't looking forward to the meeting with William Bates, or explaining to the disagreeable fellow why she had disappeared three years ago when he had wanted to shackle her with that reprobate guardian. She wanted Georgina there with her in case he got nasty about it, or tried to deny her her inheritance because she had flown the coop, as it were.

But Drew was waiting for them in the front hall, and when she raised a brow at him, he explained, "One of the twins is sick. A nasty cold apparently, but you know how mothers are. Georgie won't leave his side, so she asked me to fill in as your escort today. She didn't think you'd mind. She said something about me being a much better intimidator than she is, if the lawyer gives you any trouble."

"She told you what the problem might be?"

"That you didn't follow the fellow's advice?"

"It wasn't advice. He was actually going to hand me over to a known reprobate who was supposedly going to act as my guardian, when I *told* him my father was alive and that I didn't require a guardian. The man wouldn't listen to reason, though."

"So you simply left England?"

"Well, what would you have done under the same circumstances?" she countered.

He actually smiled. "Probably the same thing. Shall we go?"

It wouldn't have taken long to reach William Bates's office if Margery hadn't spotted one of her old friends on the street and asked to be let out of the coach for a few minutes. They waited for her, but it didn't look as if Margery wanted to end her reunion quickly.

"Are you always this impatient when you visit solicitors?" Drew asked her. He'd noticed her tapping her foot.

"I've only ever visited one, this one, and—" She paused to sigh. "Bates was my mother's solicitor. As a child, I recall him always being quite rude when my mother would go to see him and take me with her. He was so condescending, it was like he was treating her like a child."

"My oldest brother, Clinton, who handles most of the business of my family's shipping line, has told me about arrogant, rude lawyers, but also that they're not all like that. Why didn't she hire a different lawyer?"

Gabrielle smiled. "That's a good question. Probably because she never even thought to. He was her father's man, too. Loyalty, I suppose, was why she tolerated him, and because she didn't have to deal with him often. But I'm just guessing. She never seemed to mind him, or even notice how rude he was. I did, though, and I never liked him, ever, which is possibly why I'm nervous."

"Then let's get it over with. You don't need your servant for this. As the brother of your sponsor, I am an acceptable chaperone for you, you know. Let her enjoy some time with her friend."

Gabrielle didn't even have to think twice about it. Having Drew alone to herself, even if she did have some business to take care of first, was an unexpected boon. It would be a nice chance to get to know him a little better. And he was being amiable for a change. Not one insult or questionable tease—so far. Had last night made a difference to him, too? Was he finally ready to call a truce?

She called out to Margery that she could take her time and enjoy a nice visit with her friend, that she'd meet her at home later. She then told the driver to continue on.

They turned a corner and the morning

sun entered the coach and caught the tips of Drew's hair. Such lovely hair he had, and just now, it seemed sprinkled with golden dewdrops . . . God, he was so handsome, and she suddenly had an overwhelming urge to touch him. He wasn't even looking at her, was glancing out the window. Would he feel it if she leaned forward and touched him? Of course he would, and how could she explain that? She couldn't. She'd be caught red-handed and embarrassed. Or he'd sweep her into his arms and kiss her . . .

"We're here," he said.

"Where?" she said.

He gave her a knowing look and one of his sensual smiles. Oh, good grief, he couldn't *know* that she'd been thinking about touching him, could he?

He helped her down from the coach, taking her hand in his, putting his other hand to her waist to make sure she didn't fall. Such an ordinary thing for him to do, and yet she felt his hands on her so keenly. She didn't want to move on, didn't want to lose that touch. They were standing so close. She wondered if he realized that she wanted him to kiss her. Such yearning she felt, it must have been reflected in her expression. But having arrived at their destination, Drew was all business now and simply ushered her straight into the building and upstairs to Bates's office.

She was disappointed, especially after Drew had given her that knowing look and smile. Then to so dismiss her from his mind that he wouldn't even glance at her. That was why she was a bit sharp when she gave Bates's clerk her name. And she probably would have been quite sharp with Bates as well if she'd been shown right in to him. But she was asked to wait, to take a seat, that he would see her shortly.

She didn't sit down. She paced. Drew, watching her for a moment, started pacing with her. When she realized what he was doing, she stopped and chuckled. The tension left her. She even sat in one of the chairs lining the wall.

She wasn't kept waiting long, but the clerk said, "Your companion, unless he is a relative, will have to wait out here."

Drew simply ignored the fellow and led her into the office. William Bates was sitting behind his desk. He didn't rise at her entrance. A big man who overindulged in food, nearly bald and with florid cheeks, he hadn't changed at all. He was even wearing the same scowl he'd worn at their last meeting.

"Do you realize I could have had you declared dead, Miss Brooks?"

She stared at him in amazement, not because he was trying to intimidate her again, but because he didn't intimidate her at all now. Good grief, she couldn't believe how formidable he'd seemed when she was younger. It was a wonder she'd had the nerve to defy him and leave the country like she did. But he was just a large man who liked to pretend he was more important than he was.

"Nonsense," Gabrielle replied. "I sent you a letter, informing you that I was leaving England to live with my father."

"And merely assumed that I received it?"

"Whether you did or not is irrelevant. I left because you tried to deliver me into the hands of a man who was unfit to be anyone's guardian."

"You were underage!"

"I was not without a living relative!"

"A relative who did not live in England!"

She leaned forward, her hands placed on

his desk, and gave him a tight little smile. "There is no need for us to argue, Mr. Bates. I've returned to England, which is all that matters. And I'm old enough to receive my inheritance, so if you have documents for me to sign, produce them now. Otherwise, begin immediately the transfer of my mother's estate to me." Gabrielle took a card out of her reticule and laid it on the solicitor's desk, "This is the name of the bank to which you can transfer my funds."

"Now see here—"

"Just do as the lady says and transfer her funds," Drew said.

"Who are you, sir?" Bates demanded.

"Drew Anderson, a relative of the Malorys," Drew replied. "Do I need to mention titles?"

William cleared his throat. "No. No, indeed. That family is well known in this town. This matter will be expedited with all due haste. Good day, Miss Brooks." He nodded, and then stood respectfully as she rose and left the office with Drew close behind her.

Outside, as Drew helped her back into the coach, she thanked him for his assistance. He chuckled at her.

"You're joking, right?" he said. "The way

Georgie made it sound, I thought I was going to have to slam a few heads together today. But you didn't need any help in there. You handled the situation as if you deal with lawyers every day."

She blushed at the compliment. "He just wasn't as frightening as I remembered him being."

"Nonsense. He still tried to cow you, but you didn't let him. I wouldn't have said anything, but I just love throwing around that word 'titles.' It gets no reaction back home, but here it can produce some really amusing results. Now how about a ride down the Mall in Hyde Park before we return home, since we finished here early? Or maybe even a boat ride? What's the name of that lake one of your kings created in the park?"

"It was Queen Caroline, wife to George II in the last century, who had the Serpentine created. And that's a rather nice idea, actually, though it looks like it will be raining soon. Are you sure?"

"As long as it doesn't downpour, we won't melt."

That giddiness was returning. What an unexpected delight. She'd come downstairs this morning dreading the confrontation with William Bates, and not only did that go surprisingly well, but she was getting to spend the day with Drew as well.

They rode to the lake in Hyde Park. There were no boats available to rent when they got there, so they walked along the shore instead.

"I take it you're rich now?" Drew asked when they stopped to feed some ducks.

"Not at all," she replied, watching the way his jacket stretched taut as he bent over toward the ducks. "My mother's inheritance leaves me quite comfortable, though, and there's the cottage that's mine now."

"Cottage?" He seemed surprised as he glanced back at her. "Why did I picture you growing up in a mansion?"

She laughed. "Perhaps because I did. A cottage here doesn't necessarily denote size. My mother's house was quite large with extensive grounds."

"You liked living here?" he asked. "Or did you prefer the Caribbean?"

"I much prefer the warmer climate in the islands."

He hooked her arm through his to continue the walk, very proper, and yet that was the only warmth she was thinking of. It was very hard to concentrate on conversing with him when their shoulders brushed together and she could feel the heat of his body so close to hers.

"Then why come here for a husband?"

"My father wanted me to have this coming out because it's what my mother would have arranged for me had she lived. But why do you find it unusual? I am English, after all."

"What sort of man are you looking for? Give me a few clues and I'll keep an eye out for candidates."

He help her to find a husband? She almost laughed. He was probably teasing, so she replied in a light tone, "I probably want what most girls want. I'd like a husband who is tall, and handsome, and witty. Oh, and it would be nice if he enjoys traveling."

She'd just described him. She wondered if he'd noticed. It didn't sound like it when he chuckled.

"I think that has to be the first time I've ever heard that as criteria for a husband," he said. "Why traveling?"

"Because I enjoy it."

He raised a brow. "Do you really?"

"Why does that surprise you?"

"Because most women I know don't like going to sea. They either find it frightening, or just don't want to go far from the comforts of home."

"Then they've never manned the wheel!"

His look said he was sure she was teasing now. "Well, you'll have to strike old Wilbur as a contender for your hand, then. He seems a man who'll never set foot aboard a ship."

"Nonsense. What makes you say so?"

"I've seen him dance with you," he replied. "He's got two left feet. Can't maintain a good balance aboard a ship with two left feet, now, can you?"

She did laugh at his teasing this time. He just grinned and tossed a pebble into the water. Hyde Park was still in glorious full bloom and the lake was beautiful at this time of the year, but she noticed only vaguely, since her eyes barely moved off of Drew. She still found the breeze off the water a little chilling whenever he stepped away from her, but she wasn't about to mention that she was cold and risk ending their outing, or, actually . . . No, she wasn't going to make him think about keeping her warm. She couldn't be that bold; well, she could, but they were in a public place.

"What about you?" she asked. "Do you often come to England?"

"My brothers and I try to get here at least once a year, ever since my sister took up residence here. We opened a Skylark office in London after Georgie married, so England is once again one of our regular trade routes."

"Where do your normal routes take you?"

"The Caribbean. I'll be returning there when I leave England. I was going home to Bridgeport, but only because I was going to meet Boyd there. Since he showed up here instead, I'll be returning to business as usual."

She grinned. "You favor the Caribbean, too?"

He grinned as well and admitted, "Yes, but then it's not such a long trip from there to our home in Bridgeport, Connecticut."

"Your ship is docked in London, I take it?" At his nod, she asked, "What's her name?"

"*The Triton.* She's a beauty, sleek, and fast for her size," he said with obvious pride.

"How long have you captained her?"

"I was twenty when I first took command of her," he replied.

"Isn't that a name from Greek mythology?"

"Indeed. Most of our ships carry similar names. Our father named all the ones my brothers and I command, so you might guess, he loved Greek mythology."

"Rather prestigious names, though," she said, then chuckled. "I'm hesitant to mention the name of my father's ship. There's simply no comparison."

"Oh, come now. You've sparked my curiosity, so you have to confess."

"The Crusty Jewel."

"Ah, symbolic of nothing?"

"On the contrary. Chasing down treasure is his passion, and if, no, *when* he finally finds that pot of gold, as it were, he expects the chest to be full of old coins and jewels, all quite crusty from being buried for centuries."

She was pleased to note his smile was understanding. He could have gotten nasty there about her father, but remarkably, he'd been on his best behavior all day. Teasing, charming, and not a single mention of pirates.

He noticed one of the rowboats heading back toward the dock where they could be rented and mentioned that boat ride again, so they turned to head back. But he'd no sooner said it than the first raindrops hit them.

"So much for that," he mumbled. "Hurry, it's going to be pouring in a minute."

It was less than a minute. The deluge came almost immediately after he mentioned it. Everyone in the park was racing in one direction or another to get out of the rain. But there was simply no way she could run in the constraints of her outing dress and new petticoats, not without hiking up the skirt. She tried, though, to keep up with him, since he'd grabbed her hand to run, but he soon noticed her problem. Rather than just give up and accept the fact that they were going to be drenched before they reached the coach, he surprised her by sweeping her into his arms. He was able to run much faster then, even carrying her.

They were still drenched. As soon as they were inside the coach, they both began to laugh at their sorry state.

"That was quite chivalrous of you, but we're still soaked!" she said.

He paused in removing his jacket to brush a lock of wet hair off her cheek, making her realize that her coiffure was completely undone, wet locks scattered down her back and chest. Putting a hand to the top of her head, she exclaimed, "Oh, no, I seem to have lost my hat, too! What rotten luck, it was my favorite."

"Hold on," Drew said, and ran back outside.

She tried to stop him, but he seemed not to hear her. He wasn't gone long, though, and he shouted at the driver, "Back to Berkeley Square!" before he reentered the coach and dropped a very bedraggled hat on the seat beside her. "See what I'm willing to do for you!"

That was rather unexpected. "Thank you," she said as she gave the ruined hat a forlorn look. "I might be able to salvage the feathers, after they dry."

"I'd buy a new one, but that's just me."

She chuckled and glanced up at him, then drew in her breath. He'd finished removing his jacket. His white lawn shirt was plastered to his skin, revealing every sinewy muscle across his wide chest and powerful arms. Her eyes met his and the laughter died abruptly. She barely had time to notice the heat in his gaze before his arms were around her and he was kissing her.

Oh, God, she'd known instinctively that a kiss from him would be more exciting than she could imagine. Again and again, his lips moved softly across hers, drawing her carefully into his sensual web. She couldn't think, didn't want to. And then his tongue gently nudged her mouth open and suddenly the kiss was much more intense, infinitely more tantalizing. There was so much passion in his kiss now that she felt a moment's alarm . . .

"Drew, I don't think—"

"Don't think," he cut in. "Just let me warm you. You're freezing."

Was she? She hadn't noticed! But his mouth returned to hers and the passion was immediately there again. She wrapped her arms about his neck. He cradled her head with one hand while the other was rubbing up and down her back, but also pushing her toward him so that her breasts were pressed against his chest. If she could have gotten any closer to him, she would have.

When they finally separated, the air felt like steam between them. It's possible it was, they'd generated so much heat while kissing each other. She didn't even realize they'd reached the Malory townhouse until Drew took her hand, helped her down from the coach, and led her to the door. He could have done anything he'd wanted with her there in that coach, she'd been so inflamed by what he'd made her feel, but all he'd done was kiss her—and warm her in such an exciting, delightful way. Later, she would be grateful that's all he'd done. But right then, she was just disappointed that the ride had ended.

"See, I've brought you home safe and sound," he said with a tender smile.

She didn't get a chance to reply. Someone suddenly hailed her and she turned to find the Honorable Wilbur Carlisle stepping out of his carriage.

What rotten timing for Wilbur to discover he had the courage to enter the lion's den after all. "Good grief," she said, glancing down at her bedraggled state. "I need to change first. I don't want him to see me drenched like this. Can you explain to him what happened, Drew?"

"Deal with one of your suitors?" he said. "Not a chance, sweetheart—unless you'd like me to tell him you've taken yourself off the marriage mart?"

"No, I haven't—unless you're asking me to marry you?"

He merely laughed and opened the door for her. "Go dry off. I'll have Artie inform your young swain that you'll be keeping him waiting for a while."

Chapter 17

Wilbur didn't mind waiting for her at all, or so he claimed when she joined him later. Still annoyed that Drew had laughed when she'd mentioned marriage to him, she wasn't removing any names from her list just yet. So she was glad to see that Wilbur had come to call. His confession last night, of why he hadn't come around sooner, had smacked of cowardice which had disturbed her. But that he'd shown up despite his fears indicated he had a good deal of courage after all.

That night Georgina took her to a dinner party, a rather large one. She met a young earl for the first time who would have made a fine addition to her list, but she was quickly warned by several ladies that while he'd been a prime catch, he'd gotten engaged early in the Season. A shame. Arriving at the end of the Season really did have its disadvantages.

There were quite a few bachelors who were still available and they flocked to her as usual to vie for her attention. She caught Drew glowering at her at one point. Jealous? She'd like to think so, but she couldn't get it out of her mind, how he'd laughed at the subject of marriage. She wasn't giving up on him. After those heated moments with him in the coach today, she was more determined than ever to move him to the top of her list. She just guessed it was going to take much more than their brief acquaintance to get him to seriously consider marriage. But today had certainly been a good start.

"Whatever became of your father? I'd heard he was lost at sea."

Lady Dunstan, one of the pillars of London society whom she'd met earlier that week, had whisked her away from her many admirers and out to the terrace for a quick stroll. She'd been telling Gabrielle about the upcoming ball that she was giving. Lady

Dunstan had wanted to personally make sure she would be attending it, since she was such an unexpected success, so late in the Season.

But that question took her by surprise, unrelated as it was to their discussion of the ball. "No indeed," Gabrielle answered. "I've been living with him in the Caribbean ever since my mother died. He has no reason to return to England now that she's gone."

"Of course. I hadn't considered that. I'm glad to know he's still alive. Why, I'd never met him! Wanted to, though, since I knew your mother. But he always seemed to be off sailing here or there. What was it that kept him a—"

"Ah, so here you are!" Georgina interrupted, and put her arm through Gabrielle's. "Come inside, m'dear. There's a new arrival you simply must meet. If you'll excuse us, Lady Dunstan? So looking forward to your upcoming ball!"

Georgina quickly pulled her away, whispering, "From what I just heard, I'd say I rescued you in the nick of time. That lady is a notorious gossip. I should have mentioned it sooner. You didn't tell her anything about your father that we'd rather not be known, did you?"

"No."

"Good. Try to avoid her if you can, and if you can't, simply prevaricate! Be as scatter-brained as you have to, but do not tell her anything that she can sink her teeth into."

Gabrielle understood and avoided the lady for the rest of the evening. Later that night, as Margery helped her out of her evening gown, she debated discussing the situation with her and trying to come up with a suitable occupation for her father. Carla had married him thinking he was in trade, but most of the ton would frown on that nearly as much as if they learned he was a pirate. Obviously, her mother had avoided the subject with her friends. She supposed she could simply do the same.

She assumed the soft rap on the door was Georgina. The two previous nights she'd come by after they got home, to find out if she'd enjoyed the evening, and if any of the young men she'd met had appealed to her. She hadn't met any new men tonight other than that young earl who was already taken. But she'd mentioned Wilbur to Georgina just last night. The lady had probably heard that he'd come by today and wanted to know if her interest had grown as a result of his visit.

So it was quite a nice surprise to find Drew on the other side of the door, rather than his sister. She certainly wasn't prepared to see him, though, and was literally holding her gown up with a hand over her breasts. And Margery practically slammed the door in his face until she was presentable again, quickly fastening her gown back up.

Gabrielle called out for him to wait. He did. When she opened the door again, he asked, "Care for a nightcap?"

She raised a brow. After the way he'd glowered at her tonight and hadn't said a single word to her on the ride home, this was certainly unexpected. But it was another golden opportunity she simply couldn't pass up. She still wanted to explore the possibility of becoming more "friendly" with him, to find out if it was even possible after his reaction today to her mention of marriage.

"Why yes, thank you," she replied, and then added with a grin, "I've really missed my daily portion of rum."

He chuckled and extended an arm for her

to precede him down the hall. She'd only been teasing about the daily portion of rum, but she had a feeling he thought she was serious. In fact, considering what he seemed to think about her, he probably assumed she was used to imbibing strong spirits. Ah, well, he had a lot to learn about her, and she hoped to give him the opportunity, because Drew Anderson had most definitely moved from the bottom of her eligibles list to the top.

She was so centered on the man walking behind her, she didn't even notice that Margery had followed them downstairs until they reached the parlor and she heard the maid yawn loudly. The house was quiet at that time of night. Most of the servants had gone to bed. She knew if she suggested to Margery that she do the same, she'd get a stern refusal. Margery took her chaperoning seriously.

A low fire had been left in the parlor, lit earlier just to take the chill off the room. Only one lamp had been left on, and it, too, had been turned down low. The heat still wasn't enough for Gabrielle, so she moved to stand in front of the fireplace, was even considering stoking the fire a bit more, but

Drew distracted her as he looked over the contents of the bar in the corner of the room.

"As I thought, no rum in this house. Your choices are cognac, brandy, or port."

"Port sounds interesting," she replied. "Don't think I've ever tried it."

"Because it's more a man's drink," Margery put in as she made herself comfortable in one of the reading chairs by the window. "And I'll have one, too, since you're keeping me from my bed."

He glanced at Margery. It looked like he wanted to laugh, his dark eyes sparkled so in the lamplight as he brought her a drink first. He wasn't even looking at Gabrielle and yet her belly started to flutter!

He returned to the bar and took his time pouring two more glasses for them. He kept glancing back at Margery. Gabrielle had a feeling that he was hoping Margery would fall asleep, which was quite possible considering the late hour.

He finally joined her by the fire, handed her the port, then clicked their glasses together. "A toast, sweetheart," he said in a low, stirring voice, and his grin turned

somewhat wicked. "To behaving like pirates."

The endearment went right to her heart,
caused a warmth to spread along her
veins—or maybe the first sip of the drink did
that. It didn't last, though. Too quickly she
recalled he'd used that same endearment
on the docks when he prevented her fall,
and other times when he was being sarcastic, so obviously it meant nothing special to
him, it was just the way he addressed all
women. He could as easily have called her
"miss," or even her name. That's how unro-
mantic the word was to him.

And then it hit her. He'd toasted to their
behaving like pirates? Did he really say
that? The remark he'd made the other night
at the ball came back to her. He'd wanted
her to prove she was a pirate by spending
the night with him. Was that the reason he'd
shown up at her door with his invitation?
Was he going to make another overture?
Maybe even kiss her again?

Her heart started to pound with excitement. She barely even noticed him leading
her to the sofa, sitting her down, setting her
glass on the table in front of them. She shivered. He noticed.

"Cold?"

She was so flustered she had to think about the question. They'd moved away from the fire, so yes, she was cold, and yet, she wasn't. Because of him. He was sitting so close to her their legs nearly touched and she could feel the heat of his body. She smiled. It was more than enough to warm her.

"No, I'm not cold a'tall," she replied.

"Really?"

He seemed genuinely surprised by her answer, which made her realize that he now associated that shiver he'd witnessed with himself. And since it was too late to correct her denial, she blushed.

She glanced toward Margery for help or at least a distraction, but the late hour, or the drink, had proven too much for her. She was fast asleep. So Gabrielle tried to wash her embarrassment away with a gulp of port and ended up downing the entire glass. Well, that helped indeed. It no longer felt like she was blushing and, in fact, it seemed silly now that she'd blushed at all.

Her giggle told him the same thing . . . Oh, good grief, she'd just giggled. She *never* giggled. She found that funny and did it again.

"Not used to port?" he guessed aloud.

"No, rum is more my cup of tea."

"Teetotaler you mean, don't you?" he teased with a warm grin.

"Yes. I mean no." She sighed, shaking her head. "Don't try to confuse me. I'm used to strong spirits, really. Just in moderation."

He ran a finger gently along her cheek. "You've softened, Gabby. I noticed it immediately last night. But today, God, that was nice, wasn't it? Dare I hope you've given my suggestion some thought?"

"What suggestion would that be?"

He leaned closer, and still his voice was soft, almost a whisper. "Do I really need to repeat it?"

As if she could forget that remark that had plagued her thoughts ever since he uttered it. But that was a temptation she had to resist. It would come to her in a moment *why* she had to resist. The port was muddling her . . . Oh, yes, she wanted him thinking about marriage, not just bedding her.

"You do know I'm not *really* a pir—"

She'd turned her face toward his to explain, but it wasn't a good time to do that.

He was still too close. And it ended up appearing as if she'd brushed her lips against his deliberately, when that wasn't the case at all. But he was quick to take advantage of the accident, pressing his mouth more firmly to hers. And she was quick to lose herself in the moment.

Had she really thought that the passion that had flared between them today had been because of the circumstances that led up to it? No indeed. Those same passionate feelings were present again now and so swiftly! It was them. It happened the moment their lips touched.

His arm went around her neck, cradling her head against his shoulder, as his lips moved possessively over hers. Her hand came up to cup his cheek. And when his tongue slipped into her mouth, her fingers moved up into his hair, gripping the soft locks as if she were afraid he was going to stop.

He did stop, but only to change direction as his lips slashed across her cheek and down her neck. She gasped. Shivers raced across her flesh as he sucked on that sensitive area. She felt pressure on her breasts at the same time and realized he was touching her there . . .

He shouldn't be. She had to tell him. She started to, but got no farther than opening her mouth before another gasp escaped her when her nipples puckered beneath his palm. She felt so much heat, from him, from herself. And that tingling in her breasts seemed to travel straight down between her legs.

"I knew you were a pirate," he said just before his tongue delved into her ear, causing her arms to go around his neck so she could embrace him, encourage him. "God, Gabby! Why did you try to hide this wild nature of yours beneath that ladylike facade? I love it! You want me as much as I want you, don't you?"

She was close to moaning. She couldn't think. The sensations coursing through her were overwhelming every one of her senses. She could see his dark eyes glinting with desire, she heard the sounds of satisfaction he was making deep in his throat, she inhaled his heady masculine scent. She tasted him with every kiss, and the way he was touching her, caressing her felt so good she wished he'd never stop. When she couldn't help but moan with pleasure, his mouth came quickly back to hers for the deepest kiss yet. Oh, God. How could she feel so many different sensations all at once?

All her good intentions, all her hopes, had gone right out the door, she was so entranced by Drew's skilled seduction. She didn't have the will to stop him, didn't want to, couldn't even muster a token protest.

So it was a blessing in disguise to hear Boyd complain, "Here now, none of that. Or are your intentions honorable, brother?"

Drew leaned back slightly, enough to break the contact, but then, as if he couldn't resist, he gave her one more kiss, his lips lingering deliciously on hers before he turned to snarl at his brother, "Shouldn't you be minding your own damned business?"

"Shouldn't you be keeping your hands to yourself?" Boyd countered with a snarl of his own. "And this *is* my business. The girl is here to acquire a husband. So are you suddenly eligible?"

Gabrielle's embarrassment to have been caught in such a torrid embrace was acute.

And sobering. She would have liked to hear the answer to Boyd's question as well, but on second thought decided she better not. A no from Drew right now might force her to strike his name from her list, whereas not knowing either way, she could at least continue her campaign to get to know him better.

So she stood up abruptly before he could speak. Margery, disoriented, had already done the same, Boyd's raised voice having awakened her.

"Don't you young bucks ever sleep?" the older woman said in a disagreeable tone, then yawned widely as she came over to collect Gabrielle.

"Yes, Margery and I are late for bed," Gabrielle agreed. "I should have no trouble sleeping now, after that nice glass of port. Good night, gentlemen."

She lagged behind Margery and wasn't quite to the stairs when she heard Boyd say accusingly, "Getting her drunk to seduce her? That's pretty damned low."

"You're kidding, right? That's standard procedure you employ as well, so don't be a blasted hypocrite."

"Standard for women who've been

around the block a few times, not for hus-
band-hunting virgins."

"Did that pretty face make you forget so
quickly who she is? The daughter of a pirate
is no more a virgin than you or I."

Chapter 18

"Miss Brooks, may I be frank?"

Gabrielle hadn't really been paying attention to Wilbur Carlisle, who was twirling her about the dance floor in Lady Dunstan's large ballroom. This was her third ball since she'd come to London, and the gown for this one almost didn't arrive in time.

It was pale lilac in color. Margery even dug out an old necklace of Gabrielle's that her mother had given her years ago, in the hopes it would cheer her up. It was a miniature painting of an English coastline that depicted a small fishing village very like the one close to where she'd grown up, so she'd always assumed the miniature depicted that village. Hung on a chain of pearls, the small oval painting was frame by a border of tiny roses that nearly matched the lilac silk of her gown. If she'd been in better spirits, she would've been pleased at how well the necklace complemented her gown.

She'd almost begged off from going out tonight, just as she'd done the last two nights. She'd pretended not to be feeling well, enough so that she wouldn't have to leave her room. It was a lie, but Georgina didn't question her too much about it after Gabrielle implied it had to do with her monthlies. And besides, she might not really be sick, but she certainly felt sick at heart.

She'd been staying in her room in order to avoid Drew. Finding out what he really thought about her last week had hurt her terribly. She could try to correct his opinion, but she had a feeling he wouldn't believe her. The aversion his family had for pirates ran too deep. And there was nothing she could do about that. They were seamen in legitimate trade. Of course they'd hate the men who tried to steal that trade from them.

But did he have to paint her with the same brush, and assume she was a woman of loose morals because of her parentage?

And yet, what had she done to prove otherwise? Drink with him? Let him kiss her and caress her? She winced at the memory of her own wanton behavior. In trying to get to know him better, she'd actually reinforced his low opinion of her, so it was her own fault.

God, she wished she hadn't been so flustered that she'd gulped down that glass of port that night in the parlor. It had gone right to her head. She never should have let him take such liberties, wouldn't have if she'd been clearheaded, well, she liked to think she wouldn't have, but oh, God, everything he'd done, his touch, his kisses, it had been so nice she hadn't wanted any of it to end. But it had meant nothing to him. If she'd learned anything from that night, it was that she'd been a fool to even consider a cad like him for her husband.

And her feelings had just got more and more downtrodden as the week had progressed, until it got so bad she had trouble concealing them and so she hid in her room instead. Drew had made no further overtures to her, not even in jest. In fact, it seemed as if having reminded *himself* of her background that night, he utterly regretted having made any at all. He'd continued to escort her and his sister to whatever party was on the agenda, but he'd also continued to desert them as soon as they'd arrived where they were going.

And she even saw him pursuing several other young women, not just once, but twice, at two different parties they attended. He didn't even try to be subtle about it. It was as if he wanted her to notice!

His sister noticed, too. Unfortunately, Georgina also noticed the effect it had on Gabrielle and took her aside to tell her, "I've been rather thoughtless in not warning you sooner about Drew. I forget sometimes how handsome he is and how easily he breaks hearts without even trying."

"It's all right. He hasn't broken mine," Gabrielle replied, forcing herself to smile.

"Good, then I'm not too late in mentioning it. I'm sure he likes you, I just don't want you to get the wrong impression and think something might come of it. It won't. While our family would love to see it happen, he's made it clear he has no intention of ever settling down."

Georgina had the best of intentions, but she wasn't telling Gabrielle anything she didn't already know. Changing Drew's firm commitment to bachelorhood had been the plan, but it wasn't looking very promising. He'd formed some wrong impressions about her somehow, and in the coach, coming and going, she'd never been alone with him to discuss his false assumptions.

But she was tired of hiding, and tired of bemoaning the fact that the one man she was seriously attracted to was the one man she couldn't have. So be it. She'd come to London to find a husband and that was exactly what she was going to do, and Drew Anderson could go to Hades for all she cared!

Drew didn't join her and Georgina for the ball tonight. Boyd was their escort, but Boyd had lost all interest in her apparently. Because he'd witnessed her kissing his brother? It didn't matter. He hadn't been on her list anyway.

She was glad now that she *had* decided at the last minute to attend the ball. With Drew off her list, she had this opportunity to learn more about the Honorable Wilbur Carlisle. So she ought to actually *listen* to him, she supposed.

He hadn't waited for her to approve his

frankness; he was telling her, "I wanted to assure you of my intentions. I don't want you to think that like some of these other chaps, I'm here in London merely to enjoy the Season. On the contrary, and I hope you can keep this just between us, I have been sent here for three years now, to find a bride."

"I suppose I can assume you've had no luck so far?" she queried politely.

"Indeed, none. Not that I haven't applied myself earnestly. But for one reason or another, well, I'm either always too late, or I'm not interested enough to appear convincing."

Three years? she thought. How depressing. Or maybe he didn't really want to get married.

She decided to be just as frank as Wilbur. "Do you really want a bride, Wilbur?"

He sighed. "I do, actually. But the pressure has been tremendous and is even worse now. You see, my father has informed me that if I don't bring home a bride *this* year, I needn't return home a'tall."

"Good heavens, really?"

"He's not in the best of health," he explained. "He wants to see me settled before, well, I *do* understand his position. I'm his only son, after all."

She began to feel uncomfortable with the direction Wilbur's frankness was taking. *She* wasn't ready to make a decision yet, even if the Season was almost over. If he proposed before she was ready, she had no idea what her answer would be.

"Wilbur, why are you telling me all this?"

"I just want you to keep me in mind, m'dear, and to assure you that my intentions are very honorable. I confess I was in such despair before you arrived. Nearly the end of the Season and my only prospects were, well, not to my liking. Then you appeared, like a breath of fresh air. Dare I say I was quite smitten?"

It was about time in his dissertation that he got romantic. No, wait, why was she nitpicking? He was a very eligible bachelor and the only one she hadn't discounted out of hand. The others she'd met were either too proper, too snobbish, or too much the dandy for her tastes. And Wilbur seemed to be a nice man, too.

He was also quite witty when he wasn't worrying over making confessions like tonight, or who her sponsor was. Before Malory's name had been mentioned when they first met, he'd been relaxed and very charming, *and* more romantic. She should be delighted that he was still available, for whatever reason, and simply consider herself lucky that he was. He was a fine catch, after all, and very handsome even if he was rather pale. Well, actually, his skin was so white it seemed odd to her.

She sighed to herself. It wasn't the first time she'd thought that since she'd come to London. With everything else she found wrong with the men she'd met, too many of them were pallid in complexion, as well, and at the tail end of summer! But it wasn't their fault that they looked odd to her, and as Margery had pointed out, a little sun could correct that easily enough. She was simply too used to men whose complexions were deeply tanned because they spent a lot of time outdoors. Yet not everyone enjoyed the outdoors as much as she did. Not everyone could be as perfectly tanned as a sea captain either . . .

Her eyes were drawn to Drew the moment he entered the room. *Goodness,* even after taking him off her list, where she never should have put him to begin with, she could still be mesmerized by the sight of him. And her stomach was already starting to flutter. What the deuce was it about him that caused that? Did she really want to give up on him just because of assumptions he'd made? When a little talk between them would clear the air and prove he was wrong about her?

How could she even hold the conclusions he'd drawn against him? Her father *was* a pirate. And her association with pirates had educated her about matters a young lady of good breeding would never know of until after she was married. So the only thing Drew was actually wrong about was the state of her virginity. A logical mistake.

Oh, *dear,* she *was* talking herself into putting him back on her list. Dare she? She'd rather not be disappointed by him again. That had hurt. But what if he didn't hurt her feelings again? What if he apologized and admitted how foolish he'd been to assume the worst about her?

The dance ended and Wilbur was leading her back to Georgina. "It seems I'm never allowed enough time with you," he said with a charming twinkle in his eye. "I hope you'll join me for a walk in the garden later, so we can continue our conversation?"

Distracted now with her eyes on Drew, Gabrielle merely nodded. Having spotted his sister in the crowd, Drew was heading toward her, too. Gabrielle didn't think he had seen her yet, but then their eyes met, and he collided with a few people who were in his path.

She frowned upon seeing that. Clumsy? A sea captain? Maybe he was clumsy when he first stepped off his ship after a long voyage, but seamen usually had a keen sense of balance. They had to, because they constantly had to maneuver on ever-pitching decks.

As she approached Georgina, she noticed that her benefactress was speaking with Lady Dunstan, their hostess, who as Georgina had reminded her before their arrival, was one of the ton's worst gossips. That lady's presence managed to distract her from thinking about Drew. She had to pay close attention to every word out of her mouth now to make sure she didn't say anything inappropriate. According to Georgina, a woman like Lady Dunstan could make or break a debutante without even trying.

"Ah, here she is," Lady Dunstan said with a smile for Gabrielle and then a quick frown at her escort. "And *you,* dear boy, really must stop monopolizing Miss Brooks—or do you have news of an impending marriage that will finally please your father?"

Gabrielle winced for the fellow. So his frank confession wasn't such a secret after all. Apparently it was common knowledge. Regardless, their hostess was definitely putting him on the spot. Gabrielle had never heard such blatant fishing. No matter what Wilbur answered, he'd be giving the lady a juicy tidbit of gossip to chew on.

But a new voice intruded, slightly slurred, definitely snide. "I wouldn't count on it, lady, unless his father doesn't mind pirates in the family."

Lady Dunstan gasped, hearing that. Wilbur paled. Georgina was rendered speechless for a moment. Having scolded her brother more than once for using that word in public in reference to Gabrielle, she was staring at him incredulously because he'd just done it again.

Gabrielle was simply furious and the glare

she turned on Drew wouldn't let him doubt it. He was drunk, and even drunk he was so damned handsome. But what shocked her more than what he'd just said was the bright spark of desire in his midnight-dark eyes as he looked directly at her.

Chapter 19

Gabrielle hurried downstairs after being told the name of the visitor waiting for her in the parlor. She wouldn't have come downstairs for anyone else. She was still somewhat in shock after last night. She couldn't believe Drew had done that to her, deliberately tried to ruin her chances for a good marriage.

He didn't succeed, fortunately. He even insisted he wasn't serious when Georgina, just as shocked as Gabrielle was, started to upbraid him. Of course, what else could he say at that point?

Gabrielle didn't buy his innocence, though. She didn't doubt at all that the re-mark was a deliberate attempt to sabotage her husband hunting. But he *was* foxed to the gills. That his inebriated state was so obvious was probably the only reason Lady Dunstan believed that he'd only been joking and had merely suggested that he leave, which he did.

Wilbur had left, too. He'd taken quick advantage of the distraction to slip away so he wouldn't have to answer Lady Dunstan's probing question. Or so Gabrielle had assumed later. She'd wanted to leave at that point, too.

"Don't let this upset you," Georgina had said, patting her hand. "My brother can be quite careless in his comments when he gets foxed, and he usually does get foxed his last few nights in port. But Lady Dunstan knows who my husband is. For that matter, she won't risk having any of the Malorys annoyed with her by repeating what she thinks was no more than tasteless joking. She knows very well that by the time the comment made the rounds, it would no longer be considered a jest. So she'll say nothing."

Gabrielle didn't hear anything beyond "last few nights in port." Drew was leaving. And she wouldn't even have known if his sister hadn't mentioned it. She was sure he wouldn't have told her. Why should he? She was nothing to him.

And yet she was crushed. First he tried to ruin her prospects, then he intended to leave before the scandal broke. She should be furious with him. She wished she *was* furious. That would be so much more preferable to feeling hurt and disappointed.

"There you are, m'dear."

Gabrielle turned to see James Malory leaving his study. She didn't tense up like she used to in his presence. Since the night of the theater when he'd bandied quips back and forth with Georgina's brothers and she'd seen how they could provoke him without dire consequences, she'd lost most of her fear of him. And his expression wasn't guarded for once. He actually looked concerned.

"How are you feeling this morning?" James asked, putting a fatherly arm about her shoulders.

She thought he was referring to the couple days she'd hidden in her room claiming illness, so she said, "I'm fine now."

"No urge to shoot anyone?"

She chuckled at the way he put it, understanding now. "You heard about what happened last night, I take it?"

"Indeed. No more than *I* would expect from one of those barbarians I'm forced to claim kinship with, but George is quite annoyed. She actually expects her brothers to behave like gentlemen. But I'll make sure there are no repercussions due to Drew's foolishness, you may depend upon it. I'm going to bite the bullet, as it were, and join you and George for the rest of the Season."

She was surprised, and touched, that he'd be willing to do that. She knew how much he hated social gatherings. "You don't have to."

"I want to. Consider this, if you will. If not for your father, I wouldn't be here, my children wouldn't be here, and George wouldn't be the happiest woman alive."

He said it with such a warm grin, she couldn't help but return it. It made her realize the debt he owed her father was more important to him than she'd guessed.

"Well, when you put it that way . . ."

"Exactly. Now run along. I believe I heard one of your suitors arrive for a visit."

She would have explained that her visitor wasn't a suitor, but James had already

turned to go upstairs, and she'd kept the
young man waiting long enough. James had
managed to cheer her up, but her visitor
was going to take her mind off last night
completely, she was sure.

"Avery! How nice to see you again!"

She held out her hand as she approached
him. He didn't see it because he couldn't
take his eyes off her face. "Good God, I
barely recognize you, Miss Brooks. I knew
you had promise, but you've far exceeded
it."

She blushed at the compliment; actually,
it was his expression that embarrassed her.
He really did appear incredulous—and delighted.

"You're looking well yourself, Avery. But
how did you know to find me here?"

He was blushing now, severely. "I'm
afraid I bring you bad news."

She immediately thought of her father,
and yet this couldn't be about him. She'd
made a point of finding out what had happened to Avery after she'd left that pirate
isle. Her father had assured her that he'd
been ransomed and had returned to England shortly thereafter to find a less "exciting" occupation. So Avery couldn't know

anything about Nathan. And he hadn't actually answered her question. How did he find her or even know she was in London, when they didn't travel in the same circles?

He could have just seen her about town, she supposed. She'd ridden in the park twice, attended a day concert, even gone shopping on Bond Street several times with Margery. She'd also gone to the less affluent side of town last week when she'd wanted to warn Richard of Malory's lethal promise. So Avery could have just noticed her out and about and merely followed her to this location.

"What is the bad news?"

"Your name is on everyone's tongue this morning. That's how I found out that you were in town and why, and even who you're staying with. Half of the town is apparently aghast that a pirate would try to infiltrate their ranks through marriage, while the other half finds it hilarious, seeing it as quite the joke on the ton. Oh, dear, so you didn't know?"

She was so shocked her complexion must have gone white, giving him that clue. "Lady Dunstan," she said tonelessly. "I was assured she wouldn't spread what she overheard last night, but obviously she thought it was a juicy enough tidbit to risk even James Malory's wrath over it."

"I don't know about that," Avery said. "Never heard of the lady. It's Wilbur Carlisle who's telling anyone who'll listen that you aren't who you pretended to be."

She almost laughed. It would have sounded hysterical, though, so she cut it off. Wilbur? Unassuming, nice, desperate-for-a-wife Wilbur? Why would he do this to her? Why wouldn't he demand proof first before launching her into a scandal? Because he felt she'd deceived him?

It's not as if she wouldn't have told him about her father if their relationship had grown more serious. Well, she might not have confessed that her father actually plied the seas as a pirate, but she would have warned him that he was in trade. Many upper-crust families would consider him a black sheep of the family, but it wasn't as if many of them didn't have black sheep of their own. And her mother's social credentials were impeccable.

She'd been so deep in her thoughts that she hadn't heard the knock at the front door, but the scuffle going on out in the hall was certainly loud enough to draw her attention. She glanced quickly at Avery and said, "Excuse me for a moment."

"Certainly."

But she no sooner stepped into the hall than she gasped, incredulous at the sight of Ohr grappling with the Malory butler on the floor. There was no contest, of course. Ohr was barely straining. He was a strapping man in his prime, while Artie was a crusty old sea dog, very slight of build.

She almost laughed, but instead prudently mentioned to Ohr, "That's not a proper way to come calling."

"It is, when you get the door slammed in your face," Ohr countered, glancing up at her.

Ohr was lying there on the floor with his arm locked around the head of the butler, who was also lying on the floor, one hand gripped tightly to Ohr's long braid. The men were clothed in a similar fashion, with scuffed boots, cut-off pants, and billowing shirts. She never had got used to the fact that the Malorys had a butler who looked and sounded as if he belonged on a pirate ship.

The two men had stopped struggling as

soon as she'd spoken. Now Artie told Ohr, "Think I didn't 'ear the cap'n say ye weren't welcome 'ere? I know m'duty, ye bleedin' blighter, and that's keeping ye unwelcome."

Ohr made a scoffing sound. "I would have been happy to stand outside the front door and wait, you old salt, if you had agreed to let Gabby know I needed to speak with her, instead of telling me to get lost."

"She were busy! I told ye that, too!"

"And I told *you* this couldn't wait."

Gabrielle tsked. "Let him up, Ohr. What is it that couldn't wait?"

Ohr got to his feet and stepped wide of Artie, in case the butler thought to throw any more punches when he stood up. Glancing back at Gabrielle, he said, "We need to talk privately." He looked too serious by half and sounded it, too.

He didn't wait for her to question him further. He took her arm and started toward the front door with her, but Artie leapt in front of it to block their path.

"Don't *even* think about it, mate," the butler warned. "Ye ain't takin' 'er anywhere, or I'll be callin' the cap'n and ye'll be wishing ye were dead."

Ohr growled, "I've had about enough of you—"

But Gabrielle interrupted him with a gentle hand on his arm and told Artie, "It's all right. He's a very good friend of mine and one of my father's most trusted men. I'll be fine with him."

Ohr didn't wait for the butler's permission. He led her out the front door to the coach he had waiting outside. She hadn't expected to go farther than down the street, where they could talk, but she didn't try to stop him.

"You've heard about the scandal already?" she guessed.

"What scandal?" he asked.

"Never mind, we can discuss it later."

"Good, because we have some decisions to make. Pierre is holding your father for ransom, and the price he's demanding is you."

Chapter 20

Gabrielle felt numb during the coach ride. There'd been one too many shocks in the last couple days.

Ohr took her to the room he and Richard had rented near the docks. Bixley, a carrot-haired Irishman and Ohr's best friend, was there, waiting with Richard. She hadn't expected that, but then she should have. Someone had to have brought the news to them about her father.

Bixley loved to hunt for treasure and seriously believed in the old pot of gold at the end of the rainbow. And since Nathan was fond of treasure hunting himself, Bixley felt he'd found the perfect home on *The Crusty Jewel.*

Richard hugged her. He looked much more normal to her, wearing his pirate garb again, his loose white shirt barely buttoned down his chest.

He gazed at her closely and demanded of Ohr, "Why does she look like she's in mourning already? What the devil did you tell her?"

Ohr took the other chair at the table where Bixley was sitting, nursing a mug of ale. "Only what Pierre is demanding," he replied.

"*Chérie,* it's not as bad as it sounds," Richard assured her. "We are only guessing that it's you Pierre really wants and that he's just using the maps as an excuse."

"Maps?" Gabrielle asked. "What are you talking about?"

Richard glanced at Ohr with a scowl. "So you really told her nothing? What did you talk about on the way here, the bloody weather?"

In his usual unruffled way, Ohr ignored Richard's sharpness and said calmly, "I felt she should hear it firsthand from Bixley. Besides, I'm hoping my friend will remember something pertinent he might have missed in the first telling."

"I didn't forget anything," Bixley mumbled. "It were a long voyage getting here. I had me time aplenty to commit it all to memory."

"So tell me what happened, Bixley?" Gabrielle said.

"It were Latice, that bastid."

Gabrielle frowned. "My father's first mate?"

"Aye," Bixley replied. "Sailed us right into Cap'n Pierre's fort while yer pa was sleeping comfy in his cabin. We didn't even have a chance to resist. Most of us woke up that night in chains."

"Pierre has his own fort?" she asked.

"He's gone rogue, Gabby," Ohr took a moment to explain. "He found an old deserted fort and has apparently been refurbishing it for years now. And as soon as it was finished, he broke off from the alliance."

"And this is where he's holding my father?"

"Yes."

"You know where it's located?"

"I don't," Ohr replied. "But Bixley does."

"They made sure I'd be able to find it again, since I'm supposed to be bringing ye back there," Bixley said. "It's a day or two east of St. Kitts, depending on which way the wind be blowing."

"Did Latice think he was sailing into a safe harbor? He hadn't heard that Pierre had gone rogue?"

Bixley snorted. "He knew. He turned traitor, lass. Who would've thought he'd have the guts to make a decision like that, eh?"

She was incredulous. Latice was, or had been, her father's first mate. He was decisive, but only about nautical matters. On the quarterdeck, he never thought twice about giving an order. But when it came to anything else, it took him forever to make up his mind, and even then he could be talked out of a decision with very little effort.

"Why would he do that?" she asked. "Fear?"

"Greed." The Irish pirate spat out the word. "Pierre promised he could have *The Crusty Jewel* for himself. But the joke was on him. Pierre don't keep his promises. He weren't about to just give away a prime ship like yer pa's."

"So what exactly are Pierre's demands?"

"He said he wants your pa's maps. Nathan was furious, as you can imagine. Told him what he could do with, well, as I said, he was furious. He weren't about to give up a collection he's worked his whole life on. His refusal wasn't going to get us out of there, though, so after he was taken away, I offered to bring the maps to Pierre. I know where they're hidden. He said no, that you had to bring them to him."

"I do have some of his maps," she reminded him. Nathan had given them to her long ago, but they were mostly the useless ones he'd already discovered led to nothing.

"Yes, but there's not many who know that, and I certainly didn't tell him, nor did your pa. Latice might have, but I don't think he even knew. No, it was obvious, at least to me, that Cap'n Pierre don't really want the maps, he wants you."

She reacted to that statement this time, as it really sunk in. Her repulsion was so great, she shuddered. Captain Pierre, the vicious, frightening man whom she'd hoped she'd never see again. But Bixley had to be wrong! Nathan's maps were valuable, after all. And Pierre already had a woman—didn't he?

"What about Red? Is she no longer with Pierre?" she asked Bixley.

"Oh, she is. She was there, too, when he was making his demands. Got furious, she did. She even threw a dagger at him. Damned if she didn't pull it out from between her breasts, too. Damnedest place to hide a—"

Ohr coughed to warn Bixley he was getting out of line. The Irishman just grinned unabashedly.

"I take it she didn't kill him, or you wouldn't be here?" she guessed.

"No, she missed. And Pierre, he just laughed, the bleedin' sod."

"I still find this—amazing," she said. "They were . . . business associates."

"They were never even that, *chérie,*" Richard was quick to correct her. "Nathan, like the other captains, only tolerated Pierre. They were glad when he broke off from the alliance. We all were."

"But he's treating my father well, isn't he? Because of their past association?"

It was immediately obvious that Bixley didn't want to answer that particular question. He spent a few moments draining his mug, even gave Ohr a beseeching look to change the subject.

"Tell me," she demanded.

Bixley sighed. "That fort he refurbished, it had a dungeon, lassie. Our men, and your pa, they're all in it. Spent a few days there meself." Seeing her pale, he tried to assure her, "It weren't *that* bad. I've slept in much worse places."

When she thought of her father being held prisoner in that place for weeks already, and that it would be even more weeks before she could get him out of there, she paled even more. "What is your plan?" she asked Ohr.

"We won't be turning you over to him," he assured her. "But we probably won't even be able to get close to Pierre's fort unless he sees you with us."

"It's completely enclosed with high walls that are guarded," Bixley explained.

"I don't care what it takes, I want my father out of there," Gabrielle replied heatedly. "We'll leave immediately."

"We could buy passage back to St. Kitts, but that isn't going to get us to Pierre's fortress," Richard put in. "It's on an island that isn't inhabited, far from the main shipping paths. What we need is our own ship and crew. No matter what plan we come up with, without our own ship, we're going to be limited in what we can do."

"Then let's get our own ship," she said decisively.

"We will," Ohr assured her. "Buy, borrow, or steal, we'll find one in St. Kitts."

"But didn't Bixley say Pierre's island is east of St. Kitts?" she reminded him. "Wouldn't we save a day or two if we sailed directly for it, rather than pass it and then backtrack after we get a ship?"

"She's right," Richard said. "A passenger ship will also stop at other ports along the way, delaying us even more."

Ohr nodded. "I suppose we would have a better chance of finding our own ship here in London. The harbor at St. Kitts is tiny in comparison. I haven't heard of any for sale here, though, and I've been down on the docks."

Gabrielle hesitated for a moment. Then a wicked smile curved her lips. "I know of one. It's not for sale, but it's sailing in the morning."

Chapter 21

Assuming the role of a pirate was rather distasteful, Gabrielle thought after she'd explained her idea to her father's crewmen. Three years ago the notion of stealing anything, much less a ship, would never have entered her mind. But it had occurred to her now because she was so worried about her father and so angry at Drew Anderson. She still couldn't believe he'd so recklessly ruined her reputation and her chances of making a good match! Well, she wasn't just going to steal his ship and become the pirate he'd accused her of being. She was going to have him at her mercy as well.

She owed him. It was that simple. And she wouldn't have the chance to extract revenge otherwise, not with him leaving. Embroil her in a scandal, then just sail off without a care? Not now he wouldn't.

It was a brilliant plan. It would solve their current dilemma of how to go about rescuing her father and at the same time it would enable her to get even with the man who'd ruined her. But then she realized that the four of them couldn't sail a ship on their own.

"We'll need more men," she pointed out.

"I'll see to it," Ohr replied.

"Where are you going to find men on such short notice who would be willing to steal a ship?"

He laughed. "There's a whole other side to this town that a young lady of your breeding wouldn't know about. Leave it to me, I'll find all the men we need."

Only Richard guessed that she might have misgivings. "Are you sure you want to do this?" he asked.

"Yes," she replied, and even offered him a grin. "It's not every day one becomes a pirate."

He laughed. Of course he would find it funny, he was already a pirate. But he wasn't finished dealing with her reservations.

"You don't really need to come along, you know," he told her. "We could find someone who looks like you. As long as Pierre *thinks* it's you—"

"No," she cut in. "If for some reason he needs to talk to me before he allows your ship to approach his fort, I'll need to be there. I'm not going to take any chances with my father's life. My presence will give us more options as we figure out a plan to rescue my father."

"And our captain," Richard said, his expression turning serious. "You've certainly proved your loyalty to him by ordering us to steal this American's ship."

"I didn't order you," Gabrielle corrected him. "I merely suggested."

He grinned to show he'd been teasing. "I know, and it is a perfect solution. We can even give the man back his ship when we're done with it. Actually, I'd as soon not get Malory on our trail if he takes our theft of his brother-in-law's ship personally. Are you sure you don't want to ask for his help instead?"

She hesitated before answering. Both

Malorys had been very kind and generous to her. As far as she was concerned, James had repaid his debt to her father in full. It wasn't his fault that she didn't succeed in her mission to find a husband. That was Drew's fault.

"No, James Malory has already done enough for me. I'm not about to ask him for more help."

"I meant Anderson."

She snorted. "Not a chance. He'd refuse anyway. He doesn't like me and I despise him."

She'd said it too quickly, causing Richard to raise a brow. "How did that come about?"

"His aversion to pirates, I suppose. He actually made sure that it became common knowledge that Nathan is a pirate."

Richard drew in his breath sharply. Gabrielle was more certain than ever that he was English, whether he would admit it or not, because he seemed to understand exactly what that meant. Ohr preferred clarification and asked, "Is that the scandal you mentioned? The man wrecked your chances for a good match here?"

"Indeed. And then he was going to sail away without giving it another thought."

"But *why*?" Richard exclaimed.

"Because he hates pirates, and he got it into his head that I'm one, too. He didn't bother to ask, he just assumed, and embroiled me in a scandal as a result. So it's going to be a pleasure to see him surrounded by pirates on his very own ship!"

"You know that will just reinforce his opinion—"

"Exactly," she cut in. "By the time I'm done with him, he'll wish he was wrong, but he'll never learn the truth that he was mistaken."

Gabrielle went back to the Malorys' for the rest of the day, but stayed in her room. If she were to see Drew before she stole his ship, she was sure she'd tear his eyes out; then his ship wouldn't be sailing at all. So it was better that she hide in her room.

Margery was incredulous when Gabrielle told her what had happened. "Don't you worry about your papa. Those are good men he picked to accompany us here. You know they'll get him out of this mess."

"Yes, I know. We'll have the voyage back

to the Caribbean to figure out just what to do."

"I'll help if I'm needed," Margery assured her. "It's just such a shame that you'll have to miss the last of the Season here. It was going so well."

"Actually . . . I didn't have a chance to tell you last night, but Drew Anderson made sure that I would be missing the rest of the Season and any other Seasons here as well. He showed up at the ball last night, quite foxed, and said in front of Wilbur and Lady Dunstan that Nathan is a pirate."

"Why would he do that!?" Margery gasped.

"I suppose protecting the innocent from the bloodthirsty could have been his drunken reasoning, but who knows. However, Wilbur took that information and spread it far and wide this morning. Having been on the brink of proposing to me, he's probably deeply disappointed after Drew's disclosure that I no longer meet his standards."

"Good God, they've ruined you!" Margery gasped.

"Oh, yes, I'm definitely ruined—thanks to

Drew," Gabrielle said with a catch in her throat.

She felt the sting of tears in her eyes. She turned aside before Margery noticed. She wanted to feel angry again. Anger was her salvation right now. But Margery knew her well. She didn't have to see the tears to know they were there.

Her friend put an arm around her waist. "Never you mind, girl. We'll find you a husband somewhere else."

She and Margery sneaked out of the house in the early evening. Gabrielle left Georgina a note, explaining her father was in trouble and she was leaving to help him. The lady might not believe that after she heard of the scandal, but Gabrielle wouldn't be around to be questioned either way. And there was only one tense moment when Miss Carla whistled as they were hurrying down the back stairs, to let them know she wasn't asleep under the cover on her cage, but no one came to investigate.

They'd packed only enough clothes that they could carry themselves in carpetbags. She'd mentioned in her note to Georgina that she could contact her solicitor about having the rest of their belongings shipped

to St. Kitts. Ohr was waiting down the street
with a carriage to take them to the docks.
He'd already purchased her two cabins for
the voyage under a false name, one for herself and Margery to share, and one for the
three male "servants" who were accompanying her. Getting her friends a cabin, too,
meant three fewer men would have to climb
over the railing tonight to hide in the hold.

It was a bold plan they were enacting. If
she weren't so furious with Drew, she'd
probably change her mind and disappoint
them all. She just wished she didn't feel so
guilty about the way she was leaving. After
everything the Malorys had done for her,
this was a shoddy way to repay them. But
she knew James would insist upon helping
if he knew, and she couldn't let him do that.
He'd done enough.

Glancing back at the townhouse, Gabrielle realized she was going to miss the Malorys. God, she'd had such high hopes when
she came to London of finding the man of
her dreams. Oddly enough, she'd found
him. It was too bad he had to be a blackguard and turn her dreams into a nightmare
instead.

Chapter 22

Gabrielle paced the small confines of one of the cabins on Drew's ship. Her nerves were acting up. She couldn't believe she was stealing a ship, let alone *Drew Anderson's* ship. She'd give it back, of course. She was really only borrowing it, or at least she tried to convince herself of that to alleviate some of the guilt that had begun to plague her. But it didn't help much.

She'd come aboard last night after they made sure the captain wasn't around. She hadn't expected *The Triton* to be such a fine vessel. With three tall masts, it was a lot bigger than her father's two-masted merchantman. Drew and most of his crew were off enjoying their last night in port, which had made it easy for the men Ohr had hired to sneak aboard and hide themselves in the hold.

She didn't get much sleep last night, though, and finally gave up trying at dawn, so her anxieties had built up until the slightest little sound was making her jump. She'd chewed each of her nails down to the quick.

It was too quiet as the ship left the harbor and sailed out into the channel, indicating nothing was happening yet, but the wait was nerve-wracking. Her tension was very similar to what she'd felt three years ago when her ship had been threatened by pirates, when she'd waited for the sounds of cannons to warn if there would be a fight. There wouldn't be any cannons fired this morning, but she was anticipating shouts, even pistol shots as command of the ship changed hands.

The sharp knock on her door startled the breath out of her and got an annoyed squawk from Miss Carla. That in turn woke Margery, who'd still been sleeping in her bunk.

It was Richard at the door. He poked his head inside to tell them, "She's ours. You can come out now."

"I didn't hear any shots," Margery said, then asked Gabrielle, "Or did I sleep through the noise?"

Gabrielle smiled. "No, there were no shots, but like you, I was expecting some." She raised a brow at Richard. "How'd you manage such a peaceful transition?"

He came inside and closed the door with a grin. "We're good." But then he laughed. "Actually, we've had practice before. Took over a ship one night right in harbor, though it was just a joke among friends. We gave it back. But it showed us how easy it could be when you have the element of surprise on your side."

"And you couldn't have told me about that yesterday?" she huffed.

"Nothing is guaranteed. But surprise tipped the odds in our favor—Captain."

She made a rude sound over his calling her that. Though they'd agreed that all major decisions would be hers, she was taking on the role of captain only to shoulder the responsibility for their theft, in case they were caught. She certainly wasn't going to try to captain the ship, even though she was an experienced sailor now and had watched her father at the helm enough times. But Ohr was more suited to the task.

"So you had no trouble a'tall?"

"Not much. Well, it wasn't easy subduing the captain. You could have warned us he was that giant you ran into on the docks that day we arrived in London. It took four of us to bring him down. He's damn good with his fists."

"You didn't hurt him, did you?" She asked it too quickly, and with too much concern in her tone. She immediately amended, "Not that I care, but no one was supposed to get hurt."

"He's fine. Had to knock his first mate out, though, when he noticed us putting some of the crew in the hold and demanded to know what was going on. He laid into us when he figured it out for himself. Damned near as big as the captain is. But he's secured as well, locked in his cabin."

Gabrielle nodded and smiled to herself as she left the cabin. She'd already decided what she was going to do with Drew now that she had him at her mercy. She was going to make him think she really was a pirate.

As soon as the idea occurred to Gabrielle,

she liked it. Not that Drew didn't already think that she was one, but just in case he had any doubts, it would be easy enough to put them to rest. And then she'd make him want her anyway. It was the perfect revenge, in her mind. He hated pirates, so much that he'd tried to ruin her in her own backyard, as it were, because of it. It wasn't even *his* bloody backyard! So she was going to make him want her so much, it would drive him crazy. And *then* she'd make sure he knew he could never have her.

She went to find out where Ohr had put him. He was in the captain's cabin. And so was Drew, tied to a chair in the back of the room and gagged. She wished he'd been blindfolded as well, but he wasn't and he was staring at her with murder in his eyes. Of course he would be. That didn't surprise her at all. Even if he didn't already have a grudge against her, he'd despise the people who'd taken his ship from him.

She moved to the table where Ohr stood bent over the charts and tried to ignore that those black eyes were following her every step. "Why wasn't he put in the hold?" she asked in a low voice.

She was only pretending that she didn't

want the captain to overhear the question. The ship was very quiet at the moment. He'd have to be deaf to not hear her.

Ohr glanced aside at her and said cheekily, "Figured you might want a little revenge, considering how rude he was to you."

Perfect! She couldn't have asked for a better answer if she'd told him what to say. A few days in the hold was part of that revenge.

But there was more. "Besides," he continued, "the hold is filled with his crew, and the last thing you want to do is put a captain together with his crew."

"Why not?"

"It would give them the incentive to quickly plot an escape with him there to make sure of it. Separated, while he'll no doubt be plotting, there isn't much he can do about it on his own."

She nodded. She supposed he was right. And she shouldn't be asking him questions like that, things she should have known, if she really was his captain. And she *did* want Drew to think she was their captain.

She was curious, though, and wondered aloud, "Was it necessary to gag him?"

"It seemed a good idea, since he wouldn't shut up," he replied.

She rolled her eyes. She could just imagine what the giant had had to say. And she'd said more than she should have. She realized that now. So she mustered a brisk, captainlike tone and asked Ohr to step outside with her so they could discuss where to put the captain. Her carpetbags arrived first, though.

It had already been decided that she would occupy the captain's cabin, since it was the biggest room and the most suitable place for them to gather to discuss any decisions that needed to be made. But that was before they'd decided to leave the real captain in it.

There wasn't a shortage of cabins. He could be moved to the one she was vacating. It might be tricky, though, as big as Drew was. If he decided to take out his current rage on them as soon as he was on his feet, someone would get hurt, and not necessarily him. But she didn't want anyone else getting hurt.

The best way to avoid any more injuries would be to simply leave the captain in his own room. She could easily have her bags put back in that other cabin. Then again, why should she have to go to him to enact her revenge? It would be much easier if she kept him close at hand.

So she told Ohr, "I think we'll just leave the captain where he is for now."

He didn't appear surprised, but then, she didn't think she'd ever seen him reveal surprise. "Are you sure?" was all he asked.

"Yes. I know you were only teasing, but you were more right than you know. I am going to get even with that man for what he did to me, and that includes keeping him a prisoner where he'd least like to be right now: in my room, where he won't doubt he's at my mercy."

Richard would have pried for more details, but Ohr wasn't like that. He merely nodded and headed to the helm while she went back in the captain's cabin.

She had to school her features before she approached the giant to stand in front of him. She wanted him to want her. That was her revenge. But it wasn't going to happen if he realized how much she despised him now. She'd have to make him think it didn't matter that much to her that he'd ruined her reputation. So a little truth wouldn't hurt, to throw him off guard and keep him there, so he'd know that she had more than one reason to take his ship. She supposed she also ought to assure him that *The Triton* was only being borrowed, that they would return it to him in good time, well, hopefully in good time. But his was a three-masted merchantman. It should make very good time in the crossing.

He didn't have to look up very far to meet her eyes. Even sitting, his extreme height was exceptional. And he was still looking daggers at her, which was very unnerving from such black eyes.

"If I remove that thing from your mouth, will you be civil?" she asked.

He made no sound, no movement, just continued to glare at her balefully. She decided to be helpful and pointed out, "A nod would suffice."

No nod. He was still too angry to cooperate, she supposed. And the look he was giving her was actually causing her some nervousness she hadn't expected, so she turned her back to him.

Taking a deep breath, she told him, "We aren't keeping your ship. I received word that my father is being held for ransom on an isle two days' sail east of St. Kitts. That he's being kept in a dungeon is quite upsetting to me. I want him out of there. I knew your ship was ready to sail. I decided it would do nicely to get us back to the Caribbean in the quickest time possible. We won't even be taking you too far off your course, nothing you can't easily correct with a good wind." She turned back around to ask again, "Will you be civil now?"

Still no nod from him and his expression hadn't changed one bit. Blasted man was making her jumpy with those unnerving eyes of his. Well, good grief. What more assurances did she need to give him? But then she put herself in his shoes for a moment and realized there was nothing she could say to make this right in *his* mind. They'd taken his ship from him, removed him from control of it. That it was temporary made no difference to him, if he even believed it was only temporary. Maybe he didn't believe her. She should find out, and the only way to do that was to remove his gag.

Having made the decision, she stepped around behind him to untie the knot at the base of his neck. She saw immediately that some of his hair was caught in the knot and pulled tight. That had to have hurt and she wasn't sure she could untie it without pulling his hair even more. As she tried, one of his curls fell over her fingers. It was silky smooth like a child's—quite startling, since there was nothing childlike about him.

The gag fell away, retained in her hand. She held her breath, waiting for him to blast her. Silence. And still he did not turn around to look at her. She stuffed the gag in the pocket of her skirt and moved to stand in front of him.

"Something to drink to get the taste of cotton out of my mouth," he said.

How reasonable! He was going to be civil.

She looked around the cabin but saw no water, or anything else for that matter.

"In my desk drawer," he said. The drawer revealed a decanter set in a wooden pocket designed to fit it, so the bottle would stay upright in the worst of storms. It was filled with some type of spirits, no doubt, but if that would suit him, it was fine with her.

She didn't miss seeing the pistol in that drawer as well, nor did she hesitate to pocket it before she returned to him with the decanter. She was surprised he'd directed

her to the place where he kept his pistol.
Perhaps he'd just forgotten it was there.

She removed the glass cork and tilted the
decanter to his lips. He had such a sensual
mouth, full, supple, quite mesmerizing. The
last time she'd stared at it, he'd been about
to kiss her, the bastard, and he had, thoroughly. God, she wished she didn't know
what he tasted like . . . She gave him only
two sips, then took her eyes off his lips.

"Appreciate it," he said when she set the
decanter down. "But I would appreciate it
even more if you'd give me my ship back."

Just like that, and so calmly, too. She
laughed and told him, "Would you indeed? I
wonder if it would surprise you if I told you
that I would have appreciated if you hadn't
tried to embarrass me at the last ball I attended in London, by letting it be known
who my father is, but, well, I didn't get my
wish . . . and you won't be getting yours."

"Embarrass you? The man you were with
that night was courting you! If he didn't
know about your father, he damn well
should have, or were you trying to get him
to marry you without telling him the truth
about who you really are?"

"You bastard! It was deliberate, wasn't it?"

He didn't answer, demanded instead, "Is that what this is about? You suffer a little embarrassment and you arrange for someone to steal my ship?"

"A little!?"

She had such a powerful urge to hit him that she actually took a step back before she gave in to it. This wasn't going well. She never should have mentioned what he'd done to her. He obviously didn't care. But he would. By the time she was done with him, by God, he would!

She took a deep breath and cleared her throat to produce a calm tone. "It doesn't matter. And you don't need to worry about your ship. I've assured you that you will get it back."

"Not soon enough, or don't you care that this will brand you a pirate?"

She smiled at him. "Are you joking? You were already certain I am a pirate. Aren't you glad to be proven right?"

"Then which one of these ruffians do you belong to?"

He said that so sneeringly, she knew exactly which role he was placing her in and it wasn't very nice. So much for her sounding commanding.

"You're off the mark, Drew," she told him. "These men answer to me. I'm their captain."

He actually laughed as he said, "Sure you are. But they'll now be answering to me—if they want you back."

Suddenly he grabbed her. She had no warning other than those words, and they were spoken much too fast for her to react. And finding herself sitting in his lap with his arms tight around her was so unexpected, she was rendered speechless. He wasn't, and his laugh was utterly triumphant.

"How does it feel with the shoe on the other foot, wench?" he asked.

"It's a rather tight fit," she said, and then she began to struggle for all she was worth.

Chapter 23

Why hadn't she seen it coming? Because he was so damned handsome? Because she'd been unable to take her eyes off of his face long enough to notice that he was straining loose from his bonds? And now he had the upper hand, was going to gain his release, get his ship back, too, and turn the lot of them over to the authorities, she didn't doubt. She'd be seeing a dungeon firsthand just like her father, instead of getting him out of his. She'd failed utterly in her task and all because this blasted American was so handsome she'd been mesmerized by his face, just like before.

She was furious with herself, but she took it out on him. "This won't work, you fool!"

she snarled at him as she strained to get out of his lap.

"Want to bet?"

The amusement was still in his tone. It didn't even sound like he was exerting any effort to hold her, and that just infuriated her even more. She tried to take him by surprise and topple them over.

He laughed at her again. "Nice try, but the chair is bolted to the floor."

She should have realized that it would be, like everything else in the cabin, but she merely hissed, "Which is where you're going to be if you don't let me up!"

"I hate to mention it, wench, but I have the upper hand here. Actually, let me re-phrase that. I don't mind mentioning it at all!"

"It's temporary and you know it! One yell and you'll have a dozen pistols trained on you!"

"No, they'll be trained on you," he dis-agreed. "You make a very nice shield. But if you don't stop squirming, you'll have some-thing else to think about."

That was a warning tone. She heard it, she just didn't grasp his meaning. She'd managed to squirm around to the side. It didn't help, he was still holding her fast, and she'd exhausted herself trying. But suddenly he was kissing her. She had no idea how it happened or why. One moment he was staring at her mouth and then . . .

The hold he had across her chest, that had locked her arms at her sides, changed. He gathered her closer for the kiss, but he wasn't holding her as tightly as he had been. She actually got one arm loose. She had to fight the urge to put it around him. Good grief, she had to fight more than that. His kiss was too sensual and every bit as nice as she remembered it being. She found herself enjoying it far too much and she didn't want to end it. Just a few minutes, God, the taste of him, the heat that shot up between them, how he could make her feel so wanton so damn quickly! Just like before, not just once, but twice before—and now . . . despising him made no difference, the passion he stirred in her was overwhelming.

She almost gave in to it completely, that's how powerful the sensations were, coursing through her. If it wasn't a matter of her father's life and death, she would have. Still, she was loath to do what was necessary now that she could. But she had to.

She found his pistol in her pocket and wrapped her hand around it tightly. And she had enough semblance of thought left to realize that she probably wouldn't gain her release if she just pointed it at him. She couldn't take the chance that it might not be loaded and he'd know it. That would just amuse him, and she'd done enough of that. Though if it was loaded, he might not believe that she'd shoot him. Of course she wouldn't. She was pretending to be a pirate, not a murderer.

But she felt some real regret when she eased the weapon out of her pocket and slammed it against the side of his head. His arms slid off of her, dropped to his sides. His head fell back. She jumped off his lap immediately, her heart pounding. She hadn't meant to hit him so hard that he'd be rendered unconscious or worse, and the "worse" terrified her. If she killed him when she had only meant to startle him into releasing her . . .

But he was just stunned. Before he shook it off and got his feet loose to turn the tables on her yet again, she ran out of the cabin and grabbed the first sailor she saw and dragged him back with her. She shoved the pistol into the man's hands.

"I'm going to tie him again. If he makes any move to stop me, shoot him."

The man nodded. She'd given him the gun because she was still sure that Drew wouldn't believe that *she* would shoot him, or he'd be too angry to care. A few seconds more and they would have found out, though, because he was already reaching for the ropes at his feet when she returned and gave the order. She saw only that he sat back in the chair slowly. She avoided his eyes completely, her nerves too frazzled to see what was there, so she didn't know if he was watching the man with the weapon or her.

"You actually hit me?"

There was more surprise than anything else in Drew's tone, but Gabrielle didn't answer him. Getting him secured again was the only thing on her mind and she'd probably never moved so fast as she did in dragging his hands back behind the chair to rebind them. She also found another rope and wrapped that around him, too. She even thought briefly about getting a sack to put over his head, but since that had nothing to do with restraining him, would only have been for her sake, to keep her from getting mesmerized again, she managed to resist the urge.

Satisfied that his bonds would hold this time, she finally checked his head, hoping she hadn't broken the skin. No such luck. Blood had dribbled down through his hair and behind his ear. She dismissed the sailor, put the pistol back in her pocket, and left to find some water and a cloth.

She almost sent someone else to tend him. She knew Drew was furious. She'd almost been able to feel his rage. And he'd flexed his fingers repeatedly when she was wrapping the ropes around his wrists, as if he were thinking about squeezing the life out of her.

"Are you going to answer me now that your lackey is gone?" he asked.

She still didn't. She carefully got rid of the blood, then left a cold cloth over the swelling. He made a sound, not quite a moan, as she pressed the cloth to the side of his head. But as soon as she let go, he shook it off. She tsked and came back around to stand in front of him, finally ready to deal with his anger over his failed escape.

Crossing her arms over her chest, she said, "Yes, you dense man, I actually hit you. It was either that or shoot you. Consider yourself lucky."

"Son of a bitch," he growled low. "What'd you hit me with?"

"Your pistol. Found it in the drawer."

"Great, just great," he snarled. "That will teach me to kiss a viper."

A blush arose. She suspected that remark was merely rancor, but it still hurt. He was testing his new bonds—no, he was actually trying to work them loose again. The man was impossible.

"Stop that," she told him sharply.

He gave her a nasty look that was self-explanatory. She gritted her teeth, added, "Do I need to find more rope?"

"Do what you have to do, sweetheart."

"Maybe a conk on the head again? It certainly improved your disposition—not having one."

"Very amusing. But I think if you got near enough to me to try it, these bonds would miraculously open. That's how much I want to get my hands on you."

To put around her neck, she was sure.
And even though she *knew* he was still
nicely tied, she was just superstitious
enough not to put it to the test.

"It's too bad you're being such an uncooperative captive," she complained.

"There's any other kind?"

She glared before continuing, "I had considered leaving you to your cabin, but since
we'll be using it, it would be better to get
you behind a locked door elsewhere. Or
maybe you have some chains aboard? Yes,
chains would do nicely, don't you think?"

"You don't really want to know what I
think just now," he shot back.

But he did stop straining at his bonds.
She noticed that immediately. So there were
probably chains somewhere on his ship that
could be made use of. And a short metal
leash, one he couldn't possibly get out of,
would be ideal, now that she thought of it.

With his options dwindling, he was looking daggers at her again. Vastly disconcerting, that look, but much better than him being smugly certain that he could make her
the captive again.

"Answer me this," he demanded. "Why in
hell didn't you even try to convince me that

you were acting in an official capacity to claim my ship?"

"For what reason?"

"To pursue criminals, a matter of life or death, whatever. I'm sure you could have come up with some convincing lies."

"When you know I'm not an official?"

"You didn't have to reveal yourself. One of your men could have made the claim."

She smiled, couldn't help it, but humored him anyway. "I see, and you would have believed them?"

"Damned right I would have. I'm an American. Why wouldn't I believe it, when you English provoked us to war using similar tactics?"

"Right you are, this is an official seizure."

"Very funny."

"Just trying to be accommodating."

"Why? To keep me off balance, right up till you toss me over the side? Do I at least get ravished first?"

She drew in her breath sharply. The thought of taking advantage of him, while he was tied . . . Good grief, she needed to sit down, and fast, her legs felt so wobbly. She moved behind the desk to the chair there and dropped into it. She took several deep breaths deliberately and pushed the image of ravishing him from her mind. And she stared down at the desk. Looking at him was downright dangerous.

She had to get the feelings he incited in her under control. She was supposed to be making him want her, not the other way around!

"I was beginning to think you were serious," she said, "until your last remark. No one is going to toss you over the side, Drew."

"Even to save your own necks?"

She glanced at him again to ask, "Because you know who we are?"

"Yes."

She shook her head. "Sorry, but there is nothing that could justify killing you. And it sounds like you've formed the wrong opinion of us. We aren't the sort of pirates you're thinking of."

"What other kind are there?" he sneered.

She grinned. "We're a new breed, of course. Actually, we're more treasure hunters than pirates."

"Your reasons mean nothing to me. What you've done here is committed a criminal act and let me give you an assurance of my own. I'll have the lot of you hunted down for it, or I'll do it myself. *Now* do you see why it would be a good idea to let me go immediately?"

"I'm sorry to hear that," she said, and sighed just to reinforce her words. "I had preferred to think that you would be reasonable once you see that I am telling the truth, that you'll have your ship back. With no real harm being done, you could have just been happy to be about your way when this is over."

"No real harm?" he said incredulously. "What do you call cracking my head open?"

She tsked. "I did no such thing."

"It feels like it," he disagreed. "Come have a look."

She chuckled over that obvious ploy. "Not a chance," she told him. "Besides, it's just a little cut and bump. It barely bled at all, and I've removed the evidence."

He raised a brow. "You touched me?"

"Very impersonally. Didn't you feel it?"

"No, you're lying. What else did you do while I was stunned?"

"You mean while you were testing your new bonds? I did nothing! Really, I—"

"But you wanted to, didn't you?" he cut

in, with what could only be described as a knowing smirk. "Come on, sweetheart, admit it. You know you want to ravish me, and you've made sure I can't stop you, not that I'd really want to. So what's stopping you?"

"You will cease such—"

"Just sit on my lap, and I'll give you the ride of your life."

She shot to her feet, but it was too late. The words might have been crude, but the image had already got into her mind. She could touch him, she really could. He'd even given her permission. And the taste of him had been sweet, so very intoxicating. She could even do what he was suggesting . . .

"Stop it!" she burst out, but she wasn't sure if she was saying it to him or to herself. So she added with a scowl, "Or I will use this pistol on you again."

He gave her a feigned wounded look. "Is that any way to treat a wounded man?"

She headed to the door without answering him. She had to stay away from him until she got that image of herself straddling his lap out of her mind.

Chapter 24

"What do you suppose pirates were doing in England?" Georgina asked James.

She was trying to show him that she wasn't that upset, but she wasn't having much luck, not after he'd seen her stricken expression as Drew's crewman related the tale. The man had managed to slip over the side of *The Triton* while it was still in the channel, without being seen, and came straightaway to Berkeley Square to tell them that Drew had lost his ship to pirates, and he'd overheard them say they were heading to a small island east of St. Kitts.

"Does it matter? Pirates, thieves, whatever they are, they're still in possession of your brother's ship." And then James mumbled, "Bloody well wouldn't have happened on *The Maiden Anne.*"

Georgina pretended she didn't hear that. *The Maiden Anne* had been James's ship and he'd been a gentleman pirate himself for many a year, even capturing a few of her family's ships, as well as capturing her heart when she'd sailed with him as his cabin boy.

His tone implied he was angry. She wasn't surprised. He couldn't stand to see her upset about anything and usually wanted to kill whoever caused it. In this case there was nothing he could do, and that would just make him even more angry. Not that anyone who didn't know him well could tell. It wasn't his way to shout or rant or get emotional. Oh, no, James Malory was unique in that regard. If he was going to demolish someone, that person would have no prior warning.

"At least Boyd is here," she said. "I'm sure he'll want to go after *The Triton.*"

"Of course he will, but is that going to relieve your mind?" he asked pointedly.

He knew her too well. Of course it wouldn't. Boyd didn't captain his own ship, nor was his ship equipped to deal with pirates. But then neither was *The Triton* heavily armed.

"I've bought a ship," James continued. "It was to be a surprise for the next time you get it into your pretty head to cross the ocean."

She grinned at him. It had *really* stuck in his craw that he'd almost had to sail without being in command of the vessel. She wasn't at all surprised that he'd make sure it never happened again.

"Then you're going after them?" she said.

"Of course."

"That's an excellent plan," she agreed, already feeling much better.

"Thought you might think so."

"And I'll go with you."

"Now, George—"

"Don't even think of leaving me at home to worry myself sick."

He just stared at her, waiting for her to come up with a few other reasons he could more easily disagree with. She wisely changed the subject by pulling a note out of her pocket and handing it to him. She'd found it when she'd stopped by Gabrielle's room this morning to see if she was feeling better. Quite a shock to find her gone instead, though Drew's crewman showing up soon after with the news that his ship had been captured by pirates had made her temporarily forget about it.

He frowned at her when he finished reading it. "You think Gabrielle has taken Drew's ship?"

Georgina blinked. "Heavens no, that never occurred to me. I was merely surprised that she didn't *tell* us her father was in trouble, that she just packed up and left, merely leaving that note. You'd think she would have at least asked for your help, since you and her father had been friends."

"She probably felt she'd imposed on us enough. But the timing is rather . . . on the mark, don't you think? When did she leave?"

"This morning, no, wait, it could have been last night while we were at Tony's for dinner. She wasn't feeling well, which was why she didn't join us, as I'd told you—"

"But she was well enough to sneak off, so I'd say that was just an excuse."

"Oh, come now, you can't *really* think she'd commandeer Drew's ship. He's my brother. I befriended her. If anything, she might have asked him for help since she knew he was sailing. For all we know, he might have agreed and she's a passenger, or rather a hostage right now, just like he is. She'd have no reason to do him a wrong . . . turn . . ."

He sighed and finished the thought for her. "I see you've remembered what you told me he said at that ball the other night. Just the sort of thing to ruin the chit's chances for a good match here."

"Nonsense," she disagreed. "It didn't make the gossip rounds. And it's been two days since that ball. We would've heard—"

"You're always the last to know if you're personally involved, m'dear," he cut in, "and since you were her sponsor, you're most definitely involved. Besides, we didn't leave the house yesterday other than to go straight to Tony's for dinner and back."

"I know." She sighed. "Actually, when I first read Gabrielle's note, I thought it might be a ruse, that she's merely gone into hiding to weather the storm. I was going to ask you to find her so we could blast this scandal out of the water."

He raised a golden brow. "And how would you have done that *if* it is making the rounds already? It's not a lie, but the truth."

"A lover scorned, wanting revenge," she replied. "Very easy."

"You mean she scorned Drew and he wanted to blacken her reputation by making that remark?"

"Well, my brother did start the rumor. Which is why I'd feel so guilty if this has ruined her."

"Stop it," he demanded. "For all you know he may have been provoked."

She stared at him incredulously. "You're taking Drew's side?"

"Bite your tongue, George. I'd never. But did you never notice the sparks that would fly between those two?"

"Of course I did. They seemed not to like each other a'tall to begin with, but that changed rather quickly. It even worried me enough that I tried to warn Gabrielle away from Drew."

"But did you warn him away from her?"

She blinked. "Of course not. You know how he is. He's worse than you were, about being determined to never marry. So he knew very well she was off-limits to him."

"And that, m'dear, might have been the problem. She's a very pretty chit. If she set her cap for him, he may have indeed been provoked, or tempted beyond good sense, as it were."

She frowned. "Well, in any case, I'll send a note off to Reggie to find out for sure if there is a rumor circulating. She keeps abreast of all the current gossip, so she'd know. But still, Gabrielle only went out for a little while yesterday with one of those men she came to London with, according to Artie. And he said she only had one other visitor, a young man he guessed was one of her suitors. But if, as you say, the subject is the last to know about their own scandal, then she wouldn't know either, would she?"

"I wouldn't count on it. It's too bloody coincidental and would explain why she didn't ask Drew for his help."

"That's *if* she's on his ship."

"Doesn't matter, m'dear. Whether she's one of those pirates or at their mercy, or in hiding as you first guessed, I'll round up a crew today. So stop worrying about your brother. Whoever instigated this mess will be torn limb from limb. You may depend upon it."

Chapter 25

Gabrielle had been away from the captain's cabin too long now. It was quite possible that with no one watching him, Drew had been able to free himself while she was gone, so she took Bixley with her for backup and sent him in first. But she wasn't kidding herself. She knew that some of her eagerness to get back here had nothing to do with her concern that he'd escaped in her absence.

The captain was still where she'd left him, but she circled his chair, at a good distance, to make sure the ropes were still about his wrists before she dismissed Bixley. Drew hadn't said anything yet, he just followed her with those disturbing dark eyes of his until she got behind him. He was probably still simmering, and she didn't doubt he'd turn her over to the authorities if he had the chance, just as he'd said. But he'd have to catch her first, and how likely was that? He didn't know where she lived in the Caribbean, and it was highly doubtful she'd ever return to England now. Because of him. Because he'd carelessly blackened her name there.

Of course, there was the possibility that he was so furious about losing his ship to her, even though she'd assured him it was only temporary, that he might just hunt her down himself. He might also be angry because he'd thought they were going to kill him. That could be why he was giving her those dagger looks. Now that she thought of it, he had mentioned the possibility of his being being tossed over the side right before he'd asked if he was going to be ravished first.

She blushed again, remembering that, but at least she was standing behind him where he couldn't see it. He knew why she was back there, though, and asked with a sigh, "You really thought I'd try that again when the first attempt rubbed my skin raw?"

She frowned and raised the sleeves of his jacket to see the damage he was talking about. It was mostly just red skin, but there were a number of abrasions that had beaded blood. Why hadn't she noticed that when she'd retied him earlier? And why was her first urge to untie him and find some salve for his abraded skin?

She pursed her lips, annoyed that she'd even had the urge to soothe his discomfort, and came back around his chair to face him. She'd already given her cabin to Margery. Her friend was feeling a little seasick, which had happened before for the first couple days after they left port. So she'd been quick to offer her her own cabin, too quick. It had given her the excuse she needed to keep Drew close at hand. She just had to tell him now that he was going to be sharing a cabin with her. She was looking forward to his dismay.

But he spoke up first. "My sister and James befriended you and this is how you pay them back?"

She tsked and pointed out, "I didn't take their ship, I took yours."

"You don't think they'll take that personally? I hate to break it to you, sweetheart, but James is a man who holds grudges to the grave. The Malorys aren't a family to cross or harm, but that particular Malory is the most unreasonable and vengeful of the lot."

"Sorry, but I was witness to how much he *doesn't* like his brothers-in-law. Care to try again?"

"It wouldn't have anything to do with me, it's because my sister loves me and she'll be upset about this. He's very protective of her, you know. Gets quite unreasonable about it, actually."

"Your sister won't even find out I've captured your ship until you're free again," she replied, though he *was* starting to make her feel uneasy about James Malory. Living in his house for a few weeks, she never did get over the nervousness that man caused her.

"Never know what he'll take offense at. I sure as hell wouldn't risk him hunting me down, for any reason."

"And you won't hunt us down? Weren't you the one promising to see us all behind bars?"

"Of course, but I'll just be nicer about it than James will be."

She laughed at him. He said that in such a grumble. He was obviously annoyed that she hadn't turned so terrified over his dire predictions that she might release him immediately. And just to rub it in a little more . . .

"By the by," she said nonchalantly, "I do have some unpleasant information for you."

"Why am I not surprised?" he replied sarcastically.

She ignored that and continued, "The cabin I was going to move you to is no longer available for your use."

"So?"

"So you could have been cut loose in it, but since you now will have to remain here—"

"You can't keep me tied up indefinitely," he cut in now, his body stiff with indignation. "Or were you going to hand-feed me?"

She shook her head. "No, I wasn't planning on that. What I've decided is that you'll have to be chained in here, well, that's if we can find some chains. But I have men looking as we speak."

"Chained to your bed? And you call that unpleasant information?"

She knew he didn't mean it, but his tone now sounded intrigued . . . and seductive. He was just trying to embarrass her and it certainly worked. From the very beginning, the man had had no trouble a'tall making her cheeks burn with his risqué remarks that were so improper. Of course, they would be scandalous only in polite company, and he'd thought from the beginning that she was a pirate. He probably figured she was used to such talk, and if he did, that was a good thing. It meant he believed the role she was playing.

It was late morning. She'd requested food be delivered before she returned to the cabin. She hoped the chains arrived first, so the captain could feed himself. She needed to start behaving more like an uncaring pirate, though, so eating in front of him, and letting him go hungry while she did, wasn't such a bad idea.

As for his remark about her bed, if he really hadn't been trying to embarrass her, then she could expect more of the same and she'd rather not hear any more comments that set her mind to wondering about things she shouldn't. She was supposed to be making him want her, not the other way around. She could think of one sure way to put an end to what he kept insinuating, though—if he thought she was already spoken for. That might even further her plan, since it was human nature to want what you can't have.

She no sooner had the idea than Richard walked in, twirling a chain in his hand, a long one. Most of it he had draped about his neck. And it looked as if there was a shackle attached to the end hanging near his waist.

"Is this what you had in mind, Captain? There were two of them in the hold. I used my brilliant persuasive techniques to get one of their crew to toss it up to me. I told them it was for an Englishman," he snickered. "Americans, they carry such long grudges, they didn't even ask who."

"The war has been over for a number of years," she reminded him.

"Doesn't matter, it worked to get me the chain. I'd suggest the other for the first mate, but as big as he is, I doubt any of us would care to get that close to him to try to put it on. At least this one is already restrained."

He was referring to Drew, who'd been watching him with narrowed eyes since he'd walked in. Immediately she realized that Richard was the perfect candidate to give Drew the impression she wanted him to have.

She moved closer to Richard, patted his cheek tenderly, and said in a low purring voice, "Thank you, *chérie,* for the chain," and promptly kissed him on the mouth in what she hoped was a lover-like manner.

But she really should have discussed her impromptu plan with Richard first, because without warning him, she took him so by surprise that his immediate reaction was to push her away from him. Unfortunately, he shoved her away, which caused her equal surprise, since it landed her on her arse.

Richard was too busy wiping his mouth with the back of his sleeve to notice her new position, and was indignantly demanding, "What the devil are you doing, Gabby?"

"Sitting on the floor, blast you!"

"Oh," he said as he looked down at her, and then, "Oh!" as he offered a hand. "Sorry about that."

She slapped his hand away, got to her feet, dusted off her skirt. Drew was laughing. He obviously didn't need to ask why she'd kissed Richard; he'd figured that out quite easily for himself when Richard hadn't reciprocated even a little bit.

"Shall we try that again, *chérie*?" Richard asked.

"Not in this lifetime," she snorted. "And don't *chérie* me, you dense man."

He chuckled. Drew laughed harder. She would have liked to throw something at both of them, but most everything in the cabin was bolted down. No knickknacks, no clutter, though there were several large chests not counting hers, so maybe the captain just hadn't unpacked yet.

She pointed a stiff finger at the door and said to her friend, "Go, before I add your head to the growing number of them being bashed today."

Then, seeing Richard opening the door and taking the chain with him, she called him back. "Before you go, redeem yourself by getting the captain shackled to that chain first, and make damn sure it's secure."

Richard winced. "I need redeeming?"

She just narrowed her eyes at him in reply.

Chapter 26

Ohr and Richard joined Gabrielle in her cabin for dinner. Ohr glanced at the captain a few times and finally voiced his concern.

"You're going to leave him in here like this?"

"You mean chained? For now, yes. It will keep him from getting hurt again."

"When did he get hurt?"

She shouldn't have mentioned that, but since she did, Gabrielle decided the truth might be better than any trite assurances she could give. It would also explain why she wanted him to stay chained.

"He managed to escape," she said, then quickly added, "I managed to tie him up again. No real harm was done."

"I could just chain him to the deck instead," Ohr offered.

"Swab those decks!" Miss Carla squawked.

They laughed at the parrot. It was typical of her to say one of her many phrases if she heard a word from them. But Gabrielle should have covered the bird, as late as it was. She did that now, then returned to the table. She noticed Drew staring at the parrot's cage. He probably hadn't heard her talk before then.

As for Ohr's suggestion, it happened to be raining that night, but even if it hadn't been, Gabrielle couldn't bring herself to confine Drew topside.

She told her friends, "I'd rather he not be moved."

"You can have our cabin, then," Richard pointed out. "We can sleep in here."

She thought about it for a moment. For propriety's sake, she should do that, though it was a bit late to worry about propriety when she'd branded herself a pirate. Besides, this room, the captain's domain, and her occupying it, was about the only thing that really supported her ruse. The men were calling her captain, yes, but Drew needed to see that they were coming to her for their orders, and their frequent stops in this room today showed that they were. And how could she enact her revenge against the captain if she didn't have constant access to him?

So she shook her head. "I'll be fine here." Fortunately, they didn't argue with her, though she was sure they would have if Drew weren't within hearing distance.

They stayed with her a while after dinner, with Richard going above and beyond in an effort to make her laugh. He was still feeling guilty for ruining what she'd tried to pull off that afternoon, and she hadn't had a chance yet to talk to him about it, or assure him that it had been a silly idea on her part anyway.

The captain remained quietly in his corner all night, just watching them, and probably listening to their every word. The only restraint on him now was the shackle about his ankle. She'd removed the ropes from him herself earlier. That had been tricky, and quite nerve-wracking. She'd had to just loosen them enough so he could work them off himself while she shot out of his reach before he did.

He hadn't sat in that chair again since he'd left it. He'd stood up and stretched his long limbs for a while, which had caught her eye and nearly had her ogling him again, much to her own annoyance.

He'd sat on the floor after that, his back leaning against the bulkhead, his knees bent in front of him, feet planted far apart. He'd eaten his meal there, too, after Bixley slid a plate across the floor to him. No one wanted to get within his reach, which was wise. He wasn't nearly as intimidating as that big bear first mate of his, Timothy Sawyer, but Drew was still a really tall, muscular man, so a person would just be asking for trouble if he got within access of his long arms.

He'd taken off his boots, probably to see if he could slip the shackle over his ankle to remove it completely. It would have been too tight with the boot on under it. She'd been watching him and he was aware of it, so he hadn't tried it yet, but that just worried her enough to insist he lift his pant leg to show her.

He'd actually just stared at her. He wasn't going to comply. She'd gritted her teeth. He made the most annoying captive. Belliger-

ent, uncooperative, insulting. She decided
not to press it. It was a damned leg shackle,
after all, designed *not* to come off once it
was put on, and his legs were probably
thicker than most, as tall and nicely filled
out as his body was.

She realized rather late, after her friends
had left, that she'd have to do without the
normal necessities while she shared the
room with her captive. Well, it wouldn't be
the first time she'd slept in her clothes without removing them. She hadn't once removed her clothes on that pirate island,
when she'd been a captive herself. She
didn't mind sleeping in them now . . .

She went very still when the question entered her mind. Why make exceptions for
him? Good grief, it was actually a perfect
opportunity to start tempting him beyond
what he could stand, by showing him a little
bare skin. She just needed to garner the
nerve to do it, and the easiest way would be
to pretend. She didn't *want* him to think she
was doing it deliberately.

So very quickly, before she could change
her mind, she let her skirt fall to her feet and
she yanked her blouse off over her head.

She couldn't help but feel satisfied when she heard his sharply indrawn breath.

"Damn, woman, what the hell are you doing?" he nearly shouted.

As she stood before him in her chemise and pantalets, which showed off her derriere to perfection, she glanced over her shoulder at him and said coquettishly, "Oh, I'm sorry, I forgot you were there."

Then she turned toward him so he could appreciate the full upper curves of her breasts, which were revealed by the low-cut chemise. She heard him groan as his gaze fixed on her chest, and she had to bite back a laugh as she jumped into his bed in her skimpy underclothes. A double attack, one against his senses and another against his pride, that she could forget his presence in the room.

But if she thought that she'd managed a telling blow for her revenge for the day, she was sadly mistaken. He made sure of that.

No sooner did she extinguish the lamp by his bed and lie back on the pillow than he said, "You know this shackle is rusted?"

She opened her eyes and stared at the ceiling, not that she could see it in the dark, but it was in that direction that she stared.

He's quiet all night, but when the lamp goes out he starts to talk? she thought in irritation. She probably should have said something to him before she retired, at least let him know that his position on the floor wasn't her idea, that she would have supplied him with a hammock if he'd asked for one.

Then again, did she really want him to think she had a soft side? Before, when he'd been at the top of her list for matrimonial choices, she'd wanted him to know the real her and stop erroneously assuming things about her. But it was too late for that. Now she wanted just the opposite.

"Determined to see me get blood poisoning, aren't you?" he said next.

She gritted her teeth. She debated whether to just ignore him. Maybe he'd get the hint, or maybe he'd think she was asleep already.

"Ah, I see," his voice drifted across to her. "The plan was to toss me over the side and kill me all along?"

She sat up, but it was too dark to see him in his corner. "You should have left your boots on, you know," she pointed out reasonably.

"You think it would have made a differ-ence, when this shackle is so rusty it would have eaten right through that leather?"

She lay back down, slamming her head against the pillow twice. "This was a really bad idea," she gritted out. "If we were in warmer waters, you can be sure I'd go sleep on the deck myself."

He didn't reply. He was actually quiet for a while, which encouraged her to try to fall asleep.

And then out of the dark she heard him say, "I'm going to need a chamber pot, wench, or did you want me to relieve myself on the floor?"

Her eyes flew open even as her cheeks bloomed with color. She shot off the bed, quickly found a match to light the hanging lantern she'd extinguished earlier. He was sitting exactly where he'd been when she took over his bed. That was probably stick-ing in his craw, that she was going to sleep in his bed while he was on the floor wearing a chain. She located the chamber pot, set it down, and used her foot to shove it toward his end of the room. She then moved to one of his trunks to rummage through it.

"What are you doing?"

She ignored his offended tone. No doubt he was bothered because she was going through *his* trunks. "I'm looking for something for you to stick under that shackle," she said pertly. "I'm pretty sure I have nothing suitable, well, not without ripping up any of my clothes, which I'm not inclined to do."

"So you did hear me?"

"Certainly."

"I suppose that means you didn't intend for me to get blood poisoning?"

She snorted and tossed him two stockings she'd found. "I'd double those up and stuff them under the metal, rather than put them on. Now, if you don't mind, I'd like some quiet so I can get to sleep."

"If you wanted quiet, you should have moved to a different room."

"Putting you up on deck is still an option," she warned.

He didn't say another word.

Chapter 27

Damned woman could have tossed me some bedding, Drew fumed as he sat on the hard wooden floor of his cabin. It was raining outside—pouring, actually—and a cold draft seeped into the room from under the door. Usually Drew found the sound of rain soothing. He even enjoyed taking over the steering of his ship during storms. There was something primal about them that stimulated all his senses. He wasn't going to get the opportunity tonight.

He couldn't sleep. He'd tried, with his head against the wall. It wouldn't be the first time he'd slept in an uncomfortable place, and sitting up, for that matter. But it just wasn't going to happen here, not with a beautiful woman sleeping in a soft bed only a few feet away from him.

Actually, that was just one of the reasons why sleep was eluding him. The emotions churning in his gut were a bigger deterrent. He couldn't remember ever feeling this angry and he was having a difficult time dealing with it. But then, he'd never had his ship taken from him before.

He couldn't believe Gabby was doing this. She was so angry at him that she couldn't just ask him for passage? He'd been heading to his usual trade routes and he could have easily been persuaded to bring Gabrielle Brooks along. Well, maybe not easily. She *was* the reason he'd decided to sail a few days earlier than he'd originally planned. He'd wanted to get as far away from her as he could because of the temptation she presented.

That temptation had grown stronger over the last few weeks. As soon as she'd stopped being disagreeable, he'd started thinking of how nice she'd look in his bed. It got to the point where he'd wanted her so much, he'd thrown caution to the wind and actually tried to get her to come to his room. Stupid thing to do, that. It had just made him want her more. And she hadn't come to him. Instead, she'd continued her husband hunting. That was like adding a spark to the smoldering fire, and was probably why he'd gotten so drunk those last two nights in port, and why he had gone to that ball and foolishly tried to sabotage her husband hunt. And then seeing her with Wilbur at that ball, the one suitor she seemed to favor the most . . . he wasn't surprised he'd embarrassed her as she claimed he did. He couldn't recall exactly what he'd said, but he certainly remembered his sister scolding him for it.

He sighed to himself. It appeared that he'd succeeded and she'd revealed her true colors now. Damned woman really was a pirate. Like father like daughter. But he should have had her amenable to him already. She was attracted to him. He'd noticed it from the beginning. He could have at least cajoled her into a better sleeping arrangement. But his anger was getting in the way. The thought of trying to charm her was abhorrent to him right now. Because she held the upper hand? Because she'd stolen his ship, cracked him over the head with his own pistol, chained him to the blasted floor? Or because despite all that, he still wanted her?

He'd tasted her again, that was the trouble. Why in hell had he done that? He'd been so close to his freedom, to getting his ship back and turning the tables on these pirates, and he had to go and get tempted by a pair of lush lips. He'd simply been unable to resist kissing her with her mouth that close to him, her derriere squirming in his lap, the scent of her filling his nostrils.

He felt his manhood stir just thinking about that kiss again. Blasted wench . . .

"Broke a hole in one of the cabins," his first mate whispered. "Didn't think you'd mind, Captain."

Drew abruptly sat forward away from the wall. He was so incredulous he nearly laughed out loud. He'd been so deep in thought that he hadn't even heard Timothy Sawyer sneak into the cabin, and apparently he'd done so without waking the lady pirate sleeping across the room. He couldn't see his first mate. No light came in through the bank of windows because of the rain, and Gabby had extinguished the lamp again before she returned to his bed, so it was pitch dark in the cabin. His bed.

Damn, that infuriated him, that she was sleeping in it—without him.

"Not at all," he said in the same low whisper Timothy had just used. "What took you so long?"

"Had to make sure no one was on the other side to give warning."

"Did you release the crew yet?"

"Figured I'd cut you loose first."

"I knew I could depend on you, Tim."

"Was the least I could do, Captain, after I let them get the better of me today," the man said gruffly.

"Well, actually, I doubt anyone else would have thought to break through walls," Drew pointed out.

He was grinning, though Timothy couldn't see it. The man had been with him for quite a few years now, was usually a quiet, amiable fellow who never caused any trouble. For all his size, he had one of the milder dispositions Drew had ever come across—unless he was riled. And when that happened, all hell could break loose.

It didn't happen often, but like Drew, Timothy didn't like confinement. They'd caused too much ruckus one night in Bridgeport and ended up spending the night in jail to sleep it off. After Timothy had sobered up, he'd been like a bear in a tiny cage, frantic to break the bars, and damned if he hadn't bent them. Drew had had to pay for those damages, too.

"Let's get your ropes undone," Timothy said.

"No ropes. I got out of them once, so I'm wearing an iron shackle now."

"Now, that may pose a problem. Does the lady pirate have the tools to get you out of it? Or was it padlocked with a key?"

"There's no key, and one of her men has the . . ." Drew didn't finish. He was facing the door and saw the light appear under it. "Careful," he softly hissed, "I think we may have company arriving."

There was no time to prepare for it. The door was shoved open even as he was giving the warning. The handsome pirate stood there, the one Gabby had attempted to kiss that afternoon. Unfortunately, he wasn't alone. The tall Chinaman that Gabby seemed to be fond of was with him, and two others. One of them must have seen what was happening, or had come across that hole in the wall, and had the presence of mind to bring along reinforcements.

It was an utterly tense moment. The four pirates were armed, had come just inside the door, and all four pistols were pointed directly at Timothy's chest.

Drew was afraid this was one of those times that his first mate wasn't going to back down. He could feel his tension, and his anger, that he hadn't accomplished what he'd set out to do. And it wouldn't be the first time the big man had plowed through unrealistic odds. He was probably too angry to even notice the damn pistols and was going to get himself killed.

Gabrielle suddenly shot out of the bed, her body wrapped in a blanket, and placed herself directly between the two groups. And she was bristling with anger herself.

"I've bloody well had enough excitement for the day, gentlemen," she snarled. "So you're all going to rethink this situation and realize that sleep is much more appealing right now than spilling blood."

Drew let out the breath he didn't know he'd been holding. But it didn't sit well with him to suddenly be feeling gratitude to the lady. He had to admit, though, that had been quick thinking on her part, to realize that Timothy wouldn't try to get through her to get at her men. The big man had no trouble cracking a dozen male heads together, but he'd never harm a woman. She'd been in a sound sleep, but apparently had no trouble waking alert and ready to make instant judgments like that.

"Damned women pirates," Timothy mumbled in a subdued tone. Drew knew then that the danger was over.

"I have had just about enough of you, Mr. Sawyer," Gabby remarked. "Do you really have so little care for your personage that you'd ask to be shot?"

"Is that what I was doing?" Timothy said with an abashed look. "My apologies."

She tsked in disgust, but glanced behind her to tell her men, "Take him back—"

"To where, *chérie*?" Richard cut in. "There is a hole next to the door of the cabin he was in."

"He broke through the bloody wall?" Gabby asked incredulously. And then she sighed as she looked back at Timothy. She even gave him a disappointed look. "You, sir, are an outrageous nuisance. What am I going to do with you?"

Drew was incredulous to hear Timothy

say, shamefaced, "I won't cause anymore trouble, miss."

Drew groaned. Scolded by a pretty woman and the man was a complete push-over!

But Gabby wasn't done. "I'll have your word on it."

This time Timothy just stared at her. Perhaps he was debating whether he would have to keep his word if he gave it to a pirate.

But Gabby was too annoyed to allow Timothy much time to think it over. His prolonged silence prompted her to comment, "I'll take that as a no," and she marched over to the table by the bed to pick up Drew's pistol.

Since the woman had fooled him once, trying to pretend she wasn't a pirate when he knew now that she was, Drew really had no idea what she was capable of. For all he knew, she just might shoot Timothy to keep him from being a further "nuisance," as she'd called him.

So he hissed at his friend, "Answer her, damn it!"

She heard him but didn't remark on that, nor did her annoyed expression change.

She merely pointed out, "A standoff isn't going to let any of us get back to our beds. Will you at least give your word that there will be no further trouble tonight so we can all get some sleep?"

"That I can do."

Gabrielle mulled that over for a few moments. Frankly, she looked too exasperated to agree to only half of what she'd asked for. And Drew hated to admit it, but she looked much too fetching standing there clutching his woolen blanket around her, with her long dark hair disheveled and falling around her shoulders. But then her expression changed. She nodded. And it took Drew only a moment to guess that she'd just remembered what her young friend had told her earlier, that there were two shackles in the hold. Drew was wearing one now, but there was one left for Timothy.

Blast it! The wench wasn't happy with one man in chains, she had to shackle two!

Chapter 28

Timothy Sawyer might have walked back to his cabin of his own accord, but Gabrielle didn't trust him to keep his word, not even a little. A man as big as he was was nothing but trouble, in her mind—very dangerous trouble, and she wasn't taking any more chances with him.

She, Richard, and Bixley succeeded in shackling Timothy to the sturdiest wall in his cabin. The big man accepted his fate with surprising docility, perhaps because Gabrielle distracted him by satisfying his curiosity about her father's life as a pirate, answering question after question.

Before stepping back out of his cabin, she even told him, "Thank you for keeping your word and not causing any more trouble." He merely shrugged his wide shoulders.

It was done. And the ship was still in her control. It had been close, though.

She headed back to the captain's cabin. The night watch was doubled. Ohr had already seen to that. They weren't taking any more chances. And she'd been gone long enough getting Sawyer taken care of that she could hope Drew was now sleeping, or, if not, that he'd be quiet so she could.

No such luck.

He waited until she'd crawled back in his bed. He even let her get comfortable, rearranging the pillow a few times, smoothing out the blanket she was lying on top of. But the moment she sighed in contentment—it was a very comfortable bed—his voice drifted over to her.

"I've been sitting here thinking about what your breasts taste like."

She thought she'd misheard him at first. The man wouldn't really say something like that, and in such a conversational tone. Lovers might discuss such things, but they certainly weren't that!

But then he added, "Salty from the sea

air? Like rose petals from your perfume? Yes, I smelled the roses on you. Or would they simply taste like ambrosia?"

Cheeks burning with embarrassment now, she growled, "I'm going to gag you."

"I wish you'd try."

She knew what he was doing now, getting her angry enough to get close to him so he could turn the tables on her again. Not bloody likely.

She turned over on her side, giving him her back, but in the dark he wouldn't know that. Silence might get the point across to him, though, so she was determined not to talk to him anymore.

"Let's get back to your breasts," he suggested in a lazy tone.

"Let's not."

So much for her determination. Desperately, she put the pillow over her head and held it against her ear. Damned if she couldn't still hear him.

"I know how plump they are, Gabby. I remember perfectly how they filled my hand. But I want to taste them. I should have while I had you squirming in my lap today. That was very nice, by the way. I'm already looking forward to you sitting on my lap again.

But let's stick to your breasts for the moment. Will you like it when I taste them, do you think?"

"You must be remembering some other woman's breasts, one of those legions of sweethearts you have in every port. My breasts are puny, almost flat, so you can stop thinking about them!"

"Liar." He chuckled. "I remember every single thing about you, Gabby, how your mouth felt against mine, how passionate you were in my arms, how wonderful it felt to hold you close to me. But the question in my mind is, are you always so wanton, or was it just me that made you respond that way?"

"None of your damn business, Captain."

"Ah, but I'm making it my business, sweetheart. I'm going to find out, you know. Maybe not tonight or even tomorrow, but someday when I find you again, and I will find you again, we're going to make love. I promise you that. And I'll know your breasts intimately then. Actually, I'll know every inch of you intimately. I don't have the least doubt in my mind that it will happen."

It was on the tip of her tongue to tell him he was delusional, but a part of her, just a small part, hoped he wasn't. It was that mention of making love and his promise that it would happen. Good grief, what that did to her was amazing. Her stomach had fluttered sensually. Her pulse was already erratic from everything else he'd said. And her breasts tingled, her nipples had turned hard so quickly, just as they did that night he tried to seduce her in his sister's parlor. She could remember every one of the sensations she'd experienced that night and she shivered deliciously.

"Would you like to hear about it, what I'm going to do to you first?"

"No!"

She actually shouted. He chuckled again. And ignored her denial.

"I'm going to kiss you until your toes curl, deeply, very erotically, and you'll want to do the same. In fact you will kiss me back. You won't be able to help yourself. You'll hold me tight, clinging to me, tight enough to feel my desire pressing against you, while our tongues become lovers first. I will time it perfectly, you know. I'll drive you mad with desire before I even remove your clothes. And when I do finally remove them, it will be so very slowly. Do you know why?"

Ignore him. Say nothing. God, the room was so bloody hot now. Her clothes felt so tight she had to fight the urge to remove them herself.

"I'm going to savor every moment of stripping you naked," he told her, his voice much lower now, more husky. "And so will you, because I'm going to kiss you and touch you everywhere. No part of you will escape my attention. Your neck, your ears, your shoulders will feel my lips. Your breasts will feel my tongue. Your feet and calves, and especially your thighs, will feel the caress of my hands. And between your legs, where you'll be wet and aching for me, I'll—"

"Stop it! Please!"

"Do you want me yet?" he asked slowly, sensually. "You know you do. Come to me, Gabby. Let's make it happen now. There's no need to wait."

She bit her lip to keep from answering him. And then like a splash of cold water in her face, she heard, "I want you so much right now I think I could rip this chain off of me with my bare hands."

Nothing could have brought her out of that erotic haze quicker than the thought of him free and in command of the situation again. Not yet. She couldn't let him have his ship back yet.

She shot off the bed, dragging the blanket with her. He heard her cross the room. She wasn't the least bit quiet about it. She just wasn't crossing toward him.

He demanded, "Where are you going?"

"To fetch a bucket of cold water," she snapped, almost to the door.

"Damn you, wench, come back here!"

She didn't. And while he might have thought she was getting the water to dump on his head for the sexual frustration he'd just forced on her, she wasn't. She did find some, though, and splashed it on her own face. Then she found a spot on the deck that wasn't too windy and curled up with her blanket to get some sleep. Not very comfortable, but inside the captain's cabin was the kind of discomfort she didn't know how to deal with, so anything was preferable to that.

Ohr nudged Gabrielle's foot, which was sticking out from under the blanket she'd brought up to the deck with her. She woke slowly to find him standing beside her, offering a hand to help her up. She hadn't gotten nearly enough sleep during the night to have her mind clear of webs immediately.

"Rough night?" he asked.

It was a logical question, she supposed, after he'd found her asleep on the deck. But it didn't begin to describe what the captain of this ship had put her through last night with his talk of lovemaking.

But she said merely, "The captain got too—oh, good grief, I meant to say cabin. The cabin got too hot, so I sought a nice breeze for a while. I must have fallen asleep before I cooled off."

"Are you sure you don't want to swap cabins with us?" he asked.

"I'd like to, yes!"

Gabrielle blushed immediately. She had said it too quickly, and after that blunder she'd just made, too. How embarrassing!

But Ohr appeared not to notice how desperate she'd just sounded. He was like that, though. Even if he guessed exactly what was on her mind, he wouldn't say so, nor would she know it from his expression. He was quite possibly as good as James Malory had been at schooling his features.

But she really didn't care at the moment. She was just determined never to go through such an intensely arousing experience again. Good grief, how utterly ridiculous she'd been to think she could handle sleeping in the same room with that outrageous American. He was too handsome. Even in the dark when she couldn't see him at all, he was sinfully enticing, his voice too sensually provocative. She had no idea it was even possible to be stirred like that by mere words.

The current arrangement just wouldn't work. She had to be in control to enact her revenge. Even chained, *he'd* been in complete control last night. He'd made *her* react, he'd stirred up *her* senses. She was supposed to be doing that to *him!* But how could she if she couldn't even think straight because of what he made her feel?

And she didn't doubt it was all deliberate. He'd been trying to seduce her for one reason and one reason only, to get his ship back.

She thrust it from her mind and asked Ohr, "Did you get some sleep yourself after that trouble we had with Sawyer last night?"

"A few hours, which is all I need. I'm go-

ing to take over the wheel now—or would
you like to?"

Ohr wasn't teasing her. Steering the ship
was one of the things her father had enjoyed teaching her when she'd sailed with
him. She didn't have the strength in her
arms to do it for very long, and certainly not
in rough weather, but it was a beautiful,
clear morning, and the wind was steady, so
she nodded and followed him up to the
quarterdeck.

He left her there. She almost called him
back. Alone, she knew what she'd end up
thinking about—him—so she was relieved
when Richard came to join her a few minutes later.

"I'm usually fine being celibate," Richard
said.

He was sitting in front of the wheel, leaning back against it so he wasn't facing her.
He'd been chatting about this and that,
nothing relevant. Then that remark came
out of the blue and Gabrielle had no idea
how to reply to it, since she couldn't imagine what it was in relation to. So she said
nothing, hoping she'd simply misheard him.
No such luck.

"It's your fault, you know," he continued.

"If you hadn't tried to kiss me yesterday, I never would have started thinking about her again."

Oh, good grief, this was about Georgina Malory. She'd really thought that was over and done with. When she'd gone to warn him about what James had said, the implication being that Richard would be a dead man if he ever approached Malory's wife again, Richard had assured her that no woman was worth dying for.

She reminded him of that. "You agreed to stay away from her."

"At the time, yes, but I didn't say forever."

She rolled her eyes. He didn't notice. He was still facing out to sea.

She tried the most reasonable approach. "You know, she's a remarkable woman."

"I thought so," he agreed.

"Remarkable in that she loves her husband. A lot of women don't, you know. A lot of women marry for a variety of reasons, many of which don't include love."

"What about you?" he asked. "Are you only going to marry for love?

"Yes."

He'd already swung around and moved over, was sitting cross-legged now off to the side of the wheel so he could look up at her. "The American ruined your chances of finding true love in London. I ought to go down there and make mincemeat of him while he's chained up. Someone needs to make him sorry he did that!"

"No!" she said a bit too quickly. "Don't hurt him—"

"Ah, so it's like that," he cut in. "I should have known that kiss you gave me yesterday was just for the captain's benefit. I understand perfectly, *chérie*."

"Understand what?"

Instead of answering, he speculated aloud, "You know, if I had been able to get Lady Malory alone just once, she wouldn't be uppermost in my mind now. She'd merely be a fond memory. A single dalliance does work wonders. You should consider it as well."

Her mouth actually dropped open, she was so incredulous. She knew exactly what he meant, but she still said, "I don't know what you're talking about."

"Of course you do, Gabby. You want that captain. It's been obvious since your reaction to him on the wharf. And Ohr mentioned you slept on the deck last night.

Couldn't take it, could you, being alone with him in the same room? I certainly wouldn't be able to, if the woman I wanted was in such close proximity."

She ground her teeth together in frustration. "You're making assumptions without thinking. I might find him attractive, but then any woman would. That doesn't mean I can do anything about it. Unlike you men, we women need a ring on our finger first."

He raised a brow, possibly because her tone had sounded so prim and proper. "Do you really? I never would have taken you for a stickler for—"

"What the deuce did I return to England for except to find a husband?" she cut in. "If I didn't need one first, there were any number of times I could have fallen from grace, as it were."

"So why didn't you?"

"I swear, Richard, I'm not going to have any teeth left before this conversation is done. You know bloody well what you're suggesting just isn't—"

"It's done all the time, *chérie*," he interrupted this time. "You just led a sheltered life where the scandals from the wicked city never reached your ears. But consider, scandals only involved the women who got caught. You can't imagine how many others fell from grace, as you put it, without anyone being the wiser, including the husbands they eventually settled down with."

"You know that from experience, do you?"

He grinned and wiggled his brows in a suggestive manner. "But of course."

He turned to stare out to sea again. He was only teasing, she reminded herself. If she took him seriously, she'd end up thinking about his outrageous suggestion, and she didn't dare tread down that path.

"Take my advice, Richard," she said in earnest. "Forget about that particular lady. Even if she wasn't happy in her marriage, there's more to consider, like how many pieces her husband would cut you into. Malory was serious, you know. He *would* kill you. So do yourself a favor and stop thinking about his wife."

She thought she heard him sigh forlornly. "Easier said than done. Try it yourself," he added as he stood up to leave. "You'll see."

She got the point. Leaving the cabin last night hadn't stopped her from thinking about the captain. It was a wonder she'd gotten any sleep at all. But then, while her situation was like Richard's, there was a major difference. She might still want Drew just as Richard wanted the man's sister, but she also despised him now. And how the deuce could she still want a man she despised? "Darned body urges that had nothing to do with common sense," she grumbled as she turned the wheel a little too sharply.

Chapter 29

Gabrielle's new cabin was much smaller than the captain's, but that was to be expected. There was a decent-sized bed, a standing wardrobe for her clothes, a small table with two chairs for dining, and even a writing desk. No nice bank of windows like Drew had, but she didn't expect to spend much time in the cabin, so it didn't matter.

Ohr had seen to moving her carpetbags again without being asked, but he'd forgotten about Miss Carla, or maybe he'd left her behind deliberately because he really hated that bird. Most of Nathan's crew felt the same way. But Gabrielle wasn't going to use the excuse of fetching the parrot to see the captain again.

She poked her head out the door and got lucky, seeing Bixley passing. "Can you fetch Miss Carla for me, please?" At his wince, she added, "Oh, come on, she's caged. Your fingers are safe."

"I was thinking of my ears," he replied with a chuckle, and hurried off to comply.

She made room on the writing desk for Bixley to set the cage when he returned. It only took a moment later for her to learn how the captain had amused himself during the day.

She'd been sure she knew all of Miss Carla's repertoire by now. After three years, she'd taught her quite a few phrases herself. But no sooner was the bird set down on the desk than she squawked and said "Coward" quite precisely.

Bixley raised both brows at Gabrielle when he heard the bird, and he mumbled distinctly, "That's a real bad word to be teaching it, Miss Gabby."

She didn't blush until then. She'd merely figured that Drew had picked that word because he thought the parrot was hers. He'd also probably picked it because he figured it would matter to her, she being a supposed pirate and all, that he was calling her a coward because she had avoided him all day. Throwing down the gauntlet, as it were. If she really were a pirate it might matter to her, but since she wasn't, it didn't.

"I know better," she said. "She didn't learn that word from me."

"Ah," he replied on his way out the door. "The American was ornery, then."

Indeed, and a lot worse, she realized not ten minutes later when Miss Carla said, "Time to get naked, wench."

Good grief! An entire phrase like that in one day? She was incredulous, and had to allow that perhaps her father had taught the bird that one long ago and she'd just never heard it before, since she'd never started to remove her clothes in front of the bird before. That's what she'd started to do, to get ready for bed.

And yet, the phrases her father had taught Miss Carla were mostly derogatory and indicative of his dislike for his wife. In particular, the phrase the bird most favored was "Carla's a witch."

Gabrielle was surprised when Margery showed up a while later. "Are you sure you're feeling better? I can manage for a few more days if you're not."

"I'm fine now," Margery assured her. "It's more annoying than anything else that it takes me so long to find my 'sea legs,' as you call them."

Gabrielle grinned. "We can't all be sailors."

Margery snorted, then moved to Gabrielle's bags. "Let's get you unpacked. At least this cabin has a wardrobe to put your clothes in. And here, you'll be needing these. If you're going to be gallivanting about the decks like you usually do and helping out as needed like you *also* usually do when you're aboard ship, then you'll be wearing these just to give me some peace of mind," Margery said.

"These" were one of the cut-off britches Gabrielle had obtained back when Nathan first started letting her sail with him. They were a snug fit, very comfortable, and she wore them with a long-sleeved shirt that hung nearly to her knees, to keep it from being known just how snugly the pants hugged her backside.

Gabrielle lifted a curious brow. "Peace of mind?"

"Indeed," Margery huffed, but then confessed, "I've already had nightmares about you tripping over your long skirts and falling right over the rail. And don't you even think of denying it could happen, young lady. We both know it *has* happened before."

Gabrielle laughed. Trust her friend to remember that one single time the wind had caught her skirt just so and tangled it in her legs enough to trip her, and indeed, she'd been too close to the railing when it happened and had stumbled right over it. Being at sea at the time had required her having to be fished out and then having to deal with the crew's laughter when she came up looking like a drowned fish. She'd gotten a pair of britches from Richard that very day and had had more made when she got home.

"You're lucky I thought to pack them," Margery continued as she shoved the britches at Gabrielle.

"But why did you?" Gabrielle asked. "I wasn't sailing with my father."

"I know, and I even hoped you wouldn't need them, but truth be told, I had visions of you telling that captain of the ship we took to England how to run his own ship and showing him just how it's done."

"I wouldn't have!" Gabrielle laughed.

"No, but you might have used that as an

excuse just because you like the sailor's life too much. I'm actually surprised you restrained yourself."

"I had too much on my mind that trip to even notice how the ship was being run."

"Now, now, don't you worry none about getting yourself that husband," Margery said, guessing accurately what had been on her mind back then. "We'll get back to the matter of looking for one soon enough once we fetch your father out of that dungeon."

Gabrielle sighed. "It's a shame I had to leave all those pretty new gowns behind."

"I packed a few," Margery said, and took one out to show her.

"But I'm not going to have an opportunity to wear them on this trip."

"Who says you're not? Just because you're going to wear those britches to keep you safe while on deck, doesn't mean you can't dress for dinner at least. There'll be no forgetting you're a lady."

Gabrielle grinned. "Actually, for this voyage I'm a pirate."

"I'll concede—a lady pirate. And here's that shirt you wear with those britches." Then Margery tsked, looking at her hair, which she'd merely tied back with a ribbon today. "I'll help you fix that in the morning."

"Not a chance. It's just a waste of time doing up a fancy coiffure aboard ship. The wind will just rip it down."

"That's only because you won't stay off the deck," Margery huffed.

"Swab those decks!" Miss Carla put in her two cents.

"Oh, hush, you daffy bird," Margery said, and headed toward the door. "I'll see you bright and early, Gabby. Get a good night's sleep."

Afraid to hear any more out of Miss Carla for the night, Gabrielle rummaged through the wardrobe for one of the petticoats Margery had just hung up and draped it over the bird's cage. A cover of any sort usually worked to shut her up. Now, if she could just quiet her thoughts as easily, then she might get some sleep.

Chapter 30

Gabrielle dreamed about Drew that night, that he was kissing her. The dream seemed to go on endlessly, too, and brought back every one of the sensations his real kisses had made her feel. She even remembered the dream, too clearly, when she woke the next morning. She blamed it on that blasted kiss in his cabin. And she woke feeling nearly as flustered from the dream as she had been from his attempt to seduce her. Well, it wasn't quite that bad. She didn't think anything could be that bad, as hot and bothered as he'd made her feel the other night.

She joined her "officers" for the morning meal. Drew was looking a bit glum now after her desertion. He *seemed* to be ignoring them, just staring off into space. He'd been unable to hide a brief moment of surprise, though, when she showed up. After yesterday, he'd probably thought he wouldn't be seeing her again.

He couldn't help but hear the camaraderie between her and her friends, the laughter, Richard's usual teasing that could get risqué occasionally, and today was no exception. All harmless, but Drew wouldn't know that. The men certainly weren't treating her with the respect Drew might figure a "captain" was due, but she'd already decided it would be impossible to try to enforce that for an entire voyage just for his benefit, when the easy bantering was normal for pirates and this was how they were with Nathan, too.

And she'd gotten comfortable, too, donning the britches Margery had insisted she wear. Maybe that had accounted for Drew's brief look of surprise. He may not have ever seen a woman wearing britches before.

Gabrielle didn't leave the cabin when her friends did. She continued to lounge at the table where they'd eaten. She stretched out her feet and crossed them under the table.

Leaning back in her chair, she even locked her hands behind her head. In no way did it look like she might still be there to finish the meal.

Drew made no pretense about watching her now. As soon as the others left and they were alone in the room, his dark eyes latched onto her and stayed there. He might have been trying to disturb her with his perusal, but she didn't allow it to work. The conversation she was going to start was going to be entirely in her favor today. She wasn't going to give him a chance to start in on *his* campaign again.

She stretched a little so that her breasts were molded more firmly against the thick cotton of her shirt. Just a little. She didn't want to be obvious that she was showing off her attributes to him. That she wasn't tightly bound beneath the black shirt wasn't for his benefit, though. She wasn't pretending to be a boy, after all, and never had tried to conceal her breasts when she dressed in her ship's togs, as she called them. The shirts she wore were thick enough to keep her modest, with a thin camisole beneath them.

She gave Drew a curiously innocent look

now and asked, "Do you really think I'm a coward, just because I decided that I prefer to sleep naked, as I usually do, and I went off to find a cabin where I could do that?"

His incredulous expression made her want to crow with laughter, but she kept her features schooled. It was a legitimate question, after what he'd taught her parrot to say. Of course, she hadn't needed to elaborate.

After a moment or two he said, "You could have slept naked here."

She gave him a thoughtful nod. "Yes, I know. And it probably wouldn't have bothered me to do so. But I was afraid it might disturb you, and it's not my intention to deprive you of sleep. I'm sure you'll have no trouble sleeping with your new roommates."

He snorted, but it was telling, how quickly he changed the subject when he asked, "Who's this Carla person that the parrot calls a witch? That wouldn't be your real name, would it?"

Gabrielle laughed. She couldn't help it. He was still trying to annoy her with insults. It didn't work at all this time.

"Miss Carla is the parrot's name," she said with a grin. "But just so you don't go thinking she was taught to insult herself, you might as well know that Carla is also my mother's name."

"Ah, I see. How nice," he said, sarcasm thick in his voice. "You call your mother a witch. I'm not the least bit surprised a pirate would disrespect her parent that way."

She gritted her teeth for only a moment. She was *not* going to let him annoy her. "That's a natural conclusion," she allowed, "even if it is wrong. I loved my mother. It was my father who didn't like her very much after the bloom wore off their marriage. And the parrot belonged to my father long before he gave her to me, so Miss Carla acquired most of her vocabulary from him, not me."

"How did such a mismatch even occur? A pirate marrying an English aristocrat? Or was that just a lie you made up so you could snag a lordly husband? Are you even legitimate, or just a pirate's bastard?"

"I don't care how derogatory you get about me," she said stiffly. "But you'll bloody well keep your derision off my parents."

Since it must have sounded like the threat she intended, he asked, "Or what?"

"You might want to keep in mind that there is still a plank here with your name etched on it."

He chuckled, confident now that she wasn't serious, despite her sharp tone. "So why did he marry her?"

Gabrielle had to take a moment to regain her composure. Damned man had done it to her again, aggravated her enough to lose control.

"He was treasure hunting at the time. He considered her a shortcut to what he was after."

"You have to be joking."

"No, he takes his treasure hunting quite seriously," she replied.

"I suppose the better question would have been, why did she marry him?"

Was he really interested in her family, or just trying to distract himself? Part of getting her own composure back was to discompose him again, and she'd done that with subtle enticements she'd witnessed other women practicing more blatantly, a slow sweep of her long lashes, a look she hoped was sensual, a lazy stretching of muscles that weren't cramped—but he didn't know that.

She shrugged. "She married for one of the more common reasons."

"Love?"

"No, because she wanted children."

"Ah, *that* reason." He chuckled. "So how many siblings did you end up with?"

"None. That may have been part of why the bloom wore off so quickly. My mother never actually said so, but I gathered that she thought she could get my father to settle down and give up the sea. She didn't become dissatisfied with her marriage until it became clear that he would never do that. I do know that she despised the fact that he was always away at sea and never around when she needed him."

She was touching closer to home, apparently, since his reply was rather defensive. "Comes with the territory, sweetheart. She shouldn't have married a pirate if she wanted a man in her bed every night."

Blasted with double barrels! It amazed her how he uttered sensual, provocative remarks so easily and naturally, while she had to work so hard at it. He said things to her that he would *never* say to a lady. Ironically, she'd heard much worse in recent years and had become immune, or at least there was very little that could make her blush anymore—until she'd met Drew Anderson. He could make her blush without even half trying.

She fought to keep the pink out of her cheeks now by answering him without inflection. "I see you're under a mistaken assumption. My mother thought she was marrying the captain of a merchantman. She didn't know what his real occupation was. She died a few years ago without ever finding out. Now it's your turn. Since marriage has been the subject of your curiosity, care to tell me why you're so dead set against it?"

He grinned. "Can't you guess, sweetheart? You're a pirate. You know what it's like, sailing from port to port. Most sailors have to come home to a single port for marital bliss, the one they've made their home in, where their wife is waiting. And yet how many ports do they sail to where they either drown their sorrows, missing their wives, or are unfaithful, then miserable afterward in their guilt. I'm never falling into that trap. I love the fact that no matter which port I sail into, there's a woman waiting for me with open arms."

"Ah, I see. I had thought perhaps you had loved and lost, and that's why you abhor marriage, but I forgot that you're merely a true Lothario at heart."

"I don't abhor marriage. For some men it's the perfect state to be in. I just realized long ago that it wasn't for me. I'm happy in my life. Why would I want to change that?"

She shrugged and said offhandedly, "I don't know, things happen."

"Yes, they do. But take my mother, for example. She knew exactly what she was getting when she married my father. She knew he'd rarely be at home. And while she seemed happy enough, raising so many children, I used to catch her in moments when it was obvious how lonely she was, even miserable, missing my father. I was pretty young when I decided I'd never do that to a woman."

It made her sad to know that he *was* serious. He believed every word he'd just said. But that left no room for love. Did he really want to go through his entire life without experiencing true love?

"There were two ways you could have abided by that decision. You could have just decided not to go to sea instead," she pointed out.

"You're joking, right?"

She gritted her teeth. "Yes, of course I am."

"The sea is in my blood, sweetheart," he added, just in case she missed that point, then gave her a knowing look. "You changed the subject too soon. Were you serious before? Your mother really never knew your father was a pirate?"

"Why does that surprise you? When my father visited us, he didn't bring his crew along, which might have given her a clue. They are a ribald, rowdy bunch, after all. Besides, he was on his best behavior whenever he was in England."

"What about you? How long have you known?"

"Not until my mother died and I left home to find him," she replied.

"So only a few years? My, you adapted very quickly, didn't you?"

His sarcastic tone was back. She'd told him things she shouldn't have, she realized too late. "Fortunately, I'm a quick learner," she replied offhandedly, trying to correct his impression of her.

She stood up, stretched sensually, then walked over to stop near him but just out of his reach. His long legs were stretched out across the floor and crossed at the ankles. His arms were crossed over his wide chest. His expression was actually wary for a moment, with her stopping so close to him, but it quickly turned sensual.

"Ready to ravish me?" he asked.

It was fortunate that his expression had warned her he was going to say something like that. She was able to reply calmly, even with a little feigned regret, "Sorry, but you're not my type."

His short bark of laughter said he didn't believe her. "Then who is? Richard?"

She managed a grin. "Good grief, no. I was just playing around with him the other day and merely took him by surprise. He's a good friend. We actually joke around like that a lot."

"Then that pallid English snob?"

"Who? Oh, you mean Wilbur? No, I found him rather boring, if you must know. Besides, even though you're an American, you seemed a little too at home in the London ballrooms for my taste. I want a man who will go horseback riding on the beach with me, who will dive with me into crystal-clear coves and explore coral reefs, a man who will get as excited as I do about chasing after lost treasure. I want a man who will swim naked with me in the sea on a moonlit night and make love to me on a sandy beach."

Gabrielle realized dreamily that she really did want all that. But she'd managed to stun Drew. He'd been hanging on every word of her romantic fantasy.

Seeing that she'd turned the tables on him, she said abruptly, "Now, can I get you anything before I leave you to your lonely confinement?"

He replied abruptly, "Don't leave yet."

"Sorry, but I have a nice hot bath waiting for me."

"Actually, I'll take one of those myself."

"Very well, I'll have some buckets of water brought in to you. If you're a good prisoner, I'll even have them set down for your use, rather than tossed on you."

Her tone implied she was dealing with a child, even the words did. It was deliberate on her part and it was obvious by the sour twist of his lips that he didn't like it.

She left him then, but not before she stuffed her hands in her pants pockets in a casual manner. She knew very well that would lift the back of her shirt so he could see just how snugly the pants molded to her derriere. Innocently done, or so it would seem to him, and she had to fight back a laugh when she heard his groan as he watched her saunter out of the cabin.

Chapter 31

"If Miss Carla tells me one more time to get naked, she's going to find out just how cold that ocean is out there," Margery said in a huff when she entered the captain's cabin for dinner that night.

Margery was the last to arrive. Richard, Ohr, and Bixley just stared at her incredulously. Gabrielle drew in her breath so fast she choked on it, and she started coughing. Drew, sitting on the floor in his corner of the room, leaned his head back against the wall and closed his eyes, but there was a definite smirk on his lips.

Then Richard started laughing and Bixley said with a leering grin, "That ain't a half-bad idea, wench."

The Irishman probably wasn't joking. He
and Margery shared an easy relationship
that included sexual innuendo, a private
drink now and then, and, Gabrielle suspected, more intimacy than that on occasion.

But Margery wasn't going to be distracted with ribald banter and demanded,
"Where did Miss Carla pick that up, I'd like
to know? She said it a half dozen times today when I was in and out of Gabby's
room."

Margery was glaring at the three pirates,
one of whom she'd suspected was the
guilty party. But Gabrielle saw no reason not
to put the blame where it belonged.

She pointed toward Drew across the
room and said, "You don't need to look any
farther than over there for your culprit. He's
been trying to get me in his bed since he
met me." She grinned to let them know she
found that amusing, even added, "It's too
bad he doesn't have one now."

Drew actually blushed. She found that interesting, but it was probably no more than
that three unpredictable men were staring at
him now, all humor gone. It was Margery he
ought to be worried about, though, and she

even went over and kicked the foot he had stretched out on the floor.

"You'll be keeping such notions to yourself, Yank, if you know what's good for you. Our Gabby isn't for the likes of you."

Drew pulled his bare foot back to rub it and replied, "Who is she for, then?"

Gabrielle went very still. She was about to interrupt, but Margery was too quick with her rejoinder. "For the husband she'll be having soon, which won't be you, now, will it?"

Margery returned to the table. Drew mumbled something, but no one caught it and he was ignored after that.

Bixley started reminiscing about how long he'd been with Nathan. "Ohr vouched for me, but from that very first meeting, Nathan treated me like an old friend. He's like that. Sees the good in everyone. I love that man like a father."

"You just love treasure hunting," Ohr scoffed.

"Well, there's that, too." Bixley grinned and teased his friend. "Tell me you don't. Go on, I dare you."

"I just like sailing with Nathan," Ohr said.

"You aren't the only one who loves him like a father."

"That's right, you never did finish searching for your real father, did you? When that's what brought you to this part of the world."

Ohr stared across the room. Gabrielle thought for a moment that he might be looking at Drew, but his gaze seemed focused on something far more distant. He said quietly, "I found him, or rather, found out he's dead."

"Oh, Ohr!" Gabrielle cried, and moved around the table to hug him. "I'm so sorry."

He patted her back. "Don't be. It's not as if I ever knew the man. And he had another family. I may make myself known to them someday—or I might not. I have my own family now," he ended, and gave Gabrielle a fond smile as she returned to her chair.

He meant her and Nathan, and Nathan's crew. Richard confirmed that when he threw a napkin at Ohr and said, "I already claimed this family as mine."

And Bixley pushed Richard out of his chair with the rejoinder, "Too bad, mate. We were with Nathan before you showed up."

"Now, now," Margery intervened. "Nathan's got a heart big enough to include all of you."

Gabrielle suddenly felt tears welling in her eyes. They'd spent so many nights bantering like this, with Nathan quick to join in the fun. But he wasn't here now, he was in some dark, dank dungeon and . . .

"Don't cry, Gabby," Drew suddenly said. "Your father will be back with you before long."

Everyone turned to Drew, surprised by his remark, which had sounded quite tender. The man immediately clammed up, probably annoyed with himself for speaking at all. And the rest of them repeated the sentiment until they had her laughing again.

After dinner when she left the cabin, Richard followed her out. They stopped to lean against the railing. A bright moon was peeking out through a light bank of clouds. It washed the deck in soft light and reflected beautifully on the water. She usually loved nights like this at sea, when the moon kept the dark at bay. Such a peaceful setting, but hard to appreciate it with so much turmoil inside her.

Without looking at Richard, she addressed some of that turmoil. He was her closest friend, and he'd already guessed the attraction she felt for Drew, so she told him a bit more than she was going to tell the others.

"I was actually considering marriage to him. Can you believe it? And I even knew he was a confirmed bachelor, but I was fool enough to think I could change his mind and get him to propose. But all he was interested in was a brief sojourn in my bed."

"I will assume, out of loyalty, that he got nowhere near your bed?"

She snorted by way of answer. "I don't even think he was serious about it."

"But do you think that's why he wanted to ruin your chances for a good match?"

"Trying to come up with that answer just makes me see red. I have no idea why he did it."

"Some men are like that, *chérie,* especially if they take it personally, their failure to seduce the woman." Richard peered at her closely. "You wanted him to try harder?" Her blush wasn't obvious in the moonlight, but Richard had just been teasing and continued to speculate. "He's a very handsome fellow. He may be used to conquests without much effort."

"I don't doubt he is," she agreed. "But that certainly wouldn't justify—"

"No, you misunderstand," he cut in. "Emotions don't need to be justified when they take over. It can be as simple as he couldn't have you, so he made sure no one else would either. But I know you, Gabby. You're not just going to shrug this off, are you?"

"No. Believe me, before this voyage is over, he'll regret what he did, I promise you. I'm going to make him want me so much, he'll be devastated when I wave good-bye."

Chapter 32

The following morning Gabrielle saw evidence that Richard had commiserated with her after their talk about Drew. She didn't doubt that it was Richard who had caught Drew unawares with a fist to his cheek later that night. The bruise was only slight, though. And as it turned out, it didn't last more than a week.

That week passed with annoying slowness. Gabrielle knew why the time was creeping by for her. She allowed herself only a little while alone with Drew each morning after breakfast with her friends, to work her wiles on him, then spent the rest of the day eager to see him again and counting the

minutes until she could. But she forced herself to stay away, to stick to her plan.

Unfortunately, it didn't seem to be working. While the expression in his eyes might
become quite heated when he looked at her
now, he seemed too preoccupied with his
own agenda—escape by any means—to
really notice her subtle seduction. The man
still thought he could entice her with the
sensual descriptions of what he'd like to do
to her in order to get her to come near him.
He was in effect doing what she was doing!
It was just that his motive was different from
hers.

He tried romantic words, he tried crude
words, he tried combinations of both. If she
hadn't heard it all before in one form or another from pirates, she never would have
withstood the sexual onslaught. But she did
withstand it. Mostly. Although she usually
left him in a hurry to find some cool air for
her face.

Having others present didn't help to keep
her eyes off Drew either. That morning he
was exercising when she came in, bending,
stretching, walking around the narrow arc
the chain allotted him. The single glance he
gave her with those dark eyes as she

passed him stirred the butterflies in her
belly. And even after she sat down and Ohr
began chatting with her, her eyes were con-
tinually drawn to the play of muscles on
Drew's long legs, the taut stretch across his
back and buttocks. She had to force herself
to stop looking at him.

She might have to get bolder. She might
have to pretend that she was the one
succumbing. But she was limited in what
she could do for the simple reason that she
couldn't touch him. She didn't dare get that
close. But there was so much more she
could have done to heat his desire to the
desperation point if she had full access to
him.

And then she realized there was one way
to get around the restriction, at least temporarily, and she leapt on the idea the moment it occurred to her. She enlisted Richard's help. He laughed when she told him
her plan. He, in turn, brought in four other
crewmen to help—it was going to take that
many.

Drew couldn't doubt something was up.
The tub arrived and was filled with hot water. Towels, soap, more buckets for rinsing,

everything needed for a bath. And then the men just stood there looking at him.

Gabrielle came in, and with hands on hips she said, "It's time for a bath, Captain."

"Go ahead," he replied with a wicked grin. "I'll enjoy the show."

She chuckled. "Not me. You. You stink."

He sat abruptly forward. "The devil I do. I've been using those measly buckets of cold water I've been given."

"Not diligently enough, obviously. But come now, you can't deny you'd like a nice hot bath."

He didn't deny it, and eyed the tub across the room. "This shackle isn't going to reach that far," he pointed out.

"As rusty as it already is, we don't dare get it wet."

"You're removing it?" he asked with interest.

"Don't get your hopes up. It's only temporary, and you know damn well you can't be trusted without some restraint. So let these fellows assist you and it will be over with before you know it."

She left the room again. She knew that would give him the wrong impression. He'd think one of the men was going to wash him

when he realized he couldn't do it himself
with his hands tied behind his back.

She didn't return until she heard him
shouting. He'd been left alone, sitting in the
tub, hands and feet tied. She raised a brow
at him when she entered.

"How the hell am I supposed to get clean
like this?" he demanded.

She tsked to make it sound as if this
wasn't the plan. "Did the men get squeamish? Couldn't bring themselves to touch you
so intimately to get you clean?"

"How should I know?" he grumbled. "I
didn't ask."

She kept her eyes off his bare chest as
she approached the tub. This wasn't going
to work if she ended up getting mesmerized
by his magnificent body.

"All right, this will only take a few minutes,
so no maidenly airs, if you please."

"You're going to wash me?" he asked incredulously.

"I don't see anyone else here," she said,
and then stepped behind him. But first she
removed her shirt so it wouldn't get wet—
and made sure he saw her.

She heard a choking sound. "Gabby,
don't—"

"What? Now *you're* going to get squeamish?"

She was enjoying the ploy immensely. She should have thought of this sooner. Able to touch him now as much as she wanted with the pretense of helping him, she was going to drive him mad with desire.

She lathered her hands. She wanted no cloth between her skin and his. And then slowly, sensually, she began to rub his body, over his shoulders, down the corded muscles on his arms, which were very taut, pulled behind his back. She devoted a long while to his back, slipping her fingers under his arms, near his buttocks. He did try to grab her with his fingers, but she was slippery now and merely smiled to herself.

Carefully she sloshed some water on his head, then built up a lather in his hair. He groaned with pleasure. She couldn't help but smile in satisfaction as she rubbed her fingers through his hair, massaging his scalp, his temples. She didn't want to stop, but there was a time limit. She'd told Richard to return precisely twenty minutes later. Whether she finished washing Drew by then or not, that would be the end of it. And she'd already lost track of the time, she was so engrossed in what she was doing.

She rinsed his hair. And now, before she lost her nerve, she proceeded to wash his chest. She didn't come around to the front of the tub to do it. She wasn't going to let him accuse her later of deliberately enticing him by standing in front of him without her shirt on. But she had to lean against his back in order to reach his chest. He groaned as her breasts pressed against his back and, her hand slid over his chest. He turned his head toward her, trying to reach her lips with his. He couldn't do it, not without her help.

"Kiss me, Gabby. You know you want to."

She drew in her breath. She did. Oh, God, she did. She looked down at his lips as she ran her hand over his muscular chest and then moved it lower. She heard him inhale sharply and was even leaning closer to him when the three raps sounded at the door, warning her she had about thirty seconds to get her composure back.

She toweled herself quickly, slipped her shirt back on, and practically ran out of there. And that would be the last time she attempted anything so foolish. While it had accomplished what she'd hoped, to wildly inflame him, she just couldn't get that close to him, touch him like that, without having that same spark burn her.

She dreamed about him often, nearly every night. She wasn't even surprised that she did, since he filled so many of her thoughts during the day. But none of those dreams were as arousing as the one she was having tonight.

They were lying in bed, in the narrow bed in her cabin. He uttered the phrase, "Time to get naked, wench," and she felt like laughing because it was just a dream and she could do anything she liked in a dream. But it was a potent dream. He was lying on top of her and kissing her. He pulled her nightgown off. She thought he might be naked as well because she felt such heat and such pleasurable new sensations between her thighs with him lying on top of her, but she wasn't going to open her eyes to check. She was afraid she might wake up if she did.

She didn't want to wake up, not yet. Before she did, she wanted to learn as much

about his lovemaking as he'd teach her,
which was silly, because she couldn't
dream about something she didn't already
know. So it must be her wishing that made
him so tender when he caressed her, running his hands up and down her body. And
she did have full knowledge of his kiss. It
was the same in her dream as she remembered it, the heady taste of him, his tongue
thrusting boldly into her mouth in a most
passionate manner.

She must have forgotten some of the
things he'd promised to do to her, because
not all of his actions now matched his
taunts. She was naked already; he hadn't
slowly removed her clothes as he'd said he
would do. He'd said she would kiss him
back, though, and she was. He'd said she
wouldn't be able to help herself and she
didn't even want to try. He'd said she would
hold him tight, even cling to him, tight
enough to feel his desire pressing against
her, and oh my, yes, that part had been in-
corporated into her dream.

But there was so much more than what
she remembered from his taunts, because
her dream was letting him kiss and touch her
everywhere, along her neck, over her shoul-

ders—her breasts. His mouth devoted a great deal of time to that responsive area of her chest, finding out everything he'd said he wanted to know about her breasts. She never could have imagined how scorching his lips would feel, though, or the thrilling excitement that raced through her entire body. He'd said he was going to drive her mad with desire and it was quite possible that he was. No, that was supposed to be while he removed her clothes—oh, the order didn't matter! She was enjoying herself too much to mind that she wasn't getting it right, everything he'd said he would do to her.

He licked at her nipples. They'd tingled before just from his words and they did again. He licked at her belly button. He licked between her legs. Oh my God, so much pleasure. He really was going to drive her mad—no, wait, where the deuce did that come from? Her knowledge of lovemaking was broad, but it didn't include that!

She started to wake up, to struggle out of the dream, but then he was kissing her mouth again, soothing her confusion. And she remembered, it was just a dream, just a dream. He was chained in another room, he couldn't possibly be here in her bed with her.

That thought went straightaway when the pain arrived. So did all semblance of sleep and nice dreams. She was staring up at Drew Anderson in the soft glow of lantern light and realizing that he'd done it again.

He'd ruined her, literally this time. She couldn't imagine how he'd managed to escape, but he was definitely in her bed, lying on top of her, both of them buck naked, and he'd just stolen her virginity.

"My God, what have you done?" she said as she pushed against him. "How did you—"

"Shh, I just want to pleasure you."

His words were a catalyst. She felt them stir her even in the midst of her panic. "You've won!" she cried. "You've won everything, your ship back and me in bed with you!"

"No, sweetheart, I promise you'll win, too. Remember how you aroused me during the bath this morning? Now it's my turn to do the same thing to you, but I will finish what I start, and you won't be disappointed. Let me show you. Just let me love you."

But there was no humor in his expression,

no gloating because he'd won. In fact, she couldn't read it at all, so she had no warning that he was about to kiss her again.

He'd been treating her carefully, not wanting her to wake too soon, but now that she was awake, he released all the passion that she'd stoked to life during the week. She thought she'd failed to arouse him. Apparently not.

That kiss got past the shock of what was happening, and coupled with his words, it stoked her own fires back to life with amazing swiftness. Such scorching heat, his mouth locked on hers, his tongue ravishing inside it, one hand behind her head holding her there, not letting her escape any part of that kiss. And now she didn't want to escape.

Her arms went around his neck. He'd slipped his other hand between them to tightly squeeze her breast, knead it. And she could still feel him below, between her legs, thickly filling her, but unmoving, cautiously waiting. Yet the knowledge of what was there, what felt so good inside her, sent out a wave of pleasure, that uncontrollable flood of sensation deep in her belly that he so often stirred.

She pressed up against him, pulling him in deeper. That felt so nice she did it again, and again. And oh, God, it was suddenly too much sensation coalescing inside her all at once. The explosion of pleasure was beyond anything she could have imagined and it continued blissfully as he did some thrusting of his own, then, incredulously, built and exploded around her again just as he reached his own climax.

He was still after that. Gabrielle didn't think she could have moved a single muscle herself. She was so drained, so replete, so wonderfully content. She'd wonder why later. But now the only thing she was capable of was sleep.

Chapter 33

Gabrielle had no idea how long Drew had let her sleep. It was still dark outside the single porthole the cabin contained, so the sky gave her no indication. And actually, he didn't wake her at all, at least it didn't appear so. He was sitting at the little table that could squeeze in four for a meal, but more comfortably sat two.

The chair he was using was turned toward the bed, so he'd probably been watching her at some point. Right now he was staring in the vicinity of his feet, which were crossed and stretched out before him. He looked deep in thought. His expression wasn't guarded: he was frowning.

She'd barely moved, just turned her head

enough to locate him in the room. She was quite sure he didn't even know she was awake, which suited her just fine for the moment. She still had no idea how he'd gotten loose from his chain. Someone had to have helped him, but who, when his own crew were secured? It had to have been one of the new men that Ohr had signed on in London. Maybe one of them had known Drew or one of his crew and had just bided his time to help them escape. And if he was loose, then his men probably were, too, and that meant her men were . . .

God, she was afraid to even guess what the Americans had done to reclaim their ship. They wouldn't have been warned as her crew had been, to make sure no one was hurt. They'd have no reason to go easy on "pirates." Just the opposite, especially after spending a week incarcerated. Ohr? Richard? Were they even still alive?

Then a new thought snuck up on her that was just as disturbing, but in a different way. What had occurred in that bed. She could even still smell him there, the scent of him surrounding her, reminding her of her fall from grace. What an absolute fool she'd been to even think that could have been a dream. Well, she'd known it wasn't a dream after his first few kisses and caresses, so she didn't even have that as an excuse. Not that there could be any excuse, no matter the reason, to absolve her from the simple fact that she'd *wanted* it to happen.

She thrust those thoughts aside as well. She had to turn this situation back around to her favor. Her father's release, maybe even his life, depended on it, not to mention she was going to end up in a dungeon herself if Drew had his way. And while he was distracted with his own thoughts, she had the perfect opportunity.

She didn't even need to form a plan. She still had Drew's pistol tucked away in one of her bags. She just had to get to it before he could stop her.

She shot out of bed and leapt toward her bags. She opened the right one and bent over to rummage through it.

He didn't yank her away from it. He didn't even move. "Looking for this?" he asked.

She glanced over her shoulder at him, saw the pistol in his hand, pointing toward the ceiling. He must have searched the room for it while she was sleeping or, more likely, before he even came near her bed. He wouldn't want to take any chances now that he was free.

Immensely disappointed that the only easy way to regain control was gone, she straightened and slowly turned around to face him. Only then did she realize that she was standing there naked. His eyes dropped immediately to her breasts and stayed there.

She didn't panic or expire of shame, it was too bloody late for that. She did reach behind her, pulled a robe from the wardrobe, and slipped it on, denying him the view he seemed to be enjoying so much. He sighed to show his disappointment, but she didn't buy it. It sounded too exaggerated.

Belting the robe, she spat just a single word at him. "How?"

She didn't need to elaborate, he knew exactly what she was asking. And *now* he was grinning. God, he was so pleased with himself, the blighter. It was enough to turn her stomach.

"An excellent question," he replied. "I'd even tried it myself, but with no luck."

"What?"

"I'm getting to that," he said, and continued to take his sweet time about it. "You see, there's a little something you didn't know about my first mate. Timothy has a very real problem with confined spaces. We spent the night in jail once after he'd nearly demolished a tavern and he actually bent the bars, trying to get out. If you must know, I'm surprised he lasted this long."

"You're saying he actually got out of that iron shackle we put on his ankle?"

"No, he's still wearing it as far as I know, it's just no longer attached to anything that hinders his movements. He waited for your crew to get lax with the assumption that no other trouble would occur, before he yanked his chain off the wall and easily removed the wood that boarded up the hole he'd previously made in his wall."

"What have you done with my crew?"

The grin remaining prominent on his lips, he said, "What do you think?"

"If I knew, I wouldn't be asking," she snarled.

He chuckled, still immensely enjoying their changed circumstances. "Your men were safely tucked away in those pleasant accomodations you supplied for my crew. And then I came straight here to take care of you."

And he'd certainly done that. They both grew quiet and thought about what they'd done in this room last night. What a fool she'd been to believe his sweet, seductive words! But she wanted so badly to know what his lovemaking would be like.

His amusement immediately departed, he asked hesitantly, "I don't suppose it's your time of the month?"

She glared at him. She'd seen the smeared blood on her thighs, too, before she'd closed the robe. "No, it isn't."

"If I had thought, for even a minute," he said, his tone quite sober now, "that you were a virgin, that wouldn't have happened."

She found that doubtful, considering what a scoundrel he was, but she merely said, "And why did you take it for granted that I wasn't a virgin?"

"Because you're a damned pirate."

She couldn't find fault with his logic, when that's what she had wanted him to think, but her tone was still bitter when she replied, "Ruined one way or the other, there's not much difference as I see it."

She was talking about the scandal he'd left behind for her in England, as well as what had occurred between them last night. But she had a feeling he didn't realize that, that he had only the one thing on his mind when he rejoined, "I'll make that up to you."

"How can you? It's not something you can just give back, you bastard."

"No, it isn't," he agreed. "But my amends would be to not have you tossed in jail with the rest of your crew when we make port."

Was that actual guilt she was hearing in his voice? If it was, then she had an edge and needed to try to use it.

"That isn't going to do me much good when I still have to rescue my father."

He slanted a single brow upward. "You'd rather go to jail as well?"

"Of course not, but I can't get my father out of that dungeon by myself. I'll need help."

"So that tale you spun about him was true?"

She sighed. Had he really thought she'd lied just for an excuse to take his ship? Dense man, pirates didn't need excuses.

"Of course it's true, and it's a bloody fortress he's being kept in. And the ransom Pierre is demanding is more than I'm willing to pay."

"You don't have the money? I thought you came into an inheritance."

"If that was the demand there would be no problem, but that isn't what Pierre wants. He's asked for my father's maps, and I have to be the one who delivers them."

"So what you're saying is you're too self-ish to give up some old maps for your fa-ther's life?"

She gasped. To go by his expression, he seemed to regret having said it. But he'd said it, revealing his real opinion of her, and despite the fact that she despised him as well, it still cut her deeply.

"I didn't really mean that," he amended.

"No, you're right. Pierre will kill my father, but he won't kill me, so in a way I am being selfish by not giving him what he wants."

"Do you even have the maps?"

She waved her hand impatiently. "They aren't important, they're merely his excuse. This isn't the first time he's tried to get his hands on me."

Drew sat forward. "Wait a minute, you're saying *you* are the ransom?"

"Did I forget to mention that?"

He reacted to her sarcastic tone by sitting back again and crossing his arms over his chest. Then he shrugged to show he couldn't care less. "If it's not a position you want to be in, I'm sure you'll figure a way out of it. You pirates are nothing if not resourceful."

She remembered his brief moment of guilt and said, "*You* could help me."

He actually burst out laughing. "Nice try, wench, but not a chance."

"Your brother-in-law, James, would have," she pointed out stiffly.

"Then you should have asked him."

She gritted her teeth. "You could at least leave me my crew."

"Forget it. I warned you what would happen when you stole my ship. And there's only one reason you're not going to jail with the rest of them. I'd keep that in mind because it's a decision that *can* be reversed very easily. So I'd drop it if I were you."

He wasn't going to give any ground, obviously, and she wasn't about to plead with him, so she started walking back to her bed. "I'd appreciate it if you'd leave now and let me get some sleep," she said frostily.

He laughed again, but this time there was too much male satisfaction in it, which was all the warning she needed to know she wouldn't like what he was going to say next. For once, she wished she was wrong.

"There's no lock on the door of this cabin, but you'll be glad to know I'm going to give you the same courtesy you gave me, wench. Shall we?"

He'd stood up and was holding his arm out to indicate the door. She marched stiffly toward it, but stopped when she realized she was wearing only the robe and nothing under it. While it might not make any difference to him, she'd rather not finish the voyage half dressed. Nor was she going to count on his supplying her with a change of clothes, so she went back to the wardrobe and stuffed some of her garments into her carpetbag before she headed to her new prison.

Chapter 34

"Same courtesy" really had been the key phrase. Gabrielle had actually assumed she'd be put in the hold with her crew, but that's not what she'd done with Drew, and he was giving her back tit for tat exactly, including the same area of his cabin that he'd occupied—and the shackle.

He put the damn thing on her himself and seemed to take an inordinate amount of pleasure in doing so. Unlike Timothy's chain, Drew's was still firmly attached to the wall. It had been removed from him normally, the tools that had opened it still lying there on the floor. So it was in good if rusty shape, for her use.

But Drew didn't need to use the tools. He

pulled a padlock out of his pocket that he must have found before he went looking for her, proving that this had been what he intended for her before he even entered her cabin. Had he intended the lovemaking, too, or had that, at least, been spontaneous? She wasn't going to ask.

She tried to ignore his fingers touching her leg as he fastened the cold metal around her bare ankle, but like everything else that had occured tonight, she had no luck with that either. She watched him, though, with a mixture of rage and bruised feelings. There was a tightness in her chest, but she couldn't imagine what was causing it. Indigestion, she hoped.

He glanced up to smile at her when he was done. She glared back at him. He chuckled softly and moved over to his bed. He removed only his boots and shirt to sleep, stretched widely with his arms, then almost dove at the soft mattress. It was a wonder the bed didn't break with that much weight falling on it. Turning over on his back, he crossed his arms behind his head. His sigh of pleasure filled the entire room.

But less than a minute later he said, "Damn, I can smell you on my pillow."

"So wash it," she shot back.

He laughed and turned over, facing away from her, and about ten minutes later she heard some quiet snoring. She ought to make some noise to wake him. He'd certainly tried to keep her awake when their positions had been reversed, and with the most outlandish descriptions of how he wanted to pleasure her, too. She was going to have to give that some thought. Tit for tat in that regard? After all, just because he had his ship back didn't mean she was going to abandon her plan of revenge. Although how she could ever make herself attempt to entice a scoundrel, no, a *blackguard,* no, a *devil* like Drew Anderson, she didn't know. She shook her head and took stock of her surroundings.

He'd left burning the lamp that was bolted to his desk. So she could see to get settled in? No, he probably just forgot to extinguish it, or maybe it was a habit of his, to sleep with a light. But it made it easy to see that the bedding he'd been given was still there for her to use, as well as the chamber pot, which was thankfully empty at the moment, and his empty plate from dinner.

Her eyes went back to the chamber pot

and stayed there with a frown. Good heavens, how was she going to manage that now? Would he give her any privacy at all? If he didn't, she'd make him wish he had. She'd just have to forget the word "embarrassment" for a while.

She started to change her clothes to get more decent to sleep but stopped, deciding she'd rather have the loose comfort of the robe. Actually . . .

Why not? She took the robe off, too. Let him have an eyeful in the morning if he bothered to look. It might make him wild with desire, which she could then nip in the bud, because she wasn't about to let *that* happen again. The more he wanted her, the closer she'd get to her revenge. But what if he didn't want her anymore, now that he'd had her? Damn, she hadn't thought of that. Well, she wouldn't know the answer to that until another day. For now, she had to *try* to get some sleep herself.

With a sigh she lay down and wrapped herself in Drew's blankets—bloody hell, she could smell *him,* too. She was going to have to demand fresh bedding. Tomorrow. Pulling her legs up to curl into a ball, she felt that cold iron scrap against her ankle.

She sighed again and sat back up to examine the metal constriction; precisely, she tested how rough the shackle was going to be against her skin. It had abraded his. She'd like to avoid that if she could. It had been much tighter on him, of course. It had been built for a man's foot, not a woman's. She moved it to see how much give and take she actually had, then stared incredulously as it slipped right off her foot.

She had to put her hand over her mouth to help conceal her laughter. And she didn't waste a moment, immediately slipping her robe back on and tiptoeing straight to the door. And she found it locked tight.

She silently swore a blue streak to herself as she returned to the bedding on the floor. She heard Drew mumble. He'd heard her. But he didn't wake and she glared furiously at his naked back before she got back under the blankets. She even slipped the shackle back over her foot. There would be other opportunities when that door wouldn't be locked. She smiled and looked forward to tomorrow.

Chapter 35

Gabrielle woke to find herself alone in the captain's cabin. Not much light filtered into the room from the bank of windows. It was morning, but a glance outside showed the sun was covered by dark clouds, which suggested a storm sometime that day.

She dressed quickly in the clothes she'd carried in last night, her ship's togs. It was the first time she'd ever had the room to herself, without Drew or one of her friends being present. She took advantage of that and went straight to Drew's desk to rummage through it. She was disappointed to find nothing that she might use as a weapon. A woman's garter, probably a memento of one of his "sweethearts in every port." A miniature of Drew's sister Georgina. Lots of invoices that were all ship or cargo related. No weapons, not even a letter opener.

The ship's logbook was on top of the desk, though. It hadn't been there while she'd occupied the cabin. She glanced through it now to see if he had updated it this morning, but the last entry had been made the morning he'd set sail from London. She hadn't expected to find any personal thoughts in it anyway. These books served a purpose, were a record of their ships, not their captains.

She looked toward his trunks next, but since she had no idea how much time she was going to have alone, she moved quickly to test the door instead. And frowned to find it still locked. Why? Did he know the shackle didn't fit her? Had he put it on her foot merely symbolically, a little revenge of his own? Blast it. She certainly wasn't going to get out of the room this way.

She'd formulated a plan last night. But it had been based entirely on the assumption that she wouldn't be locked in this room permanently. Now what? Wait until he was asleep, then bash him over the head again so she could get the key out of his pocket? Did he think she wouldn't? Bash him over the head, that is. The chamber pot could be quite handy for that, being the heaviest item in the room other than the lantern hanging from one of the support posts. Or did he really not know that the shackle didn't fit her?

She didn't know what to think now, but she did know that she didn't want to hurt him again, which left her with options that she didn't like at all. The trouble was, she'd had hopes where he was concerned, so her emotions were still involved. If they weren't, then she wouldn't even give bashing him over the head again a second thought. But she'd actually moved him to the top of her list of men she'd like to spend the rest of her life with. He'd ruined that when he'd ruined her, but the anger she'd felt had only masked that disappointment. It was still there, lurking under the surface of her bitterness. But still, despite what he'd done to her, she wanted to leave him with a broken heart, not hurt him physically.

With a deep sigh, because she obviously wasn't going to get anything accomplished for the moment, she moved back to her pile of bedding on the floor. She caught the aroma of food this time and found the plate that had been left for her. It had been covered with a large napkin nearly the same color as her blanket, which was probably why she hadn't noticed it sooner. And it was immediately apparent to her, even before she tasted the breakfast, that Drew's cook was definitely better in the galley than hers.

Gabrielle was quite bored by the time Drew showed up several hours later. She'd come to no further conclusions, though she did finish her search through the cabin— and his trunks. Which turned out to be at least interesting, if annoying. The annoying part even amazed her when she figured out that it was nothing other than old-fashioned jealousy on her part. But then, one of Drew's trunks contained nothing but women's belongings.

Everything in it looked new. A parasol, a silk purse, a gaudy fan, a pretty if cheap locket on a chain, and other assorted baubles. There were also at least half a dozen lacy scarves, but all identical, which made her realize that all the items were probably presents. For his many sweethearts? The thought made her want to burn the entire contents of that trunk, and she even glanced briefly at the lantern hooked to the post. If the smoke wouldn't travel and cause an alarm, she probably would have done it.

When Drew finally walked in around noon, she was sitting on her pile of blankets, leaning back against the wall, her feet flat on the floor, her knees bent in front of her. She gave him a sultry look as he crossed the room, but she was so furious it probably looked more like a glare.

He needed no practice for sultry looks. The one he turned on her made her catch her breath and scramble quickly for a distraction before that sensual stirring in her belly got the better of her.

"I'm bored," she blurted out.

That brought their reversed circumstances immediately back to his mind and had him smirking. "Too bad," he said as he continued across the room to the table that had his charts spread out over it.

He studied the one on top for a few minutes, made some notations on it, then moved over to the desk and got comfortable in his chair, legs stretched out under the desk, fingers twined with his hands resting on his belly. He wasn't planning on ignoring her. As soon as he was settled, his eyes came back to her.

She glanced away before she caught his look, but she could feel his dark eyes moving leisurely over her now. As long as she didn't actually meet his gaze, she should be able to avoid getting flustered by him again. She could hope.

While he wasn't there, she'd managed to avoid thinking about last night and the amazing pleasure he'd given her. It was much more difficult to push it out of her mind when he was present and stirring her senses with the attraction to him that she couldn't seem to shake.

"Now, explain to me why I should make an effort to amuse you, when you didn't exactly relieve my boredom when I was sitting where you are," he reminded her.

"I don't recall you mentioning it," she said with a thoughtful frown, then raised a brow at him. "Still working on tit for tat, are we? If you want to get specific, I didn't steal your virginity either, as it happens, but *you* certainly added that new wrinkle. You ruined me socially, stole my virginity. No decent man will want me now!"

"You're a pirate!" He almost laughed. "No

decent man would have married you any-way."

She sucked in her breath. "What a rotten thing to say, and it's not even true! A man who'd had a chance to fall in love with me might have overlooked my father's occupa-tion. But not now, after you stole my virgin-ity."

He coughed, sat forward, and no longer looked the least bit comfortable. But he did point out, "I didn't steal it. Your cooperation was delightfully noted."

"I thought you were a dream, you bloody sod!" she snarled at him.

"Did you really? Many ladies who share my bed say the same thing—that I'm a dream."

He sounded too amused now. "That's not what I meant!" she snapped angrily. "I really thought I was dreaming."

"Did you?"

"Yes."

"I wish to hell I had dreams like that." He grinned. "But now that you mention it, I've always found lovemaking to be the perfect remedy for boredom. Care to while away the afternoon in my bed?"

"*That* isn't going to happen again!"

He shrugged. "I'm sure you mean that quite sincerely at the moment. But you've had a taste," he said. Then, with complete confidence and a winsome smile, he assured her, "You'll want more."

"Possibly," she allowed, then added with her own shrug, "Just not with you."

His lips tightened just enough for her to notice. She was delighted to know she'd struck a chord at last. And now would be a good time to change the subject, before she got caught up in that same chord.

"What have you done with Margery?" she asked.

"I assume you mean your maid?"

"Housekeeper," she corrected.

"Whatever," he said with little interest. "I've allowed her to retain the cabin she was using. She's fine. She slept through the commotion."

"May I see her?"

"Want to start bargaining for favors?" he countered with a roguish grin.

She drew in her breath and glared at him. "What I want is to be put to work to occupy my time. There isn't much that I don't know how to do on a ship."

He actually seemed to give it some

thought, then said, "The decks need swabbing."

She nodded, thinking he was serious. "It wouldn't be the first time I've tackled that job."

"Are you joking?"

"No." And then she sighed. "But I suppose you were?"

"Of course I was. You're not leaving this cabin until we make port, sweetheart. Sorry, but I don't trust you any further than I can see you."

"I don't have my crew at my back, so what are you worried about?"

"That you'll try to get them at your back again. And this isn't up for debate, so forget it."

"But—"

"Want me to remember that I was gagged some of the time while I was your captive?" he cut in sharply.

She got the point and shut up—for now.

Chapter 36

Drew had the three miscreants brought before him on the quarterdeck, the three he'd shared his cabin with after Gabby had taken the cowardly route and moved out of it. One of them had planted a fist in his face last week when he'd been sleeping. He'd never been able to guess which one had done it, nor had he asked, since he'd been in no position to retaliate or protect himself at the time. But that situation had changed nicely.

They each had their hands tied behind them. He made them wait nearly an hour before he approached them to get his answers.

He knew them by name now, after sharing the cabin with all three of them. Bixley looked wary about why Drew had had them brought up from the hold, but then Bixley was the last one he would suspect of having a reason to assault him when he wasn't looking, as it were.

Richard was wearing a cocky grin as usual. The Frenchman, if he even was French, which Drew suspected he wasn't, appeared not to have a serious bone in his body. He was always joking about something with his friends, including Gabby. That might have annoyed Drew; hell, it did annoy him.

Ohr was the enigma among them. He seemed to be close to Gabby, but he wasn't demonstrative. The man kept his emotions, whatever they were, strictly to himself.

Of the two, Drew suspected Ohr was the one who'd hit him. Richard was too happy-go-lucky. Nothing appeared to bother him; in fact, he reminded Drew a lot of himself. But Ohr was too serious. There was no telling what emotions simmered beneath his quiet demeanor. Drew intended to find out, though.

"What's this about, Captain?" Bixley asked in a nervous tone when Drew moved over to stand in front of them.

He didn't answer immediately. Suspense could make the men uneasy, which would benefit him. Besides, having the upper hand with these particular fellows was distinctly satisfying, so he was in no hurry to rush through the interrogation.

"Relax," he finally said. "I just have some questions for you. I merely have to determine which of you will have the answers."

"Sounds puzzling," Richard remarked.

"Probably just needs some sails fixed," Bixley put in. "And I'm the man for that."

"My sails are fine," Drew disagreed.

"Not fine enough for that storm that's a-brewing. I can smell it in the air."

"He's got eyes, Bix. He can see there is a storm heading this way."

"But he hasn't fixed those sails yet," Bixley countered. "They'll be ripped to shreds if—"

"Are you actually telling me how to run my ship?" Drew cut in incredulously. He'd wanted these three nervous about why he'd summoned them, but all they wanted to do was talk about the ship!

"We're sailors, Captain, same as you," Richard said with a grin. "If we see something wrong with a ship, we're not going to keep it to ourselves."

"I'll fix the damn sails," Drew replied. "Now answer me this. Which one of you planted your fist in my cheek last week while I was sleeping?"

Bixley started to laugh. "So that's what that bruise was from? Wondered about it. And here I'd been thinking ye tripped over yer blankets in the dark."

Drew wasn't the least bit amused. He moved to stand in front of the Irishman and said, "Shall we start with you, then, Bixley?"

"Start?" The man blinked and, his expression turned wary again.

"Why not?" Drew said. "It's called process of elimination. I'm sure you've heard of it."

"Ain't heard of it, and don't care to be in the front of the line to be experiencing it, either. It weren't me that punched ye in the dark."

"No?" Drew said calmly, then glanced at Ohr, then Richard, but those two were both wearing blank looks now. So he added with a sigh, "As I thought, we will have to find out the hard way, then."

The punch knocked Bixley down.

Sprawled on the deck, he made no move to get back up for more.

Richard spoke up. "There's no need for that. If you want a fight, untie me. I'm the one you're looking for."

Drew nodded and signaled the men he had standing by to take Ohr and Bixley back to the hold. He was somewhat surprised. Perhaps there was more between Gabby and the supposed Frenchman than he'd thought.

Bixley grumbled at Richard as he was helped to his feet, "Speak up sooner next time, eh."

Richard winced and mumbled, "Sorry, Bix."

Drew studied Richard's handsome face as the other two men were led off. He felt anger rising up for what he was starting to suspect. What would stir up fighting emotions in the Frenchman? Drew had done nothing more to Gabby than kiss her a few times in England before he sailed. He'd *wanted* to do more, but she hadn't cooperated.

Richard grew uncomfortable under the extended scrutiny and finally said in a sharp tone, "What? It was just one bloody punch."

"I wouldn't have guessed you," Drew said now that he and Richard were alone.

Richard grinned. "Neither would I, if you must know. It was an impulse, quite unplanned."

"Why?"

Richard shrugged. "Felt you deserved it and more."

Since Drew felt nothing of the kind, he snarled, "You want a piece of me? Let's hear the reason."

"Are you joking, man? After what you did?"

That took Drew by surprise and brought forth a thoughtful frown. "I know what I've done recently, but we're talking about last week when I was a prisoner in chains unable to *do* anything other than stew."

"I told you, it was just an impulse."

Drew didn't buy that, but he gave Richard a thoughtful look. "Why do you pretend to be French?"

The man just grinned wider. "Why do you assume I'm not just because my speech might change a bit occasionally? Maybe I'm a Frenchman who grew up in London."

"Maybe you're a liar."

Richard shrugged. "What difference does

it make, eh? We all pretend to be something we're not."

"Even Gabby?"

"Gabby is whatever she wants you to think she is," Richard replied cryptically.

Drew snorted. "Which means?"

"That if you want to know about her, you should be asking her, not me."

"Then let's get back to you and your blasted reason for attacking me."

"Sorry, can't oblige you, Captain. I've been sworn to secrecy. How about you just accept my apology and leave it go at that?"

"How about you satisfy my curiosity before I beat it out of you?"

"Have at me, then. I don't betray my friends."

"You're saying she's just a friend?"

"You thought otherwise when she was thinking about marrying you?"

That word "marrying" in reference to him actually had Drew taking a step back. The very thought of marriage made him shudder. But he was finding it hard to believe that Gabby had entertained those thoughts. And, in fact, Richard could be feeding him a pack of lies just to throw him off track.

But he was still curious enough to ask, "Did she tell you that?"

"I've said too much already," Richard rejoined. "I'm saying no more."

"So it wasn't jealousy that had you attacking me?" Drew persisted.

Richard snorted. "You don't listen too well, Captain. She's my best friend. Whoever she ends up marrying will be fine with me, well, as long as it's not you."

"Then you *are* jealous!"

"No, I just don't like what you did to her. I tried to give her some excuses for it, but I didn't really believe any of them m'self."

Drew ground his teeth together. He was so frustrated at the moment, it was a wonder he hadn't knocked the pirate on his ass yet. But then it occurred to him . . .

"I got her drunk to try and seduce her, but my blasted brother interrupted us, so I didn't get very far. Is that what this is all about? Did she think something else happened while she was tipsy?"

Richard shrugged. "She never mentioned that, so I've no idea."

"What *did* she mention?"

"Nice try, Captain, but that secret is going with me to the grave. So have at me or send me back to the hold, because this conversation ends now either way."

Richard was taking it for granted that Drew wouldn't lay a hand on him. His confident tone said as much. Drew should have disappointed him, if for no other reason than to get rid of the frustration he was currently feeling over learning next to nothing from this futile exercise. But he let him go. He was going to have to take this subject up with Gabby instead, obviously. But she wasn't exactly in an appeasing frame of mind either, so she would probably just make his frustration a lot worse.

He should have just put her in the hold with her crew. It was no more than she deserved for trying to steal his ship. But she'd given him more pleasure than he'd expected when he found her sleeping in her cabin that night, an experience he couldn't get out of his mind.

God, that had been sweet, but making love to her had its drawbacks, too—in particular, that that one time with her should have been enough for him, but it wasn't. With every other woman, once was just fine. He revisited his many sweethearts merely for convenience, not because he was eager to see them again. But with Gabby, he wanted more. Despite his guilt.

And that was another thing that perplexed him. Who would have thought a damned pirate would turn out to be virginal. That still amazed him. But it was kind of sweet, too, that he was the first man for her. Another new experience for him, though, because it certainly wasn't something he looked for in his women. Just the opposite. He preferred women with a good deal of experience. They knew the game, and that marriage wasn't one of the prizes.

Had Gabby really thought about him for a husband? He smiled and shook his head. He was going to find out.

Chapter 37

The storm that had been threatening all day arrived that afternoon with a vengeance. Gabrielle had been hoping that it would just blow away, or at least that *The Triton* would outrun it, but neither occurred.

In the middle of a violent torrential onslaught was the one time she didn't like being on a ship. Actually, ever since she'd lived through that hurricane that struck the islands, she didn't like rainstorms no matter where she was. But being at sea added an extra element of danger. Sinking.

It was a fine ship, though—sturdy, well maintained. The creaking of its planks was minimal. Even the sharp dipping and careening didn't get out of hand, at least not right away. It was inevitable, though. And so was Gabrielle's nervous reaction, made ten times worse by the fact that she was locked in a cabin. If the ship did go down, she wouldn't even have a chance to find a dinghy, piece of wreckage, or any other sort of raft where she could then hope for rescue. No, she'd be going straight down to Davy Jones's locker.

She sat there huddled in her blankets for the longest time, watching the few things in the room that weren't nailed down roll back and forth across the floor and, at one point, halfway up the wall. That had been a terrifying moment, when the ship dipped almost horizontally as it rode down that one particularly huge wave.

Even the lantern went flying off its post in that moment of gut-wrenching fear. The glass in it shattered as it rolled across the floor and smashed against the wall, leaving a trail of spilled oil in its wake.

She stared at it with a mixture of horror and relief. The fire probably would have been instant if the lantern had been lit. While she'd actually thought about it, if she were going to start a fire to try to make her escape, this absolutely wasn't the time to do it, when Drew and his crew were fighting the elements to keep them afloat and wouldn't notice a fire until it was too late. But at least she'd had the wits to extinguish it when the storm began, leaving only the lamp that was secured solidly to Drew's desk still burning.

She wished she could sleep through the storm. That would be an ideal way to put her worry aside, to just wake up when it was all over. But it was impossible to even try in her position on the floor, where she was holding tight to her chain to keep from being tossed about just as much as everything else was that wasn't nailed down. She could probably find better purchase in Drew's bed, at least a softer cushion for all the sliding she was doing. But that was one place she wasn't getting anywhere near, now that it was his again.

She didn't expect to see him again until the storm was over. Night had arrived, though it was hard to tell with that solid sheet of rain outside the windows and nothing but black clouds beyond it. Several more hours passed, but the storm still gave no sign of abating.

And then a cold blast of wind and rain entered along with Drew. He had to shove the door to get it to close. He didn't bother to lock it again. He turned and leaned back against it as his eyes located her. He didn't look the least bit worn out or downtrodden after spending hours out in that downpour. He looked exhilarated, full of vim and vigor, as if he could take on anything without batting an eye.

He tossed off the rain slicker he'd been wearing, though it hadn't kept him from getting soaked. "Are you all right?" he asked.

Her nerves shot, she said, "No, I'm frightened, I'm cold, I'm hungry, and my arse is bruised from all this tossing about. I'm bloody well not all right."

She expected him to laugh and call her a ninny. Instead he amazed her by making his way to her, kneeling down beside her, and drawing her into his arms. She didn't have a single urge to resist the closeness he offered, even though he drenched her with his wet clothes.

He made himself comfortable against the wall, then pulled her halfway across his chest. He took a napkin out of his pocket, opened it to reveal a handful of cold sausages cut in little chunks. He put one in her mouth.

"Leftovers from breakfast," he said. "The galley is closed for the duration, so there won't be a full meal, probably not until tomorrow. You should know that's standard procedure."

"Yes, I know," she replied as he fed her a few more chunks that took the edge off her hunger.

"Are you really bruised?" he asked.

The question made them both think of the last time he'd asked about her bruises, when she'd accused him of leaving her with some after their first meeting on the docks. The thought made them grin at each other.

"No, just a bit sore," she admitted. "I doubt I'll feel it tomorrow. Be careful crossing the floor, though. We haven't been steady enough for me to try to pick up that glass that broke from your lantern yet."

"I should have thought to remove that lantern when the storm started."

"You weren't here to do that. I was, but all I thought to do was turn it off."

She realized too late that she'd just admitted that she could move about the cabin just fine, that the shackle was no restraint for her at all. But he gave no indication that he caught that slip, merely fed her a few more sausages before he ate some himself.

She shouldn't be sitting like this with him, pretty much cradled in his arms, but she couldn't bring herself to move yet, she was so comfortable. His wet clothes had been cold to start, but where her body was pressed to them was now warm from her own heat. In fact, steam could have risen between them, it was getting so warm.

There was simply no way she could ignore the body she was leaning against, or not think of what it had done to her the other night. The kind of pleasure he'd introduced her to had been beyond her comprehension before then, but now . . . she simply couldn't get it out of her mind. He'd said it himself, she'd had a taste, she'd want more, and damned if he hadn't been right.

The way he was holding her now brought back so clearly the memory of how his hands had felt moving so sensually over her bare skin, she nearly drew in her breath. And his mouth, God, the feel of it, the heady taste of it. He'd made her tremble, he'd made her skin tingle deliciously, he'd made her throw caution to the wind and accept everything that he offered.

She shivered, remembering just how sweet her surrender had been. He felt it.

She'd only vaguely heard the clap of thunder that had just occurred, but he guessed that was the reason. "You're afraid of the storm?"

"I never used to be, but we had such a bad one a few years back, they called it a hurricane. People died. Whole buildings were ripped to shreds. I'd never seen anything like it and hope to never see anything like it again."

"This was in the Caribbean?"

"Yes, after I'd been living with my father for a while. It tore through those warm waters with a vengeance. St. Kitts wasn't the only island it hit. It left a wide path of destruction behind it."

He pulled her a little closer to him. "I think I remember that one. I only just missed it myself, had sailed back to America a few days before. But I heard about it on my next trip and witnessed some of the damage. Some areas still haven't recovered."

She nodded. "One of the smaller villages on our island was like that. With every single house demolished in it, the survivors simply packed up and moved elsewhere. But even in our major town, it took months and months for us to get rid of all the debris and rebuild. I forgot what it was like to sleep back then."

He glanced down at her in surprise. "You actually pitched in to help?"

"Margery and I did." But then she grinned and tried to make light of it, so it wouldn't sound so unpiratelike, and added, "It was either that or wait forever for the butcher shop to reopen."

He didn't laugh. He touched her cheek with the back of his fingers, almost like he was telling her he knew she wasn't as bad as she pretended to be. It made her uncomfortable when he showed her this tender side of him. It also reminded her that she was lying in the arms of the man she still meant to get even with.

"I think I'm fine now," she told him, sitting up to lean away from him. "It even sounds like the wind has died down a bit."

"No it doesn't. And maybe I'm not so fine now," he replied as he pulled her back against him and firmly fastened his mouth to hers.

That damn quickly, all of the amazing passion that she'd felt the other night was back to inflame her and push away all of her resolve. She put her arms around his neck and returned his kiss wholeheartedly, and did some improvising of her own, tasting him with her tongue. He was so intoxicating! She even turned slightly, enough to press her breasts hard against his chest. His groan was sweet music to her ears.

It wasn't long before he stood up, lifting her in his arms, and carried her to his bed. Without pausing once, he seemed not to even think about the shackle. What a cold dousing it would have been if it had still been attached to her ankle and had pulled them back. Nothing prevented him from laying her on his bed and stripping out of his wet clothes with such haste. She certainly didn't. She was too busy watching him with bated anticipation as each piece of clothing was tossed aside.

This was her first real unobstructed view of his tall, splendid body in all its glory. When she'd bathed him she'd tried not to look so she wouldn't succumb to her desire for him, and when he'd made love to her before, he'd already been on top of her by the time she realized he was really there bare naked. But now she was amazed at how much it thrilled her to see him like this. He was so lean and muscular. There was no part of him that didn't ripple with muscle as he moved, from his wide chest that tapered to those lean flanks, to his strong arms. Such long limbs—even his legs were proportioned just right to the rest of his fine, athletic physique. It took her breath away, how handsome he was.

She laughed when he dove onto the bed because it bounced them a few times. He did as well. But then he was rolling them over and he began to swiftly remove her clothes.

She placed a hand over his and shyly reminded him, "Didn't you promise to remove my clothes slowly?"

He brought her hand to his mouth and kissed the back of her fingers. "I remember. I'll try, Gabby, but I have to confess, you make me feel like an untried youth, I have so little control when I get near you. This isn't the first time. There's nothing more I'd like to do than savor every delicious moment with you, but my God, you fill me with such passion!"

She felt some of that passion now as he kissed her, again and again. But he tried, he really did, to remove her clothes slowly. He even kissed her arms and legs as they were exposed. He just got rid of her shirt rather quickly so he could fasten his mouth to her breasts, which drove her a little wild herself.

A few times he gasped, "My God, woman, you are so beautiful," as he gazed down at her breasts, and again when he turned her over to kiss the small of her back and ran his hands slowly up the back of her thighs.

She shivered deliciously. His touch was so gentle, his mouth so hot, such an extraordinary contrast.

"I think you're beautiful as well," she said, and he laughed.

What they were doing was even more beautiful. The wonder of his touch dazzled her as he caressed her arms, her neck, her cheek; even her toes didn't escape his notice. But the passion was there, just under the surface, barely contained. She felt it when he finally gathered her close and kissed her deeply, and it seemed the passion caught up and overtook her before it did him.

It all happened so fast, she had no time to

think about anything other than the pleasure that she knew was only moments away. And there it was, exploding around her the very moment he entered her. Good God, so quickly it happened, so sublime, and it lasted so long, she was even still throbbing around him moments later when he stiffened and plunged deep for his own climax.

Her sigh of contentment was almost a purr. She didn't want to move, didn't want to think, didn't want to consider what she'd just done—again.

"Sleep here where you'll be comfortable," he said with a kiss to her brow just before he left the bed. "I'll go get rid of the storm for you."

Half asleep already, she did hear him and smiled over that whimsical comment. Battle storms just for her, would he? What a silly, sweet man.

Chapter 38

Gabrielle woke to sunshine pooling across the floor. The storm was over. If Drew had returned to the cabin, it wasn't to wake her. She had the room to herself and dressed quickly, then immediately checked the door. Still locked.

She sighed and moved back to sit on her blankets, but changed her mind and moved to his bed instead. She made it up neatly first, then sat in the middle of it. Much more comfortable, and why not? Obviously, if he'd thought she was shackled to begin with, he knew better now and wasn't going to try to restrain her in some other way, well, other than the damned locked door.

Her plan for revenge wasn't working. How

the deuce was Drew Anderson going to go mad with desire for her if she kept letting him make love to her? She was going to have to change her strategy. Never mind making him just want her so much it would drive him crazy, she was going to have to make him love her instead.

It was a daunting thought. It would be much harder to accomplish, she was sure. Lust had been easy. She'd already managed that, just not with the intended results. But was it even possible for a man to fall in love and not consider marriage? Well, yes, a Lothario like Drew, he was probably the only man who could love a woman and not give a single thought to marrying her. And once she was gone, he'd go on to his other women, and with each one of them he'd be thinking of her instead. Perfect! She'd bloody well haunt him for the rest of his life!

But how was she going to get him to love her? She'd wanted it to happen in London, but it hadn't. Of course, he hadn't been around often enough to get to know her there. Here, keeping her in his cabin, he'd set himself up so he couldn't avoid her. So let him get to know the real her? Including giving up her ruse and confiding that she wasn't really a pirate?

No, maybe she shouldn't go that far. The ruse still allowed her to be more bold than she would be otherwise. And how much sweeter her revenge would be if he fell in love with her while still thinking she was a pirate.

She hadn't made a firm decision by the time he returned to the cabin that morning. This time he looked exhausted. Well, he'd been up for over twenty-four hours and then some, and had probably spent most of that time fighting to keep his ship afloat.

The chap who usually delivered their meals followed Drew in and set a large tray on the table. Gabrielle bolted out of the bed and went straight to the tray, which contained two plates filled to the brim with breakfast fixings. She sat down immediately and started eating.

Glancing up, she found him grinning at her. "What?" she said. "You think those few sausages you fed me yesterday satisfied my hunger?"

"That has a nice ring to it, doesn't it?"

"What does?"

"That I fed you."

She knew instantly that his thoughts had taken a sensual turn, though she couldn't imagine why. She pointed to the tray and asked, "Aren't you hungry?"

"I'm starving," he replied.

But he was still just standing there staring at her, and this time she blushed. He was talking about lovemaking again. How could he even think of that, as tired, and hungry as he must be?

She decided to pretend she didn't understand his double entendre and turn the screw a little at the same time. "I enjoyed sleeping in your bed last night," she said around a mouthful of fresh, warm bread dripping with sweet jam. "That was quite possibly the best sleep I've had in weeks. It was certainly the most comfortable. Thank you for thinking of it."

His face actually flushed. She was, of course, just talking about the bed and he knew that, but, apparently, it didn't stop him from thinking about what they'd done there.

After a few moments in a mere conversational tone, he mentioned, "It's long been my habit to celebrate after surviving a storm

like that, so I'm having some guests to dinner tonight. Since you're sharing my cabin,
I suppose you'll have to join us. I'll have a
dress delivered to you later today, after I get
some sleep."

She sighed. They were having a perfectly
normal conversation and he had to throw in
that "I suppose" remark to remind her that
she was a prisoner, not a guest.

"Why?" she asked, her tone a little stiff
now. "I have no one to impress."

He shrugged. "Most of the women I know
enjoy dressing up, I merely thought you
might like to."

He said no more, and after his exhausting
night, he climbed into bed and was almost
instantly asleep. Gabrielle spent most of the
remainder of the day pacing about the
room, mulling over her new plan to make
Drew love her, and trying to ignore his presence.

She finally gave some attention to him
again when she found herself inadvertently
stopped next to his bed. He was snoring,
not loudly and not steadily, just off and on.
He really was exhausted. She could probably make all sorts of noise and he wouldn't
hear it. She could even touch him and he

wouldn't wake, so he wouldn't know. Damned trusting of him, to leave himself locked in with her when she wasn't restrained.

She could very easily leave the room right then. A little bash on the head with the chamber pot and she'd have the key out of Drew's pocket within seconds. She'd seen him shove it there after his man dropped off the tray of food and left, and he'd relocked the door.

So simple. But the middle of the day wasn't a good time for her to try to sneak down to the hold. Besides, every muscle in her body was resisting hitting Drew over the head. She just couldn't bring herself to do that again. Which didn't mean she was giving up on escaping. He could well sleep until dark. If she had the key . . .

She stared at the pocket where her freedom resided. Drew was lying on his side. He was twisted a bit, his bottom leg stretched out straight, the top one bent. The pocket with the key in it was the top one. If his pants weren't so snug, she'd have no trouble slipping a couple fingers in there to extract the key. But the pants were snug. Very. They clung tightly to his derriere in that position, defining his back cheeks. A very nice arse Drew Anderson had.

She rolled her eyes over the thought and got back to her pacing.

Chapter 39

There were four of them dining that night in the captain's cabin. Drew's first mate had been invited, which was expected. Timothy had come for dinner the night before as well. But the fourth man bowled Gabrielle over when he entered with the first mate. Richard! She was so glad to see him she didn't think how it might look when she threw herself at him and hugged him excitedly.

Gabrielle did get off two quick whispered questions before she noticed Drew staring at her. "All of you are all right?" she asked.

"As well as can be expected in our crowded accommodations," he replied. "But our host kindly provided appropriate dinner attire." Richard swept a hand over his freshly washed white shirt and black britches.

"But what the devil are you doing *here*?"

"Your guess is as good as mine, *chérie*," he whispered back at her. "I was told, warned was more like it, merely to act like I am *not* a prisoner."

She glanced at Drew upon hearing that, but he just smiled and sat back to watch the reunion. Richard leaned toward her. "And may I say how lovely you look tonight, Gabrielle." He eyed her simple pink ball gown with the dramatic décolletage. "I imagine our captain provided your attire as well. He wants to enjoy himself tonight." Richard winked at her. Gabrielle blushed, but she didn't try to speak to Richard privately again. Drew had to have some reason for including Richard other than she'd be glad to see him, and that reason worried her.

The food arrived soon after Richard's arrival. It took four crewmen to carry in the assortment of platters, and one came in with an armful of wine bottles. Richard, glad to be out of the hold, started drinking more than he ought to. Gabrielle barely touched the wine herself.

Drew had ordered excellence from his cook, and by far it was not a meal one might expect to have at sea. Roast beef offered with two different gravies, glazed onions and carrots, three different rolls to choose from, Yorkshire pudding, roasted potatoes, and even a salad topped with a creamy garlic dressing. Gabrielle was going to *have* to find out how Drew's cook managed to keep lettuce fresh at sea, she really was.

The mood turned quite festive with such hearty food before them. It even began to feel like a real celebration. Richard relaxed and amused the group with his usual banter. Gabrielle stopped worrying that he'd been brought there for some ulterior reason. And even Drew seemed to be enjoying himself.

"By the way," Timothy said to Drew during a lull in the conversation. "On one of those ships we spotted briefly right before the storm, the lookout swears he saw your sister and brother-in-law on its deck."

Gabrielle blanched, hearing that. Drew, on the other hand, burst out laughing.

Drew began, "I hate to say I told you so—"

"Yes, I'm sure it breaks your heart, so don't," Gabrielle cut in tartly, thoroughly annoyed by his amusement. "The lookout was probably mistaken anyway."

And Richard joined in, "Oh, I say, is that Lady Malory he's talking about?"

"Oh, good grief, Richard," Gabby snapped. "Forget about her!"

Her friend winced, but then shrugged. "I've *tried,* Gabby. Really I have, but I just can't forget about my one true love."

Drew sobered now and demanded, "Is he talking about my sister?"

"Why yes, he is," Gabrielle fairly purred at the captain, though her eyes were glaring at him. "Fell quite head over heels for her. Won't listen to sound advice, like her husband is going to break every bone in his body if he gets anywhere near her."

"James will have to stand in line," Drew growled as he stood up and took a step toward Richard.

That was unexpected and had Gabrielle instantly regretting that she'd provoked him. She leapt between the two men to try to defuse what she'd instigated.

"Oh, stop it," she told Drew. "Georgina nearly slapped Richard's face off the last time they spoke, so nothing untoward has or will ever happen between them. She's a bulwark of resistance where any other man is concerned, simply because she loves her husband. You ought to know that."

It was a tense moment. Drew obviously took protecting his sister seriously. Every line of his body said he was ready to rip Richard apart with his bare hands. But he *was* paying attention, thankfully, and Gabrielle's last remark took the edge off his anger.

"I could have done without that reminder," he said as he moved back to his seat.

Richard had drunk too much wine to be wary. "You should have let him have at me, Gabby," he said. "He's been itching to ever since he thought you and I . . ." The thought made him laugh before he finished it.

"That isn't why I wanted to rip your head off," Drew replied rather calmly, considering the subject matter.

"Ah, that's right, it was because you couldn't remember why Gabby can't go back to England."

Gabrielle drew in her breath sharply. "Richard, that's enough."

But Drew sat forward to ask, "Why can't she go back?"

"With that rumor making the rounds that she's a pirate? Give it a good guess, Captain. I'm sure you'll figure it out."

Gabrielle sat back and closed her eyes. She had a feeling she knew now why Richard had been invited to dinner. Drew had been fishing for information, obviously, something he thought they were keeping from him. Instead he had caught the one subject guaranteed to bring her anger back in full force.

Chapter 40

Timothy tried to redirect the conversation to neutral subjects, but only he and Richard participated. With Drew just staring at Gabrielle, and she just staring at her plate, the tension in the room could have been cut with a knife. They left soon after, with Richard making a joking comment about being eager to get back to the hold, where the air wasn't so frosty. Her anger had prompted that remark. With her scandal on the table, as it were, there was no way Gabrielle could conceal that anger from the man who'd caused it.

Alone with him now, he sat back in his chair, his glass of wine in hand. And he was still just staring at her. Waiting for her to explode? Another few moments and she probably would have.

But he lifted a tawny brow first and said casually, "Odd how I wasn't the only one to guess, isn't it?"

"Guess?"

"Or maybe not so odd," he continued in the same tone, as if she hadn't raised a question and wasn't glaring at him. "I mean, look at the company you keep. And how often did you visit them in the seedier side of town?"

She snorted. "You don't know where my friends resided, and besides—"

"But I do," he cut in. "I followed you one afternoon. Not for any reason other than I was bored that day and, well, maybe a little curious. I must say I was a bit surprised at how easily you and your maid rebuffed those ruffians who tried to make your acquaintance that day. Thought I might have to reveal myself to intervene, but no, I suppose I'd back off, too, if I had two women angrily swinging their purses at my head. It didn't take me long to realize you must be used to that sort of attention."

She vaguely recalled the incident he was talking about, the day she'd gone down to the wharfs to warn Richard that Malory was going to murder him if he even so much as saw Richard again. She'd been very upset with Richard, enough to take it out on anyone who tried to delay her from reaching him so she could tell him just how upset she was over the very real threat now hanging over his head.

But what the devil did any of that have to do with the scandal that Drew had left her with? Or was he just trying to delay addressing that, or hoping he could entirely avoid giving her a reason for what he'd done? It was even possible that he didn't have a reason, that he'd just done it on a lark.

And then, in the same casual tone he was maintaining, he said, "You know, sweetheart, if I didn't make those assumptions about you myself, I never would have kissed you that day we went to the park."

That was so unrelated in her mind to the subject at hand that she couldn't fathom why he'd even mention it to her. And then she realized that the "subject" hadn't really been introduced yet, so he was talking about something else entirely. Or was he?

A bit confused now, she demanded, "Why?"

"Because if I thought you were a virgin, you'd be off-limits to me. So I convinced myself you weren't, for the simple reason that I *had* to taste you. To be honest, it was driving me crazy. Perhaps you can understand that, now that you've had a taste yourself?" She glared at him, causing him to shrug. "No? Well, at the time, I wanted you to have the morals of a pirate, because I knew that was the only way I could have you."

"And because of what *you* wanted, it was perfectly fine to ruin my good name in the country of my birth?" she fairly shouted at him.

He sat forward so abruptly that he sloshed his wine on the table.

She mimicked what he'd said that night at the ball. " 'I wouldn't count on it, unless his father doesn't mind pirates in the family.' "

He laughed. "I was merely joking. And you said it yourself, that it merely embarrassed you."

"Of course it did, but no one there took it as a joke, you ass. What you said made the gossip rounds immediately. Everyone in London thinks I'm a pirate now. Because of you!"

"But you *are* a pirate."

"No I am not!"

She hadn't meant to say that and give up her ruse this soon. But she'd let her anger get in the way because he *still* didn't look the least bit contrite over what he'd done.

Defensive was all he looked, and sounded, when he pointed out, "What the hell do you think stealing my ship was, if not pirating?"

"Just desserts!" she snapped back. "You made sure I couldn't make a good marriage in England, so I took your ship as payback."

"So that was all lies you fed us, about your father needing rescuing?"

"No, that was killing two birds with one stone." She smirked. "A perfect solution for two dilemmas."

"One dilemma. You said that you prefer the islands. That's where you should have looked for a husband, not in England."

She gasped. Was he really trying to remove himself from blame with an excuse like that?

"It was my father's wish that I find a good

match there. It's his hopes, as well as my own that are going to be crushed when he finds out that isn't possible now."

"He aspired too high for a pirate."

Her eyes rounded incredulously. "And you think that exonerates you? Forget about my father for a moment and consider what else you did with your *joke.* My mother's good name was without blemish. So was mine, for that matter, but in fact there's never been a scandal associated with her family. However, in blackening my name, you've also dragged hers through the mud."

Was that finally a remorseful blush rising up his cheeks? Obviously not, because all he said was, "Then she shouldn't have married a pirate."

It was the last straw. She stood up and leaned across the table to shout at him, "She didn't know, you bloody bastard! He took pains to make sure she never knew. I told you that! He took pains to make sure no one in England knew, and why, you might ask? To make sure her good name was protected! But without a moment's hesitation, you just blew all his efforts out of the water, didn't you? On a lark. No, wait, what did you call it? A joke!"

He actually flinched, then said with a sigh, "For what it's worth, that wasn't my intention, so I suppose an apology is in order."

"You suppose?" she bit out. "Well, I *suppose* you won't be surprised when I don't accept your apology. There's nothing you can do to make amends for what you've done, well, unless you help to rescue my father. Then I might, though probably won't, but *might* forgive you."

"Done," he said without hesitation. "But there'll be no 'probably' about it. When he's freed, we're even."

Chapter 41

Gabrielle went to sleep that night on her blankets, a little in shock. She'd said nothing else to Drew, too afraid he might change his mind. She hadn't expected anything to come of her threat to not forgive him unless he helped her rescue her father. She wasn't even sure why she said it. His cavalier attitude up to that point warned she'd be wasting her breath. But, good grief, he'd actually accepted.

After the shock wore off, she had to allow that his guilt must be a lot worse than he'd let on to her. Or maybe he didn't really think there'd be any danger involved. She probably should warn Drew that he could be risking his life and his ship. Pierre was a real pirate, after all, not just a dabbler like her father, who was really a treasure hunter at heart. But if she warned Drew, he might change his mind.

It wasn't much of a dilemma. She'd have to mention it. It would be dishonorable not to. But she was going to wait and see what ideas Drew came up with first for the rescue—just in case he backed out on the deal after she explained fully what he was getting himself into.

The surprises didn't end with his proffered help. The next morning on his way out the door, he told her, "We have a deal, so I'm going to call on your honor, if you have any, and request that you stay away from the hold. Your crew will be released soon enough. You don't need to help in that regard."

All of which made no sense to her until he continued out the door—and left it open. Giving her freedom of his ship? Incredible! But before she started jumping for joy, she examined what he'd just said. Her crew would be let go, but let go for what? To be transferred to the nearest jail? Or to help with the rescue?

He was gone before she could ask, and frankly, she'd rather savor her triumph for a little while before she found out if she still had another rescue to accomplish. But really, Drew would be a fool to not make use of her men, now that he'd agreed to help. Surely he realized that at least.

She didn't bother to change clothes, to take her first steps outside of her brief prison. She was still wearing the dress she'd been supplied with for dinner last night, had been too dazed to even think of changing out of it to sleep. She got curious looks from his crew. Apparently, Drew hadn't told them yet that some of the pirates were no longer being detained under lock and key. But none of them tried to stop her, and after she moved to within sight of Drew, the matter was settled in their minds that he had allowed her the freedom.

She still had nothing to occupy her time, though she wondered if Drew would really object if she just started helping around the ship. She'd have to try that later, but for the moment, she simply enjoyed the sun and fresh air after being denied it for several days, and the view of the quarterdeck, where Drew was manning the wheel. He was such a big man. His extraordinary height and breadth would give most men pause, but he'd never intimidated her. He'd inspired many different responses in her, but fear wasn't one of them.

His love of the sea was obvious. He had an exhilarated look about him, as if there was no other place he'd prefer to be. She'd seen that look on her father, too, many times. But seeing it on Drew made her feel a little sad. No wonder he'd decided never to marry. No woman could ever come close to what he felt for his ship, and the sea.

Not that she cared anymore. Good heavens, no! She wouldn't marry him now if he begged her. But she did realize that most of her anger toward him was gone. She wasn't sure if she could even continue any sort of revenge against him now. If he did end up helping to free her father, they would be even, like he'd said.

Timothy stopped by to have a word with her that turned into quite a few. The first mate apparently loved to talk once he got started, about ships, about his hometown— Bridgeport, Connecticut—about anything that came to mind. With nothing else to do, Gabrielle certainly didn't mind listening to him.

As he was winding down he said, "I was

surprised to find you out and about this morning."

"Gabby didn't tell you about the deal she and I struck last night?" Drew said, having come up silently behind them. "She managed to use her powers of . . . persuasion to gain her freedom again."

Gabrielle was speechless. What Drew had just said, or rather implied, was horrid, and no doubt a deliberate attempt to embarrass her. But Timothy was even more embarrassed, and with red cheeks, he muttered something and hurried off.

"That was fairly close to an accurate explanation, don't you think? It shut Tim up," Drew said, as if he'd been doing her a favor instead of profoundly embarrassing her.

If one of his crew hadn't walked past them just then, the first words out of her mouth would have been rather shrill, but she managed to keep her voice down as she demanded, "*Why* did you do that?"

"What?" he asked with a perfect display of innocence as he made himself comfortable against the railing next to her. "You looked like you needed rescuing. When Tim gets started like that, he'll talk your ear off."

So he *was* going to pretend he'd been

doing her a favor? She just didn't buy it. Nor was she going to let him slip by with an excuse like that.

"I didn't need rescuing, but even if I did, why the devil would you say a thing like that?"

He gave a careless shrug. "It was the first thing that came to mind."

"Liar," she snarled. "That was a deliberate attempt to make him think the worst of me!"

He noticeably stiffened at that. The charge of "liar," which had been hasty on her part, would offend most men. He was apparently no different.

His annoyance was there now in his derisive tone when he shot back, "You seem to manage that well enough on your own, sweetheart."

She gasped sharply. "How dare you?!"

"Easily enough," he replied. "Besides, I could have thought of a number of other things that would have been much more damaging than a mere insinuation."

"Such as?"

"The truth."

"The only truth is that you got into my bed when I was sleeping and took advantage of the fact that I thought you were a dream."

The mention of that night abruptly changed his demeanor. A lazy smile spread across his face. "That was one hell of a nice dream, wasn't it?"

She'd never seen a man turn sensual so fast, but Drew managed it with ease. From offended ire to seductive charmer within seconds! His eyes got heavy-lidded with a lambent glow. And the turning of his lips, just so, warned her that he was done with the original subject and was going to pursue in earnest the new one she'd unwittingly introduced.

"I'd prefer not to think of it," she said stiffly, trying desperately to ignore that fluttering in her belly that his sensual look aroused in her.

He chuckled. "You can try, but you know you won't succeed."

"Stop it," she said.

She wasn't done upbraiding him or she would have walked away. But she made an attempt to at least give him her back. If she wasn't actually looking at him, her pulse would slow down and she could think clearly and—

He slipped his arm over her shoulder and beneath her neck, so that his fingers were able to caress her cheek with a feather-light touch. It caused gooseflesh to spread along that side of her body.

She squeezed her eyes shut, fighting the sensations that threatened to overpower her. He'd managed to pull her back against him with that arm, and the weight of it rested on her breasts. He wasn't even touching her nipples, but they responded anyway; tingling and tightening, as she imagined his fingers on them.

"Face it, Gabby, what we shared was so nice, it's worth repeating—many times."

So husky his tone! But it was those potent words that were shredding her resistance. She had to give it one more try before she succumbed completely to the desire he was so easily provoking.

"You wanted Timothy to assume the worst. Why?"

He sighed over her stubborn persistence. "I'm crushed that you're still dwelling on that," he said, though he didn't sound the least bit crushed. "I was just teasing you, you know. I figured we're close enough now that you wouldn't mind. And besides, my crew knows me very well. You've spent several nights with me in my cabin. They already assume we're lovers."

Just teasing. Something she really wouldn't have minded if they really were lovers. But they weren't.

She started to point that out when she said, "We aren't—" only to have the thought interrupted when he swung her around abruptly and kissed her.

She should have seen it coming. She should have had her willpower firmly in hand before his lips touched hers. What willpower? Her resistance crumbled relentlessly and soon she was slipping her arms around his neck and nearly purring as he gathered her closer.

There was a chuckle as another of his crew passed by them. She didn't hear it, but he must have, because he whispered against her lips, "Let's go to the cabin and continue this in private."

If he hadn't suggested that, if he'd just taken her to his cabin without mentioning it, she probably wouldn't have been able to muster a protest. But his words broke the trance he'd put her in, and in that one moment of clarity, she was able to tear herself out of his arms and hurry away from the temptation he presented.

Chapter 42

It took a while for Drew to get his body back under control. He remained at the railing where Gabby had left him. Stubborn wench! They weren't going to be at sea forever. They should be taking advantage of every minute they could get alone. So why did she fight it?

They'd shared one of the more enjoyable nights of his life—twice—and he knew damn well she'd felt the same about it. The damage was done. She was no longer a virgin. There was no *reason* for her to deny herself that pleasure. But she was obviously going to. Because he'd ruined her chances for a good marriage in England?

Damn, he hadn't meant for that to happen. He'd been drunk, yes, but that was no excuse. That he was ending his visit with his sister sooner than he had to had him annoyed, too. Because of Gabrielle. Because he had to get away from her before the temptation became too much for him. Because she was still husband hunting and immune to his charms and it was starting to irritate the hell out of him.

His guilt was extreme now that he knew what his careless words at that ball had done. "Payback," she'd wanted for it; that had been the word she'd used. He recalled all the temptation she'd presented him with when he'd been in chains and unable to do anything about it. How often she'd shown off her curves with a supposed innocent stretch of her limbs. The unusual looks she'd thrown at him that he might have called sexy if he hadn't thought she was immune to him. The silly wench had *wanted* him to want her, to drive him mad with lust so she could have more revenge in denying him. And she'd nearly succeeded.

Did she really not know that he'd already wanted her so much it was barely all he could think about? And having her hadn't changed that one bit.

He really did need to get as far away from Gabrielle Brooks as possible. This voyage couldn't end soon enough for him. And yet that wouldn't end it. He'd promised to help her free her father. Damn. But he had no choice in that. He did owe her something for inadvertently embroiling her in a scandal and after taking her virginity, too.

The honorable thing to do would be to . . .

He stopped the thought before it started. It wasn't the first time it had snuck up on him since that amazing night in her bed. An unexpected virgin demanded certain things of a man, after all, the least of which was to make an offer to turn the occurrence respectable. And if Gabrielle hadn't stolen his ship, he probably would have been foolish enough to make that offer, out of guilt, out of—lust, or for whatever reason. His guilt would have prevailed.

She would have refused, of course. She wanted nothing to do with him. She had stressed that from the start. Or would she? Her friend had said that day that she'd entertained thoughts of marriage to Drew. Was that a lie Richard had came up with to get him to stop questioning him about that punch?

He sighed and headed back to the quarterdeck. He'd never been in such a muddled state of mind over a woman before. And jealousy! Where the hell had that come from? But he couldn't deny it. First that fop Wilbur, then her friend Richard, now his own friend Timothy, who he knew damn well didn't entertain any thoughts about her. Why was jealousy rearing its head now, when Drew had never experienced it before? Well, he could only assume that it was because he wasn't the least bit done with her himself.

Lovers! Gabrielle no sooner entered Drew's cabin, where her eyes moved straight to his bed, than the fury she'd felt up on deck returned with a vengeance. Everyone on board thought she and Drew were lovers and he found that amusing!

It was too bad he didn't delay returning to his room that evening, since she apparently needed more than a few hours to get her emotions under control. He probably realized that when she began throwing things at him the moment he walked through the door.

He ducked the first missile she launched but wasn't as lucky with the second, which prompted the sharp command, "Put that down!"

She didn't. She was standing behind his desk with two drawers open, which gave her a wealth of items that weren't nailed down to throw at him. An inkwell was next. She wished it had splattered all over him, but it was securely stoppered and didn't even break. Then she aimed a well-worn nautical book at him.

She paused only long enough to hiss, "We aren't lovers! We are never going to be lovers! And you damn well better let your crew know that!"

He'd been on his way to reach her but stopped abruptly at that demand. He even grinned now, the blackguard.

"We've made love twice. Sorry, sweetheart, but that officially makes us lovers."

"The devil it does!" She snorted and hurled a handful of old coins at his head.

One coin caught him on the cheek and prompted him to move again, quite quickly. In fact, he was around the desk and behind her, dragging her hand out of the drawer before her fingers could close on the next missile. Safety, his own, prompted him to grasp her other hand as well and place both of them at the small of her back, where he had no trouble keeping them. That position put her rather close to him, so she still struggled for her release. It wasn't going to happen.

"I think you owe me for this gash on the cheek," he told her.

She didn't believe there was one there, but she eyed both his cheeks first before she said, "What gash? You're not bleeding, more's the pity."

"Feels like it."

"It probably won't even bruise, which wasn't the idea a'tall, so don't think I'm done!"

He tsked. And he was putting so little effort into restraining her in that position that his voice was almost soothingly calm.

He said, "Your problem is that you're as frustrated as I am. You couldn't get this angry over a little teasing if you weren't. It's got nothing to do with what I said. It's got everything to do with your desire—for me. Admit it. You want me, Gabby."

"I don't!"

"Liar. I happen to recognize the signs— since I just went through it myself. For

God's sake, I was even jealous of Tim today for spending time with you!"

She stopped struggling for a moment and said, "Now who's lying? A man with a sweetheart in every port wouldn't know the meaning of jealousy."

"I would have been the first to agree with you—before I met you," he said.

"Timothy is rather sweet, like a big, lovable bear," she said provokingly.

His eyes narrowed. "You're *not* making me jealous again, wench."

"Wasn't trying to," she insisted, then said heatedly, "And let go of me!"

She shouldn't have made that demand. It brought it immediately to both their minds, just how close she was to him. His arms were already around her. Their chests were already touching. He didn't have to move very far to bring their mouths together.

She saw it coming and tried to turn her head aside. "Don't—"

"Stop?" he teased, finishing the thought for her.

"No, don't—"

"Kiss you here?" he finished again, brushing his lips against her chin. And then, cupping her cheek, he tilted her head up to him.

"Or here?" and she felt a feather-light brush against her cheek. "Or do you want me to kiss you here instead?" he added deeply.

His lips pressed firmly against hers now, one hand slipping around her neck to support her head, the other moving down her back to her derriere to press her closer against his arousal. What a token resistance that had been! And her anger did not keep her from responding, oh, no, just the opposite. Gripping his shoulders, she kissed him back with all the heat she'd been feeling for the last several hours, and the passion that exploded between them was amazing.

He'd been correct. She wanted him. Too much, apparently. She even helped him get their clothes off. She wasn't sure who dragged whom to the bed. And they didn't leave that bed for the rest of the day.

They didn't sleep, though. Later, they were sitting on the bed, both cross-legged, both naked. He was running his hands softly up and down the insides of her thighs, caressing her. He wasn't trying to excite her. They'd already made love. He was just touching her very softly, continuously. He did that a lot, now that she let him.

In fact, his hands were rarely far from her when they were together now.

And then out of the blue, with no previous conversation to give warning of what was on his mind, Drew said, "Will you marry me?"

Without thinking, she said, "Yes, I will."

He probably wasn't expecting such quick compliance, because he asked, "Why?"

"I rather like the life at sea. I figure from you, that's what I'll get."

He apparently didn't like that answer, because he said, "Try again."

"That isn't enough reason?"

"Admit it, you just want to make the rest of my life as miserable as you've—"

He sounded as if he were teasing, but that struck such a nerve that she cut in rather sharply, "If you weren't serious, why the bloody hell did you propose?"

She probably shouldn't have put him on the spot with such a pointed question. It turned him defensive, and frustrated, to go by the hand he raked through his hair.

"It was the honorable thing to do, all things considered," he said.

"My acceptance was for the same reason—all things considered. But if you weren't really serious, then I'll decline."

He should have looked relieved at that point. Instead he just looked more frustrated.

"Fine," he retorted. "Don't say I didn't ask."

She stared at him incredulously. "You call that asking? I'd call that begging me to refuse."

"You're not going to worm your way out of this. You accepted. I'm holding you to it!"

He lay down and turned a stiff back to her. She did the same. An hour later, his backside was touching her derriere. Thirty minutes later, their legs were entwined. About one minute after that, they were making love again, and not another word was said about his odd proposal.

Dinner came, and with an annoyed shout from Drew, it was left outside the door. Darkness came, filtered only by a little moonlight through the bank of windows. Sweat came and soaked the sheets, but they barely noticed. And Gabrielle came, again and again, each orgasm more powerful than the last.

It was a day she'd never forget.

Chapter 43

"I've noticed it, you know," Margery said in a sage tone. The older woman had been let out of her cabin about the same time Gabrielle had gained her own freedom.

"Noticed what?" Gabrielle asked.

"How happy you've been recently."

Gabrielle was standing next to her friend near the bow of the ship. They were watching a rather large moon making an appearance on the horizon. It was one of the more beautiful things the ocean offered on a clear night, bright moonlight reflected on its waves. She almost wished Drew were standing with her instead. Almost.

"Happy?" Gabrielle replied with a slight

frown. "I won't be happy until my father is freed."

"Well, of course," Margery said. "That goes without saying. But I think you're liking the captain more'n you let on, aren't you?"

Gabrielle grinned now in answer. She couldn't very well deny that anymore, or at least she couldn't deny she liked making mad, passionate love with him. Drew, unprovoked, at his most charming, was devastating to a girl's senses. And he hadn't been provoked for a while now. And he'd definitely been at his most charming.

"Have you and he . . ."

Margery couldn't bring herself to elaborate, even as outspoken as she usually was, but Gabrielle got the point easily enough, since it was a subject often on her mind. She didn't even blush when she replied, "Yes."

"I was afraid of that," Margery said with a disappointed sigh.

Gabrielle noted the disapproval but didn't take it to heart. It was expected. While Margery didn't adhere to the proper way of doing things herself and had had many lovers over the years, she took her role as chaperone seriously and wanted only the best for

Gabrielle. But life had its little curves and this was one of them.

"I thought the first time was a dream," Gabrielle admitted, and at Margery's doubtful look she laughed and said, "No, really. And I can't deny it was the nicest dream I'd ever had."

Margery rolled her eyes, but then her mind went off on a different track and she asked with a suspicious frown, "This isn't part of your revenge, is it?"

"No, I'm done with that. He and I finally talked about it, and he admitted he didn't intentionally stir up the scandal. And he's making amends for it, by helping with Papa's rescue, and also by not throwing *me* in jail for stealing his ship. Besides, you know very well I didn't really want to settle down in England when I consider the islands my home. England was Papa's idea, not mine, and even so, I don't think it *really* mattered to him. He was thinking of my mother, because it's what *she* would have wanted for me. So Drew kind of did me a favor in ruining my chances for a match there."

Margery snorted. "No one but *you* would see it that way now. But why did you get so angry about it to begin with, then, if you felt he did you a good turn?"

"Because that isn't what I thought a'tall. Not then, anyway. I thought he'd made that remark deliberately, which made it a direct attack against me, and a nasty one at that. *That* was deserving of revenge, especially since he was sailing off and leaving me there to sink in that scandal. But he didn't even know his remark made the gossip rounds."

"Well, I've said it before and I'll say it again, that anger wasn't doing you any good, so I'm glad you've given it up."

"So am I," Gabrielle agreed, and it was the truth. Not being angry and not fighting with that man had some really nice benefits.

She and Drew had sort of an unspoken truce, ever since that day she tossed half the contents of his desk at him. Neither of them said anything of the wrongs they'd done each other. And the truce had a profound effect on her. She felt so bubbly inside she might have called it happy, if she could think of a reason why she should be happy. She couldn't. Except, well . . .

"He asked me to marry him."

"Well, good, at least I won't have to draw

and quarter him now for taking advantage of you."

"I think I refused," Gabrielle was forced to admit. "I'm not really sure, though."

She remembered that night clearly. It was over a week ago, the same day they'd had their last fight, before their truce began. And it had definitely been an odd proposal. He'd gone from "doing the honorable thing" in asking, to getting upset when she accepted, to getting even more upset when she changed her mind and refused instead. And then he'd finished off by leaving her in doubt as to whether they were engaged. He was holding her to it? That's what he'd said. But he'd said it in a moment of anger, so he probably didn't mean it.

Unfortunately, Margery wasn't going to let her off after a remark like that and demanded, "What do you mean, you aren't sure?"

Gabrielle tried to shrug it off by saying, "I accepted, then changed my mind, but it sounded like he's going to hold me to my first answer."

"Good for him and fie on you for refusing," Margery huffed, then said, "At least marry him for propriety's sake. If you want to divorce him later, fine, just make sure you aren't having any babies first."

Now Gabrielle blushed. She tended to be outspoken herself, but Margery always won hands down in that department.

And why hadn't she thought about babies as a natural consequence of enjoying herself in Drew's bed? Because not once had she thought that far ahead, and besides, if she had stopped to think about what she was doing, she knew damn well she would have stopped doing it.

She'd been sleeping with him every night since their truce started. She hadn't asked permission. He hadn't invited her. She'd just gotten into his bed each night without thinking, as if she belonged there. And they'd made love every one of those nights. That's what she didn't want halted with too much introspection. The voyage was going to end soon enough, in a matter of days. They were already passing through Caribbean waters. So was it too much to ask, to have just a little sensual bliss uninterrupted by reality?

But a baby? Good grief, she really should have considered that. And the thought had her picturing herself holding a little Drew in

her arms. He'd be the most beautiful baby
ever created, she thought as she felt her
heart skip a beat. The baby was not even
born, and most likely not even conceived,
and she already loved the child! What the
deuce was wrong with her?

"Pretty moon, isn't it?"

Gabrielle jumped, startled by Drew's sudden presence beside them. Margery mumbled something about getting to bed and
left them alone. The moment she was gone,
his arm slipped around Gabrielle's waist and
drew her to his side.

It was the first time he was making a
"public" display of affection. The only other
time had been when he'd kissed her as they
stood on the lower deck, which had been
witnessed by all and sundry. It wasn't that
there hadn't been ample opportunity, since
she'd been spending most every day with
him up on the quarterdeck. He'd even let
her take the wheel for a while, after she'd
convinced him she knew how.

But he was all business when he was up
there, commanding his ship. Besides, he
did mention one night that he didn't want
his men yearning for port any sooner than
was reasonable, that they got sloppy when

they were rushing to end a voyage because they had women on their minds. She'd gotten the point.

"That's one of the prettier moons I've seen in a while. I often saw really big moons on the horizon, nice and full, in St. Kitts. We had some magnificent sunsets, too, right off of our beach."

"You lived on the beach?"

She nodded. "Papa has a small house on the coast, not too far from town."

"It sounds a bit too perfect. I'm surprised you wanted to leave it."

"I didn't," she said, and said no more.

He must have read the end-of-subject tone, because he didn't address it further and said instead, "I'd love to walk with you on a beach sometime, any beach as long as the weather is balmy."

Was he remembering that romantic fantasy she'd mentioned to him? "Chilly walks on the beach aren't bad," she pointed out. "I've done that before in England, when I was much younger."

"Possibly, but they won't allow for swimming naked with you in the water, and I really doubt you'll find any crystal-clear coves with coral reefs to explore along the English coasts."

He did remember! She glanced up at him with a grin. "You're probably right, though I never checked. I didn't even learn to swim until I moved to the Caribbean to be with Papa. He taught me."

His fingers grazed her cheek softly. "I'm jealous. I think that's something I would have loved teaching you."

She might have laughed if his tone hadn't turned so husky. She caught her breath instead and had to fight the urge to turn toward him and start kissing him. But she could feel his fingers in her hair. She'd lost her ribbon, so it was loose at the moment. He touched her so often! Half the time she didn't even think he was aware he was doing it. He just couldn't seem to keep his hands off of her.

To get her mind off of that, she asked, "Have you given any more thought to our plan of action once we make port?"

"Yes, before we sail to Lacross's stronghold, we're going to stop at Anguilla to find a woman with the same color hair as you, and reasonably the same shape, to make him think it's you on board my ship. Then I'll go in with the maps."

She glanced at him. "Wait a minute, are you implying that I'm not going to be there?"

"Not implying, stating a fact," he replied adamantly. "After what you've told me about this pirate, you aren't getting anywhere near him."

"But he doesn't even want the maps," she said. "I told you that, too."

"All supposition," he reminded her. "He *did* ask for them, his only stipulation being that you show up to deliver them yourself. So the fake you is present and accounted for, just not leaving my ship, the maps get handed to Lacross, and then your father gets released. All nicely accomplished with no one getting hurt."

She rolled her eyes. "And if he doesn't release my father until I'm standing in his presence?"

"He can't very well renege just because I deliver the maps to him."

"Like hell he can't. Don't for a minute assume he's honorable. I need to be there in case your plan backfires and he ends up holding you hostage, too."

"Does that thought . . . distress you?"

She blinked, then frowned. Was he fishing for a declaration of some sort? That she was worried about him? That she cared about him? She pushed the thought away, didn't want it in the same conversation that Pierre was in.

So she said, tongue almost in cheek, "Of course it distresses me. If you get captured, then I'll have two hostages to rescue, won't I?"

He laughed, pulled her closer, rubbed his cheek against hers on the way to whispering by her ear, "I find it charming that you'd rescue me."

She slipped her arms around his neck and smiled as she replied, "I'd have to rescue you so I could shoot you for being dumb enough to get captured in the first place."

He burst out laughing. "Damn, Gabby, you are wonderful for the disposition. I don't think I've ever laughed as much as I have since I've known you."

"I bet you say that to all your sweethearts," she replied with feigned coquetry.

He gave her that stomach-fluttering smile of his. "No, I don't believe I have. Only to you."

Chapter 44

They arrived much sooner than Gabrielle had expected, the very next day. They docked on the island of Anguilla late in the afternoon. Colonized by English settlers from St. Kitts back in the 1600s, Anguilla wasn't far at all from her home, which could have been reached before dark.

One of Drew's crew told her Anguilla was one of his trading stops, so she figured that was why Drew picked it, since things there would be familiar to him, whereas St. Kitts might not be on his usual route.

She never did summon up enough nerve to broach again with Drew the question of whether he was going to let her men go. If he'd said no, that would have ended their truce right then and there. And besides, she figured, now that he'd agreed to help, he would be foolish not to make use of all available men, particularly those willing to go above and beyond in their effort to free Nathan.

Regardless, she was almost holding her breath, standing there at the rail, waiting to see the hold opened and if her friends would be marched off to a dungeon or given their freedom. She'd been forced to come up with a few alternative courses of action, just in case.

Since it was a British-controlled island, and Drew wasn't the least bit British, there was a slight, though very slight, chance that she could turn the tables on him, if it came to that. Richard could sound like the veriest English nabob if he had to, after all. And the English authorities would be inclined to believe one of their own before they would an American. But she was praying it wouldn't come to that. The last thing she wanted to do was land Drew in jail when her truce with him was still in effect.

She'd reason with him before that, rail at him, bribe him, cajole him, even throw the contents of his desk at him again if necessary. She just needed at least one plan in case everything else failed.

And then Richard strolled over to say, "What rotten luck, to be let out now. I was losing to Bixley at whist. Needed a few more hours to break even at least."

She was too thrilled to see him standing there without a guard to immediately grasp what he was saying. But as soon as she'd given him a relieved hug, she realized he was actually complaining about being set free, and sounded quite serious about it.

"You were given cards to pass the time?" she asked.

Richard chuckled. "We've had all the luxuries we could have hoped for, *chérie*. Cards, dice, some of the best damn food I've ever eaten, and still hot, straight from the galley. Nathan needs to steal Anderson's cook, he really does. We were also given hammocks, and, you won't believe this one—even a bath."

"How'd you manage that?"

"Well, there was an old tub down there. Ohr asked for enough water to fill it. He wasn't really expecting he'd get it, but damned if the buckets didn't get lowered to us, one by one." He laughed with the memory. "We drew straws for the order of us all using that single tub. I didn't do too bad, got it second."

She'd worried herself sick and they'd been having the time of their lives? A vacation was what it sounded like! Drew *could* have told her, the bloody sod. So could her friend, for that matter.

She slapped Richard's shoulder. "Why didn't you tell me that when you were let out for that dinner?"

He shrugged. "I thought you knew. These Americans, they weren't treating us like prisoners, well, other than the lock on the hatch, which Ohr was determined to break, by the way, until I was able to assure him you were fine with the new arrangements."

And it had obviously looked like she was doing fine at that dinner that Richard was brought up to join; she hadn't told him differently that night. But it was just as well her friends hadn't tried to escape, since it looked like they weren't going to be carted off to a dungeon after all.

"Where is Ohr?"

"Right here," Ohr said at her back.

She swung around with a glad cry and threw her arms around him. "I was so worried! And I was afraid to ask about you. I didn't want to bring you to Drew's attention."

Richard chuckled at her. "I don't think we were far from his thoughts, Gabby. He even brought us up on deck one day, determined to find out who had bruised his cheek late one night."

She went still, hearing that. "He did? And what did he find out?"

"Nothing," Richard replied. "Told him I was sworn to secrecy."

"I suppose I shouldn't be surprised that you'd done it," she allowed, recalling her own curiosity. "I'd wondered about that bruise myself."

"He's treated you honorably?" Ohr asked, looking too serious by half. She didn't doubt for a minute that if she gave him the wrong answer, he'd go right for Drew's jugular the moment he saw him, and he might not even wait that long.

So she said, "Very much so, after we figured out that what he did in England wasn't intentional. He even offered me marriage."

She really shouldn't have added that, since both men were now staring at her, waiting for her to elaborate with the response she'd given Drew. And since she still wasn't sure about the results of that unexpected conversation with the captain, she ought to just tell them that she'd refused him. Of course, if Drew ended up mentioning it to one of them, that they were engaged . . .

But she couldn't go far wrong with the truth, so she continued, "I refused him. He didn't like that answer and probably considers us engaged." And then she shrugged. "I *might* reconsider, but I would rather not decide until after Papa is free."

"Nice to know I still have the option to run like hell."

Gabrielle winced at the sound of Drew's voice. Was everyone going to sneak up on her today?

Drew sounded as if he was joking, but he probably wasn't. He'd made that offer, for whatever reason, without much conviction, and got adamant about it only when she'd given him answers he wasn't expecting.

She turned around to see his grin, and before she could make a reply, his arm slipped about her waist. That was a clear indication to her friends that they were more to each other than she'd been letting on.

But before she could correct that impression, Drew added, "Shall we adjourn to the inn to formulate our plans? I already have a perfect one in mind, but I'd like to hear what you think of it."

And just like that, he took full command of the rescue and had Richard and Ohr's support. And later, when they heard his plan, those two were all for leaving her behind and out of Pierre's grasp. Which probably would have been just what happened—if James Malory hadn't shown up.

Chapter 45

"Is this even accurate?" James asked, looking over the drawing Bixley had scribbled to give them an idea of what Pierre's stronghold looked like.

No one answered him for a few moments. They were all in shock that he was even there, and James hadn't offered any explanation for his presence yet. Looking rather dashing and even piratical with a flowing cravat tied loosely over his full-sleeved lawn shirt, high black boots, and no jacket, he made Gabrielle remember the time the Anderson brothers had let it slip that James was an ex-pirate. Seeing him now with his darker tan from the ocean crossing, his hair windblown, she no longer doubted it.

Drew finally exclaimed, "What the devil are you doing here, James!?"

The look James turned on Drew was quite intimidating. It certainly had Richard slumping lower in his chair to try to avoid James's notice. Gabrielle cringed as well.

"I'm here at your sister's behest," James said in a calm tone. "She worries about you. Bloody well can't imagine why, but she does." And then he tapped the drawing on the table again and repeated his question, "Is this accurate?" And they guessed, at least Gabrielle did, that he must have overheard them discussing some of their plan before he joined them.

Bixley hesitated in answering the question, but then nodded. "The fort was recently refurbished."

There were many more questions. Having James Malory asking them was making Bixley think long and hard about every word out of his mouth before he gave any response. Malory seemed to have that effect on people—including Gabrielle. This was the James Malory she'd first met, the one who'd so frightened her, not the one she'd ended up liking toward the end of her stay in London.

She would have been biting her nails if she wasn't trying very hard not to look guilty. She was dreading the moment when his questioning turned to her, and it would. She was sure of it.

But so far he hadn't asked her a thing. He'd merely looked at her hard, then looked just as hard at Drew sitting next to her on the sofa in the gathering room at the inn, and obviously came to his own conclusions about why they were there together.

Unfortunately, James hadn't come alone. Georgina walked in only a few minutes after him. She was hatless, her brown hair braided down her back. And she was wearing a skirt and a loose comfortable shirt that was belted on the outside and was so big on her it might well have been one of James's shirts. She looked marvelous, as if she had thoroughly enjoyed the sea voyage.

She took one look at the couple on the sofa and said, "Well, this is a relief. Both present and accounted for. So there weren't any pirates involved after all?"

Richard, that rogue, grinned and raised his hand to draw Georgina's attention to him before he remarked, "I wouldn't say that."

Georgina had merely glanced at her husband and asked, "Does he count?"

"Most definitely," James replied, then added, "Though he'll wish he didn't."

Richard didn't say another word after that, realizing that James was no longer talking about pirates, but Richard's interest in his wife. Georgina realized that, too, but she merely tsked on her way to her brother for a hug.

It had taken a few moments for Drew to get past his new amazement, but now he demanded, "What the devil are *you* doing here, Georgie?"

"You really have to ask, when one of your crew showed up to warn us *The Triton* had been overrun by pirates? Or was that not the truth?"

"It was true, but you didn't think I could handle that on my own?"

She actually blushed slightly. "Well, certainly, but that wasn't my only concern. Gabby disappeared, leaving a note that her father was in trouble. We gathered she might be with you, but since she is our responsibility, we couldn't just guess about it, we had to make sure."

Gabrielle was the one blushing now. She

hadn't expected ever to see the Malorys again, so hadn't expected to have to deal with the guilt she felt for the way she'd sneaked off.

"I was desperate," Gabrielle tried to explain. "Having just learned that my father had been in a dungeon for nearly a month, and it might take that long again before I could get him out."

"We understand, Gabby," Georgina said.

She might have said more, but James, studying the drawing again, said to Bixley, "High walls *and* a gate?"

Bixley nodded again. "Pierre keeps it locked, and manned, too."

"Bloody hell," James mumbled, but then in a resigned tone added, "Very well, I haven't climbed any walls in a while, I suppose I'm due."

"You're due for no such thing," Georgina countered, and moved over to stand next to her husband. Then she suggested, "Why don't we just blow those gates up? Our ships can get close enough, can't they?"

It was beginning to sound like Malory was taking over the rescue operation. Gabrielle wasn't surprised that he would put himself in charge. He was a man who wouldn't just participate, he'd command, organize, give orders, and shoot down any objections. And he wouldn't bother to ask if his help was needed.

James tapped the drawing now and dryly asked his wife, "Did you fail to note these cannons on the walls, m'dear?"

She glanced down at the drawing, said just as dryly, "It's an old fortress. Those cannons are probably ancient and unusable, wouldn't you think?"

"No, ma'am," Bixley put in before James could give his opinion. "Pierre refurbished that place. It's like new, well, aboveground it is. He did no work on the old dungeon, other than to make sure the doors would lock tight."

Georgina said "Bloody hell" as well and moved over to the group of sofas to sit next to Gabrielle.

Gabrielle felt the need to elaborate on Bixley's information and told James, "According to Ohr, Pierre added a few more enemies to the count when he turned rogue. It forced the other captains in the alliance to change locations. They didn't like that. It had been a really nice settlement they'd built up over the years that no one knew about. Most of them were even calling it home. But they didn't trust Pierre not to give away its location, so they moved out."

"Would any of these other captains help with this endeavor?" James queried.

"They might. But it would take a while to locate them and—"

"And time is of the essence," James cut in, but not unkindly. "I understand your concern for Nathan when you don't know his condition or how he's been treated all this time. But we have two ships now to pull this off. You can stop worrying."

"He says that all the time," Georgina whispered beside her. "You'd think he'd know by now that it doesn't work, especially since I'm here for that very reason. A woman won't stop worrying until there's nothing left to worry about. Well, at least that goes for me."

"And me," Gabrielle agreed.

Chapter 46

Two plans were formulated, neither of which included hiring a look-alike to take Gabrielle's place. Drew was annoyed. He'd liked that plan because it kept her out of harm's way. But when he'd argued the issue, James had pointed out that if something went wrong with their plans, and it became necessary to confront Pierre directly, Gabrielle would be useful in luring the pirate captain out of his fortress.

Georgina wasn't that lucky. She'd had her way about not staying home in England, but that had been a safe voyage. They hadn't even been caught in that bad storm, had been able to avoid it entirely. And James had enjoyed her company on the crossing, as he knew he would, which had influenced his decision to allow her to come along. But now that the rest of the trip involved danger, he couldn't be budged about her safety. She was going to stay at the inn in Anguilla—where Drew thought Gabrielle ought to be.

They wouldn't be gone for more than a day, though, possibly not even that long, so his sister wouldn't have long to worry about them. According to Bixley, Pierre's stronghold was only a few hours away.

The two plans were nearly identical, just a matter of timing. They could try to break Nathan out in the dead of night, when most of the fortress would be sleeping, or they could use Drew's ship, and Gabrielle's presence on it, as a distraction while just a few of them climbed the back walls and sneaked their way to the dungeon.

"It's not just my father who needs to be rescued," Gabrielle reminded them. "The rest of his crew is with him. He won't leave them behind."

As Pierre and his guards would surely notice that many men trying to sneak their way out over the back walls in the bright light of day, going in at night was really the only option. They would leave for the docks after a hearty dinner and a brief rest.

Drew had hoped to spend those few hours with Gabrielle, but his sister had other plans for him. With a look that promised he'd wish he was elsewhere, she'd dragged him outside where they wouldn't be disturbed.

"I've a bone to pick with you," she began.

"I gathered as much."

"What the devil do you think you're doing? Do you even know that you embroiled that girl in a scandal in England with your careless reference to pirates at that last ball you attended?"

"It wasn't intentional, Georgie. But yes, she informed me of that fact."

Georgina blinked. "So she *did* know about it before she left?"

"Indeed. To hear her tell it, it gave her the extra incentive to take my ship—killing two birds with one stone, was the way she put it."

"Revenge?" she guessed. "Very well, so I'm not all that surprised. Probably would have done the same thing myself under the circumstances."

He grinned. "No, you wouldn't have. She

actually knows how to run a ship, you don't, so it never would have occurred to you—"

"Oh, stop," she cut in. "You aren't going to distract me from the main problem."

"There is no problem."

"The devil there isn't," she disagreed. "She's a young, innocent—"

"Not so innocent now."

"I see," she said with a sigh, then amended, "No, I don't see, and this is exactly what I was afraid of. You know better. She was under our care. Good God, Drew, what could you have been thinking?"

"She left your care."

"And went into yours, so she was still under our family's protection, as it were, which is quite the same thing. You'll have to marry her, you know. When James finds out, he'll insist."

"Then he'll have to do his insisting with her. I already asked."

She scowled at him for not mentioning that sooner. "Why didn't you say so?"

"Because she refused me."

That took the wind out of her sails. "Did she really? I find that unbelievable."

So did he, but he said by way of explanation, "She thinks I'm a Lothario, a cad, a seducer of women."

"You *are* a seducer of women, Drew."

He smiled at her. "I wouldn't be one if I married, now would I? Or do you think marriage *wouldn't* have a remarkable effect on me?"

"What I think doesn't really matter when it comes to this." But then she asked him pointedly, "Do you love her?"

"Of course not," he said quickly. But he did admit, "I don't think I've ever lusted after a woman quite this much, though. But I'm sure I'll get over it as soon as the next wench comes along."

Georgina snorted and poked a finger in his chest. "I'd suggest you give that a little more thought, brother mine. It would be much better if you enter this marriage knowing that it's not just the right thing to do, but also what you *want* to do."

She started to walk away. He called after her, "I told you, she refused me!"

"That won't be the case after James hears about this. You may depend upon it."

Chapter 47

Gabrielle managed to avoid any interrogation of the personal sort that night with the excuse of a slight headache. And claiming that she was sure the brief rest they were all going to take would cure her of it, she went up to her room.

She did rest, or tried to, but she kept trembling with fear, with dread, and no matter how many positive thoughts she tried to concentrate on, she couldn't get the trembling to stop. Now that her father's rescue was at hand and she would be sailing to within shouting distance, as it were, of Pierre Lacross, it was all she could think about.

She hadn't voiced her fears to the others,

but what if her father and his crew were in no condition to escape? As they'd been incarcerated for close to two months, anything could have happened. And Pierre was evil! Had he fed them decently, or did he just give them mere crumbs, barely enough to keep them alive? Had he abused them in other ways, just for his amusement? Had he even kept Nathan's crew alive, when they meant nothing to him and weren't part of the deal?

She managed to get the trembling under control before she joined the others downstairs again. She had no chance to speak privately with Drew on that short voyage. He'd taken the task of steering the ship himself and was in conference with Ohr most of the way. It had been decided that Ohr was going ashore with him and James. Richard hadn't been included in the rescue party, not because he wouldn't have been useful, but because James had made an offhand remark that Richard would be left behind in the dungeon if he had his way. James had been joking. Possibly. But Richard decided not to put it to the test.

They anchored *The Triton* and James's ship in a small cove on the west side of the island, which wasn't very big. Bixley guessed they'd have a fifteen-minute walk to the fortress, most of which could be done on the beach. And there were about five hours left of darkness to get in and out of the dungeon, which was plenty of time if they didn't run into any trouble.

Gabrielle watched the rowboat being lowered into the water. There was enough moonlight peeking through the clouds to see that James was already rowing ashore from his ship. She felt calmer now, had managed to fight back her fears, but they were still just below the surface. The slightest thing could set off the trembling again.

She should have insisted on going with them. But in her few rational moments, she knew she'd only be in the way. If they had to fight their way in, she couldn't contribute much to the effort. But it was going to be pure agony, waiting for them to return to the ship.

Ohr hugged her briefly before he went over the side. "Don't worry," he told her. "You will see Nathan before the night is over."

"I know. Just be careful."

She barely had time to say that before

Drew gathered her in his arms. And in front
of his entire crew he gave her the most tender, heart-stirring kiss—the one thing guaranteed to break through the fragile control
she had over her fears. As she kissed him
back, reveling in his closeness and the delicious sensations that ran up and down her
body, she began to feel anxious. The trembling started again, but he let her go before
he felt it—and besides, he might have at-
tributed it to her passionate response. She
pressed her fingertips to her lips as she
watched him go over the railing.

"I don't see what there is to love about
him," Richard remarked at her side.

"Are you kidding? He's—"

Gabrielle stopped, realizing what she was
admitting to. Good heavens, was that why
she was more afraid than she should be?
Because Drew was walking into danger?
She loved him. What a foolish thing to do.

Richard put his arm around her shoulder.
"It will work out, *chérie.* He adores you."

"He adores all women."

He chuckled softly. "So do I, but I would
give them all up for—"

"Shush!" she told him earnestly. "Richard,
please, stop pining for another man's wife.

Malory won't tolerate another trespass. You make me fear for your life by not being reasonable about this."

"Who said love was reasonable?"

Bloody hell, Richard was right. Love wasn't reasonable at all.

She sighed and bid him good night. She hoped she'd be able to sleep during the tense wait for the men to return, but she couldn't still her trembling nerves. She didn't know how long she lay in Drew's comfortable bed, but she finally gave up on falling asleep and came back on deck—just in time to see the two boats returning, both filled to the brim with men.

They'd been successful! Her relief was incredible, almost draining. She staggered to the railing, trying to spot her father in one of the two boats, but the moon was well hidden now and the only man she recognized was Ohr. She could just barely make him out, and only because he was standing in the boat rowing to—James's ship? Why wouldn't he come back to *The Triton*? And why the devil was he standing up? He knew that wasn't safe.

Every muscle in her body seemed

to tighten. Something was wrong, very wrong . . .

She no sooner came to that conclusion than Ohr shouted, "It's a trap!" just before he dove into the water.

Several shots were immediately fired at him, the guns apparently having been pointed at him all the while. Ohr didn't resurface.

Gabrielle gripped the rail, nearly paralyzed by the sudden grief washing over her. Ohr couldn't be dead. Not her dear friend. And his warning had been too late. He'd died for nothing! Others had swum out in advance and were already climbing aboard both ships, no, just more were joining the fray, too many were already on board.

The sounds of struggles and pistol shots were all around her now. She turned and saw one man leaning over an unmoving body. He glanced up at her and grinned. She didn't recognize him, nor the man who pushed him aside to throw a dagger at one of Drew's crewmen, who was trying to escape over the side. The man went over. The dagger went over with him, embedded in his back.

She realized she had no weapon of any

sort. She didn't think Drew would have any in his cabin either; he'd been fully armed when he'd left. But his cabin was too far away anyway, and the railing was right next to her. Her only chance was to slip over the side herself.

She gave it no further thought and did that now, only to be yanked back against a wet chest and have a strong arm pressed against her neck. Her breath was cut off and she began to panic, her arms and legs flailing wildly.

Then a voice that sounded vaguely familiar said, "And just where did you think you were going, Gabby, my dear?"

She gasped out, "Avery? Avery Dobs? What are you doing here? Let me go. We have to—"

"You aren't going anywhere except into Pierre's waiting arms," he cut in. He eased his grip on her so that she could turn to face him.

His wet clothes, the smirk on his face, the conclusion hit her hard. Horrified, she said, "My God, what have you done?"

"My job."

"I don't under—You can't mean that you take orders from Pierre?"

"Why does that surprise you?" he asked. "You forget that I was on that pirate island with you and witnessed the same things you did."

"What are you talking about? We were captives!" she exclaimed.

"Yes, but there were bars on the hut where they kept us men, and I had nothing better to do than stare out of them. I became very melancholy."

"You were a hostage. Of course you would—"

"No, it had nothing to do with that. Do you know I watched them carry a chest to the main building while I was there? It was so heavy they dropped it and it broke, spilling gold coins all over the ground. They just laughed. Wealth was stored in the huts right next to us, trunks of fine woolens and silks, crates of tobacco and rum, all stolen, all stored until it could be sold."

"They were pirates! That was their business."

"Exactly," he said. "But it wasn't just the wealth to be had. It took me several months to figure it out. It was also the laughter I'd witnessed on that island, the joking, the bonds of friendship. Those men were enjoying themselves. When I thought about going back to my career on a staid English ship—where a simple mistake could get you flogged—I couldn't do it."

"You merely sailed under the wrong captains. It's not like that on all—"

"How the deuce would you know, Gabby? Not that it matters. I made my choice soon after my release, before I even reached England, and sailed directly back to the Caribbean. It took me another month to find one of the pirate captains. The first one wouldn't take me on, but he saw how determined I was and allowed me to catch a ride back to that island. Pierre was there and short on men, having barely won his last sea battle. He was willing to take a chance on me, and I haven't disappointed him yet."

"Then what were you doing back in England?"

"Can't you guess? I was sent to make sure your friend Bixley didn't delay in reaching you. I have my own ship now. It was priceless, Gabby! I'm the one who took him to England. He didn't know me from Adam. He had no idea he was sailing on one of Pierre's ships. So it was easy enough to trail him when we docked, straight to his friends, and listen in when he apprised them of your father's dilemma. Heard from them where you were staying. I wasn't going to reveal myself, but then I heard that rumor circulating about you."

"And you just had to rub it in?"

"Not at all. I figured, just in case you didn't know about it, that it would give you even more incentive to head back this way. Which it did. And then I followed you back. I lost you in that storm, but I had a feeling that Anderson would dock in Anguilla before you set out to rescue your father, since it's so close to here, and he didn't disappoint me. I was able to overhear most of the plans you made tonight at the inn. While you foolishly wasted time resting, I came straight here to warn Pierre and earn my reward."

"I thought you were a good man. I was so happy to see you when you came to the Malorys'," she said with all the contempt she could muster. "But you're just a two-faced bastard, Avery."

Unfortunately, the insult rolled off of him. He even laughed, though only for a moment. Then he stiffened. But when he spoke, it wasn't to her.

"Put it down."

She tried to turn her head to see whom he was talking to, but it wasn't necessary. Avery turned them both to place her between himself and Richard, who was pointing the pistol he held at Avery's head.

It was an excellent time for her to get out of the way. She steeled herself for the pain, then let her legs crumble so she could fall to the deck. It did hurt, but it didn't work. Avery must have been expecting her to do something of the sort, because the arm about her neck dragged her back up to cover his chest, and the point of a dagger was now pressed against her cheek.

"Nice try, Gabby," he sneered. "But don't try it again."

"You won't kill her," Richard said.

"No, but I don't care if I scar her up some. And this is your last warning. Put it down!"

But before Richard could decide either way, he was hit from behind and fell to the deck. And Pierre Lacross stood in his place.

Chapter 48

Pierre hadn't aged well in the three years since she'd last seen him. His black beard was still just as matted as before, but there was now a lot of gray streaking through his shoulder-length hair. However, it was the deep lines in his face that made him look so much older now. The life he led, the things he'd done were taking their toll on his appearance. In fact he was extremely thin now, almost emaciated. It made her think she wouldn't be completely helpless in his hands. She could fight him. She might even win. But on the way to his fortress wasn't the time to try, with his men all around them.

He said nothing to her other than the single chilling remark rasped in her ear, "I have wonderful plans for you, *chérie*."

She couldn't think about that. If she did she'd become so paralyzed by fear that she might as well lie down and die. Instead she noted every little thing around her and on the way, like they seemed to be tossing any of the men that were still alive into the hold to deal with later, including Richard and Timothy. Like the thick overgrowth in the middle of the island that made it nearly impassable. Like the hidden door in the back wall when they reached the fortress, which was carelessly left unlocked.

They were all too elated with their victory to think of taking precautions now. She counted how many candles there were in the short passage from there to the main hall. The door through which they entered the hall was also concealed behind an easily movable cabinet, and when in place, it gave no indication a secret passage was behind it.

It was telling that they didn't care she knew this. Obviously, neither Pierre, nor any of his men, ever expected her to leave that island again.

As Gabrielle looked around the large, barracks-like hall, she noticed two means of escape. One was a wide doorway, open now, which led to a large courtyard. The courtyard was enclosed by high walls. Bixley's drawing had been accurate in that respect. It was too bad he hadn't known about that secret door.

The other means of escape was an open, narrow stairway that led up to a second floor, possibly living quarters where the officers of the fortress used to reside. As it was such an old fortress that had merely been refurbished and not completely renovated, Gabrielle guessed that the kitchens were out in the courtyard, not connected to the main building, and the entrance to the dungeons was probably out there as well.

She saw all of this at a glance since she was led, or rather dragged, straight through the hall and upstairs by Pierre. The bedroom they entered was probably his, filthy, cluttered with mismatched furniture, the bed unmade, dirty dishes on a small table. That he didn't close the door when he pulled her in there was her only hope for the moment. It indicated he might not be staying.

She yanked her hand loose easily enough.

She hadn't even tried to do so before now. A little more hope. Maybe he was as weak as he looked. He wasn't even very tall. She'd forgotten that, or maybe she never noticed before because she'd never met men as tall as . . .

She couldn't think about Drew yet, didn't dare ask what had happened to him. If he was dead, she was afraid she'd just give up and not care what happened to her. All concentration and reason would be lost, and she needed all of her wits to survive this.

She moved away from Pierre. It didn't work; he followed her closely, keeping her within reach.

"I don't suppose you want the maps?" she asked, turning around to face him.

"Maps?" He chuckled. "I knew you would be amusing. No, you know why you are here."

She did; it just would have been so nice to be wrong. "Are you going to let my father and the others go now?"

"When you tried to cheat me?" he said with a tsk. "I should kill them all."

She paled, almost lost her balance, her legs turned so weak. But he laughed.

"Certainly I will release them. Do you

think I would waste food on them when I do not have to?"

"You're lying."

"You wound me, Gabrielle. Why would you think such a thing?"

His grin belied that she was insulting him. "You know they'll try to rescue me. You won't risk—"

"Risk what?" he cut in. "As long as they stay away, you stay alive, this is what they will be told. You think *they* will risk that? Besides, I will assure your papa that I will only take my fill of you, then you can go." And then he laughed again. "Red, she will not tolerate your presence for more than a few days. She is very jealous."

She was surprised that he would tell her that, but then maybe it wasn't true. She gave him a skeptical look. "Then why have you even bothered with this elaborate scheme to get me here?"

Pierre shrugged. "Because a few days may be enough for me. Or I may decide to get rid of Red and keep you. I have not decided yet. Would you like me to keep you?"

"I'd like you to go to hell."

He laughed yet again. She was definitely amusing him, which wasn't a good thing.

She needed to make him not want her around, not give him reasons to keep her.

He raised a hand to touch her. She immediately slapped it away, but he was quick and caught her wrist instead. And this time when she tried to yank it away, he proved he was stronger than he appeared.

"Do not mistake your position," he said coldly. "Your papa, he is not gone yet."

"May I see him?"

"No."

"How do I know he's still alive?"

He shrugged and let go of her wrist. "You do not. However, since I had no reason to kill him, you may assume he is. But shall we put it to the test, just how much you want him to leave—unharmed? Remove your clothes. This room is warm, you will not need them here."

She was paralyzed for a moment. She'd worn one of her thinner island skirts and a thin blouse for the trip, a matching pair that could have been mistaken for a dress. But with only bloomers and a chemise under them, it wasn't going to take her long to remove them. The door being open had misled her into thinking he wasn't going to touch her yet, that she still might have time to escape. She glanced at it. He did as well. His laughter returned.

"No, no," he said. "Chasing after wenches is one thing I will not do. If you run, I will have every last man in my dungeon killed."

She stiffened. He said that with a bloody smile on his lips, as if he were savoring the thought.

"I will be back shortly," Pierre growled as he moved to the door. "Be in that bed waiting for me, or I will have your papa brought here and flogged before your eyes."

Chapter 49

"How tight are your bonds?" Drew asked James, who was sitting next to him, tied to the same tree.

"I've been bound with better knots," James replied.

"Then you can break them?"

"Yes," James said, raising Drew's hopes, only to dash those hopes when he added, "Eventually."

"We don't have all night! You heard that bastard. They'll be back here soon. God, if it's the last thing I ever do, I'm going to kill Lacross," Drew said as he strained at the ropes around his own wrists.

"You'll have to get in line," James replied.

Drew snarled, "For once, Malory, *you'll* have to get in line."

They'd left the ships armed to the teeth. It hadn't done them any good when they'd been ambushed. There must have been twenty pistols pointed at them when they were surrounded on the beach, halfway to the fortress. Someone had warned the pirates that they were coming. The pirates had even bragged about it.

Their wrists had been tied behind them, but they'd merely been held there on the beach until Pierre Lacross showed up. Bixley knew some of Pierre's men and had hurled a long string of curses at them until one of the pirates got annoyed enough to gag them all.

"So these are the men who tried to cheat me of my prize?" Lacross had said when he arrived with another large group of men.

"You want we should kill them?" someone had asked.

"There is little entertainment in that," Pierre replied in an amused tone of voice, and then he pointed at Ohr. "That one, he goes with us. We have two ships to capture, every man will be needed. These other three will not be going anywhere. Collect them when we are done."

Ohr had been taken with them to make it possible for the pirates to easily board the ships by trickery. The pirates even sat around and waited nearly an hour just so the crews on the two ships would think enough time had passed for the rescue to have been a success. Ohr's presence with them was to give that impression.

Not a single man had been left to guard them. None were needed, since the pirates had spent the time they had to kill making sure their prisoners were better secured. More ropes had been produced. One was even used to wrap them to a palm tree. There was no doubt that they'd be there when someone came back to collect them.

It had been easy enough to spit out the gags, but the ropes were a different matter. Those around Drew's wrists had gone beyond painful, they were so tight he had no feeling in his hands now. And too much time had passed, plenty of time for Pierre's trap to have been sprung. Had Gabrielle already been captured? It was killing him, thinking about what was happening to her.

"They'll be celebrating tonight," Bixley

said, finally getting his own gag loose. "It's what they did after they captured Nathan. They jump on any excuse to break open another cask, and you heard them crowing 'bout getting the jump on us."

And they'd have a lot more to crow about now if their other trap was a success. Two more fine ships to sell or put to use, and the most beautiful woman . . .

"That might give us a little more time," James said.

"Time for what?" Drew snarled.

"To turn the tables, of course. You don't think I'm going to let George fret if we're not back by dawn, do you?"

"I'd like to know how the hell you think—"

"Quiet, someone's coming back this way," Bixley hissed.

Drew had never felt so much frustration. If he didn't break these bonds soon . . . He couldn't even feel if he was making progress, but he was straining for all he was worth.

He could make out six men coming down the beach toward them, laughing, taking their time. So the trap had been sprung successfully?

"Told you they'd still be here, that it didn't

matter how big they were," one of the pirates said to his buddy as he bent over to cut the rope from the tree. "No one ties knots better'n I do."

"Let's go, mates," another man said, nudging Drew with his foot. "We've a nice dungeon waiting for you."

James had gotten to his feet the moment the rope fell away from his chest. Drew slid up the tree trunk to do the same. With his longer legs, both of which had fallen asleep, it was a bit slower going. He stamped some feeling back into them. Bixley got to his knees first and didn't move further, so someone yanked him the rest of the way.

James shook his head back to toss his hair out of his face. That was when he was recognized.

"Don't I know you?" one of the pirates said to James. The man was older than the others.

"Highly doubtful," James replied, and turned around, dismissing the fellow.

The man persisted, came around so he could see James's face again, and insisted, "You look damn familiar. I'm pretty good with faces. I never forget—"

"Senility changes that," James cut in

dryly. "So let me put it in terms even a child can understand. You don't know me, you have never known me, and, most important, you don't *want* to know me."

That got some chuckles from the pirates' friends and a taunt from one of them. "Thinks 'e's too good for the likes o' ye, Mort."

Annoyed now, Mort stepped closer to peer up at James, and then his expression turned to one of surprise. "I'll be damned. I told you I never forget a face. You're Captain Hawke! I knew it! I sailed with you for a couple months, but you were too wild and dan . . . ger . . ." The word trailed off warily as Mort tried to step back, but he wasn't quick enough.

"Should have remembered that as well, old chap," James said as he slammed a fist into Mort's face.

Drew was as surprised as the pirates were that James was free of his bonds. Another of them went down with an amazingly fast right to his cheek, before any of them even had a chance to move. The last four pirates still standing then tried to converge on James. Drew managed to trip two of them with one long leg. Bixley fell on one of them to keep him down, while Drew kicked the other squarely in the face, knocking him out. James had already dropped another, sent him flying several feet, actually. The last man standing panicked and tried to run. Drew tackled him, but with his own arms still bound, he was having trouble keeping him down. And James wasn't coming immediately to give him a hand, as he had gone to dispatch the pirate that Bixley had a leg-lock on. But Drew was angry enough to head-butt the fellow. Not the preferred way to do it, but it worked.

Drew rolled over to see that all six pirates were no longer moving. The entire fight had taken less than a minute, but then James Malory always had been fast, and lethal, with his fists.

Getting to his feet, he told James, "Nice work, but you could have given me a little warning."

"Didn't I?" James replied. "Thought breaking Mort's jaw would give you a clue."

"The ropes?" Drew said impatiently. Now that the tables had been turned, so to speak, he didn't want to waste another minute getting to Gabrielle.

James took a dagger from one of the pirates and came over to slice through his ropes. And in a moment of compassion that he rarely revealed to anyone other than his wife, he said, "She's going to be all right, Drew."

"I know. She has to be. But I'd rather see that for myself sooner than later." He didn't add "before he hurts her," but it was there in his mind and added extra speed to his race to the fortress.

Chapter 50

"If he touches you, I'm going to have to kill you."

It wasn't just the words that told Gabrielle she had company other than Pierre. So did the blade pressing against her throat. Yet again? Did all of Pierre's friends have a fixation with throat cutting?

Gabrielle had been lying on the bed where Pierre had told her to wait, but she'd been unable to bring herself to remove her clothes. She opened her eyes to see the woman with one knee on the bed, leaning toward her. The bright red hair was a dead giveaway.

She'd never met or seen Red before, and was surprised to find that she was a handsome woman, too pretty for someone like Pierre. She did have a few scars on her left cheek, but they weren't very wide and were faded, barely noticeable. Somewhere in her middle thirties in age, she was wearing men's clothes that fit her snugly. Too many of the buttons on her shirt were left open, showing off a pair of hefty breasts that were barely covered. A small black scarf was tied around her head to keep her wildly disarrayed hair out of her face, and so the linked gold loops on both ears dangled freely.

Her remark struck Gabrielle as bizarre. The woman must know that was Pierre's plan.

"Why don't you kill him instead?" Gabrielle asked curiously.

"Kill him? I love him, that bastard."

"Then help us to escape."

Gabrielle's hopes shot up when Red actually appeared to give it some thought, but then she shook her head. "That isn't one of my options, which are simple. I either kill you, or make you less appealing. You want the choice?"

It sounded like angry bravado, so she ignored the threat and asked, "How did you get in here without him seeing you?"

"He wasn't watching my door. I just waited until he went outside to relieve himself."

"If you're not going to help me, then you might as well kill me. The man I love is, God, I don't even know if he's still alive!" Gabrielle cried.

Red stood up straight with a snort. "How melodramatic, like I'd fall for that. But you needn't worry about your father. I like that old buzzard. I'll make sure he's released."

A little compassion in the midst of murder? She had a feeling Red might not be as bloodthirsty as she was making herself out to be, and that gave her more hope than she'd had all night.

"Thank you," Gabrielle said. "But I wasn't talking about him."

"Then who . . . ?"

They both heard the footsteps approaching the door. Red panicked and leapt over the bed to crouch on the other side of it. What Gabrielle felt was worse than panic. She was out of time, her brief reprieve gone.

The door opened. Pierre swayed there for a moment before he regained his balance. His eyes were glassy. He was drunk.

But he didn't sound it when he said, "You

don't follow orders well, *chérie,* but you will learn. I am sorry to have kept you waiting, but I could not resist savoring this triumph for a little while. Too long, I have wanted you. And for too long I thought you were out of my reach. But not anymore, eh?"

She'd heard the gasp when he said he wanted her. It wasn't hers. She could imagine what Red felt hearing that—if she really did love him. But what had the woman expected to happen? Had she really just closed a blind eye to the outcome of his scheme, hoping it wouldn't come to pass? Or was she as helpless to do anything about it as Gabrielle was?

Gabrielle said nothing, couldn't get any words out past her fear and revulsion as he approached the bed. The sound of a pistol shot outside in the courtyard made Pierre pause.

"What are those fools doing?" he growled. He added a few French expletives as he left to find out.

Gabrielle realized the distraction might be her only chance to escape. She bolted off the bed and was halfway to the door before she remembered Red might try to stop her. She glanced back. Red was standing on the other side of the bed. She looked furious, but it wasn't because Gabrielle was attempting to flee.

"Go on, go!" Red spat out. "Get out of here while you have the chance!"

Gabrielle hesitated. "What will you tell him?"

"Tell him? After what I heard him say to you, he'll be lucky if I don't kill him. I'm done with him!"

Gabrielle didn't waste another moment. The hall below was empty. Whatever was happening in the courtyard had drawn all of the pirates outside. More shots were being fired before she reached the outer door, and what she witnessed in the courtyard was pure mayhem.

The men from the ships! They were everywhere, fighting with whatever weapons they'd found, and some of them just with their fists. She saw Ohr, oh, thank God, he was alive! She realized he must have released the men from the ships. But she looked frantically for just one man in the crowd. The tallest man there—she would have spotted him immediately if it were daylight, but in the moonlight it took a few moments for her eyes to lock on him, and her knees went weak when she did, so much relief filled her. Drew, pounding his fist into some pirate he was holding by the shirt-front. He was all right!

She almost ran to him, had to fight back the urge to do so. He looked so magnificent, swinging his fists, leaping from one pirate to the next. She knew it wasn't a good time to interrupt him, but it was the perfect time to find her father, while the yard was in such chaos that no one would notice her.

She made her way carefully around the edges of the fighting, had to pause only once when two men fell nearly at her feet, grappling on the ground. The first door she found that looked like it might be the entrance to the dungeon just led to a cold cellar. The second door was the right one. The narrow stairs were lit by a torch hanging there at the top. There wasn't much left of it, but there were a half dozen fresh ones in a basket on the floor just inside the door. She lit a new one. The brighter light illuminated the large ring with a single key on it, hanging from a hook on the wall. She grabbed it and descended.

That there was only one key worried her, but she understood when she got to the bottom of the stairs. There were only two doors off the long corridor down there, one on each side of it. Military cells designed to hold many prisoners together. One was open to a big empty cell not in use. The other was locked. She could hear voices on the other side of it, discussing the commotion up in the courtyard.

"Papa?"

"Gabby?" she heard from deep in the cell, then closer as he moved to the door. "My God, what are you doing here?"

She dropped the torch to fight with the lock, her hands suddenly trembling. "I—I figured it was my turn to rescue you."

She was starting to cry, but she couldn't help it. She'd been so worried about him all these weeks, her worst fear being that Pierre, as evil as he was, wouldn't keep Nathan and his crew alive.

"Tell me you're all right?"

"We're fine. The food has been plentiful, exercise once a week, though we could have done with a change in odors."

She got the door open, was able to see for herself. Her father stood there grinning at her with his long hair and beard. She started to laugh as she hugged him. "Look at you, you're shaggy."

"I swear I asked for a barber, but they thought I was joking," he teased. "But how did you get here, and what's happening up top?"

"I brought a lot of help. James Malory and his American brother-in-law, and both their crews."

"Pierre?"

"I don't know," she had to admit. "They're still all fighting."

He took her hand. "Let's get out of here. Damn, I hope Pierre is still alive. I want a piece of him myself."

Chapter 51

Drew had never been this frantic before. He'd fought his way to the main building, but after he got inside and searched the few rooms upstairs where he'd been sure he'd find Gabrielle, all he found was a red-haired woman angrily packing her belongings.

"Where did Lacross take the woman?" Drew demanded of her.

She only gave him a brief glance before she said, "I let her go when the shooting started. If she's smart, she's hiding."

He ran back downstairs and outside. He saw immediately that more men had shown up and were helping to fight the last few pirates still standing. From the look of them, he guessed they were the prisoners, released from the dungeon, and he didn't have to guess who'd let them out. He saw her, standing back out of the way, and started running to her.

Gabrielle saw him racing across the courtyard to her. She helped him close the distance and threw her arms around his neck when he reached her. Her feet left the ground, he hugged her so tightly, and then he was kissing her, and kissing her, and he wouldn't stop kissing her.

"My God, when I thought he'd gotten his hands on you—" he began.

She said at the same time, "I was so frightened when I thought you'd been captured!"

"We were, but James got loose and turned the tables—"

"Oh God, Drew, a few minutes longer . . ."

"He didn't touch you?"

"No, the pistol shots drew him away. And with no one left in the hall to stop me, I found the dungeon and released my father."

Having said it all, she began trembling in reaction. Drew felt it and tried to soothe her. His own panic had receded now that she was safe and in his arms. He gathered her closer, kissed her gently, ran a hand through her hair.

"You can thank Ohr for the timing," he said in a soothing voice. "Bixley showed James and me a secret entrance, but with only the three of us, we would have had to be more cautious—actually, James had to hold me back. I wasn't exactly thinking straight by then, I was so worried about you. But then Ohr arrived at the front gates with the men from the ships, and we were able to get the gates opened for them before the main force of pirates began pouring out into the courtyard. Where's your father? He's all right?"

She looked out into the courtyard and spotted her father breaking some board he'd found over the back of—was that Pierre? It was, and it looked like Nathan had the situation well in hand. Most of his crew were around him. Some were already tying up those pirates they'd already subdued. Some of them were also beating on Pierre. Lacross was being passed among them. She even noticed Avery had been captured and added to the growing number of pirates already trussed up.

She glanced back at Drew with a smile.

"Yes, they were treated rather well, though that wouldn't have been Pierre's doing. They *used* to all be friends, the two crews, well, not quite friends, but more than passing acquaintances when they shared the same base."

Hesitantly now, he told her, "I was going to ask your father's permission to marry you."

She went very still and leaned back to glance up at him. There was something in her eyes. Amusement? Tenderness? Blast it, he couldn't tell, and he was suddenly feeling quite out of his depth. He'd never in his life lacked confidence with a woman before. But then he'd never felt this way about a woman before, either.

"Drew, do you love me?"

"My God, Gabby, do you really need to ask?"

"But your sister was so certain you would never want to get married."

"My sister doesn't know about the hell you've put me through while I was figuring it out."

"Hell?!" she gasped, and tried to push out of his arms indignantly.

He stopped her from leaving his arms

completely and cupped her cheek tenderly. "I know that it's the most important thing in my life right now to not lose you. I know that you're in my thoughts, day and night. I know that I went a little insane at the thought of Pierre hurting you. I know that you drive me crazy with wanting you. I know that I want to protect you, to cherish you . . . I know very well what all that means, Gabby. I love you so much it hurts."

Her grin came slowly, but grew quite dazzling. "Let's go find my father so you can tell him all the reasons why you want to marry me."

"Er, I'll give him just the one reason, if you don't mind. Fathers tend to take exception when lust gets mentioned in reference to their daughters."

"You can leave that part out."

"Come to think of it, fathers have the power to say no, too. You're really going to make me do this?"

"Me? You were the one who said you were going to ask his permission," she reminded him.

"It was just a thought. I don't think I was serious. I was just letting *you* know what was on my mind. Your acceptance was all I needed."

"Stop worrying. He won't be too angry when he hears about that scandal in London."

Drew groaned. But then he noticed her grin just before she put her arms around his neck and pulled his mouth down to hers. "You deserved that bit of teasing for making me wait so long to hear that confession," she said against his lips.

"Then you'll marry me?"

"I was ready to marry you in London!"

In that moment when he kissed her, they were oblivious to everything around them, including the cheer that went up from their friends who were watching them. Near the barracks, James found Nathan, who was wrapping a rope around Pierre. The pirate was barely conscious from the beating he'd weathered. He'd just finished being passed around among Nathan's crew. Each one of them had laid a fist or foot to Pierre in repayment for his hospitality.

"I would have simply broken his neck," James remarked.

"James Malory!" Nathan exclaimed as he looked up. "Gabby said you were part of this rescue. If I'd known you were going to get involved, I wouldn't have spent all these weeks worrying!"

"I hope that rope means you're going to string Lacross up?"

Nathan glanced back at Pierre and shook his head. "No, he deserves a worse fate than that. I'm going to turn him over to the English authorities in Anguilla, where he'll spend the rest of his life in prison."

"In that case, if you don't mind?" James said, then bent down to lift Pierre's head off the ground long enough to crack his cheek open with his fist. Now he was uncon-scious.

Nathan chuckled. "Still the same old Mal-ory, eh? Damn, it's good to see you again! You not only saved my life and the lives of my men, but most important, you saved Gabby."

"I believe I did that!" Drew said as he and Gabrielle joined them.

James raised a tawny brow, but then he said magnanimously, "I'll allow that my brother-in-law did do his share of head bashing today. Nathan, this is one of my wife's younger brothers, Drew Anderson."

"It's a pleasure, sir," Drew said, warmly shaking Nathan's hand.

"No, the pleasure is definitely mine," Nathan replied. "But you, James! You've more than repaid your debt to me. I merely asked you to help Gabby find—"

James interrupted with a gesture toward Drew, who was fervently kissing Gabrielle again. "I think we can safely surmise that I *have* fulfilled all requests."

Chapter 52

Gabrielle married Drew Anderson in a small chapel near her home in St. Kitts the very next day. She would have been willing to wait if he had wanted to track down his brothers, so they could be present for the happy occasion, but he wouldn't hear of it. The moment he had received her father's permission, which had been a painfully awkward experience for him, he'd asked where he could find the nearest priest. And besides, his sister and brother-in-law were there to represent his family.

She'd been so amused by how difficult it turned out to be, for him to speak with her father. He'd been in a tearing hurry to do so: then, when faced with asking the question, he'd stumbled over every word. And she knew exactly why. It was that word "marriage." He really had thought he would go through life merrily avoiding such a binding tie. It was a bit of a shock for him to accept the fact that he *wanted* to get married. But she didn't doubt he did. He just preferred to view the event as a way of keeping her forever, rather than of joining the matrimonial ranks.

She'd been able to wear her mother's wedding gown for the ceremony. A full layer of pale pink lace over powder-blue satin, the combination gave the lovely gown a lavender hue, and to complete that illusion, the sheer veil that trailed behind her was lavender, which nicely complemented her midnight-black hair. The gown was one of the few things that had belonged to Carla that she'd brought with her on her first trip to the Caribbean. She hadn't taken it back with her to England when she'd gone there to hunt for a husband, simply because deep down, she'd hoped she wouldn't find one. How quickly love had turned that notion around.

Her father recognized the gown. She hadn't thought he would. When he'd come to collect her to escort her down the aisle, he'd told her, "Your mother was a beautiful bride in that gown, but you, my dear, are a vision. Are you sure about this man? He's barely left you alone long enough for me to ask how you feel about it."

She'd chuckled at him. "Yes, very sure. I didn't know it was possible to be this happy, Papa. And I'm the one who wouldn't let him out of my sight. Men tend to get cold feet for the silliest reasons when it comes to matrimony."

He grinned. "So do women, but I don't think you have anything to worry about. It's obvious in the way he looks at you that he loves you very much. Now let's get you married. Let me straighten your veil. And what's that around your neck that you're hiding?"

"Oh, I'm not hiding it, I just forgot to pull it out when I put the gown on," she said, and lifted the locket out to rest in the center of the square-necked lace bodice of her gown. "It's something Mama gave me a long time ago."

"I'll be damned," Nathan said, staring at the miniature painting. "So that's how they hid it, by making a piece of jewelry out of it."

"What?" she asked, and then gasped as

she guessed, "The missing piece of your map?"

He started to laugh. "Indeed."

"But how does a picture of a village help? I've seen the rest of the map, it has no identifying marks other than the X where treasure is buried. Even the shape of the island it's on is ambiguous."

"Yes, but that is what was missing. One single landmark that can be located. I only need to find an island now with a fishing village like that on its southern coast and likely nothing else on it other than recently built—" He stopped and slapped his forehead. "And I know exactly where it is! I've been there. It doesn't even have a name yet, but we stopped there for supplies a few years ago. The villagers bragged that the island belonged to them, that no one else wanted to settle there."

She grinned at him. "That's one treasure hunt I don't want to miss. Why, I never would have been born if you hadn't had the other parts of the map and gone to England to look for that missing piece."

Her father had that look in his eyes that he always had when he was on the scent of treasure. Excitement, mixed with eagerness, mixed with joy. Nathan Brooks was never happier than when he'd figured out one of his maps.

"That's true enough," he agreed. "I had no other reason to return to my homeland. But your soon-to-be husband doesn't strike me as a treasure hunter, and I'm sure he'll be wanting to go off with you for a little time alone to celebrate the start of your new life together—unless I tell him that I'll be giving this treasure to you as a wedding gift. Think he might want to come along then?"

She laughed. "Probably not. But when he sees how much I want to, he might agree. The man does like to please me. But are you sure you want to give this one away? You've searched so long for it."

"Aye, but it was one of your ancestors who buried it and devised such an elaborate scheme to hide it that he didn't even share the information with his own family. Your mother never knew about it, and she was the last of his line. It's fitting that it go to you."

Hearing it put that way, Drew agreed that they could go along, and he didn't need much cajoling. He just insisted they sail on *The Triton,* rather than *The Crusty Jewel.*

Ironically, the *Jewel,* which Latice had betrayed his captain and shipmates for and then been denied, never had been put to use. It had been sitting in the bay in front of Pierre's stronghold, along with three other ships that Nathan had claimed as recompense for his incarceration.

But Drew had mentioned something about not being comfortable making love to his wife with her father in the next room. Gabrielle just grinned knowingly. It seemed to be universal, the reluctance that captains had to sail on ships other than their own, and she didn't doubt her husband felt the same way.

Gabrielle didn't mind missing the excitement aboard *The Crusty Jewel* as they followed in its wake. She already thought of *The Triton* as her home. And besides, they'd spent their wedding night aboard her, and Drew did no more than cast off the next morning before he returned to their cabin to keep her pleasantly occupied.

But it wasn't a long trip. It was barely mid-morning when they anchored beside the small island. And then came the tricky part of counting the steps and making sure they had the right spot to start digging at. Two hundred and fifty-eight steps due north of the grinning skull, the legend on the bottom of the map said, but they had to find a skull in the vicinity of the X. It turned out to be a skull and crossbones scratched into a flat stone on a rocky ledge. It took until midday just to find that! But the delay kept the excitement high. This was going to be the mother lode of all treasures, the one that had been the hardest to track down. And while it had already been given to the newlyweds, every man there was thrilled to be present for the discovery.

Spanish doubloons was the most common guess. Artifacts from the old world was another. The map was several hundred years old, after all, drawn up during the heyday of piracy on the high seas. And while the owner of this particular treasure hadn't been a pirate himself, he'd been an English lord who had been sent to rid the seas of pirates. So it had always been assumed that the treasure he'd buried had been confiscated from one of the pirate ships he'd captured.

Drew stood behind Gabrielle with his arms around her waist. She leaned back against his chest as they watched the digging.

"You won't be disappointed if they find nothing?" he asked her.

"Of course I will," she replied in a light tone. "But this isn't going to be one of the empty treasure chests. With the last piece of the map passed down through my family without them even being aware of what it was, this treasure has to be intact."

He kissed the side of her neck. "I hope you're right, sweetheart, for your sake."

She heard the doubt in his voice but ignored it. She was too excited to entertain any negative thoughts.

And then one of her father's crewmen lifted the chest up high with a shout of glee. It was a small chest, barely a foot square. And there was no lock on it that would have to be broken. The man quickly handed it to Nathan, who wasted no time in opening it.

With all of his crew gathered near and holding their breath in anticipation, their gasps of disappointment came simultaneously. Gabrielle's shoulders slumped slightly. Empty. She really hadn't believed this one could be empty.

It wasn't. Drew walked her over to Nathan, who gave her a sheepish grin. "It looks like I've given you a bunch of mementos for your wedding gift," he said as he handed her the chest.

Gabrielle glanced down to see a pile of old letters, a dried, pressed rose, a velvet ribbon, a lock of hair, and an assortment of other odds and ends. Even a baby's tiny stocking! None of it had any value other than to the man who'd buried the chest. To him, these things had been priceless . . .

Nathan continued, "I'm thinking one of those extra ships I just came home with might be more fitting. Take your pick, my boy, and add it to your Skylark line."

Drew nodded. "With pleasure, and thank you. But I already found my treasure."

Gabrielle turned around slowly. With the look in Drew's dark eyes, she couldn't mistake his meaning, and tears of happiness formed in her own eyes.

"You mean that, don't you?" she said softly.

"With all my heart, sweetheart . . . my wife."

She wrapped her arms around his neck

and kissed him. It took only moments before she was so involved in that kiss that she forgot they had an audience.

Her father cleared his throat and said, "I forgot to mention this deed that was on the bottom of the box. I'm not too good at reading Old English, but it looks like you now own this island."

Gabrielle's eyes widened, and then she squealed in delight, squeezing Drew tightly in her excitement. Drew burst out laughing at how quickly she got distracted by some real treasure.

When she finally calmed down she told him, "I love it! Look around you, it's beautiful here. And did you notice that little waterfall on the way here?"

"Can't say that I did, probably because my eyes were on you."

She grinned and snuggled under his arm. "We might want to build a house here, a place for us to come home to between voyages."

He looked down at her. "Between voyages? Do you mean that?"

"You thought I was joking when I said I liked the life at sea?"

"It had crossed my mind."

She grinned. "Someone should have warned you not to marry a woman who loves the sea—and loves even more a captain who sails it."

5-14-07
Reel good
realy HK
Sue K. 3-12-24
Good Book

no
9-21-07